To My Good Buddy
Guitar Player And
Motor Cyclist
MARTIN BUSLER
Merry Millennium

GRASS ROOTS

When the Cookies are Passed

in the

GRASS ROOTS

of

The Nation's Summer Capital

BY
Richard C. Harrison

Four Seasons Publishers
Titusville, FL

GRASS ROOTS

For information contact: Four Seasons Publishers
P.O.Box 51, Titusville, FL 32781

PRINTING HISTORY
First Printing 2000

ISBN 1-891929-12-7

PRINTED IN THE UNITED STATES OF AMERICA
1 2 3 4 5 6 7 8 9 10

TABLE OF CONTENTS

GRASS ROOTS

PART ONE
WORLD PEACE

Bud Green, overworked to the point of exhaustion, stumbled into Senator Blassforth's staff room only to find it deserted. He was the gopher, the junior member of the staff, sent out to gather more data. He'd left a bustling staff room with the whole staff working on an around-the-clock project for World Peace hours earlier. The sudden shock of finding the staff room abandoned jarred him into a quandary. He didn't believe it!

He faltered as his loafers scuffed across the threshold. The Preppie look had faded. The striped tie dangled askew from rumpled button-down, and the blue blazer sagged on his lanky frame. His tired eyes darted around the empty room, as abandoned desk chairs sat like a jury, waiting to pass judgment.

Finding Tilly, the senator's secretary, he blurted out, "Where is everybody?"

"Senator Blassforth took off for a vacation in the Bahamas," Tilly said, clearing her desk, and the last one to abandon ship.

It was eerie . . . the ghost town feeling of silence with it's leftover evidence of bustling activity, now laying idle.

"But what about everybody else?" Bud asked. He couldn't believe it. "We had all been working for World Peace!"

"When the cat's away, the mice will play."

Her cheery, secretarial tone of voice was little comfort to him. That empty feeling came over him. It was like the time his mother

1

went off to work when he was very young, leaving him with his grand-mother on the farm in Elmira. It was the feeling of being alone and abandoned.

"When will they be back?"

"The senator will be gone two weeks, so I don't expect the others till then."

Bud was beginning to get the idea. The overworked staff had re-acted like school children at recess. The devoted group he worked with had put World Peace on hold and rushed out to play.

Bud had been so enthusiastic when he joined the staff, the idea of taking time off, was the farthest thing from his mind. "Nobody men-tioned a vacation when I joined the staff," Bud said.

Tilly had worked for the senator's predecessor. She had been around and knew the ropes. She was older than the other staff members were. While she ran the office like a staff sergeant, she was careful not to be maternal. Without looking up she said, "Looks like a long hot sum-mer, the natives are getting restless."

"You going, too?" Bud asked.

"Yes, Olive will be in to cover for me starting tomorrow," she continued cheerily.

Determined to finish the project on World Peace, Bud was frus-trated with the interruption to his work. Then he remembered his Grandfather's parting advice as he left Elmira: *When in Rome, do as the Romans do; if you can't lick 'em, join 'em.*

Learning to work within the system was a new game for Bud. Trying to sound casual, he asked, "Where do the mice play?"

"Three of the girls in the office and I have rented a place in Reho-both Beach."

"Is it very far away?" he said, wondering where they go.

"It's the nearest ocean beach due east of Washington. It's called, 'The Nation's Summer Capital.'"

"Oh!" Bud stammered, "how do you get there?"

Tilly looked up at Bud's desperate expression. With his dark curly hair in a windblown mess, he looked like a little lost boy, who had stayed up past his bedtime. Her careful veneer melted, when she saw that he really didn't know what to do.

"If you want to go, I'm going tomorrow morning at nine," Tilly suggested. "I'll show you the way, but you'll be on your own when we get there."

Tilly's offer surprised him, and he didn't know what to say. A rule of thumb came to mind from his childhood. The gentle tone of his grandmother's voice floated across his memory, saying, "*When the cookies are passed, pause and take one.*"

Bud paused, and said to Tilly, "That sounds good to me."

"You could follow me, or better yet, if you drive me down, I can ride home with one of the other girls."

"Why don't I pick you up in the morning?" Bud offered.

"Okay, if you're in front of my apartment building at nine, I'll ride down with you and show you the way. If you don't show, I'll drive myself," Tilly said matter-of-factly.

"Fair enough," Bud said, as he left the abandoned office squaring his shoulders. Striding erect like his grandfather, Captain Green, made him look taller than average height. He was just five feet, eleven and a half inches tall in his bare feet – five twelve in his loafers. An aura of maturity made him look older than his early twenties. He had developed strength and wisdom through his grandfather's gentle guidance.

Bud Green had been a nonviolent political activist his senior year in college when his grandfather suggested that he work within the system. After graduation, he found a job on a senator's staff in Washington, DC and set out to help make the world a better place to raise a family.

Bud had never been drawn to demonstrations, but he was determined to make the world a peaceful place to raise children and he had to do it himself. He had come to Washington to make a contribution toward World Peace.

The thrill of coming to Washington, DC was overwhelming. He found a magical inspiration in the White House, the capitol dome, the statues and the wide boulevards flanked by graceful elms.

The enthusiasm and dedication of the young people on the staff carried him through long hours, day after day. It wasn't nine-to-five. It was a never-ending job that needed to be done. They lived the cause day and night. When you are immersed in a power struggle to save the world, time means nothing. Overtime is a matter of dedication.

The Senators and Congressmen didn't bother with fair labor laws. They willingly passed fair labor laws, but always exempted themselves and their staffs from them.

Finding the whole staff gone had been a shock to Bud. As the shock subsided, he realized he could use a change. His whole body, mind, and spirit needed to have the battery recharged.

Frustrated with the interruption to his work and too tired to know what to do, he had accepted Tilly's offer to show him the route to The Nation's Summer Capital. Having gotten himself into this excursion of investigating the route of the annual exodus of bureaucrats, he felt compelled to go through with it.

He'd been impressed with the sights in DC. It was time to explore the surrounding countryside. What better guide than Tilly to show him the route to The Nation's Summer Capital? Besides, he'd never had a chance to talk with Tilly for any length of time. It would be a privilege to spend some valuable time with the head honcho. She could show him the way and point out the interesting features as they went long. After all, it was just another part of "working within the system."

He dropped into bed with visions of the office staff going down the road to playland. The thrill of setting out on the open road, exploring the route to the Nation's Summer Capital, lulled his tired body into a dream of a new adventure. He was looking forward more to the journey than to the destination.

THE JOURNEY

Anxiety about an unexpected adventure woke Bud early. He'd flopped into bed feeling burned out. He straightened up his room, cramming everything, including World Peace, in the closet. Bud packed a bag and grabbed some breakfast. Then glancing at his watch, he cleared out six months of litter from his car. He didn't know where he was going, but it was time to "join 'em."

Tilly was waiting by the curb as Bud drove up at five of nine. In her freshly washed shorts, halter-top, and running shoes, she looked more like a young tourist than the savvy, matronly senator's secretary he had known.

"Well, you made it!" she said as he pulled up to the curb.

"I made it this far. I'll put your bags in the back."

"I can do that," she said, throwing her bags on the back seat. "Just go straight ahead to the beltway."

Bud had become adjusted to the congested Washington traffic. In Washington, everybody drives. There is public transportation, but that's for the public. He was a survivor of the rush hour mishmash, but easing onto the beltway, was another story.

Bud tried to get into the flow of traffic by rubbernecking in every direction while stomping on the gas. As he eased out of the access ramp the excitement built up, like leaving a pit stop in the Indy 500. Once into the flow of traffic, sports cars ducked in and out in front of him, jockeying for position as enormous trucks went rattling past

5

them on both sides.

"Doesn't anybody drive the speed limit on the beltway? Some of these cars pass me like I was backing up," Bud said.

"Police try to catch them, but now they're outnumbered."

As they raced along, the pace slackened. The traffic slowed to a creep and then ground to a halt, much to Bud's relief.

"It's too soon for the back-up to the Bay Bridge," Tilly said. "Must be an accident up ahead."

"Rather be stuck in a backup than torn apart in a wreck," Bud said, feeling relieved as he sat back and relaxed.

Tilly reached over to tune the radio, saying "Maybe I can find a traffic bulletin that will tell us what's happening."

He noticed the anxious sports car drivers stuck a few cars ahead. The sound barriers stood silently on each side of the highway. While the inner loop waited, the outer loop cars raced by in the opposite direction.

Bud could see four lanes of traffic stopped bumper-to-bumper down the hill and out of sight and winding up over the next hill. "Hurry up and wait," he joked.

A man got out of his car and walked toward them. Bud opened the window. The man asked, "Do you have a phone in your car?"

"No, I'm sorry. I don't," Bud said.

"Looks like a phone antenna," Tilly spoke up, "two cars ahead on the right." The man went to see.

Bud smiled and said jokingly, "At last we're alone."

"With a thousand weary travelers? You call this alone!"

"I meant, this is the first time I've had time on my hands since I've been in Washington," Bud said. "I've been so enthusiastic about helping Senator Blassforth work for the good of all."

"Senator's have to work for the desires of the voters in their constituency," Tilly explained.

"Don't you get excited about making your hopes and desires come true?"

"As his secretary, I work for his hopes and desires, whether or not they are mine."

"You mean it's just a job to you?"

"My job is to do what the senator wants and his job is to do what the voters want. If we don't do our jobs, they will get someone else to do it."

"Never thought of it that way," he said pensively.

"Maybe you ought to. It'll help you pace yourself, so you'll be more effective. 'Politics is local,' as they say. It's the grass roots that count," Tilly stated.

He knew what she was saying was true, but he was too burned out to consider hard facts. Talking with Tilly was exciting, so he looked around at the stalled cars and changed the subject, "Look at all those frustrated people; all dressed up and no way to get there. They ought to be riding on public transportation."

"Suburbia's too spread out to make public transportation pay. People want a house and a yard. They keep moving out past the suburbs to get more space" Tilly said. "Besides, they have a love affair with their cars."

"Cars are lousy lovers," Bud stated. "When you surround yourself with machines, you find the machines don't love you."

"Americans like the convenience and independence."

Many frustrated motorists began getting out of their cars and gathering in holiday groups. "It's like a day at the races, with all these people trapped in urban congestion, having a holiday outing on the beltway," Bud said.

"The beltway was designed to handle the out-of-town traffic. They could skirt the city instead of driving through downtown. But the suburbanites found it first."

"They sure have!" Bud said looking around, engrossed.

"Imagine driving from New York to Richmond and innocently taking the beltway."

"Blue highways must be empty," Bud said, "everybody's here."

"They're starting to move."

"Where?"

"On the next hill."

They watched each car start, like rows of little, metal ants creeping along. They were transfixed watching the movement slowly ooze in their direction and disappear behind the nearest hill. Waiting hopefully for the movement to come in sight as it reached the top of the hill, they watched in silent expectation. When the car in front of them finally began to move, they relaxed and looked at their watches.

"Wasn't so bad," Bud said as they eased forward.

"Probably another tractor trailer jack-knifed and turned over, blocking all four lanes. Getting to be a daily problem."

"Where are all these cars going?" Bud wondered out loud.

"Traffic on the beltway is like this twenty-four hours a day, seven days a week," Tilly said. "Makes you think that they pay people to drive on it."

"How long will it take us to get there?"

"Two and a half hours. Should be there by eleven-thirty," Tilly explained. "Turn on the next exit toward Annapolis. We take the John Hanson Highway, which is Route 50, East."

Bud slowed his vehicle, as it curled around the cloverleaf onto a four-lane highway, divided by a grassy median. Bud felt more at home as the suburban houses thinned out and farmland lay green and lush.

Near Annapolis, new road construction turned the road into a rollercoaster ride. Cement "Jersey barriers" zigzagged each lane of traffic through the work area, on a frightening ride.

The traffic began to thin out between the third and fourth Annapolis exit, as they crossed the Seven River Bridge.

"Why are there so many exits to Annapolis?" Bud asked, drawing her out. "Is the Naval Academy that large?"

"Annapolis is the state capital of Maryland. The U.S. Naval Academy is on that point of land where the Seven River flows into the bay. They call it, '*The Sailing Capital of the World.*'"

There was another back up as they neared the tollbooth for the Bay Bridge. Bud gladly sat back and relaxed as the traffic ground to a halt. He asked, "Is it always like this?"

"Lately, on Saturday mornings it's worse," Tilly explained. "When I was a little girl, we used to take the ferry across the Chesapeake Bay before they built the bridge."

"You must have been going to Rehoboth Beach for many years," Bud said. "Bet you're glad they built the bridge."

"Mother doesn't like to come to Rehoboth Beach anymore," Tilly exclaimed. "She says, 'They've ruined the beach when they built that bridge and let in all those nasty people.'"

"That's a good one," Bud joined in. "Sounds like my grandfather. He had a summer camp in the Adirondacks and we had to walk the last mile to get there. When I complained about the walk, he said, 'That's what makes the camp so nice.' If it is hard to get to, it won't

8

be full of tourists."

"It gets harder to get to Rehoboth Beach each year, but there are more and more people."

"You sound like a native." Bud's curiosity about the area was running rampant. "Were you brought up in Washington?"

"Yes. The District of Columbia used to be like a little southern village, back when District residents weren't allowed to vote, before home rule. Over a hundred years ago, Senator Newlands built a large summer home just over the District line in Maryland so he could vote. This started a residential community out Connecticut Avenue, now called Chevy Chase," Tilly said.

"Suburban sprawl has made Chevy Chase seem like it's nearly downtown now," Bud said, trying to sound knowledgeable.

"Yes, it's inside the beltway. Mother used to tell me that the population increased tenfold during World War II and spilled over into Maryland and Virginia. The District's city limits couldn't be enlarged, because Maryland and Virginia won't give the District any more land," Tilly explained.

"The metropolitan area must be spread thirty miles past the beltway now," he continued, trying to draw her out.

As Bud pulled up to the tollbooth, Tilly said, "You buy the gas and I'll pay the toll," as she handed him the money.

As they started over the four-mile, high-rise Bay Bridge, the view was spectacular. The sun caught the triangular sails of the day-sailor's boats. Large tankers crept up the channel. An occasional yacht or power boat left wakes in the expanse of blue water.

We check our brains at the toll booth," Tilly announced. "Turn off the air conditioner. Open the windows. Let the bay breeze blow through and relax. From here on, we're on vacation."

The refreshing fragrance of the gentle breeze, spiced with the aroma of the vast bay, encouraged Bud to relax and enjoy it. "I'm ready to sit back and unwind," Bud said, enjoying Tilly's travelogue. "Are we almost there?"

"Almost half way there, but the traffic is better once we get past the drawbridge at Kent Narrows, just beyond the bay. After that, the traffic strings out."

Fortunately, the Kent Narrows drawbridge was down and the traffic thinned out a little. As two lanes went on to the Jersey Turnpike, two lanes of beach traffic pealed off to the south.

"Just stay on Route 50," Tilly said. "After the bridge, it goes down the Eastern Shore."

"The Eastern Shore?" Bud asked, looking puzzled.

"Yes. Wealthy people have large water-front estates on the Easter Shore," she said.

"Eastern Shore of what?" Bud persisted.

"In-people call it the, 'Eastern Shore.' It's the Eastern Shore of the Chesapeake Bay. It's a nautical term. Boat people use charts on the waterways, but automobile people use road maps," she explained. "Guess you could say the Eastern Shore of the bay is the western shore of the Delmarva Peninsula.

"Delmarva sounds like an Indian name," Bud suggested.

"No. Delmarva is an abbreviation of Delaware, Maryland, and Virginia. This peninsula has a culture of its own, but three states have jurisdiction. Delaware has the upper coast, Maryland runs through the peninsula to the ocean and the bottom third is Virginia. The Delmarva natives tend to make up their own rules. They don't like the government across the bay telling them how to live. I'm beginning to feel like a tour guide!" Tilly said.

"Sorry, but I've never been to the Nation's Summer Capital. Used to go to a lake in the summer."

"Ocean is different," Tilly said. "Get in the left lane. We want to turn east on 404."

They turned onto a two-lane macadam road winding through rolling hills. The woods on each side of the road were lush and occasional farm fields were full of maturing crops. Anxious beach goers whizzed past when they found a stretch with no oncoming traffic, only to be stuck behind the next car holding to the speed limit. Bud looked it all over with interest.

A divided highway skirted the town of Denton and gave the speedy drivers a chance to get ahead. As it tapered back to one lane, Tilly said, "Turn left on Route 16 up ahead."

There was no stoplight and Bud waited for a break in the oncoming traffic and turned onto a winding road. As they rounded a curve, Bud spotted the Delaware State line:

GRASS ROOTS

"WELCOME TO DELAWARE
THE FIRST STATE
SMALL WONDER"

Bud asked, "Small wonder?"

"Almost as small as poor little Rhode Island. Delaware has only three counties at low tide," Tilly joked. "One congressman, two senators and no sales tax."

"That is a small wonder!" he said.

The rural Delaware countryside lay flat as a pancake. An occasional farmhouse sat up in the sun like a pat of butter. High cornfields and low soybean fields joined a windbreak of trees on the windward eastern side. Long, low chicken coops were strung out beside a mobile home like a string of barges so long that you couldn't see the end.

"Must be chicken country," he said, trying to sound sharp.

"The Sussex County symbol is a little yellow baby chicken. Chickens, corn, and soybeans are the major produce. The local cantaloupes are delicious, but they don't travel," Tilly explained. "You have to eat them here."

When he saw a man on a riding mower with his tiny son on his lap, Bud's heart jumped up in his throat as he gulped with envy. That's what he missed as a fatherless boy. He was determined to be there when he had a son. He glanced at Tilly to see if she'd noticed, but she was staring intently at the road ahead. Bud read a sign aloud, "'Welcome to Ellendale.'"

"Twenty-five miles an hour," Tilly read another sign. "It's like a ghost town. You never see any people unless you exceed the speed limit. It's the last speed trap before the beach."

Bud slowed to a creeping twenty-five miles an hour through the town. The main street had been widened to accommodate the highway. The sidewalks had been pushed back against the houses. One house was boarded up. It stood stately, in the middle of the few blocks of Main Street, with long front windows and fancy Victorian trimmings that suggested that it had seen better days.

"That was a substantial house in its day," Tilly commented.

"The magic that makes a house come alive is tender loving care and elbow grease," Bud remarked. "It's sad to see such a magnificent house neglected."

"Doesn't have the three important features of real estate-location, location and location. Who'd want to live here?"

Empty parking spaces lined both sides of Main Street. There were rusty signs each side of the Ellendale Post Office, reading:

15 MINUTE PARKING
FOR POST OFFICE

Bud thought, "They're ready for action, in case it should come."

Bud picked up speed at the "END 25 MILE ZONE" sign. "Is it this flat all over Delaware?" Bud said, scanning the scenery.

"Good bicycle country for errands and sightseeing."

"Did the government set up The Nation's Summer Capital?"

"Heavens no. It just happened because it's the nearest ocean. Years ago, Rehoboth Beach started out as a Methodist Camp meeting site. They build little one-room, two-story camp meeting 'tents' and some of them are still there," Tilly remarked.

"The tents are still there?" Bud couldn't help asking.

"They are little frame houses, but they were called 'tents,' because they are just one room like a tent. They have grown larger through the years with add-ons. First, a back porch for cooking, when it rains and indoor plumbing. Then, wrap-around porches, on the front and sides, that became enclosed for extra bedrooms when the resort became popular. Turn right on Route 1 and watch out for the Dover and Wilmington traffic to the beach. We're almost there," Tilly commented.

Bud turned on to the four-lane divided highway that is Delaware's route to the beach. Farms gave way to billboards advertising everything for the tourist and the traffic turned into a sprint to the finish line.

Bearing left at the Rehoboth Beach Exit, one lane crept, bumper-to-bumper, over the canal drawbridge into the tiny resort town. Bud read aloud the sign at the entrance to Rehoboth Beach, "Welcome to the Nation's Summer Capital."

"Do you want me to show you the town before you drop me off or shall we take the back way?"

"Let's see the town."

GRASS ROOTS

"Okay. Just go straight ahead down Rehoboth Avenue six blocks to the ocean. Its the world's worst traffic jam, but let's do it anyway. Everybody drives straight down to the ocean, around the U at the boardwalk, and then goes to their cottage. It's a compulsion, like moths drawn to a flame. Maybe they want to make sure the ocean is still where they left it. They have to see for them-selves that the ocean hasn't been turned off and the waves are still crashing on the shore."

They eased down Rehoboth Avenue with its two lanes of traffic each side of a grassy median with trees. The parking meters that lined each side of the lanes were full of cars. The traffic stopped for the light on Second Street, while cars turned onto the main drag in front of them. Skimpily clad bathers dodged in and out of the clogged cars. When the light turned green, Bud crept forward into the backup of the First Street stoplight.

"I like the greenery in the median," Bud said, his dark eyes glancing around. "The trees remind me of Washington."

"The train used to come down the middle of the road in the olden days. The median is where the tracks were."

When they finally inched by the First Street light, the ocean block stores seemed to scream their wares: RESTAURANT OPEN ALL NIGHT! T-SHIRTS! PIZZA! GOLD CHAINS! ICE CREAM! FUDGE! POPCORN! FRENCH-FRIES! DOLLY'S SALTWATER TAFFY!

The street made a slow U-turn at the boardwalk and Bud had plenty of time to look over the beach and see the ocean for the first time. He eased his way back to the light at First Street.

"That's the town . . . the center of activity here. Turn right when you can, get back to First Street. My garage apartment is in the Pines just a few blocks."

Bud was glad to get off the main drag. Turning north on First Street, he found two blocks of back street commercial houses before he came to the old frame summer cottages with generous screen porches. He crossed a little bridge over a small. The tree-lined inland side of the lake reminded Bud of the Adirondack lakes. On the ocean side, a six-story condominium building blocked the ocean view.

"That's the Henlopen Hotel and Condominiums," Tilly said, pointing. "The Pines start at the other side of the lake. Turn right and then left."

They pulled up in front of a large frame house, as Tilly said, "This is it." She got out of the car and reached for her bags, saying, "Thanks for the ride." You're on your own from now on. With the ocean on the east and the canal on the west you can't get very lost. Good luck and have a good time."

"Thanks for the tour."

"See you on the beach."

He was free to do whatever he wanted to do. Free to see how the government people relaxed. He had mixed feelings. The thrill of a major adventure mixed with the uneasy feeling of being a stranger in a strange town.

THE BEACH

After dropping Tilly off at her apartment, he drove through the residential section looking enviously at the people talking and laughing on the screen porches of their cottages snuggled in the trees. They were like little camps in the woods with large screen porches wrapped around both sides of the cottage.

The ocean breezes lured the summer people out on the porch. Some ate at picnic tables, while others lolled in wicker furniture with bare feet on grass rugs. Reading lamps and overflow cots welcomed night owls. They communed with nature. Looking down from their porches, waving to their summer friends walking by, securely screened from the intrusion of bugs and well wishers, they were living as though they were living on a deserted island, relaxing in the comfort of their outdoor sanctuary.

People in bathing suits walked down the middle of the streets, carrying towels and folding chairs, going to and coming from the ocean. He smiled as he watched an old couple enjoying a bicycle ride and waving to the people on a porch.

Finding his way back to the main drag, he turned into a motel. It was full, but they called around and sent him back away from the beach to an inland motel that had a vacancy.

He found the motel, signed in, took his bag up to check the room. Pulling on a knit shirt and shorts over his bathing trunks, he set out on foot to find something to eat.

On the street, he squinted in the blazing sunshine, as if he had just come out of hibernation. The same shock you get when returning to real life after coming out of a matinee movie. Everything looked bright and shiny. He walked down to the ocean block, where he had seen a restaurant called the Country Squire.

Going into the restaurant, he groped in the dark to find his way, because the contrast of the bright sunlight outside made it seem like he had entered a dark cave. As his eyes adjusted to the inside light, he found a bright, cheery atmosphere.

There was a long bar the whole length of the wall on his right and a row of booths on the left wall. He sat down in a booth. A bunch of papers stuck in a glass turned out to be menus. He was interrupted as he looked over the menu.

"Hi. My name's Rose."

Looking up into a welcome smile, he said, "Hi. My name's Bud."

"Well, Bud, are you thirsty or hungry?" she asked.

"Both." She wore a healthy tan and her eyes had flecks that were dazzling.

"What would you like?" Rose asked.

At the moment he liked talking to Rose, his only friend in town. She was down to earth and her warm smile put him at ease. "What are you offering?" Bud asked.

"Everything on the menu. Tell me what you want to drink and I'll give you a little more time to make up your mind."

"Just a cola, I guess."

"Be right back."

He watched her walk over to the bar. She kidded with the bartender, got the cola, and brought it to his booth. "Here's the cola. I'll be back in a minute to take your order. Okay?" Rose asked.

"Okay!" He smiled a boy-am-I-glad-to-meet-you smile and watched her walk off. Her evenly tanned legs had a naturally coordinated walk. Her khaki shorts, Izod shirt, and sailing shoes fit her personality. She was the kind of person you could have a good time with: sports, movies, whatever. She didn't appear to have a negative bone in her body.

He sipped his cola and looked around at the other people. At the front end of the bar, a group of young men and women were talking and laughing. At the middle of the bar was an older man with a baseball hat with a tractor advertisement that Bud tried to puzzle out by looking in the bar mirror. Two barstools away sat "Mr. Muscles" exhibiting his tattooed arms in a tank top.

There was an older couple having lunch with a younger couple. Bud studied their noses to see if they were <u>her</u> parents or <u>his</u> parents.

"Ready to order?" Rose said, reappearing.

"What do you recommend in the sandwich line?"

"They're all good. I had a turkey on whole wheat."

"That's what I'll have."

"I'll put in your order."

It wasn't long before she brought the sandwich and a bill. "Will there be anything else?"

"No. That ought to do it," Bud said, with a gentle smile, and added, 'except . . ." Eager to talk to her more, he had blurted out one embarrassing word and choked up.

Waiting for him to continue, she looked him over, his erect stature, his dark eyes. "Except. . . ?" she asked.

"Oh, how late do you . . . ?" He looked down shyly.

Moved by his modest dignity, she came to his rescue with, "I'm on the late shift today. Going right home to bed when I get off. Maybe I'll see you on the beach tomorrow?" she offered.

"Where do you go . . . I mean, to the beach?"

"I usually go to fisherman's beach, just past the north end of the boardwalk. There's more room there."

"I'll look for you tomorrow on fisherman's beach."

"See you on the beach," she said as she went back to her customers. "Enjoy your lunch."

Admiring her fluent stride from table to table, he finished his lunch. He paid the bill and went back out into the bright sunshine to look over the area and find Fisherman's Beach. The pedestrians swarmed up and down the sidewalk wearing bizarre costumes reminding him that he was in a resort town. He picked his way through the crowd to the boardwalk.

The seagulls swarmed over the foot traffic. The sun warmed his skin and the gentle breeze welcomed him to the beach. The hot sun painted the skimpily clad bathers with sharp contrasts, like a movie poster. No subtle details distracted their minds. Chatting in glossy oversimplifications, the hoard of strangers, reacting to the bright contrasts, caught the spirit of having a good time. The breeze supported elaborate, colorful kites and fluttered the flaps of the scattered umbrellas.

A rag-tag mob of day-trippers crowded the beach, leaving no room for the hungry seagulls. The sunbathers assumed every position on folding chairs, towels, and on the sand. Bud studied the body surfing and boogie boards in the waves. Frisbees and a volleyball game painted color and action into the beach scene. The foot traffic on the boardwalk flowed north and south, at a right angle to the street. Bud impulsively started wandering north on the boardwalk. Sidestepping preoccupied strollers and hurrying adolescents, he began to observe the boardwalk action.

The body language on the boardwalk was entirely different. On the street, half of the people were on their way to buy something, pushing past the leisure strollers.

The boardwalk crowd looked like an endless group of refugees from the rat race, sauntering along aimlessly. They wore a weird collection of outfits from the old gentlemen in knee socks, town shoes, and shorts to the teenyboppers in skimpy string bikinis, flaunting their navels. There was the motorcycle bunch, the college clique, the little tots with their grandfathers, the young lovers, the new parents proudly carrying their baby, and single refugees like Bud.

Each generation group and social strata of humanity coexisted on the boardwalk, because they only had eyes for their own strata. Little kids, playing under the feet of lovers making out, aren't aware of the action-taking place. Each faction is looking for someone compatible to merge with or take over.

Once they are on the boardwalk, the ocean seems to fade and the makeshift shops are the center of attraction. The focal points are the electronic video games and the ice cream vendors.

The last six blocks of the boardwalk were narrower. There were a couple of high-rise condo buildings. Then two old houses set back from the boardwalk, proudly resisting change. One of the old houses belonged to the Pennsylvania Railroad and the other was the Village Improvement Association.

At the end of the boardwalk, the ocean caught his eye. The waves crashed on the beaches between the jetties. Muscular, tanned lifeguards sat on a high stand in the middle of each beach watching the bathers. The lifeguards had posted little red signs near the jetties warning the bathers to stay off the jetties.

The long jetties seemed to grow out of the dunes under the boardwalk and pointed out into the ocean like extended fingers. The sand built up on the south side of each jetty, but left a deep drop on the north side. Heavy wooden beams bolted to two rigid lines of pilings on each side, forming a beeline from the dunes down to the water past the low tide line.

At the north end of the boardwalk, Bud took off his shoes, tied the laces together, and slung them over his shoulder. He went down the steps to the sand beach and headed for the ocean.

The loose sand made him feel that he was doing the treadmill dance step. While one foot swung forward, the other foot seemed to slide backward. He climbed up on the jetty and balanced his way toward the water. He had to jump off before the jetties rose too high above the sand.

Just over the jetty, surf fishermen had cast their lines out into the ocean. Their fishing poles were secured in tubular holders stuck in the sand. After climbing over the jetty, he was careful to avoid the fishing lines as he walked along the water's edge. The ocean was cool and felt refreshing on his feet.

He climbed over the next jetty and started back to the water's edge again, when a striking young lady blocked his path. She looked familiar and when she said, "Weren't you at Senator Blassforth's fundraising dinner? he knew where he had seen her.

"Yes, I was," he said, trying to remember her name. "I'm Bud Green."

"Missy Mannerly," she said. "How long are you down for?"

"At the beach? Oh, I don't really know. Maybe a week."

It was obvious from Missy's deep tan that she had been there since the season started and it was painfully obvious from Bud's pale complexion he'd just arrived. Starting to ask how long she was down for, he quickly changed to, "Where are you staying?"

"Mummy and Daddy have a house on Pennsylvania Avenue."

The old work pressures tightened up the muscles in the back of his neck. He remembered that Senator Blassforth had been able to sell four dinners for the fundraiser to Mr. Mannerly, because the senator had asked Bud to sit with Missy at the dinner. Bud, "Are your parents on the beach today?"

"No. Daddy's gone back to town and Mummy's cleaning house. We're having a party tomorrow night. Why don't you come?"

"What time is it going to be?"

"Cocktails and finger food. Sixish."

"What number Pennsylvania Avenue?"

"Oh, you will come then! Number nine."

"I'll make a point of it."

A friend came up to talk and Missy said, "Bud, this is Betty Brass. Betty, this is Bud Green. We met at a political rally for Senator Blassforth."

"Missy always knows the most handsome men," Betty said with a sweet smile. "Welcome to the Nation's Summer Capital."

"Thank you," Bud said, feeling better talking to a couple of lovely ladies with the ocean washing his toes.

"Where are you sitting?" Missy asked.

"I was just walking up the beach," Bud answered.

"Why don't you come and sit with us when you finish your walk. We can catch up on what you've been doing. It's the pink umbrella and we have lots of chairs."

"Thank you. I just want to walk a little farther. Nice to meet you, Betty." They all waved and smiled as he started walking up the beach. He wasn't ready to jump back into a social swirl of politics.

Bud walked up the beach, dodging the darting waves washing up on the sand, with the good feeling that he belonged. "*So this is how it is in The Nation's Summer Capital*," he said out loud to himself.

He would have walked forever, if it weren't for the jetties that separated the beaches. Each jetty was a barrier for the strollers at the water's edge.

As he approached each jetty, he angled away from the water edge, trudging up into the loose sand, until he came to the high tide mark. The high tides had washed over the jetties, piling up the sand against the jetty. He could step up on the jetty and balance along the top until the sand was close enough to jump down on the other side.

After about five jetties, he turned back. As he jumped off the second jetty on the way back, one of the girls from the office was waiting for him. "Hi, Bud," she said. "We waved to, but you were looking at the ocean."

"I didn't see you. Tilly showed me how to get here, but she said I'd be on my own when I got here."

"Well, you don't have to be antisocial. Come say hello to the rest of the gang."

They walked up the beach to where the others were gathered. They all waved a greeting to Bud, except a girl lying on a towel tanning her back. Bud was fascinated with her agility, as she reached back to tie her bra straps while lying on her stomach.

"We waved to you, but you walked right by."

"I didn't see you."

"Tilly said you were here somewhere."

"You all cleared out in a hurry. Guess I was buried in my work. Didn't realize that everyone was going to drop everything and leave. I was lucky to catch Tilly as she left the office."

"We have to catch a ride with anybody who will drive across the Bay Bridge. It gets too scary when there's a wind storm."

Tilly spoke up, "They built the bridge high enough for the tall ships to sail under it. I'm afraid it will blow over."

"And they built the second bridge so close to the old one," another girl spoke up, "that when one blows over, it'll take the other one down with it like a domino."

"There's a beautiful view from the top of the bridge," Bud said. "I guess I was taking in the sights."

"What have you been doing down here?" one girl asked.

"I'm going to the mannerly party tomorrow night," he said.

"What a socialite!" another girl said.

"Aren't you all going?"

"We haven't been invited."

"I wish I wasn't invited. I don't like the social side of politics. I just came down here to see what's going on."

"Must be tough to be so much in demand." The girls teased.

"Well, ladies, my public needs me," Bud joked. "I'll see you all later." They smiled and waved goodbye.

As he walked on down the beach, he was happy to know so many people in a place that was new to him. The office ladies weren't self-conscious in their skimpy bathing suits. Next time he saw them in their office clothes, he would remember the trim figures in the bikinis.

As he made his way over a jetty he heard a familiar voice. "Hi!" Missy waved to him. "Going my way?"

"If you're headed south," he said.

"Let's go sit under my umbrella. I want to know what you've been doing since I've seen you."

"Lead the way," Bud said, nonchalantly.

Bud and Missy chatted about everything and everybody they knew in common. When she said, "Let's go swimming," he took off his shorts and shirt and they raced into the surf. After a swim they talked some more, sitting in the sun until he was dried off.

As people started leaving the beach, Bud said, "Well, guess I'd better get going. Glad I ran into you."

"See you tomorrow," she said with a pretty smile.

Back at the boardwalk, he slipped on his shoes and found himself heading for the Country Squire. It was happy hour and the place was jammed. He tried to elbow his way through the gang around the bar. When he asked a busy bartender about Rose, the bartender yelled over his shoulder, "She's here somewhere, but happy hour's a madhouse."

Looking around at the noisy crowd, he decided to leave. He had a long walk ahead of him through the town to his motel. The first day on the beach was an exciting new adventure, but the sparkling sea kept reminding him of Rose's sparkling eyes.

He picked up some fast food near his motel and ate it in front of the TV. After a shower, a movie was just starting on the TV. It had been a long day. The fresh air and exercise had relaxed his body. The light sunburn felt warm and comfortable, like Rose's smile. He lay down on the bed to watch the movie and fell into a deep sleep.

ROSE

Bud woke when the bright coastal sun danced across his eyes. He crawled out of bed, turned off the TV, dressed for the beach, walked to the nearest place serving breakfast. As if he had a pressing mission, he ate quickly and left.

He strolled down to the boardwalk. The morning crowd was a different world. Runners and joggers ignored the people who were on their way to breakfast. The seagulls were walking around in the sand and scavenging last night's leaving on the beach. Tired shopkeepers were getting ready for another day.

He found himself at the north end of the boardwalk. He had been retracing his steps of yesterday, but looking over the bathers. Over the jetty he scanned the beach area until he found what had subconsciously drawn him to this spot.

Rose was sitting on a towel in a bikini applying suntan lotion to a healthy body. Her hands moved sensuously over her smooth skin. She twisted agilely to reach hidden areas. Bud watched from the water's edge for a moment. It was fisherman's beach and he knew how the fish felt when they are being reeled in. His feet had started moving in the direction of the lure.

"Good morning, Rose," he said as he walked up to her.

"Well, if it isn't Bud," Rose replied.

"You're a sight for sore eyes," he said, smiling because she even remembered his name!

"Thank you," she smiled. "The beach is more fun when you know somebody."

"Yesterday, I ran into someone I knew, Missy Mannerly," Bud commented. "She goes to the next beach north of Fisherman's Beach."

"That's Snob Beach, where the wealthy people from Washington go," Rose explained.

"Do you have names for all the beaches?" Bud questioned.

"Unofficial names, like girl's boarding school nick names. The next one is Deauville Beach and then Cuba, where the young surfers hang out. Henlopen Acres Beach Club, then North Shores, and the state park used to be called Whiskey Beach until the state police clamped down on drinking on the beach. Now its called Gay Beach," she said.

"I didn't walk that far up the beach. Missy wanted to know what I've been doing since we met in DC at a fundraiser for my boss. Nice to know somebody, but didn't come here to talk shop."

"Won't you sit down," she said, moving to one end of her beach towel.

"I'll just sit in the sand." It felt so comfortable talking with Rose. With Missy he felt he was on stage. After some small talk, he felt more confident. "Do you have to work tonight?"

"No, this is my day off. Why?"

"I'm invited to the Mannerly's party at the Pennsylvania Avenue cottage and I don't want to go alone. Would you go with me?"

"Never seen the Mannerly's cottage. But won't Missy be upset if you bring someone else?" Rose asked rather seriously.

"I might be upset if I'm alone. I came down here to get away from politics," Bud explained.

"I'd love to see the Mannerly cottage. And maybe I'll find out if I'd like to go with you. What time is the party?"

"Sixish. Cocktails and finger food."

"Sounds fancy. What do I wear?"

"I don't know. I've never been there. I think I'll change from my bathing suit before I go."

"Hope so," Rose said scowling. Then smiling, she exclaimed, "I mean, is it going to be the dress-up crowd from the Pines?"

"Probably so, but this is a resort area. I think I'll dress casually. Where do I pick you up?"

"I live out on the highway, behind the bay. It's about ten minutes away. I'll write out the directions for you."

"Pick you up about a quarter to six, then," he said.

"That'll be perfect."

Bud jumped with a start. A screaming siren rose to an ear-shattering pitch. The high-frequency wail was sustained, like the climax of a soprano solo, then, slowly, began to wind down.

"What in the world is that?" Bud asked excitedly, as the siren rose again to its highest pitch. "Do we evacuate the town or is it a drowning?"

"It's just the volunteer fire company," Rose said calmly.

"Why does it have to be so loud?" he asked, as the siren wound down again.

"That's how they call the volunteer firemen," she said, as the siren wound up to the top of its scream again.

"It just keeps going up and down," Bud worried.

"Yeah," Rose laughed. "They used to blow it five times for the rescue squad and ten times for a fire. The rescue squad now is radio controlled and the men wear beepers," she yelled over the continuous rise and fall of the siren. "The first volunteer to arrive at the fire station can turn it off. But he wants the others to come and help, too, so they all let it go ten times."

"I'd think it would disturb the people. It's so loud!"

"If your house was on fire, you'd be glad to hear it."

As the tenth wail slowly wound all the way down through the contralto range, sliding on down into a baritone and fading out, Bud looked around. No one seemed to pay any attention to the siren. They had all become accustomed to it.

To Bud, the siren became a friendly reminder that the people of the town cared. Town's people helping each other in time of need. Volunteers coming to the rescue of their neighbors.

Bud and Rose talked and swam and he bought her a hot dog. They spent a wonderful day together on the beach. Rose decided to go home about three o'clock, so Bud left at the same time.

"I'll pick you up around a quarter of six," Bud said.

"I'll be ready. See you then," Rose said, waving good-bye. Bud walked back to his room at a happy pace singing a tune to himself. He hadn't been this excited about a date since he left Cornell University. The long hours of working for World Peace on the senator's staff, had nearly obliterated his social life.

He bathed and dressed in khaki slacks, a knit shirt, and loafers. He had meant to buy some boat shoes, but he had been so full of himself on the way through town he had forgotten. He decided to drive around and explore the area out on the highway. He drove past Rose's house both ways, looking it over.

She had about five acres with a stately old farmhouse near the road. He was surprised to see a mobile home beside the old farmhouse and two extremely long chicken houses out in back. The woods were cleared around the chicken houses. The farmhouse sat in a little cluster of shade trees. The mobile home lay across the lane from the farmhouse.

At twenty minutes of six he pulled into the lane. A black Labrador retriever barked and came out from under a pick-up truck to greet him. The dog wagged his tail and looked expectantly at him, so Bud got out of his car and petted the dog's head. "Good. Good dog. Good dog."

Bud was surprised to see the trailer door burst open and Rose come hurrying out. She wore khaki slacks, a knit shirt, and boat shoes. "The dog's name is Roamer. He's very friendly. He's our doorbell. You're early."

"Better than late. Roamer and I have made friends. He's a good dog," Bud said.

"Well, you're lucky," Rose said. "I'm all ready to go."

"Who lives in the farmhouse?" Bud asked.

"We used to, but it gets too cold in the winter," Rose answered. "Dad bought the mobile home and we moved into it. It's warm as toast in the winter and cool with central air in the summer."

"Ought to fix up the farmhouse and live there."

"You can fix it up, if you're so interested," she glared. "Fix it up and live there in the winter, if you're so clever."

"That's what I'd do, if I stayed around here," Bud said looking serious. Then with a smile, "Ready to go?"

"Ready when you are," she said sweetly.

They drove back to Rehoboth Beach and found 9 Pennsylvania Avenue. The large old wooden beach cottage was the third house from the beach. It had been the fifth house from the beach before the

'62 storm.

The wrap-around porch was lit up like a country inn, and tinkling piano music floated over a murmur of conversation. Bud and Rose went up to the porch door.

When Mrs. Mannerly opened the screen door, Bud said, "Hello, Mrs. Mannerly. I'm Bud Green and this is Rose Gardner. I met Missy on the beach and she invited us to your party."

"Oh, yes. Please come in. Missy will show you where everything is and introduce you around," she beckoned.

Going in, they found Missy standing right behind her mother. Missy had on a Lily dress from a popular Florida shop and looked smashing.

"It's so good of you to come, Bud," Missy said. "I didn't see you on the beach today."

"I got involved with old friends on another beach. Missy, I want you to meet Rose Gardner. Rose, this is Missy Mannerly."

Bud worried introducing them. *If Missy was upset because he had brought a date, she was able to cover it beautifully.*

Missy said, "Rose, let me show you the bar and the food." She took Rose by the arm and led her to the bar and food table, as Bud followed.

Betty Brass was at the bar. "Betty, I want you to meet Bud's date, Rose Gardner. Rose, this is Betty Brass."

"How did you manage to get such a charming man?" Betty said.

"We're old friends," Rose copied Bud's line, trying to keep everyone happy.

"Bud, you remember Betty Brass?" Missy said.

"Of course, Betty, how could I forget such a charming lady."

"Compliments will get you everywhere," Betty quipped. "Bud, I want you to meet Geoffrey Johnson. Geoff, this is Bud Green and Rose Gardner."

They shook hands all around with pleasant smiles. "This is a lovely party," Bud said to Missy.

"Thank you for coming."

When someone else spoke to Missy and Betty, Bud and Rose looked around. The room was full of older gentlemen in summer blazers and ladies in colorful summer cocktail dresses. Two uniformed waitresses passed canapés on silver platters. It was obviously a catered affair.

They started strolling from room to room, eating hors d'oeuvres and sipping their drinks.

The house was a display of summer elegance. The antique wicker furniture was freshly painted to match the decor. Large watercolors of nostalgic beach scenes from the Rehoboth Art League adorned the walls. Beach bric-a-brac filled every niche. It was a trip to old aristocratic beach life.

"This is a charming house," Rose said, trying to make conversation.

"Mr. Mannerly bought this house for entertaining," Bud said, sounding derogatory. "I'm sure it's all deductible."

"I meant, it was nice of you to invite me. I've heard so much about the Mannerly House and their parties. I've lived here all my life, but this is a summer house for Washington people."

"Sorry," Bud said apologetically. "I came to Washington to work for World Peace, but I feel like a deductible item in a power struggle. I need a rest from politics."

Rose turned to him and said, gently, "It's a lovely party," as her eyes sparkled. "Let's just enjoy it while we're here."

This simple remark surprised Bud. He became enamored with her genuine lust for life. Her easy manner had gone right to the point. "You're right," he agreed. "I like your spirit."

There were no familiar faces in the sea of humanity. Everyone was polite and friendly. "Where are you from?" "I used to know someone from there." "Excuse me. I see an old friend. Oh, hello, Charles. How have you been?" People faded in and out of their conversations.

After an hour and a half of social niceties, Bud said, "Let's get something to eat. I'll take you to dinner."

"I've eaten so much finger food, I'm stuffed."

"Then, let's go for a walk along the beach," Bud suggested.

"Sounds good to me,"" she said.

They found Missy, thanked her, and said they wished they could stay, but they had to go. Bud found Mr. and Mrs. Mannerly near the front door and thanked them. Mr. Mannerly said, with a warm smile, "Thank you for coming. Give my regards to the Senator Blassforth."

The night air smelled fresh and balmy. The party noise slowly faded as they walked toward the beach. Bud took her hand as they climbed up on the little boardwalk to the beach and he didn't want to let go once they were on the flat boards. She pulled him toward the sand beach away from the crowd.

"Didn't mean to cut you off at the party," Rose said. "Hope I didn't upset you."

"You're so right. I guess I'm just tired of the polite nonsense of political parties. Thanks, I needed that."

"I enjoyed being there," she said, raking the warm sand with her fingers.

"Have you always lived out on the highway?"

"My father used to live in Rehoboth Beach. He went to the Rehoboth High School in town. The Rehoboth Country Club used to be in town."

"Why'd he move out on the highway?"

"Real estate prices rose so high that now sixty percent of the home owners in Rehoboth Beach live in the Washington area. It wasn't the same little town anymore and the prices offered for houses were irresistible."

"You must hate the tourists."

"No. They've brought prosperity to us. They work fifty weeks a year to have two weeks here. Then, they go away and let us have three seasons here all to ourselves."

"I envy you, living here year 'round."

"And I envy you in the fast lane in the Capital City."

"I'm just a country boy, trying to work for World Peace within the system," Bud stated.

"What's this World Peace business? Sounds radical."

"I just want to try to make the world a better place to raise children. I'm not comfortable talking about myself. Let's talk about us."

"Us? What about us?"

"What I mean is, I think you're very special. I'd like to get to know you better."

"We're doing that right now."

"Have you decided whether you'd like to go out with me again?"

"Evening isn't over yet, but it's been good so far."

"You're waiting for me to make my move?" he asked.

"Something like that. Or not make any moves just yet."

"I just want to relax and enjoy doing whatever you'd like."

"That's sweet of you, but I'm not a city girl. I just enjoy every day as it comes. Should be going home soon," Rose said. "Have to be up early tomorrow."

"Okay. I'll take you home to bed," he said, trying to sound gallant while dropping a subtle claim on her.

He held her hand as they climbed up the sand to the little boardwalk over the dunes. The party was breaking up as they came to Bud's car. They drove home in silence, each wrapped in their own thoughts. As he turned into Rose's lane, the black lab came out to greet them.

"Roamer, you take good care of things," Bud said as he went around to open Rose's car door.

She had jumped out, saying, "I'm not used to gentlemen since the popularity of women's lib."

"We both need some practice."

She walked toward the mobile home. At the door, she turned and said, "Thank you for taking me to the Mannerly party."

"My pleasure," he said, bending to kiss her. She offered her cheek and he liked that. "See you tomorrow?"

"Have to work early. Why don't you come by for a late lunch and we'll see."

"I'll be there about two."

"Good night."

"Bye."

Bud hopped into his car and zipped off feeling on top of the world. He drove around aimlessly, feeling too awake to go back to his room. He found a place to park near the beach.

Settled in the sand, he gazed at the moon, basked in the evening breeze, and thought about Rose. It was as if he didn't have a care in the world. He had forgotten about World Peace and politics.

Bud woke up late. He had slept like a baby, ignoring the early rays of the sun. As he started for breakfast, he noticed that the steady breeze made the weather feel about ten degrees cooler near the ocean. *That's why they all come here*, he said to himself, *to get away from insufferable heat and humidity of DC.*

The Avenue Restaurant on the corner of First Street was an old establishment that had grown into a large masonry building. It looked neat and clean. He was ready for its sterile ambiance. Scanning the breakfast menu displayed in the front window, he toyed with the words "break" and "fast"" Don't want a fast break, I'm ready to break the nightly fast, he mused.

As he went in, Bud was surprised to see an orator standing at the far end of the dining area. His surplus army work pants hung on his wiry frame. His sharp, dark eyes scanned the breakfast crowd as he said, "When you Denton Dagos come here, you look like a bunch of Delaware grits."

Bud wondered if the orator was referring to the people from Denton as day-trippers or was using a slang term for Italians. The hostess seated Bud at a little table.

"Who's giving the speech?" Bud asked, as he sat down.

"Oh, that's just Crazy Eddy," the hostess said. "He comes by every morning. Sometimes I wonder if he is crazy like a fox. Everyone lets him do whatever he wants. He's entertaining and he's harmless."

"Well, I'll listen to the entertainment, then."

"Your wait person will be Jane. She'll be right with you."

Crazy Eddy was building to the climax of his oration. "You don't talk shop down here. The national debt isn't Pines Talk."

A young lady in a waitress uniform came up to Bud's table, interrupting Bud's concentration with, "My name is Jane and I'll be your wait person this morning."

"Crazy Eddy is quite an entertaining speaker."

"Not if you have to listen to him every morning."

"Oh, he isn't that bad, is he?"

"No, I just get tired of working around him. May I take your order?" she asked. Bud ordered a big breakfast.

He'd found another piece of the puzzle of the Nation's Summer Capital. Crazy Eddy played the role of the village idiot, but it was an envious role. The local people were fond of him and they protected him from the tourists. Ignorance is bliss, and Crazy Eddy was happy as a clam, but he wasn't ignorant. He had probably been a top executive when something snapped in his brain and he's been happy ever since.

After breakfast Bud strolled leisurely through town, looking at the shops. It was a small town with big city overlays. *The Washington Post* was everywhere.

There was a crowd on the boardwalk. The bathers had come out early in the bright sunshine. They were running up to the boardwalk for sodas, pizza and ice cream. He decided to explore the boardwalk in the other direction.

Bud turned south. As he walked along looking at each shop on the boardwalk, the sounds of FUNLAND caught his attention. He became intrigued with rides and games of every description going full force. It looked like an acre of carnival rides and slots under roof and open to the boardwalk to lure the strollers.

The new computerized slot machines overshadowed the older mechanical challenges. He strolled through the amusement area past the bumper cars, carousel, shooting gallery, and aerial rides. He wandered past rows of mechanical and electronic games with their coin slots sticking out at him. He was glad to see the games of skill, like skeeball, were still part of the scene.

The popular games of chance were a combination skeeball and a racehorse game and something called Whack-a-Mole. Little moles randomly pop up in one of five holes while the players try to "whack" them with a padded mallet. One little tot missed every one, while regulars tried to outwit the moles. Flabbergasted with the ridiculousness of it, he decided to ask Rose to try it with him.

He finally found his way out to the bright sun again and went on down the boardwalk. He estimated that the boardwalk was about a mile long. As he neared the south end, the shops had not replaced the large homes sitting back from the boardwalk.

At the end, he could see a stretch of sand before him and a couple of large houses. He took off his shoes, tied the laces together, slung them around his neck, and went down the steps to the beach. There were very few bathers this far from the center of town.

Each beach had a lifeguard, sitting on a white lifeguard stand, watching the swimmers. Bud sat down in the sand to watch the bathers. The waves were crashing out about twenty feet from shore. He watched the swimmers dive through the waves and come up in the rolling sea, past where the waves were breaking.

He decided to try battling the waves. He took off his shirt and shorts. He put his shoes on top of them to keep them from blowing away in the brisk beach wind.

He waded out, keeping an eye on the waves. As a big wave built up to crash on him, he dove into it and came out the other side. He swam around, letting the cooler water lower his body temperature. As his body relaxed, his nervous system went idle, and his mind was distracted with the ebb and flow of the waves. *It doesn't get any better than this*, he thought to himself.

Floating on his back he watched a sea gull glide into the wind as though it was hovering and then bank into a turn that carried him swiftly away. Two puffy white clouds stood out against the deep blue sky.

An idea struck him. This would be a good place to try body surfing. His toes touched the bottom, as he was getting set to catch the next wave. He started swimming frantically as the wave built up. He was on the crest of the wave when it broke and surged him shoreward.

Suddenly the support seemed to give way and jammed him head first into the sandy bottom with a boiling motion. He stood up a little dazed and waded heavily ashore, dripping wet and wiping his eyes. He felt like a shipwreck victim wading ashore on a deserted island.

He flopped down on the sand. "Tomorrow I'll bring a towel," he said, out loud. A young boy and his father were body surfing. Bud watched them with interest, feeling a little envious. The boy wiped out just the way Bud had been, but the father seemed to know when to put his feet down and try to stand up.

The bright sun warmed his skin as he stared at the breaking waves. The rhythmical crashing and washing ashore lulled him into a restful trance. Mother nature had captured an overworked idealist.

Three young children came romping back to the beach to take out their aggressions on the ocean, spraying sand. Bud dug into his shoe to find his watch. *One-thirty! Better get going!*

He pulled his shirt on over his dry shoulders. He carried his shoes and shorts up to the boardwalk. By the time he reached the center of town, his bathing trunks were dry enough to put on his shorts. He brushed the sand off his feet, put on his shoes, and headed for the Country Squire. He stopped a minute inside the door to let his eyes adjust to the darker restaurant.

"Look who's here," Rose said, smiling.

"I've been out in the sun and I can barely see in here. How are you, Rose?"

"I'm fine. Are you hungry or thirsty?"

"Little of both. How about a cola and tender loving care."

"Take any seat and I'll bring you a cola."

Bud found a seat and looked around as he adjusted to the light. He watched Rose carrying his drink to him.

"Here you are," Rose said smiling.

"What time do you get off?"

"Not so fast! Give me a minute to catch my breath."

"Sorry. Been thinking about you ever since last night."

"Thank you for taking me to the lovely party. I'm not much of a party girl, but I did enjoy seeing the Mannerly's house."

"Just meant that I'd like to talk to you some more and I didn't want to bother you when you were working," Bud explained.

"We're not busy now. I can take off whenever I want. If you're going to have a sandwich, I'll get one for myself. I'll sit down and eat with you, if I may?"

"That would be delightful. I'll have the same as you're having, whatever you recommend."

"You may be sorry," she said, going back to the kitchen.

Bud looked around at the few stragglers at the bar. The lunch crowd had left. Most people were on the beach, enjoying a beautiful day.

Rose returned with two sandwiches and a glass of milk for herself. She took off her apron and sat down.

"Have you ever played Whack-a-Mole?" Bud asked.

"Oh, my! From the sublime to the ridiculous!" Rose said.

"It's so bizarre that it caught my attention. Have you tried it?"

"Heavens, no. But I'm willing to try anything once."

"Anything?" he said, provocatively.

"I said 'once.' If I've already tried it once, it doesn't count. If you're thinking what I'm thinking."

"What are you thinking?"

"Whack-a-Mole!"

"Well, let's try it."

"All right, if you'll stop talking about it. Is that what you wanted to talk about?" she asked.

"Not really. You said you had graduated from the University of Delaware. What did you major in?" he asked her.

"English major and a minor in Marine Biology. Why?"

"Do you like waiting on tables?"

"I've just graduated and I need some time before I start on my career."

"What are you planning on doing?"

"I'm planning on eating my sandwich with you," she dodged the question as her eyes flashed a gentle smile, "and walking down to Fun land, so we can Whack-a-Mole."

"Like your attitude," Bud said, enjoying her ability to stay on track. "Let's enjoy our lunch."

"Like your attitude, too."

After lunch he wanted to pay for her lunch, but she said it was free. They walked down the boardwalk to Fun land and watched the others play Whack-a-Mole. Then Bud paid for two players.

When it started, Bud whacked frantically at the diving moles while Rose calmly and deliberately caught a couple of them as their heads popped up. Exasperated, Bud whacked away blindly.

Suddenly it was over. Rose had won easily and accepted a fuzzy stuffed animal.

"You sure you've never played this before?"

"Never. It just takes a cool head and a steady swing."

"Hasn't anyone ever told you not to lob to the gentleman's back-hand."

"Not in this day and age. Hey, this was your idea."

"What would you like to do now?"

"Is this like a date?"

"Sure hope so."

"Let's sit on a bench and look at the ocean. Seen a lot of people doing that, but I never seem to have time."

"Shall we get an ice cream cone and eat it on the bench?"

"Chocolate marshmallow?"

"I'll get the cones and you select the bench."

When Bud came back with the ice cream cones dripping on his hands, they sat down and went to work on them.

"Have you always worked in politics?" Rose questioned.

"I hate politics. I was working for World Peace, until the senator went on vacation. The whole office staff dropped everything and came down here."

"Working for a senator is working in politics."

"So I've found out. I spend as much time at parties as I do working for World Peace. Just trying to work within the system."

"You don't seem to like what you're doing."

"I seem to be all alone with the idea of World Peace."

"You aren't some kind of fanatic, are you?" she asked.

"I guess I was in college, but I'm trying to find my way at the moment. It's a personal thing," Bud rattled on. "I just want to help make the world a better place to raise a family."

"You're right," she pointed out. "World Peace starts at home. To really work, it has to start in the grass roots, as you politicians call it."

"You mean it works from the bottom up?"

"Doesn't everything in a democracy?"

"Just hadn't thought about it that way."

"Well, when you do, let me know what you've found out."

"I like talking to you. You might know something I need to know."

"I know one thing. I'm keeping my options open this summer, to answer your question that I ignored at lunch. I'm not ready to start my career just yet," Rose said emphatically.

"I like that idea. Maybe I should hang in there with my job and see how things work out."

"Patience is a virtue, possess it if you can. Often found in women, but seldom found in man," she laughingly recited.

"That rhymes, but I'm surprised to hear a modern liberated woman quoting a sexist poem. Sounds like an old wives' tale."

"Don't be so impatient with old wives' tales, unless you can do better," she chided him.

"Okay, give me a minute." Bud puzzled out a rhyme for her, "Chauvinism is a problem, avoid it with acumen, sometimes found in man, but always in a woman."

"How did you do that?"

"I've written a lot of slogans for World Peace."

"That sounds like a slogan for war," she responded.

"Let me rephrase that for you," Bud said, changing the subject. "May I take you to dinner tonight?"

"You have to give me a little more time," she said. "I'm not used to the fast lane."

"Neither am I, but I'm going back to Washington at the end of the week and you're the best thing that's happened to me since I left Elmira."

"Elmira? Where's that?"

"Little town in New York. Lot like this town, except big city people don't visit there. It's not 'upstate New York' where the New Yorkers live," he related. "It's what they call the 'Southerntier,' more like inland Delaware."

"Full of chicken farmers?"

"Yes, and dairy farms and truck farms."

"Sounds nice to me."

"Nice place to be from, as they say."

"Maybe you ought to work with the grass roots of Elmira?"

"I'll think about that, too. Now, what about dinner?"

"Boy! Talk about impatient! Where do you want to eat?"

"You pick the place and I'll take you."

"Have you been to the Lamp Post?"

"Not yet, but I'm ready, willing, and able."

"Pick me up around six?"

"I'll be there."

Bud walked Rose back to her car asking, "What do I wear?"

"You can come just the way you are, if you like. It's a resort town."

"I'll take a shower and put on slacks. See you at six."

Rose drove off and Bud started walking back through town. Thinking about the Grass Roots and Rose, he walked right by the shoe store and forgot to buy the boat shoes again.

He showed up at Rose's fifteen minutes early. He got out and played with Roamer. Rose's brother stuck his head out of the trailer door, and said, "I'm Rose's brother. She said you're early. She's getting dressed."

"I'm Bud Green. There's no hurry."

Bud and Roamer walked all the way around the old farmhouse. It stood solidly on its foundation, but there were a lot of little things that showed the neglect of abandonment.

Rose came running out, saying, "You're early!"

"Sorry. I just wanted to look over the old farmhouse."

"Well, take a good look," she said sarcastically.

"I just did," he replied. "Roamer and I checked it out."

"Okay. I'm ready if you are."

They hopped into Bud's car and drove off. "The LampPost restaurant is out on the highway where Route 24 comes to Route 1," Rose said. "Route 1 is the highway that goes down the barrier reef between the ocean and the bay, while Route 24 skirts the inland side of the bay."

"Sounds easy enough," Bud said. The next thing he saw was a sprawling building with the right sign. An oversized lamp hung on a post in front of the building. Bud pulled into the parking lot that surrounded the rambling roadside restaurant.

The double-entry doors were enclosed in a glass windbreak that told Bud it was a year round restaurant with regular help. There were two dining rooms and a bar off the waiting room. The hostess greeted them as they entered into a large foyer and waiting room, with. "Do you have a reservation?"

"No, we don't," Bud replied.

"It'll be a few minutes. Let me put you on my list and you can wait in the bar, if you like."

Bud put his name on her list, so they went into the bar, found a table, and ordered wine. It was a friendly place. The locals ignored the national news on a TV hung high in the corner of the room. Tanned workmen with baseball hats sat at the bar. The attitude adjustment hour had them talking and laughing.

Bud and Rose sipped their wine, smiling shyly, and making small talk. Bud wanted the evening to be a treat for Rose and he tried to treat her like royalty. Rose felt at home there and had settled in to enjoy the evening.

It wasn't long before the hostess appeared and showed them their table. Bud carried the half-full wineglasses to the table and even pushed Rose's chair in for her.

"You may order whatever you like tonight. This is my treat and I want you to have a memorable evening," Bud said.

"Oh, goodie! I'll have to read the whole menu, in that case. Oh, this is going to be fun," Rose said eagerly.

Rose looked around to see who was there. Bud looked at the decor. The walls were decorated with handmade, pioneer farming tools.

Windows, divided into several with little panes, covered the outside wall. The curtain colors blended well with the wood paneling.

The tabletops were hatch covers from the victory ships of World War II. They had been dipped in shiny polyurethane. Even the handgrip holes were filled with clear plastic. Bud felt a rustic authenticity and simple honesty in the ambiance.

When the waitress brought their dinner, Bud tasted his meal. "These are delicious crab cakes," he stated.

"Naturally. Some places have a good view of the water and not so good seafood. They sell you the view. But the Lamp Post doesn't have a view, so they have to have good seafood."

"That's an interesting theory. I'll remember that."

When they had finished, there were only empty plates to clear away. As the waitress asked about coffee and dessert, the band started setting up.

"Let's have dessert and coffee until the band starts," Bud suggested. "I haven't heard a live band in ages."

"Why not. I can go back on my diet tomorrow."

When the band started with a low, walking bass in an easy tempo, they listened. The singer, Bunky Eye, moved to the mike in the blue spotlight and sang, "Put Your Head on My Shoulder." The dance floor quickly filled with an odd assortment of couples.

Both Bud and Rose slid their chairs back at the same time, with the synchronized body language of a happy couple. Together they were drawn to the dance floor by the mood of the music. He took her in his arms and drifted with the easy beat. She put her head on his shoulder. Floating gracefully in unison, oblivious to the sea of dancers, they felt alone together.

The whole world had become so soft and gentle, so right, so easy. The magic of this unforgettable moment colored the rest of the evening. For the first time in his life, he just went with the flow. Serendipity had taken over.

Rose had spent every summer of her life in Rehoboth Beach. She knew better than to get involved in a summer romance, but she was cherishing the moment.

Bud had discovered true happiness and peace for the first time. He wanted to go on dancing forever.

When the music stopped, Rose stepped back, aglow with bliss.

"You dance so well, I don't ever want to stop," Bud said. "I could go on all night."

"So could I, but I have a big day tomorrow."

"One more dance. Then I'll get you home in time for a good night's sleep."

"One or two, but no more, should quit while it's still fun."

"Your wish is my command," he said, still trying to sound gallant.

Rose smiled as the music started again. They were drawn together again by the magic of the music. When the music stopped a second time, Bud said, "Our dessert is here."

They smiled into each other's eyes over dessert and coffee. Bud dutifully called for the bill, paid, and drove her home.

When he walked her to the door, they kissed goodnight. She squeezed his hand. "Thank you for the lovely evening," she said, turning to go in.

Bud was left alone with Roamer. He gave the dog a pat on the back, singing, "Roamer is a misnomer. I think I'll call you Homer." Glancing at the stately old farmhouse basking in the moonlight, he slid into his car. He drove off singing, "Put Your Head on My Shoulder," all the way back to his motel.

Everything seemed right with the world. He slipped off to dreamland, with a happy fantasy of Rose in his arms. Reason had flown out the window and rhyme had taken over. *Dancing flames smolder, with your head on my shoulder.*

LOST ROSE OF SUMMER

The next morning Bud went looking for Rose. When she wasn't at the Country Squire, he remembered she had said, "I've got a big day tomorrow." Last night, Bud had been so carried away with Rose, he had forgotten to ask where she would be.

That feeling of being left behind came over him, as if he had lost his best friend. How could he have missed this most precious connection? *Maybe she went to the beach.* With hope in his heart, he went to look for Rose on the beach, but ran into Missy Mannerly instead.

""Hello, stranger," Missy said as he was walking up the beach. She wore a different bathing suit every day. The style was tastefully modest and traditional. "You look like the cat who swallowed the canary."

He was taken by surprise. She was right, but Bud didn't know it showed. He blurted out, "Oh, Missy. Thank you for the nice party. We had a good time."

Missy ignored the "we" word. "Thank you for coming. I'm glad you enjoyed it."

Bud found himself trapped in polite society again. Missy was a beautiful girl, but he was searching for Rose. Feeling indebted by Missy's hospitality, he nervously raved about her party. "Your beach house is beautiful. The people were all very pleasant. The wicker was unbelievable. The beach bric-a-brac was fascinating. But the best part was the paintings."

"Every time Daddy goes to the Rehoboth Art League, he can't resist buying another painting."

"They are an overwhelming collection of interesting scenes of this area."

"Well, why don't you stop by and look at them when you can see them without all those people in the way. Just drop by when you have time."

"That's very kind of you." He said, but he was thinking, *How did I get into this?*

"What about this evening?"

"I'll have to check my schedule," he said, trying to stall. "Why don" you give me your phone number? I'll call you when I get back to my motel," Bud stated.

"It's 227-2227. It must be awful to have to keep a schedule while you are at the beach."

"Most of the staff are down here and I like to let them know where I'll be."

"Oh, I didn't know the others were here, too."

"Yes. This is the Nation's Summer Capital."

"I've heard that, but I thought it was just a Chamber of Commerce slogan."

"Seems to be where the action is in the summer. You and I are here and we seem to be in the middle of the political arena most of the time."

"Do you have to make everything sound like a power struggle? Lighten up, as they say."

"You're right. I'll check with the rest of the staff, if I can find them on the beach. I'll get back to you."

"Let me know."

"I'll call you first," he exaggerated, as he left.

Bud walked on up the beach, hoping he would find Rose, before he ran into the group from the office. Maybe Rose had gone to a different beach. Why does life have to be so complicated, just when everything was going so right? Looking over all the bathers on the beach, he spotted the office gang.

"Here comes the socialite. How was the party, Bud?" said a voice in the crowd. The office group hung together. They took turns teasing him, as if each one was speaking for the group, while Tilly silently watched and listened.

"All right. A lot of stuffy old people all dressed up." Bud went along with the friendly abuse. This familiarity made him feel like part of the group.

"Don't give us that. Heard you showed up with a townie."

"What do you mean by townie?"

"A local girl. A native girl."

"She's just a friend. A very nice girl."

"Listen to conquering hero smitten by a local beauty."

"Oh, knock it off."

"Heard you took her out dancing last night."

"Where'd you hear that?"

"It's a small town. Heard you took her to the Lamp Post."

"It's a nice place."

"If you like that kind of crowd. Last time we were there, women in sequin pants suits from Pots Net, danced together."

"What a bunch of snobs. You all sound jealous. Just 'cause you weren't invited to the Mannerly's."

"We were invited to a party in our neighborhood."

"Well, if any of you would like to see the Mannerly house, I'll take you there this evening. Missy invited me to take a closer look at her paintings."

"You may want us to go along with you, but I'm sure Missy wants you all to herself."

"You've had your chance. I don't understand all this hanky-panky. I invited you, but I don't like all this maneuvering."

"Watch the hanky-panky expert maneuver out of this one."

"Well, I did tell Missy that you were in town. And we check with each other's whereabouts in case we're needed."

"We'll be checking on you, but you don't need to check on us when we are on vacation."

The end of the sentence was interrupted, by the volunteer fire company's siren, raising to its high-pitched wail.

"Siren is so loud," Bud yelled over the screaming siren.

Tilly spoke up, "First time I heard it I was in the hardware store, about to pay for my goods when it went off. A great big man, at the cash register, jumped over the counter and ran out."

"What did you do?"

"We didn't know what to do. We just went out and watched the fire engines drive off. I went home and came back later and paid, when things had quieted down."

"Guess we should be thankful that the town cares enough to come to their neighbor's rescue," Bud said.

"You'll get used to hearing it," Tilly said.

"Gets better each time. Well, gotta be going," Bud said.

"Yes, we know," the office gang chided him.

"See you later."

Bud walked on up the beach, still looking for Rose. When he saw a young girl coming out of the water scowling as she pulled up the high-rise sides of her string bikini, he worried about the unpleasant look on her face as though the string bikini was about to slice her in half. He hadn't noticed her alluring figure, until she turned the other cheek.

He walked much farther up the beach this time. Each jetty was different. Some of them were easy and some were a challenge. Past the city limits, there was a row of umbrellas and chairs set back on the dunes of the Henlopen Acres Beach Club. The people sat and read or relaxed in an orderly row.

The enormous stone jetty, bordering the north side of the Beach Club, looked forbidding until he found a paved walkway over the jetty, high on the beach. Walking on, the North Shores' beaches looked exciting.

People sat or laid, helter skelter, wherever they wanted. A large catamaran, pulled up on the beach, flapped its colorful sail in the breeze. Bud was lured toward the old watchtowers, left over from World War II, looming up ahead. They looked like cement silos standing by themselves on a lonely stretch of sand. Relics of the threat, of an invasion by enemy submarines in World War II that seemed so remote in this day and age.

The towers stood out on the beach and looked quite near. As he went on, they were much farther than he had estimated. When he finally came up to the first one, he was tired from the long walk. Exploring the perimeter, he found it all boarded up.

He tried to decipher the weathered graffiti, but it was too far-gone. Looking back, the North Shores' bathers were so far away, they were colorful specks on the sand. He had come a long way.

GRASS ROOTS

Watching a lone sea gull gliding over the water, he sat down to rest.

He thought of Rose. Why hadn't he had sense enough to ask her where she would be? Maybe she was on the late shift. It was time to go back to the Country Squire to see if she had come in. He was hungry, anyway. But he wanted to avoid Missy and the office gang, until he had talked to her. Maybe he could walk inland and find his way back.

He staggered to his feet and started trudging back down the beach. Walking on the wet sand nearest the water's edge to get better traction, his inland hip was overworked. At low tide, the steeper slope of the sand made him feel like a side-hill cow.

The sun was warm on his shoulders and the brightness was dazzling. He was an explorer retracing his steps, looking for a way to avoid hazards.

After he passed the Henlopen Acres Beach Club, he turned inland. Coming to a road, he walked south. The road went along the beach and then turned inland by the Henlopen Hotel, the masonry high-rise landmark at the north end of the boardwalk. He knew this would lead him back.

The road skirted a lake and turned south over a bridge. It was the bridge where he had driven Tilly that first day, only four or five short blocks from the main drag. His pace quickened as the sights became more familiar.

At the Country Squire, he asked for Rose. "She took the day off," a waitress said. It was late for lunch and he was hungry. He sat down and ordered a sandwich. What should he do? When the waitress brought his lunch, he asked for a phone. She pointed out the one on the boardwalk, just down the street.

He gobbled down the sandwich and headed for the phone. No one was at home at Rose's house. He decided to walk back to his motel to shower and dress. He had been spinning his wheels all day, getting nowhere. *Might as well be ready, just in case.*

He had stopped in the shoe store on the way home and bought a pair of boat shoes. When he was dressed, he called Rose's house. No answer. He called Missy to get it over with and Missy answered.

"Oh, hello. Missy?"

"Hello, Bud. What time are you coming to see the pictures?"

"Well." He didn't know what to say. "I could come over in a few

45

minutes."

"Perfect. We can have a drink and you can browse."

"Sounds good. I could use one."

"See you soon. Bye."

He decided to drive to Missy's house. There would be a place to park and he could get away easier. Missy waved from the porch as he drove up. "You can park in the driveway," she called to him.

He pulled into the driveway and went in.

"Hello, Bud. So nice to see you again. Won't you come in?"

"Nice to be here," he mumbled. Stepping into the lap of luxury was scary. The Mannerly's were kind and generous, and Missy was fun to be with. But Bud didn't want to get in over his head.

"Promised you a drink. What would you like?"

"What do you have?"

"Anything you want." She noticed that Bud hesitated as if he was at a loss for words. She led him in to the bar, reciting, "Scotch, bourbon, gin, or vodka. Beer, wine, or soft drinks."

"Do you have some white wine open?"

"Sure." She took a bottle from the little refrigerator under the bar. She poured it into two stemmed wineglasses. She handed one to him and she took the other. "Feel free to wander around the house and look at the paintings whenever you like." As she started out of the room, she added, "Let's sit down for a minute on the porch and talk."

He followed Missy out to the porch. He had the feeling that they were alone in the house.

They sat down and each took a sip of their wine. Missy asked, "Did you major in political science?"

"Heavens, no. I have a bachelor of arts degree."

"Are you planning to make a career out of politics?"

"No. I don't like politics. I had been working for World Peace, so I joined the senator's staff."

"Doesn't pay much, does it?"

"You rate people by the amount of money they make?"

"Mummy and Daddy use the Green Book, *The Social List of Washington.*"

"Like the *Four Hundred in New York*, seems so old fashioned."

"It's very good, actually, when you need to make up a party list and send invitations. The troublemakers are already weeded out for you. It makes your party a success," she boasted.

"Seems so superficial," Bud said, "letting a stranger decide who your friends are."

"How'd you have me rate people?"

"By their accomplishments. By what they stand for and by what they do."

"You can't do much in this country without money."

"I hadn't thought of it that way."

"Well, that's the way it is. Perhaps I should rephrase the question. Have you thought about your financial future?"

"Financial futures have more to do with living within your means than how much money you make." Annoyed, Bud pontificated, "Nothing exceeds like excess!"

"Didn't mean to upset you," Missy said pouting.

"This isn't beach talk. Have you thought about the seagulls and the ecological chain?" Bud said almost dramatically.

"No, they're just there. Daddy says 'Ecology is the root of all evil economics.' It just isn't practical," Missy replied.

"Maybe I can figure out a way to make it pay."

"Wouldn't an established job be easier to do? Daddy has some businesses in the Midwest. He's always looking for someone to run them," Missy suggested.

"Guess I was taught stewardship. I want to do something to help civilization and nature. Make a contribution."

"You sound like a dreamer."

"Well, some dreamers had to paint the pictures, before your Daddy could buy them."

"Artists like to starve. They're not very practical," she said. "But here I'm talking too much, when you wanted to look at the paintings."

"Good idea. Let's enjoy them."

Bud put his glass down, got up, and looked around. Missy politely did the same. "I don't want to disturb the rest of the family."

"You won't. Mummy and Daddy have gone to cocktails with an old friend."

The paintings were unusually well done. Some scenes were familiar and some he had never seen. "Where is this," he asked.

"Oh, that's McQuay's store, by the bridge over the canal, as you come in to Rehoboth," she said.

"Guess I had my eye on the traffic. I'll look for it next time."

Bud was pleased to see Rehoboth Beach in an exhibit. When they found themselves back on the porch, they sat down again.

"That was delightful," Bud said. "Thank you." An urgent feeling that he'd be beholden for the treat was bothering him.

"Glad you enjoyed them. I like to look at them when I'm home alone."

"Would you like to go out for dinner?" he said. Feeling obligated to return her courtesy, he was getting in deeper.

"Oh, let's just walk down the boardwalk and get a pizza or something at Grotto's," she suggested.

"Sounds like fun," Bud said, relieved that Missy hadn't selected a fancy restaurant. They finished their drinks. Bud stood up when Missy got up to carry the glasses to the kitchen.

"Ready to go?" Missy said when she returned.

"Yep," Bud said, following her out.

On the street, she hooked her arm in his and steered him to the boardwalk. They dodged the evening crowd of unfamiliar faces as they marched toward the center of town. He felt like a lamb being led to slaughter. He looked around at the unfamiliar faces in hopes that the office gang wasn't around.

Near the center of town, the ocean's crashing waves were drowned out by a penetrating, throbbing sound. The busy foot traffic on the boardwalk turned toward the street. Two boys, with the car radio on full blast, crept around the U-turn, in a desperate and over enthusiastic search for girls.

Missy led Bud into Grotto's Pizza Parlor. A smiling hostess seated them at a table by the window, across the street from the Country Squire. Bud thought, *So far, so good.* He began to relax as they studied the menu.

"I like mushrooms and anchovies," Missy announced.

"I'd like a plain slice or two," Bud said.

"We can get a small one, six slices, half plain and half with the works," Missy said.

"Sounds perfect," he agreed.

The waitress appeared and took their order. As soon as she left with their order, Missy watched Bud's eyes wander around the room, studying the other patrons. When he finally looked at her, she asked, "Where did you meet Rose?"

It seemed like casual conversation. "In the Country Squire across the street," he said.

"You picked her up?" Missy asked looking surprised.

"No. She works there, waiting on tables for the summer."

"A waitress?"

Missy's probing was becoming uncomfortable. *What's the matter here?* Bud stammered, "She just graduated from college and came home for the summer."

"She's a townie?"

"Yes. Her father grew up in Rehoboth Beach, but they've moved out on the highway, just out of town."

"You said you were old friends."

Oh, oh, here it comes! Better change the subject. "Don't usually think of either of us as old." Bud replied coyly.

"You know what I mean!" Missy pouted.

"Do I sense a little bit of jealousy?"

"Me? Jealous? Of a local waitress?"

"She has decided to wait until the summer is over before she starts on a career," Bud explained.

"Everyone seems to be in limbo career-wise," she complained.

"It's summer vacation time. You and I are both taking time off. Let's talk about you for a change," he changed the subject.

"What about me?"

"You look so attractive when you try to cross-examine me."

"Oh. Now."

"You always dress so nicely. I like your happy face. You are fun to be with," Bud said.

Fortunately, the waitress brought the pizza before he went any further. He was getting in too deep again.

They each selected a slice and tasted it.

"You're right," Bud, said. "This is the best pizza I've ever tasted."

"Glad you like it," she said.

When they had finished, Bud asked, "Would you like to stop at the ice cream store for dessert?"

"Let's just walk on home. I'm sure we have some ice cream in the fridge," Missy replied.

"Good idea," Bud said. He wouldn't run into anyone he knew at Missy's house.

As they left the pizza parlor, the sun was setting. Golden waves dotted the ocean. The overhead lights on the boardwalk popped on automatically as darkness descended on their sensors.

Missy fumbled for his hand. "That pizza was divine," she said, giving his hand a little squeeze. "I'm sorry. Didn't mean to be so inquisitive. How can I make it up to you?"

"No problem," Bud said.

Missy's house was dark. She led Bud in turning on a couple of porch lights. "Let's look in the fridge," she said, leading him by the hand through the dark house.

In the dark, she turned suddenly, grabbed him, and kissed him with ardent passion. He was caught off balance. By the time he gained his equilibrium, a hungry lust stirred in him.

Groping in the dark had turned into an exciting exploration by Braille. Their preliminary fondling, interrupted by a sudden electrifying crack of a car door slamming, split them apart.

"Where are your parents?" he asked, a little breathless.

"Obviously, they haven't returned from the cocktail party," Missy said, pulling herself together. She slid her hand around his waist, in the dark and pulled him to her.

What a time to get lucky, he thought. A week ago, he'd have welcomed any chance for intimacy or just fooling around, but with Rose in the picture, it didn't seem right. He was thinking, *Never rains, but it pours*.

"When do you expect them to come home?" Bud asked nervously.

"It's sort of Russian roulette," Missy whispered. "They don't stay out after dark very often."

"We should be looking more proper, in case they pop in on us," he said, trying to untangle himself. Bud hadn't intended to get involved with Missy. He had started out being polite to her as part of his job. Things had gotten out of hand and he was feeling responsible.

"Yes. You're right," she said, letting go of him. "I'm sorry to be so forward."

"Took it as a compliment. A most enjoyable one, at that."

"Thank you for being so kind."

"Got a big day tomorrow. Going to have to go home soon."

"Thought you were on vacation."

"I am, but I have to go back to Washington in a day or so. Have to be ready for the campaign," he said as he headed for the lights on the porch and Missy followed him.

"Wish you didn't have to go," she said disappointedly.

"So do I," he said, as he turned to face her at the door.

"Hope I see you again soon. Thank you for everything."

She came right up to him and he bent forward and gave her a proper goodnight kiss.

"Thank you," he said, waving goodbye on his way to his car. He backed the car out and waved again as he escaped.

Back in his room, he glanced at his watch. It was too late to phone Rose again. Knowing he had to wait until tomorrow to try to find Rose, he tossed and turned a long time before falling asleep.

PART TWO
THE RAINBOW

Bud woke to the sound of a gentle rain. He would have liked to snuggle back down in the covers, but his unfinished search for Rose inspired him to leap up. He rummaged through his bag for something to wear in the rain.

Putting on yesterday's shorts, shirt, and the waterproof boat shoes, he went out on the little balcony and held out his hand. The light sprinkle felt warm and harmless.

He set out for town, hiding his anxiety by singing in the rain and enjoying its refreshing patter on his bare head. The freshly washed air was fragrant.

He strolled down to the Country Squire. He sat down in his usual place to wait. The same woman he'd talked to the day before came up to him. "Well, how are you this morning?"

"I'm fine," he lied. "Is Rose working today?"

"Think so. I'll see if she's come in yet. Would you like a cup of coffee while you're waiting?"

"Okay," he said.

The rain had driven a lot of people inside. They were sort of milling around, waiting for the rain to stop. She brought the coffee, saying, "I'll see if I can find her for you."

Watching the people, he took an anxious sip. "Damn!" The hot coffee burned his lip and he jumped, spilling some on the table. A few drops had fallen on his shirt. He'd rather have had juice and some breakfast, first. He looked around to see if anyone had been watching him. They were all wrapped up in themselves. His embarrassing mishap had gone unnoticed.

Finding a napkin he wiped up the spilt coffee. "Should have stood in bed," he grumbled to himself. An old quotation, but he couldn't remember where it came from or just what it meant.

"Look what came in out of the rain," Rose said.

She had suddenly appeared from nowhere. Bud stammered, "Hello, Rose. I looked all over for you yesterday."

"Took the day off, because I had to go to Dover. Ran a lot of errands and didn't get home much before bed time."

"I missed you," Bud said, looking forlorn.

"That's sweet. I see you're really into that coffee."

"I spilled it. Was it ever hot!"

"Have you had breakfast?"

"No, but when can I see you again?"

"Tell me what you want to eat. When I bring it to you, I'll have a minute to talk. Okay?"

"Hot cakes, sausage, juice, and a glass of milk."

"Be right back."

He watched her athletically coordinated walk as she strode back to the kitchen. He was fascinated with the smooth rhythm of her hips. The movement made exotic little creases that danced on her khaki shorts.

He was oblivious of the crowd gathered around the door. He was pondering the mysterious attraction of Rose. There wasn't any one thing that he could put his finger on. She just seemed to be altogether in a healthy way.

Her mind, body, and nervous system all worked together in harmony. It was such a refreshing combination, that he never seemed to get enough. He was completely preoccupied with the idea when Rose reappeared with his breakfast.

"Here you are," she said, placing his breakfast on the table with an easy graceful movement and a little flourish.

"Thank you, Rose. Do you have a minute to talk?"

"What's on your mind," she asked, putting down her tray.

"I looked everywhere for you yesterday."

"I know. You just said that."

"What I mean is that I wanted to see you again and I didn't know how to find you."

"Well, you've found me now."

"When can I see you again?"

"You're seeing me now."

"Okay. When do you get off from work?"

"About four or five, today. Why?"

"Just thought we could do something together."

"Why don't you stop back around four o'clock and we can talk about it. By then the rain may have stopped."

"That's what I wanted to hear," he said with a sigh of relief. The furrows in his brow cleared and he smiled. "I'll be here a little ahead of time."

"Don't rush. I'll wait for you."

"Don't want to let you slip away again."

"We'll talk about it then. Enjoy your breakfast."

Bud gobbled up his breakfast in a happy state. It was a big relief to find Rose again. He left feeling on top of the world.

Outside, the few pedestrians sprinted for cover in the rain. The hard rain was over and the wind had died down. Bud started to walk toward the boardwalk, but ducked into a bookstore to get out of the sprinkle.

He browsed among the books. You can't tell a book by the cover, he thought to himself. When he saw an attractive cover, he picked up the book and looked through it. He hadn't had time to read a book since he had arrived in Washington. He wanted to get back to reading.

There were a lot of attractive books displayed on their side with their front covers showing. When he came to an attractive looking cover, he read the dust jacket blurb. It was a slow, engrossing process. When he finally found himself near the door, he looked out.

The rain had let up enough to venture outside. The sun peeked out between two clouds, making the wet pavement sparkle. As he came to the boardwalk, he stopped transfixed in his tracks. An enormous rainbow arced out of the ocean, across the heavens, curved over the land, and faded inland. Both ends of the rainbow were out of reach.

It was spectacular and subtle at the same time. The whole spectrum of colors were there, but they were ethereal. The filmy colors were translucent and yet vibrant. He had never seen such a moving sight. He just stood there in awe gazing up at it.

Other people began to stop and look. Bud wanted to share it and he thought of Rose. As the sun became stronger, the rainbow began to fade and soon it was over. It was like an omen.

Bud decided to sit on an empty bench. There was no one on the beach. The wet sand was puddled. The ocean washed in and out as waves were breaking near the shore. He wondered what the beach looked like in the snow. *Did the ocean ever freeze over*?

A couple of daring sunbathers ventured forth. Bud watched them spread out their towels and settle down. Others began to follow them out on the sand. They were like seagulls, playing follow the leader and competing for position. Soon the beach was full of summer activity again.

They all danced to mother nature's song. Bud looked up, but the rainbow had gone. In Washington, it was business as usual, whether there was rain or sunshine. He liked the idea of nature playing an active part in life.

Walking north up the boardwalk, looking at the ocean, he nearly ran into a jogger. Being involved with two women had been troubling him. He decided to walk on the road until he was past Snob Beach.

There were paths from the road, over the dunes to the beach. Taking the third path, he felt safe that he had gone past Missy's pink umbrella. Scanning the beach from the top of the dune, he spotted two of the office staff.

They greeted him as he approached. "Hi, Bud. Did the rain cramp your style?"

"Enjoyed a walk in the rain. Weather here is a big event. Everything at the beach depends on the weather. In Washington, the weather doesn't seem to matter. Did you see the rainbow?"

"We just got here. When was it?"

"You must have just missed it."

"Here," one girl said, stretching out a towel, "sit down and tell us what you've been up to."

"I'm going to have to go back to town soon. I didn't have time to plan this trip and I'm running out of money."

"Call the office and have your check sent down here?"

"Well, I came down on the spur of the moment. I just walked out.

I have cleaning and laundry to do up there. Sort of get it together before the senator returns."

"We'll miss your tips on the activities of the elite."

"I haven't had a minute to myself since I've been here. I'm not complaining. I've been received royally, here. I'll be back. That's for sure."

"Sound like you've been having a good time. We envy you."

"Hope it hasn't been too good a time."

"Tell us the juicy parts."

"Isn't much to tell and I think I'd better leave it that. Quit when I'm ahead."

"You're no fun. How have you been making out with Missy?"

Bud blushed. "I just looked at her paintings. Her father has an extensive collection of Rehoboth scenes."

"We're getting close. You blushed when we asked about Missy and making out."

"What do you want me to say? We had a wild fling and her parents came home unexpectedly and caught us in the very act of the thing itself?"

"That's better. When did it happen?"

"Didn't. Just thought you wanted some juicy fantasy."

"Tell us the real stuff."

"I have to get out of here. You people are up to no good," he said. He stood up and thanked them for the use of the towel.

"Have you been in the water today?"

"No, but I'll try it and let you know how it is. Who's up for a dip?"

"You go in first and tell us if there are any jelly fish."

"When you see children out in the water, there aren't any jellyfish. Okay? Keep an eye on my things." He took off his shorts and shirt. He dropped them on the sand and put his boat shoes on top of them. "If I'm not back in fifteen minutes, call that good-looking female lifeguard."

"Get out of here," they called after him as he went down to the water. The sun had warmed the air and the water felt chilly on his toes. He stood ankle deep looking at the horizon.

A man chased his child's beach ball that had blown into the water. There was a land breeze and the ball danced on the waves in front of him. The man tried to swim after it, but it was heading straight for the British Isles. The man swam after it with the old college try, but gave up and turned back just before the lifeguard whistled at him and motioned him to shore.

Bud waded out till the water was up to his knees. Soon it was up to his waist. He had seen others standing waist high and imagined they were peeing in the ocean. So there would be no doubt, he dove into a big wave and swam out over his head.

The luxurious feeling of bobbing along with the waves was a relaxing sort of therapy. He was safe from the pressures of his social life. Blue sky stretched as far as you could see. He was a little spot in a mammoth ocean, a water bug making tiny rings of concentric circles in the ocean's vast surface.

Time floated by, till one of the office staff girls called from the water's edge, "Hey, Bud. How are the jelly fish?"

He looked around for signs of a menace, but saw nothing. "I haven't been stung yet," he yelled back. Wondering how long he had been in the water, he waded ashore to look at his watch.

"Here. Dry yourself off with this towel," she said, handing him the towel he had been sitting on. He took the towel, turned away from the wind, and shook the sand out of it.

"Just need a corner to dry my face and hands," Bud said, as he dropped the towel and fished his watch out of his shoe.

"Use it all you want. It's an extra towel."

"Look at the time," Bud said. "I've got to get going."

"Ah ha, you have a date with Missy, or is it that other girl you took to the party?"

"None of your business. Thanks for the use of the towel." He grabbed up his clothes and started for the dunes. Stopping on the little boardwalk that led to the street to brush the sand from his feet, he wished he had dried off all over. The polished beach sand in his shoe had ground against his foot the day before and worn a sore on his foot.

The wet sand clung to his feet. He patiently brushed off as much as he could. He finished wiping his feet dry with his shirttail and put on his shoes. Back on the road, he walked along with his shorts and shirt in his hand. At the Henlopen Hotel, he angled back to the boardwalk again. He put on his shirt and shorts and headed for his rendezvous with Rose.

"You're a little early. Can I bring you something to eat or drink?" Rose said as he entered the Country Squire.

"I'll just sit down and wait, if I may. There's no hurry."

"Suit yourself," she said, going on with her work.

He wanted to sit down and collect his thoughts. He felt he was in a friendly place. It had become his home away from home. The barstools were filling with local workers. All the parking meters were full, so the drinkers must have walked in. They had probably just gotten off work at one of the shops, or were taking a break in a long day, before the evening crunch.

A bunch of young men and women, up from the beach, hung out near the door. There was a dart game going on back near the rest rooms. The TV, hung high for all to see, had a baseball game in progress, but no one was watching it. There was a lot of chatter and laughter from all directions. The happy mood was clear, but the words were blended and garbled. It was a pleasant sound with no distractions.

What was he going to say to Rose? He had told her he missed her. She was something very special to him. He cared for her a lot. He wanted to be with her. He didn't want to say something stupid, like "I love you." There must be a more descriptive way to tell her how he felt.

This was ridiculous, because he would soon be leaving town. Still, he wanted to express his appreciation. She had always been straightforward, very up front with everything. Her attitude was so refreshing.

"Sorry to keep you waiting. It has been busy since lunch," Rose said, interrupting his thoughts.

"Hi, Rose. Gee, it's good to see you."

"Let's go sit on a boardwalk bench and get some air."

They went out and walked along until they found a vacant bench. As they sat down, Bud asked, "Did you see the rainbow?"

"Yes, the whole crowd walked out to the bandstand in the median for a look. It was spectacular!"

"Never seen one quite so clearly and so large, so glorious! I stood there like a tiny grain of sand, looking up in awe."

"I like the way you talk."

"I like everything about you, Rose. Everything is so easy."

"Well, let's not get carried away."

"I have so little time and so much to say. I'm going back soon, and I want to see you again."

"Well, I'm here, now."

"I know and I am thankful. I hope you'll let me take you out to dinner one more time."

"When do you have to leave?"

"Day after tomorrow. Can we go out before then?"

"You bought me dinner last time. Would you like to come to dinner at our house?"

"That'd be nice, but you and I seemed to hit it off when we went out together, just you and me. Really want to take you out once more. Which evening is better, tonight or tomorrow night?"

"Tomorrow would be better for me, but I have a lot to do between now and then."

"Don't let me hold you back. You go and do what you have to do and I'll pick you up around six tomorrow night." Bud stood up and pulled her up to get her started.

"Better get going," she said, with a gentle smile. "I'll see you around six tomorrow."

She turned, waved goodbye, and hurried off. Bud watched her thread her way through the strollers on the boardwalk. She slipped through the crowd with the ease and balance of a running back breaking away for a touchdown.

When she was gone he sat back down. Having settled a date, he could relax and enjoy the end of the vacation. Sticking his legs out straight in front of him, he leaned back on the bench. Stretching his arms up, he locked his hands behind his head. The late afternoon sun to his back, he gazed at the ocean. The superstructure of a large ship glistened on the hazy horizon.

The ocean was a gigantic new friend. It was a whimsical new bond, like the mouse that befriended the elephant. The fantasy was absurdly delightful.

As the sunbathers began to leave the beach, the bathing beauties changed into beasts of burden. Packing up their gear, the women slipped on tops and stepped into shorts or skirts. When they had gathered their things into a beach bag, they picked up their towels and blankets. Stepping leeward, they shook the sand out of them and folded them. Last they folded the beach chairs; the way nomads fold their tents. With an ingenious dexterity, they loaded themselves up and trudged off the beach with a staggering pack horse gait.

The men seemed to travel light. Pulling on their shirts and carrying their shoes, they were ready in no time. One man had to dust off the *Wall Street Journal*. Bud pictured him in a pinstripe suit, wearing over-the-calf hosiery, because all the hair on his lower legs was worn off.

Having followed the flock in their summer migration to the beach, Bud felt accepted as one of them. Like the geese, they each had their own personalities, but had flocked together in a caravan to get here. His was an occupational influence that had brought him here, but it passed for heredity with the "in-crowd."

The swimmers had all left the water. The lifeguards were going off duty. The sun cast a long shadow across the sand. The gentle breeze was cool. Bud sat forward and stretched. The show was over on the beach.

Standing up and turning around, a herd of tourists trooped past him on the boardwalk. Some with bare feet and some with city shoes. A quiet group of Mennonites walked down the steps to the beach. The men and boys all wore the same outfit; except the men wore natural beards under their homemade black felt hats. They had rolled up their black pants enough to wade in the water. Black suspenders made X's on the back of their white shirts.

Each woman wore her hair in a bun with a little starched, white cap, as if it was a badge, the way nurses do. Carrying their shoes and stockings, they held the sides of their full black skirts up to ankle length.

Bud didn't want to stare at them. He turned to walk back to the middle of town. He sauntered along, inspecting the shops and the people. He was taking mental pictures for his scrapbook.

When his stomach clock went off, he decided he should find a different place to eat. He had seen so many restaurants on his walks home, he decided to try the first one that looked good.

The Summer House looked fresh and summery. A doorman held the door for him, greeting him with, "Good evening."

"Good evening," Bud answered, wondering what he was getting into. The music was modern, but not too loud. A double curved bar was to the right. White wooden lattice, with hanging ferns, formed a canopy over the bar, giving it a fresh-air look.

The bar stools were full of happy young people, relaxing and talking. Booths lined the other walls. There were a few tables in the front window with white wicker chairs around them. It was a good place to be seen for the lonely newcomers.

A waitress with a green "Summer House" apron asked him if he would like to eat. She showed him to a booth and gave him three menus. One menu had fancy drinks, mostly creations with unique names that were house specialties. One menu was a dinner menu, and one was the sandwich specials.

"Can I get you something from the bar?" the waitress asked.

"Just a cola. I have a lot of menus to read."

She wrote on a little pad and went to get the cola. The sandwich menu gave an elaborate description of their hamburgers. He decided on the option of lettuce and tomato. When she came back with his cola, he ordered the special hamburger.

"How do you want that cooked?"

"Medium rare."

She wrote it down, picked up the menus, and left.

Bud watched two young men in alligator shirts approaching a young woman sitting at the bar. One of the men used dramatic moves as a means of expression. His masculine look was contrived casual with his collar up and shirt tail out, making his buddy look neatsy tidy.

The girl swirled around with glee, her tan legs still wound around each other, because of her miniskirt. They were all glad to see each other. They all jabbered at each other, laughing and making dramatic gestures. The men stood around her while she squirmed as she swiveled back and forth on the tall bar stool. They were friends, but it was hard to tell how friendly they were. It looked to Bud as if they had all systems set on go.

"Here you are," the waitress said, setting a large plate on the table. It was an open-faced sandwich with the lettuce and tomato artistically arranged on the side beside a mound of potato chips and a pickle. "Can I bring you anything else?" she asked carefully placing a bottle of ketchup beside it.

"Looks like plenty to me," Bud said. "Thank you."

He put the lettuce and tomato on the hamburger and took a bite. It was delicious. The lights dimmed slightly as the music became a little louder. The noise level at the bar rose along with the music. *This place is really sophisticated*, he thought. The subtleties were smooth and well done. Perfect for someone on the make. Bud was content to be an observer, already torn between two women.

There was too much activity to think of the next day or the next moment. He ate slowly, watching the young adults at play.

As he paid his bill, he noticed the lights dim a little more and the music became slightly louder. It was time for him to go back to the motel and get himself together.

The streetlights and colorful signs pierced the darkness as he walked back to his room. He found the room in disarray. That morning, he had rushed out looking for Rose. He turned on the TV as he went around the room gathering his belongings.

He sorted the clothes to take to the Laundromat the next. When he was organized and ready for bed, a movie started on the TV. Propping the pillows up for a back rest, he settled down for the show.

It was an action movie with car chase scenes. At the happy ending, he turned it off and hit the hay.

Early beams of sunshine on his face woke him up. He leapt out of bed, dressed, and grabbed up his dirty laundry. Outside, he threw the laundry in the back of his car and drove out on the highway in search of a Laundromat and breakfast. His plan was to put the clothes in a machine and eat while they are washing.

With the clothes in a washing machine, he found a fast-food restaurant, picked up a *Washington Post* and looked at his watch as he sat down to breakfast. After breakfast, he put his clothes in the dryer and drove out past Rose's house to take another look at the old farmhouse.

He had timed the dryer just right. It stopped just as he was going in to get it. He spent some time folding his laundry so it wouldn't be wrinkled. Menial tasks had become satisfying to him. They gave him instant gratification.

Back in his room, he laid out his clothes for the evening. He put on clean shorts over his clean bathing trunks, a clean knit shirt, and his new boat shoes. He grabbed a towel as he danced out the door.

Walking to the beach, the familiar shops looked bright and beachy in the brilliant sunshine. He headed straight for the boardwalk and turned north, striding along with a purposeful air. He was free of worries and ready to make his good-byes.

At the north end of the boardwalk, he took off his shoes and headed for the water's edge. Scrambling nimbly over the jetty, he scanned the air for fishing lines. He spotted the pink umbrella up on the dune.

He found Missy in a different bathing suit. "Good morning," he said with confidence.

"Hello, Bud. Haven't seen you around lately."

"Been busy with the staff. Have to go back to the rat race tomorrow."

"I'll miss you."

"I'll miss you, too, but duty calls," he exaggerated.

"Won't you sit down and chat a minute?"

"Sure," he said, selecting a chair beside Missy.

He was comfortable talking with Missy now that he was ready to leave. They talked about little things. Neither of them had the courage to mention their little passionate embrace.

When the sun became uncomfortably hot, they took a dip in the ocean together. She was always pleasant company, when there was no threat of political obligations.

They sat down again, by the umbrella, until the sun had dried his trunks. Bud stood up, found his towel, and said, "This has been very pleasant. I'd better see if I can find the rest of the staff on the beach."

"Thanks for coming up to visit. Wish you could stay."

"So do I. Thanks," he said, walking on up the beach.

Over the next jetty, Bud spotted the office staff sitting on the beach. They were eating lunch.

"Now, the reason I've called you all together today," Bud started talking in the tone of voice often used by the senator's chief of staff, Bob Barker, "is, what are we having for lunch?"

"Well, if it isn't Bud. What have you been up to?"

"I've just checked out all the socialites and they're all behaving," Bud quipped.

"I can't eat the other half of my sandwich. Why don't you eat the other half, Bud?"

"What kind of sandwich is it?"

"Look, it's free. Just take it and eat it."

"Okay," Bud said, taking the sandwich.

"We're serving iced tea today. Want some?"

"Sure."

"To what do we owe the honor of your visit?"

"Glad you mentioned that. I'm going back to the rat race tomorrow."

"Why are you leaving so soon? The senator won't be back for almost a week."

"Running low on money, for one thing. I left on the spur of the moment, when you all abandoned the office, just to see the Nation's Summer Capital. Motels cost more than staying where you are. Next time, I'll plan ahead."

"You were so buried in your work, you ignored the summer. You have to be ready to go, when the time comes."

"If you give me your phone number, I'll let you know what's happening in Washington."

"We don't want to know, but Olive knows where to call us."

"Left everything in a mess. I have to get organized."

"Well, when you've gotta go, you've gotta go."

"Been in the water?" he asked.

"We're waiting for you to test it for us."

They teased each other in a friendly way all afternoon. Bud went swimming and some of them joined him. Bud felt at home with them in his new summer playground.

He left the beach about four o'clock to get ready for his date with Rose. He walked back to the motel in time for a shower enjoying the end of a perfect beach day.

He put on fresh clothes and drove to Rose's house. Roamer greeted him as he pulled in the lane. Rose came out, ready to go to dinner. "Hi, Bud. You're right on time."

"You look lovely," he said, opening the car door for her.

"Where are we going?"

"How about the Lamp Post?"

"All right."

Bud waited till they were there to say what was on his mind. When they had ordered their wine, he couldn't wait any longer.

"Finding you is the best thing that had ever happened to me. I'm afraid I'll lose you when I go back," Bud blurted out.

"Love letters in the sand wash away with the tide," she said with a gentle smile.

"You make it sound like a summer infatuation."

"I'll always remember the good times we've had, but I know you have to get back to Washington."

"I don't want to get back into the rat race I was in. Can't we keep in touch?"

"Pen pals with *A Tale of Two Cities*."

"What can I do to let you know how I feel?"

"That's easy. All we have to do is enjoy the evening."

"That's what I like about you. I'll drink to that." Rose's easy wisdom turned the tide. Both Bud and Rose had a magical evening together. It was comfortable to have such a good friend of the opposite sex.

When he was home alone, Bud went back over the evening in his mind, relishing the joy of each moment. What made it so, so right, so easy?

They liked being with each other very much. Wondering about love, he didn't know if he would like being in love, but he loved being in like!

RICHARD C. HARRISON

THE LONG, HOT SUMMER

Bud was anxious to take his good feelings back to town. The change of scene had produced a miracle. Relaxing in the bright sunshine with refreshing ocean breezes had charged his batteries. The ocean's grand expanse distracted his thoughts and his lucky encounter, flooded his world with a rosy hue.

There was no hurry to get back. As a matter of fact, he didn't really want to leave, but it was time to go. His finances were becoming questionable. He could squeak through another day or two. He had spent too much money on Rose. He wouldn't last another day if they went out to dinner again.

Besides, the senator would be back any day now. Bud needed to get his office clothes in shape. He had left on the spur of the moment. The cleaners and Laundromat were on his mind.

Wondering how he was going to get home, Bud asked about directions for the drive back to Washington. "Route 1, left on Route 16, right on 404, and right on 50. You can't get lost going back. Just follow the signs to the Bay Bridge."

After checking out of the motel, he threw his bag in his car and walked to the nearest restaurant. He treated himself to a leisurely breakfast with the *Washington Post*. He dawdled over a newspaper article with an extra cup of coffee.

As he strolled back to his car with the newspaper under his arm, the morning sun warmed his back. It was a beautiful day for a drive.

GRASS ROOTS

The clear blue sky and gentle wind put a spring in his step. He felt like a new man in this magic resort town and was ready to bring back these good feelings to his work.

Throwing the paper on the other seat, he hopped into his car and started for Washington, eager to explore the well traveled route that the staff was accustomed to. At first the sights were familiar, but soon Bud wondered if he had gone past his turn. "I've got plenty of time to get lost. I'll go another half hour, before I get worried," he said to himself.

Sure enough, a sign said, "BAY BRIDGE," with a left arrow. "That was easy," he said to himself, as he turned onto Route 16, "Just have to have faith." The Milton outskirts had a familiar look. He remembered the wooden yard signs that looked like the east end of a heavy farm woman pointing west as she bends down to pick crops. Stopping at the faded red light, he remembered he'd stopped there with Tilly.

As he drove along, the flat land, the chicken houses, and the farmer's fields full of corn and soybeans, were reminders of Delaware. The corn had grown taller in a short time.

Slowing down to twenty-five miles an hour through Ellendale and then Greenwood, he looked around at the tiny towns. It was so slow, he felt as though he was creeping along. He smiled at the rusty post office signs, "15 MINUTE PARKING FOR POST OFFICE." There were no parked cars within the town limits.

Out of town, the pace picked up again. Bud was reassured he was going the right way, when he saw the "WELCOME TO MARY-LAND" sign with a footnote, "Drive gently."

The two-lane road came to a dead end at Route 404. When he stopped at the stop sign, there was another, "BAY BRIDGE," sign with an arrow pointing to the right. He waited for the string of to pass so he could pull out. The caravan of returning vacationers was growing longer.

At the bypass around Denton, the road branched out into two lanes each side of a grassy median. The caravan fanned out to fill the lanes. It was the anxious drivers' chance to pass the slower vehicles. They tailgated in the fast lane.

There were pickups pulling large boats on trailers, station wagons packed full of beach gear, and families crowded together in sedans with their gear in car-top carriers. A happy group of vacationers heading home.

The road soon tapered back into a two-lane road, wedging the caravan back into single file. Winding through a hilly section, people settled for the lead cars pace. Soon they slowed for the intersection at Route 50. It's the main highway from Ocean City, up the Eastern Shore of the Chesapeake Bay to the Bay Bridge.

The stoplight held up the heavy traffic on Route 50, as they crept around the turn that fed into the four-lane divided highway. It was beginning to feel like Washington traffic.

An extra lane had been added to each side of the median as the suspension towers for the bridge came in sight. There were two bridges side by side, the two-lane bridge he had driven over going east and a three-lane bridge going west. It ought to be called the Bay Bridges, like London Bridges, he mused, or was it London Bridge is falling down. He remembered singing London Bridge is Falling Down as a child.

Having learned the rhyme as nonsense syllables, when he was a small child, it sounded like "London Bridges." He remembered dancing around the room, singing, and imagining that all the bridges in London were falling down. Also, the staffers on the beach, worrying about the domino effect, said, "If one bridge blows over, it will take the other with it."

Crossing the bridge was like returning to the main land. It felt as if he was leaving a serene isolated island and going back to the hustle-bustle of civilization.

This morning he'd started out causally dressed in shorts and a polo shirt, with fresh sea air in his lungs. Sunbeams streaming through the windows on the driver's side reminded him of the ocean. He wanted to come back to town refreshed and rejuvenated, but like the Delaware cantaloupe, it doesn't travel well. You have to leave it there. You can't take it with you.

After the tollbooth at the end of the Bay Bridge, the other cars revved their engines, challenging each other to get to the fast lane. It was a contagious energy and the race had started. "They're off and running!"

Noisy diesel tractor-trailers rattled by, sounding like freight trains. The hot pavement was distorted on the horizon by elastic heat waves.

GRASS ROOTS

Heavy traffic filled his nostrils with exhaust fumes. The thick humidity, intensifying the heat of the sun shining in the car window on his bare arms and legs, made him perspire uncomfortably.

The frustration of being caught up in the hustle-bustle of the traffic came over him. Slamming on his right turn blinker, he looked around frantically for a chance to switch to a slower lane. "Welcome to the rat race," he yelled at the other cars.

When he was able to get to the slower lane, he settled into a slow burn, resigned to following the car in front of him, until he came to the beltway. The traffic slowed a little on the access ramp to the beltway. Filing on to the five-lane race, he merged left until he was next to the fast lane. Going with the flow of traffic while staying within the fifty-five mile an hour speed limit was a constant hassle.

Turning off on his exit, he was almost home. The traffic in town was still congested, but at least the pace was slower. He was grasping for a tattered shred of his relaxed beach attitude when a car cut right in front of him.

"That did it," he yelled, jamming his brakes and loosing his cool. The sudden reminder, that the commuting in Washington is always a competitive sport, finished off his good beach attitude.

He pulled into his street and parked, with a sigh of relief. Grabbing his bag, he went in. Three young men had rented a three-bedroom furnished house on Capitol Hill. They each had a bedroom and an agreement about keeping the kitchen clean. Bud had worked such long hours, he rarely saw the other two tenants. One of them traveled most of the time. The other man was gone every weekend; his wife and children were still in Richmond, too far away for a daily commute.

An investor had bought the house, after the '67 riots, and had given it a cosmetic face-lift. The plumbing and wiring were very old, but still functioning. The house had seen better days, but dividing the rent three ways gave them a convenient place to live within their budgets.

Bud had found the house listed on the staff bulletin board. It was near enough to his new job and the price was right. It was just another little house on the fringes of Capitol Hill.

Bud went up four steps to the front door. The afternoon sun was hot on his back. He let himself in and threw his bag on his bed. The room looked drab compared to the beach houses. Having been used to bright sunny rooms with an airy feeling, he felt the dark walls were closing in on him.

He sorted out his clothes, one pile for the cleaners and one for the Laundromat. He had decided to go to the Laundromat first and run to the cleaners, while it was washing, get back to change the wash to the dryer, and get a bite to eat while it was drying.

This worked out perfectly. As he was meticulously folding his clothes, he ironed them with his hands. He'd discovered wash and wear clothes needed a little help to smooth out wrinkles. He drove home with his laundry and put it away in the dresser.

Looking around the room at the rental furniture that came with the house, there was a double bed with a worn wooden headboard, a padded slipper chair, a straight chair at the small desk with the phone, and the old dresser.

He'd been working such long hours, he never looked at the two pictures. The one over the bed was a framed landscape print and the one over the desk was a mysterious abstract. The windows on the corner walls provided cross ventilation. The pull-down shades had always been at half-mast behind filmy curtains.

His room looked neat because everything had been crammed into the closet when he left town. Rummaging through the closet, the briefcase surfaced. The briefcase he had carried to the office the day of the exodus.

Taking the briefcase over to the desk, he made an effort to reconstruct the work he had been doing for World Peace. The half-finished reports and copies of maps had to be sorted out. He sat and reread the reports, referring to the maps. As he read, his mind wandered back to the beach.

Yawning and stretching, he decided there was plenty of time tomorrow to look over the reports, when his mind was fresher. He was soon in bed and sound asleep.

Waking with the sun pouring in the other side of the bed, he wondered where he was. Sitting up and looking around, he found himself back in his Washington bedroom. Last night's papers were on the desk, where he had left them. His clothes were piled on the slipper chair. The curtains hung still and breezeless in the open windows.

GRASS ROOTS

The sheets stuck to him when he tried to get out of bed, damp with perspiration. "Looks like another hot, humid day in Washington," he mumbled to himself as he got up and rummaged through his bag for toilet articles. After a shower and shave, he contemplated another trip to the Laundromat with the sheets.

When he was dressed, he decided to go out for a bite to eat, just to get out of the house. The beach routine had not worn off. He wasn't eager to get back into the rat race.

Reading the Washington Post on a stool at the Pancake House, he was in no hurry to go much of anywhere. He had a list of things he needed to do. The first thing on his list was reread the report on World Peace, and the second was to stop by the office while the sheets were in the washing machine.

He went back to his room and tried to sort out the report. It was strange working at the little desk in his room, because he'd done most of his work in the field or at the office. He was too restless to be thorough. Leaving the piles of papers on the desk, he decided to check in at the office.

Bud's car seemed to know the way to the office. Like a horse heading for the barn, the car went straight to the office as if it was on automatic pilot. He didn't remember driving.

Olive said, "Well, good morning, Bud. What brings you here so early?"

"Just thought I'd check in. When's everyone due back?"

"The senator'll be back in a couple of days, but I haven't heard from him, yet. The staff probably will be here at the same time. Your paycheck's in your folder."

"What's happened since I've been gone?" Bud asked as he pulled open the file drawer and pulled out his paycheck.

"The senator has ordered a poll of his constituents' issues, but the results aren't in yet. When we know the results, you can be sure we will all hear about it," Olive said.

"How has the weather been here?"

"Looks like a long, hot summer. Natives are restless."

"The Nation's Summer Capital's beautiful this time of year. Have you been there?"

"Yes, I go every year when Tilly gets back. I'm ready to go, but I have to cover for her until she gets back."

"If you need me, give me a call."

"Thanks, Bud. Don't work too hard."

"Just want to get ready for the senator's return," he said as he went out the door.

He drove straight home and reread all of the reports. He worked on them in his room until his stomach clock announced it was time for lunch. He had been so engrossed in the project, that he had lost track of the time.

He went out to eat, needing a break. The old enthusiasm for a contribution to World Peace had been rekindled. He'd seen a light at the end of the tunnel luring him on. When he'd eaten, he went back to his room and submerged himself in desk work.

He was so engrossed in his project that he didn't notice how hot and humid his dingy little room was. He really needed to concentrate and there were too many interruptions in the air-conditioned staff rooms at the office.

He sat erect at the desk to make sure the perspiration that dripped off his nose didn't drop on his important papers. Working in his underwear in the privacy of his room for a noble cause, his mind had blanked out the city heat. The report began to pull together in a viable package. He stood up to stretch, like an artist standing back to get the big picture. Admiring the stack of papers that would save the world, he realized his muscles were stiff. What his grandfather used to call "Double feature cramp."

He found a fan in the closet, crawled under the desk to plug it in, and turned it on. In a sudden lunge, he seized the papers as they were about to blow around in disarray. He put a book on top of them, rather than turn off the fan. He hadn't realized how hot and humid it was.

He looked at the bed, realizing he'd forgotten to go to the Laundromat. He was relieved when he felt the sheets and found they had dried. Glancing at his watch, it was time for a late bite to eat before bedtime.

The next day, he put the finishing touches on his report. It was ready to present to the staff. It was a grand moment for. First, he had time to get his personal things in order. The cleaners and the laundry were next. He even shined his loafers. He laid out his office clothes on the desk chair and read the report in bed. Tomorrow, he would be

GRASS ROOTS

ready for the senator's return.

The morning of the big day arrived. He leapt out of bed as the first rays of the sun began to light the sky. He showered and shaved, humming a little tune. He dressed carefully, put the papers in his briefcase, and set out to tame the world. Stopping for a quick breakfast, he scanned the Washington Post for any late breaking news and drove to the office.

Tilly was back at her desk busy reviewing the schedule for the day and quickly perusing Olive's notes. She glanced up, saying, "Morning, Bud. Glad you're here early. There's a staff meeting scheduled for this morning, soon as the others get here."

"I'm ready. I'll be at my desk," he said to the top of her head as she organized her desk.

Bud sat down at his desk, took out his report, and started rereading his masterpiece. One after another the research staff drifted in. The chief of staff worked directly with the senator. He was the liaison between the speechwriters and research staff. The girls at the beach were mostly typists/receptionists. They were a motley crew of jacks-of-all-trades.

Barker Champion, the senator's chief of staff, burst into the room. "Let me have your attention," he announced in a rich, booming voice. "I have copies of the results of the latest poll. There are some new issues and we'll have to work on them. Each of you will be assigned a different issue to work up ASAP, which means as soon as possible, if not sooner. Any questions?"

"This isn't a question," Bud said, "but I've finished my report on World Peace."

As he handed it to the chief, Barker Champion said, "Good work, Bud. I'll read it before I show it to the senator." He held it up for the rest of the staff to see. "This is the kind of work we need," he said. "Turning back to the polls, the issues that are important to our constituents are: jobs, minimum wage, and abortion. Who has a preference?"

"Can the senator save the army base? That provides jobs for them back home," Ed Eager spoke up.

"He tacked it on to the budget bill. I think it will ride through that way," Barker said. "Why don't you see what you can come up with about jobs?"

"I'll get right on it."

"I'll dig out the senator's speech on the minimum wage in the Congressional Record," Sam Sly suggested.

"Good. We can use it in our next mail-out. Bud, you are so good at research. See what you can find out about abortion."

"I don't know anything about abortion," Bud complained bitterly, making the others laugh.

"Haven't you ever gotten a girl in trouble?" Ed joked.

"Okay," Barker boomed, "knock it off. We've got work to do on these new issues. See what you can come up with, Bud. Now, here are your copies of the new poll. Let's get cracking!"

As Barker left the room, everyone mumbled as they glanced at the poll results. Bud was stunned. He laid his copy of the new poll on his desk and stared blankly out the window.

He had poured himself into World Peace for so long, he was disoriented with his new assignment. *Why me? I don't know where to start! Never even used the word and I don't want to start now.*

He had been assigned to dig into an issue that had been part of the female mystique. If it wasn't a forbidden area for men, it was, to say the least, morally offensive.

He looked around the room at the other staff members, busily planning their new strategy. Pork barrel politics was not his bucket of blueberries. He picked up his poll results, stuck them in his briefcase, and went out for some air.

The morning sun cast angular shadows between the buildings as he wandered aimlessly down the sidewalk. The majestic elms arched over head, shading the walk. He walked right past his car and out into the mall. When he found a park bench free of pigeon droppings, he sat down and put down his briefcase. There was a wild-looking homeless man walking around talking to himself. Bud knew just how he felt.

A gentle breeze blew a piece of newspaper across the expanse of green grass. He wished his assignment was over and had become yesterday's news. Busy people walked by, on their way to work. He wondered what inspired them. *Money? Power? A challenge?*

At the other end of the wide expanse of green, the towering Washington Monument pointed to the heavens. A ring of flags at its base flapped gaily in the breeze, obscuring his view of the reflecting pool at the Lincoln Memorial.

Two nicely dressed women carrying brown bag lunches found a bench near him and chatted excitedly while they looked over the contents of their lunch bags.

The screaming wail of a siren caught his attention. He had forgotten about the downtown traffic around the perimeter of the mall. He stood up to see if it was an ambulance, fire truck, or police. Trying to look nonchalant, he took hold of the arm of the bench. A DC police car siren screamed, "Whee wha whee wha," sounding like Nazi SS terrorists. A mocking bird over his head imitated the "whee wha whee wha," scorning the authorities. Craning his neck to see the mocking bird, he realized his leg had fallen asleep and his back was stiff. He had no idea how long he had been sitting there.

Edging toward his briefcase, he stooped to grab the handle, steadying himself with the other hand on the arm of the bench, and regained his balance. The feeling was coming back to his leg with this activity, so he set out gingerly trying the stagnant muscles as he walked.

He found his car, threw the briefcase on the other seat, and drove home. The rental house had little charm. It was just a place to stay for some busy young men. He let himself in and looked around at the used furniture. He noticed how dark and dismal it was.

He went to his room, took the poll results out of his briefcase, and laid them on the desk. He loosened his tie, hung up his blazer in the closet and sat down in the slipper chair. The curtains hung straight down by the open window. He kicked off his loafers and put his stocking feet up, on his neatly made bed. He had been so inspired that morning, but now he couldn't get up any enthusiasm for this new project. He just didn't give a hoot.

He took the newspaper out of the briefcase and sat back down. He worked on the crossword puzzle for a while and then started on the comics. Then losing himself in the syndicated columns, Dear Abby and Irma Bomback, he relaxed and felt better. He felt "less worse," as his grandfather used to joke.

He got up, sat at the desk, and dutifully read the results of the poll. He wondered how thorough the poll had been. Maybe there was a message from the grass roots in the statistics. With this in mind, he started jotting down notes. *Go to the library and look up the history of the abortion issue. Call the archives the newspaper. Check the Congressional Record index.*

After a couple of fruitful calls, he was on his way. He picked up copies of articles and took them to the office. He sat down and scanned the articles, just to get the feel of how they were written. After making sketchy notes on the word processor, he started reading a medical book on abortion he had checked out of the library.

It was a hideous topic and the technical text was gruesome. When he became callous to the repulsive topic, he scanned through the text for ideas. It became repetitious and monotonous and he drifted off to sleep.

He was a pioneer taking women and children through the wilds unexplored territory, when cannibals surrounded them. With a desperate move, he spearheaded an escape route through the enemy lines, cutting his way through a wall of human flesh, dragging his canoe behind him. They almost made it, when he saw a spear flying through the air directly toward his heart, in slow motion. He was frozen in fright, unable to move, as he watched the deadly missile coming closer and closer, heading straight for its target.

It was curtains! He was going to be a goner! The terror built and WHAMO'

He woke up in his office chair. He looked up at the computer screen. It was covered with Z's. He had fallen asleep and his left hand had dropped down on the Z key. Because of the automatic repeat feature, it had printed several pages of Z's on the computer's memory while he was asleep.

The evidence was splashed across the screen for everyone to see. Looking around to see if anyone had noticed him asleep, he marked a block at the end of the Z's. Scrolling up to the top of the Z's, he marked the beginning of a block and deleted the block in one swell foop.

He printed out a hardcopy of his notes and threw the book and articles in his briefcase. It was getting late. There was no use fighting this obnoxious subject anymore this day. It was time to quit.

At this point, he would have quit his job and walked out on everything, but Champion had accepted his report on World Peace. He had to hang in there, so he could help them expedite it.

He picked up his briefcase automatically as he stood up to leave, flipping off the word processor. The screen went blank, the way his mind had flipped off as he'd drifted off to sleep at his desk. His mind was still blank when the car took him home. He carried the briefcase in to his room, set it down beside the desk, and went out to eat. The evening air was balmy. The street lights artificially reflected on the tree's leaves as they fluttered in a gentle wind.

He had enjoyed walking to the restaurants in Rehoboth Beach. He started exploring his Washington neighborhood on foot. In a few blocks, he spotted a neon sign. Walking toward the sign, the words began to take shape. Alfeo's Italian Restaurant turned out to be cozy, the service was warm, and the food was delicious.

By the time he left the restaurant, his mood had moderated and he strolled home, whistling a little tune.

The next day, Bud decided to make a simple preliminary report to Barker Champion. He told Tilly that he was waiting to talk to Barker.

"Bud, what can I do for you?" Barker said as he walked up to Bud's desk.

"I have found a consistent trend in the articles I've been research-ing and I think it is time to pass it on, verbally."

"Okay." Shoot!"

"Well, every time a judge or politician takes a stand on the abor-tion issue, it causes big demonstrations in opposition. The best thing to do now is not to take a stand."

"We have to take a stand. It's a grass roots issue."

"There are women's rights activists and religious fanatics that think it is none of your business. They really don't want politicians messing with their women's rights and their religious beliefs."

"Where do we take a stand on the issue?"

"We need to stay out of this issue. Take a stand not to take a stand."

"We have to take a stand!" Barker insisted.

What a jerk! Bud thought, realizing he wasn't getting to Barker. "Just wanted to tell you what I've found."

"I've got a meeting," Barker said, glancing at his watch. "Keep up the good work."

Bud knew that Barker would never be able to see this issue from the women's point of view or the religious view point, but he had felt a moral obligation to try to tell him. Bud had found the issue very distasteful from the beginning. World Peace was difficult enough, but at least his heart was in the goal. He didn't have the interest or the stomach for this new issue, but at least he tried.

Clearing the air with this confrontation with Barker made it possible to follow his assignment on a day to day schedule, until it came to a head at the end of the summer. The senator's Labor Day speech was a smashing success, until a reporter asked him as he was leaving the stage where he stood on the abortion issue. Shooting from the hip, he ignored Bud's research, and said he was against it.

Bud was upset when he heard about it, but he was fed up with the whole subject. He told Barker Champion about shooting from the hip to reporters. His constituents said they didn't think that politicians had any business dealing with abortions. They were neither for nor against the issue. They just didn't want it to be a political football.

This was a little too subtle for Champion. *Either you are for something or you are against it. How could you take a stand to not take a stand?*

Bud didn't like the issue in the first place and he left the office before he blew up. He went home and sat down, trying to cool off. He was jerked out of his thoughts by the telephone's ringing. No one had ever called him at home before.

"Hello?" he said inquisitively.

"Hello, Bud. This is Missy, back from the beach."

"Well, well. Did you have a good summer?"

"I missed your smiling face."

"I'm sure you found other smiling faces there."

"What I'm calling about is, I have been invited to a benefit dance party and I don't want to go alone," Missy said. "Daddy has paid for the tickets, including dinner, drinks, and dancing, at the Sulgrave Club, next Saturday night."

Bud remembered his grandmother's old saying, "When the cookies are passed, pause and take one." Bud paused, and said, "I'd be delighted to accompany you. What do I wear?"

"Blue blazer, gray flannels, button-down shirt, and striped tie. You know, the *uniform* you always wear."

When Bud first came to DC, Barker told him, "If you wear the uniform, you can eat free in Washington." For once, maybe Barker was right.

Bud said to Missy, "That sounds like fun. I'll pick you up around 6:45 p.m."

"Thank you. I'll be looking forward to it."

Missy was a pleasant distraction from his work. She called in the nick of time. This new project was so repulsive, he had no intention of working overtime and neglecting his social life.

MISSY

Looking forward to dining and dancing with Missy, made Bud's work days more bearable. On the day of their date, he left the office early. Stopping at the car wash on the way home, the feeling of flushing all evidence of office grime, made him smile.

At home he showered and dressed in fresh clothes. With a final check in the mirror, he smiled back at his reflection and headed for the door. The humidity had lifted and the city cooled down for the evening. On the way to Missy's house, the radio was still into a news broadcast. He turned it off and whistled a happy tune.

Missy opened the front door, saying, "Hello, Bud. It's good to see you." Her charming smile and elegant gown were a welcome change from his distasteful assignment.

"Nice to see you looking so beautiful."

"Thank you. You're right on time and I am ready to go. Just let me get my purse." She called out, "We're leaving now."

"Have a good time," echoed from the back of the house and they left.

Bud escorted her down the walk and held the car door while Missy seated herself. When he walked around and sat beside her, she asked, "How was your day?"

Starting the car, he said, "Don't ask."

"What's the matter? Has World Peace taken a turn for the worst?"

"Not working on World Peace. I've been assigned a new project and I hate it."

"What is your new project?"

"Can't even bring myself to talk about it."

"Oh, come on! It can't be that bad."

"How was "your day?" Bud asked.

"Don't try to change the subject. Let's see. Let me guess. I bet it's the abortion issue."

"Bingo! You've got it."

"Where do you stand on the issue."

"I don't have any opinion on it, because it is a feminine or religious issue. How do you feel about it?"

"I don't think a bunch of old men should be sticking their noses into something that is none of their business."

"I like that. May I quote you?"

"You most certainly may, anytime, anywhere."

"Now, how was your day?" Bud asked a second time.

"I floated through a bunch of simple tasks, thinking about our date tonight."

"So did I."

"Turn here," she said, pointing to the right. "We can look for a place to park on the street or they have valet parking."

"Valet parking sounds good to me."

"I like it, but Daddy doesn't like anybody else driving his car, so we usually have to find a place to park and walk."

Bud pulled into the circular driveway and stopped in front of the door. The doorman opened Missy's door as the parking attendant opened Bud's door and handed him a claim check. Missy waited for Bud and they went in together.

This was obviously a grand social event. Party people stood on the marble floor of the large foyer, waiting to go through the line of dignitaries. Bud and Missy took their place at the end of a line. Missy went first, greeting each one, and introducing Bud to them. Warm smiles and strong handshakes made him feel welcome.

Each new name lasted until the next smiling face, until they all became a blur in his mind. He remembered his science teacher, saying "Pay attention, because there will be a test later."

A fifteen-piece orchestra was playing big band music, in a bright society two-step, reminiscent of Lester Lanin's businessman's bounce.

The ballroom had elaborate chandeliers sparkling above a generous dance floor. The party goers were all gathered around the tables that surrounded the dance floor.

It was a treat to hear a live band with a solid beat and such crisp phrasing, but the in-crowd took it for granted and talked over the music. They had come to expect handsome bouquets of flowers under glistening chandeliers and a good orchestra.

Bud was surprised at their Blasé attitude. From deep in his memories, his grandfather's warm hearted advice surfaced, "When in Rome, do as the Romans do."

A waiter in tails with a silver tray asked, "May I get you a drink?"

Missy said "Madeira" and Bud said "White wine."

"Bud, you remember Betty Brass from the beach."

"Of course. Its good to see you again, Betty," he said. Her Low-cut dress showed off an expensive tan.

"Missy always finds such handsome men," Betty remarked.

"You mean there are others?" Bud joked.

"Oh, I was just teasing. Its good to see you again, Bud," Betty said, and turning toward her escort, "You remember Geoff Johnson. He was at Missy's party at the beach."

"Oh yes," Bud said, smiling in recognition. As they shook hands, he said, "Bud Green."

"What do you do in Washington?" Geoff asked.

"I'm on Senator Blassforth's staff. I came back from the beach early, because he is up for re-election. What do you do?"

"I'm a law clerk at Johnson, Meadows, Barnsworth, and Brass. It Isn't very exciting, just corporate law. The clients all go away in the summer, so they were very generous with my vacation this year."

"I really enjoyed Rehoboth Beach. I didn't want to leave."

"Was it your first time there?"

"Yes."

"Where are you from?" Geoff asked.

"Elmira, New York."

"We drove through there once, on the way to Maine."

"It isn't on the way to anywhere."

"I know. We were going round about to visit an aunt. It is a picturesque countryside with quaint farms on rolling hills, as I remember it," said Geoffrey.

"I remember learning to drive on those winding roads, as a kid," Bud's dark eyes smiled warmly. "Where are you from?"

"I'm a native. There's a little group of us who were born and grew up in the District of Columbia. We've been accused of being an exclusive clique of cave dwellers," said Geoffrey.

"I've heard the graduates of Miss Shippers dancing school have to tell the new presidents how to act," Bud laughed.

"That's about the size of it," Geoffrey said as he glanced around looking for Betty.

The waiter reappeared with the drinks. Missy and Bud took their drinks saying, "Thank you."

Scanning around at party goers, it looked much like the same crowd that was at Missy's house at the beach. It was a mixed bag. Mostly older people wearing the in-town uniform.

Missy picked out a table and told Bud where to sit. He held her chair for her and pushed her in and sat down. Missy greeted the others and handled the introductions. Bud watched the others take their napkins and put them in their laps. He followed suit.

The dinner was a magnificent spread. The polite table talk was easy to fall into and everyone seemed to be having fun. It's was a nice change from the office. Bud listened to the orchestra and his mind wandered, missing some of the conversation.

As the music stopped, Bud couldn't miss Betty's remark to Geofrey across the table from him. "Watch what you're saying!" she said, sharply.

"Eat your vegetables!" Geoffrey snapped back at her, sounding as though he was mimicking his mother. It was so ridiculous, everyone at the table burst out laughing. Geoffrey was either a deadpan comedian or a snide snob. Bud enjoyed the sophisticated banter and Geoffrey's sharp tongue gave it spice.

After several courses and the dessert and coffee had been served, the people became restless. A host went up to the bandstand to give a little welcoming speech. They had reached their financial goal. "And now I'll turn the microphone over to the orchestra."

A Glen Miller tune started people toward the dance floor and Bud said to Missy, "Shall we dance?"

"Thought you'd never ask," she teased, with a smile.

Bud's jitterbug was rusty, but Missy had it down pat. The music went from one song into another. Bud had anticipated a break in the dancing, but the music was continuous. "Don't they stop between songs?" Bud asked.

"They used to stop between songs, but now they don't. They just keep playing. It started with the debutante balls to keep the youngsters dancing so they wouldn't have time to wander out into the boxwood gardens."

"They have to stop sometime," Bud said, sounding breathless.

"Let's cut in on Betty and Geoff." She caught Betty's elbow and switched partners.

After two more tunes, Betty said, "Would you like to sit down a minute?"

"Let's do it," Bud agreed. They walked back to their table and took two chairs side by side. They chatted until Missy and Geoff joined them.

Missy panted, "Geoff can really jitterbug and I didn't want to stop."

"Seems to be the one thing I do well," Geoff said with a modest grin.

As they sat around, chatting, and dancing some more, Bud felt at ease with the party group. It was very posh and a lot of fun. All you had to do was look and listen to fit in. The others were easy going and Bud felt so comfortable with them that he forgot about his worries.

"This has been a splendid evening," Missy said at midnight, pushing back her chair. Bud and Geoff stood up and Betty picked up her purse.

"Good to see you again," Bud said to Geoff, shaking hands. "Nice to see you, Betty." Betty stood and turned to him, bending slightly, so he kissed her cheek.

As Missy led the way to the front door, Bud searched through his pockets for his claim check. A parking attendant took the claim check and rushed off. Bud reached for his wallet, found a dollar, and folded it into the palm of his hand inconspicuously.

A collection of spirited party goers gathered on the front steps. It was an outgoing bunch, full of friendly jokes, waiting for their cars. When Bud's car pulled up, the doorman opened the car door for Missy. Bud slipped the parking attendant the folded bill and slid into the driver's seat.

As they pulled out, Bud said, "Thank you for the delightful party."

"Thank Daddy. It was nice of you to take me."

"It was my pleasure."

"You are fun to go with. You always know what to say and it makes me proud of you."

"You're the one who knows the ropes. I feel confident when I'm with you. Would you like to stop somewhere on the way home?"

"Thank you, no. Do you mind if I go straight home? Daddy and Mummy will stay up until I get home."

"Not at all. I think we've done enough for one night."

They rode in silence, until Bud spoke up. "Sorry I was so short when you asked about my day."

"I don't blame you. I get upset every time someone mentions the abortion issue."

"Well, your party cheered me up. Thanks, I needed that."

"Glad you enjoyed it."

Bud walked her to the door, kissed her good night, and said, "Thank you again for the lovely evening."

He had forgotten all of his problems until he went home to his rental house. Missy had been good for him.

Bud found himself back in a frustrating routine. He read the articles on the abortion issue in the newspaper and caught the news on the radio and TV. It was an explosive issue. There was a lot of coverage.

No matter how often this strange word was bantered around, it never became part of his vocabulary. He shuddered when the space shuttle "aborted" their mission. He knew how to spell it and pronounce it, but he had never said the obnoxious word aloud.

By Friday evening, his spirits were at a low ebb. He called Missy.

"Hello, Bud. How are things going?"

"I found a new restaurant that I liked. It isn't fancy, but a cozy little place. I want to share it with you. Would you go to dinner with me?"

"I'd love it. When?"

"How about tonight?"

"Hold on a minute. Let me check with Mummy and Daddy," she said putting the telephone down.

Bud waited patiently, listening to her footsteps going and coming.

"They're going out to dinner tomorrow night, but Mummy has our dinner ready to put on the table now."

"What time tomorrow night would you like to go?"

"You are so sweet. How about sixish?"

"Pick you up around six, tomorrow. It's not a fancy place. We don't have to dress up."

"Sounds divine," Missy said. "See you tomorrow. Bye."

He hung up, pleased with the idea. He had to eat anyway, and he could pay Missy back and get out for an evening of fun.

He decided to walk to Alfeo's Italian Restaurant and check it out while getting his dinner. The waiter welcomed him as if he remembered him.

"Bringing someone here tomorrow evening to show them your resturant," Bud said.

"When I see you coming, I'll drop everything and make sure that it all goes well."

"We won't need any special treatment. " Just a cozy corner to ourselves.

He rolled his eyes, knowingly. Then, he said, "What can I get you from the bar?"

"Nothing. I think I'll just order dinner tonight, but when I come tomorrow, we'll have the full treatment."

Bud studied the menu, planning what he would order tomorrow. When the waiter came back, Bud asked, "What is your specialty of the house?"

"Many good things. Caesar salad! Fettuccini Alfredo! Veal scallopini!"

"Sounds delicious. I'd better save them for tomorrow night. Just bring me spaghetti and meatballs with garlic bread and the house salad."

"Good choice," the waiter said, reaching for the menu. "Let me look this over some more," Bud said, drawing the menu back towards him.

The waiter drew his hand back, smiling, and went to put in his order. There were three or four empty tables. Bud wondered if the restaurant would be crowded on Saturday night. The dining room was small, but seemed to be adequate for the regular crowd.

GRASS ROOTS

It was a neighborhood place, where customers were greeted like friends stopping by to visit them. The friendly atmosphere was what appealed to Bud the last time he came in. They would find a way to make the evening work out.

On the walk home, the moon tried to compete with the bright streetlights. The pale glow was no match for the bright lights. The tops of the trees above the street lights, basked in the moon and an occasional rooftop had a delicate sheen.

He walked home, contented with his upcoming date with Missy and forgot about the office. The next day, he sprang out of bed. He had some errands and laundry to do. He cleaned out the car in preparation for his date. It was happy work, a labor of love.

By six o'clock, he pulled up in Missy's driveway, all set to go out to play. Missy opened the door, saying, "Come in a minute and I'll get my purse." She led him through the stately foyer to a formal living room. Then she said, "Make yourself comfortable and I'll be right back."

He looked around at the polished furniture and the ornate decor. Each item in the room seemed to be an antique treasure. The walls were adorned with elaborate, gilt framed paintings of majestic landscapes by old masters. The buoyant carpet felt like a lush cushion of fresh sod under his feet.

He had been primed for action, but a feeling of being fair game in the open season came over him. The overwhelming display of wealth, tradition, and power was too much for him. He'd never lived in such elegant surroundings. An uncomfortable idea struck him, that Missy was at home here. He could never provide such a setting. If he could, he wouldn't want to.

"Sorry to keep you waiting," she said, rushing into the room with her purse, "I had to check the doors."

"You have a magnificent home."

"It's a bit much, but I've gotten used to it. Shall we go?"

"Why not," he said, following her to the door.

As they settled into the car, Missy asked, "How was your day?"

"Saturday has become my favorite day. I spent the whole day getting ready for this moment."

"You told me it wasn't a fancy restaurant. You said not to dress up."

"You always look dressed up to me."

"I must be old fashioned. I don't know how to dress down."

"Dress down?"

"Yes You know, jeans. A friend of mine was invited to an informal party, so she went in jeans. The hostess was upset and said, 'I told you it was informal, not casual,' " Missy explained.

Bud broke into song, "Dress up, dress down,

> All around the town.
>
> Boys and girls together,
>
> London Bridges falling down."

"Careful you don't trip over your light fantastic."

"And here we are!" Bud said, with a flourish, as he parked on the street in front of Alfeo's Italian Restaurant.

They were greeted as long, lost friends by the waiter. "Ah, Mr.Green, your table is ready," he said, motioning to a table in a cozy corner.

"Missy, will this table suit you?"

"Of course It's perfect."

"Can I get you something from the bar?" the waiter smiled.

"Chianti would be appropriate," Missy suggested.

"Good idea. You have a nice bottle of Chianti?" Bud asked.

"We have the best. I'll bring you one to taste," the waiter said, hurrying away.

"How did you find this friendly place?"

"I went for a walk and there it was. I enjoyed the dinner and wanted to share my discovery with you."

"You are so kind. I'm glad you thought of me."

"I've decided to stop overworking. Take a little time for myself."

"Daddy says, 'All work and no play makes Jack and plenty of it.' I'm not sure what it means, but it sounds familiar to me."

"That's a good one," Bud said. "My grandfather'd like that."

"You mention your grandfather a lot, but you never mention your father."

"My father died in the army shortly after I was born. Don't remember him at all. My grandfather's been a father to me."

The waiter appeared with the wine. He put the cork on the table, poured a little in Bud's glass, and stood back to let him taste it.

Bud scrutinized the color with his eyes, admired the aroma of the wine with his nose, dutifully took a sip, hesitated to get the taste, and said, "That's fine."

The waiter was pleased. He poured Missy's glass and filled Bud's glass. Missy took a sip and said, "You're a good judge of wine."

Bud had no idea of what made a good wine, but he had seen a man in a movie taste the wine while the waiter waited for his approval. He had enjoyed the little charade and Missy bought the act. He quickly changed the subject "Have you always lived in Washington?"

"Heavens, no. I was born Lincoln, Nebraska. When I was six we moved to South Dakota. Daddy took over a lumber company and a bank there. We moved to Des Moines when I was twelve. I went to boarding school at Madeira, when I was ready for high school. Moved here soon after that."

"You have an impressive home. Your living room looks like a museum."

Mummy collects antiques and Daddy collects paintings. You get used to it, but I think it is a little much."

"I'd feel that I had to dress for breakfast, everything's so formal."

"Daddy entertains a lot. You never know when a dignitary is staying over. I don't mind. It's kind of fun. Where do you live in Washington?"

"I share a furnished rental house with two other men. You wouldn't like it."

"Maybe I would. How do you know what I'd like?"

"It's nothing like your house."

"I'd love to see it sometime."

The waiter returned, asking, "Are you ready to order?"

"We've been talking. What do you suggest ?"

He listed his favorites. Missy and Bud made selections from suggestions and he went off to place the order.

They had a cozy evening together. The dinner hit the spot. "How about some spumoni and espresso?" Bud suggested.

"Let's go to my house for dessert. We have more variety."

"Why not," Bud said, being agreeable.

He drove her home, parked in front, and followed her up the walk. Missy unlocked the front door and let him in, flipping on lights as she went.

"Let's go look in the kitchen," she said, taking his hand. When they were in the darkened dining room, she turned to him and said, "Oh, Bud, that was a wonderful evening."

She had stopped and he had walked into her in the dark. "I can't see where I'm going," he said, grabbing her arm to steady himself. She grabbed his arm and they embraced. Two lonely people in need of affection had found each other in the dark.

The wine made it seem natural. They both had gained courage from the bottle. They didn't hear the car door slam, but the key in the front door startled them. "Oh, dear. Daddy and Mummy are back," she said, a little breathless. "Come out in the kitchen."

She led him by the hand and flipped on the kitchen light. "I'll put on my face in the powder room. You had better wipe the lipstick off with a paper towel." She vanished into a bathroom off the kitchen.

He was left alone to face her parents. He found the paper towels and did a fast scrub at the sink. He opened each cabinet under the counter, until he came to the trash can and threw the paper towel away, destroying the evidence.

He heard them come in. They put away some things and were walking toward the kitchen. As the door swung open, Missy came out, saying, "We were just going to have some dessert. Won't you join us?"

"No, we have had our dessert," Mr. Mannerly said. "You and Bud go ahead."

"It's nice to see you again, Bud," Mrs. Mannerly said.

"Good to see you, Mrs. Mannerly," Bud said.

"Missy can fix you a nice dessert. We'll leave you two on your own. Good night," Mrs. Mannerly said.

"Good night," Missy and Bud both said together.

Missy looked at Bud as soon as they'd left. "Sorry I should have known they'd be back early."

"No harm done. You made a quick recovery."

"We should have gone to your house."

"Too late now. Maybe another time."

Missy found some ice cream and cake. Sitting at the kitchen table, they ate, giggling and looking into each other's eyes.

When they had finished, Missy rinsed the dishes and put them the dishwasher.

"Guess I better be going," Bud said reluctantly.

GRASS ROOTS

"That was a wonderful dinner. Thank you so much."

At the door, she looked up at him, he kissed her good night, and she responded with eager affection. He whispered, "Good night. "

She whispered, "Thank you again."

Sunday morning Bud overslept When the first rays of sun danced into the room, he'd rolled over and fallen back to sleep. Moving to the edge of the bed, he sat up and stretched, yawning and trying to focus. Looking at his clothes piled on the slipper chair, he remembered last night.

A comfortable smile came over him as he staggered to the bathroom. The carefree ablutions on Sunday morning had become a luxurious contrast to the weekdays. Things were going so right. The dinner was a success and he had a day off to himself.

Looking forward to the Sunday paper, he dressed casually and went out for breakfast. The early sun had stirred the birds into morning activities in the fresh morning air. Walking at an easy pace, he picked up the paper and a coffee to go and headed for a park bench.

Claiming a bench in a shady spot, he settled down as though he owned the space. Carefully separating the glossy advertisements from the magazine section and comics, he made two neat piles. Spying a trash can, he dumped the ads, opened the coffee, and took a sip as he glanced at the comics.

The good feeling that he had earned the indulgence let him relax and enjoy the morning. Having read all the comics, perused the magazine section, he turned at last to the front page. With an uninterested glance at the international headlines, he looked off in a daze at the green grass and the majestic trees.

The nation's capital was a political arena. In this grand coliseum, Bud was beginning to know how the Christians felt when they were thrown to the lions. He could never change the world from the top down. The grass roots looked better every day.

Missy mentioned his father and it brought back old memories of his childhood. He desperately wanted to settle down and raise a family. Most of all, Bud wanted to be there when his children grew up.

There had been an article about abortion on the front page. Rather than read it, he had decided to put it in his brief case save it for Monday morning. He trashed the other parts of paper and wandered

91

nonchalantly back to his room.

He was beginning to appreciate what his grandfather meant he said, "Sunday is the day of rest." He should take time to commune with nature. The sun was shining, birds were singing, God was in his heaven.

A steady rain slowed the Monday morning rush hour to a crawl. A limo, creeping along trying to avoid being splashed by the other cars, had pulled in front of Bud's car. Water dripped off the sleeve of his trench coat as he fumbled for his coffee mug on the floor under his knees. He had made coffee at home to avoid going out in the heavy rain.

He parked near the office, listening to the news on the car radio and sipping his coffee. He sat there, immobile, with the motor running. Returning to work had become repulsive, like a trip to the dentist. Any excuse to postpone it, like waiting for the rain to let up, came as a welcome relief.

When the news was over, he finished the coffee, turned off the engine, grabbed his briefcase, and went in to face the music with resignation.

"Good morning," Tilly called out cheerfully, as Bud entered the office. "It's a beautiful day to work."

"Thought only water fowl like foul weather!"

"I see we are keeping our sense of humor. You must have had a good weekend."

"This job makes the weekends seem like heaven. The weekends are the one redeeming feature. Did you have a good weekend?"

"Yes. I always do I don't try to fly high with the eagles when I'm down here with the turkeys. You shouldn't take your work so seriously."

"Haven't, since they gave me a new assignment. Barker in?"

"No, but I'll tell him you want to see him."

"Thank you. I'll be at my desk."

Bud hung up his dripping raincoat and settled at his desk. He pulled the papers out of his briefcase and put them on his desk. *Maybe if I wrapped up this report, they would let me go back to what I am interested in.* He started on a half-hearted summary of the abortion issue.

GRASS ROOTS

Organizing his notes, he flipped on the word processor and was halfway through when Barker came in. "Good morning, Bud."

"Oh, Mr. Champion. How did the senator like my report on World Peace?"

"It's not a campaign issue."

"It's an important issue at any time."

"It may be to you, but it isn't to our constituents. We are running for reelection here."

"You mean I wrote that report for nothing?"

"Right. Now we're trying to dig up some dirt about the young upstart who is challenging the senator. After the election, we will get back to World Peace."

It was becoming obvious to Bud that they were not going to be implementing his program for World Peace. He had the feeling that Barker hadn't even shown his report to the senator. He was getting fed up with politics, but hadn't decided what else to do.

"I'll be through with this new issue this week."

"Good work, Bud," Barker said, rushing off.

Sam Sly had been working at the next desk and couldn't help but overhear their conversation. As soon as Barker was gone, he turned to Bud, "What's so important about World Peace?"

"What have you got against World Peace?"

"Nothing, except it won't win the election and that's a lot more viable than World Peace."

"You don't know anything about it."

"Bet you can't tell me one thing about World Peace that I don't already know."

"Did you know that we have never gone to war against another foreign democracy?"

"No, but that is an interesting idea. Okay, but don't get so uptight about these reports."

"They hired me because I had been working on World Peace for two years before I came here. I thought they were interested in the work I had been doing."

"The staff works for Barker, Barker works for the senator, and he works for the constituents. It's the grass roots that get to say what they think. Why don't you go back to the grass roots and enjoy yourself?"

"Not a bad idea. I've been thinking about doing just that!" Bud said with finality, turning back to work on getting rid of his report.

When he got home, Missy phoned to invite Bud to another society party. He was delighted to have the invitation, a welcome opportunity to forget about the frustrations of politics.

The following weekend, Bud took her to a free concert on the mall Saturday afternoon. This time they ended up at Bud's place. As he parked out front, he said, "Here is my humble abode."

"What a quaint little house," Missy said as Bud led her in.

"Rub a dub dub," Bud said, "three men in a tub."

"You don't mean you take baths together."

"No, we hardly ever see each other. What I mean is, there's only one bathroom. Three men bunk here, and never do anything to fix it up. It's just the way it was when we rented it."

"It's kind of cozy Where are the other two men?"

"One of them has gone back to Richmond for the weekend to be with his family and the other is out of town on a business trip."

"We have the whole place to ourselves," Missy beamed.

"Something like that. How about something to eat or drink?"

"No, thank you. Let's sit down and talk."

"What would you like to talk about?"

""You and your future. Why don't you sit over here on the sofa with me?"

Bud tried to explain that he didn't see any future where he was. He hadn't come to any conclusions about what to do next, but he was about ready to quit politics. He needed to get back to fundamentals.

Missy listened and asked pointed questions about his future. She was shopping for a permanent relationship, but the probing went a little too deep.

When she said, "Mummy thinks that politicians are socially un-acceptable," Bud tensed with resentment.

"What's that supposed to mean?" Bud snapped back. She had hit a trigger word.

"Politicians are like entertainers. If you're seen with them too often, people will think you're lower class."

"They'll think you aren't right-wing conservatives. They are afraid you might think for yourself."

"Oh, I didn't mean it that way," Missy said, reaching out to take his hand "Let's not fight over silly little things."

Her hand was warm and friendly. She gave his hand a gentle squeeze, gazing into his eyes with admiration. She whispered,"You look so strong and handsome when you get fired up."

His hand returned the squeeze as he leaned to kiss her. She responded with a heated embrace. There were some maneuvers that resembled parlor rugby, with considerable grappling and some gentle fondling. Panting with excitement, Missy whispered, "If only we were married. I have a lot of warmth I want to share with you."

"I'm afraid I'm not ready to support you in the manor to which you have become accustomed," Bud said, sounding a little stilted.

"We could play house starting out in a little house just like this one."

"We're playing house right here now."

"I mean when we are married."

Bud stood up trying to compose himself, stammering, "I'm not ready for marriage."

"You say that, but you act like you're ready for a marriage bed."

"We can't live on love. I'll never make enough money to be able to support you the way your parents expect."

"Isn't it time you thought about a regular job? Daddy could find something that would suit everybody."

"Everybody but me! Sure, I want to settle down and raise a family, but I don't want to go off half-cocked. I don't want to start something that I can't finish." Bud's tone of voice rose to a fever pitch, as though he was ready for a rampage. "I have to believe in what I'm doing. No one believes in the issue they assigned to me, not even the senator!"

Missy said, "I'm sorry if I upset you."

"It's not you," Bud said, calming down, "it's me . Let's talk about something else. How about a television program?"

"Let's just pretend we live here in peace and harmony, just for today. This is a fine house and I like it. I won't mention the future anymore."

"You're a sweet girl with a lot on the ball. You need a man who will take care of you. I'm just a young idealist in a political uniform who has not found his way yet. Coming here after college, I was thrilled to help shape the world. I wasn't ready for a power struggle and I think it's becoming too much for me."

"You're very special to me. You have a lot of social savvy and you're kind. I'm always comfortable when I'm with you."

"Thank you for those nice words. Think I'll look in the kitchen to see what three busy men would have left," Bud said.

"I'll go with you," Missy said, jumping up and straightening her skirt.

They stared at the barren refrigerator and then looked in all the kitchen cabinets. "When she got there, the cupboard was bare," Bud said, in a sing-song voice.

"It certainly looks like a man's kitchen. You need a woman around the house."

"That would be handy," he said with a knowing grin as he closed the last cabinet. Playfully he slipped his arm around her waist, pulling her close and giving her a warm kiss.

Missy relished the moment. A genuine smile of appreciation came over her as she looked in his twinkling eyes.

"Let's walk down to Alfeo's," Bud said. "It's a few blocks and maybe we'll work up an appetite by then."

"We can't go with these silly grins on our faces. Everyone will know what we've been up to," she said shyly.

"The waiter will be relieved if he notices. Would you do me the honor of accompanying me on a short walk?"

"I would love it . Lead the way."

They went out holding hands in the October air, singing.

> "Boys and girls together,
> All around the town."

PART THREE
NOVEMBER CHILL

A cold, damp wind put a chill on Capital Heights. As Bud went out his front door, he pulled his coat collar up to screen the icy wind. Shiny wet cars lined each side of the street. The bare large tree limbs bent in the wet wind, obscuring his view, swaying like black fingers. He took a long look, standing in the doorway, trying to remember where he'd parked last night. Seeing a familiar shape down the street, he made a dash for his car.

He was in a terrible mood. Senator Blassforth was no longer interested in World Peace. His constituents were more interested in the abortion issue. "Keep World Peace on the back burner until after the election," he'd been told. Bud stormed into the office, ready to kill.

Tilly said, "My, looks like you got out on the wrong side of bed this morning."

"Didn't want to get up at all this morning."

"What's the matter?"

"Every time I turn on the TV, I see Senator Blassforth mudslinging and badmouthing his opponent."

"Negative advertising works. Nice guys finish last."

"I'd rather finish last than lie to the American public. Some day the people will have had a bellyful."

"Let's not get too carried away."

"Abraham Lincoln said, 'You can fool all of the people some of the time and you can fool some of the people all of the time, but you can't fool all of the people all of the time,'" Bud said.

"And some nut shot him."

"The nuts always shoot the good guys. They ought to shoot mud-slingers!"

"You better talk to the rest of the staff. And calm down!"

"I'll try, but I've had it with dirty politics."

The staff members saw the look on his face as he entered the staff room. "Missy isn't treating you right?" one asked.

"It isn't Missy. It's the senator's advertising on TV."

"It's working. He's up in the polls."

"Well, he has dropped in my poll."

"You're not a voter in the senator's state and you are not the senator, so cool down and let's talk."

There were the same old strategy discussions. Bud wondered what happened to the significance of the grass roots. They went on about big money in the media. The negative advertising was becoming a high-tech campaign of mudslinging, garbage in, garbage out. An old song floated across Bud's mind, making him smile, *Stick Out Your Can, Here Comes the Garbage Man.*

His disposition didn't improve, but he was able to appear calm and cooperative. He was ready to quit, but not right away. He needed to put things in order.

The day dragged and he pretended to keep busy shuffling and reading papers. He hated being a frustrated clock-watcher. At five o'clock, he put on his coat and headed for the door. "What happened to the dedicated fanatic?" a staff member asked.

"Decided to go home at five o'clock," Bud snapped and left.

The streets were still damp, but at least it wasn't raining. He went straight home. He showered and changed clothes for his date with Missy. He couldn't bear to turn on the TV.

He'd never had a drink before picking up a date, but he poured a glass of wine. Taking it in the bedroom, he sat down to collect his thoughts.

The phone rang. "Hello?" Bud answered.

"Are you all right?" It was Missy. A staff member must have told her about Bud's attitude.

"Yes, I'm okay now. What time do you want me to pick you up for dinner?"

"I'm ready now. Anytime that suits you."

"I'll be there in about fifteen minutes."

"See you then."

He hung up the phone. Settling back in his chair, he looked around the room and relaxed. He took another sip of his wine.

Felt like everyone were in cahoots, conniving against him. Even Missy. It was the hanky-panky and manipulation he sensed. He couldn't put his finger on it, but the feeling was there.

He was ready to quit politics, anyway, so it didn't really matter. Pleased with resolving his anxiety for the moment, he took another sip of wine. He got up, took the glass to the sink, and found his coat.

Outside, the wind had dried the pavement and calmed down for the evening. The streetlights lit up the bare branches, casting a filigree of shadows on the sidewalk.

He drove to Missy's house in a happier frame of mind. The car was still warm and the "good music" station didn't have any political advertisements. He parked and went to the door.

Missy opened the door. "Hello, Bud. Won't you come in while I get my coat?"

"Of course," he said, stepping in. She selected a coat and Bud held it for her.

She called out, "We're leaving. We won't be late." From the back of the house, two voices answered, "Have a good time."

In the car, Missy asked, "Are you feeling all right?"

"Yes, I'm okay now,' Bud said, inquiring. "Why do you ask?"

"I called the office trying to locate Daddy. Tilly said you had just left in a huff."

"She's right!" His dark eyes turned pitch black.

"What's the matter?"

"Guess I'm tired of politics," he said. "They've switched from issues to mudslinging."

"Negative advertising works."

"It's verbal abuse and I find it repulsive," he snapped.

"You have to get elected before you can help anybody."

"You're right, but I just don't have the stomach for it. Don't trust mudslingers to help anybody but themselves. They've lost sight of the grass roots."

"Daddy says, 'Plants with strong roots are called weeds, while ones with weak roots are called flowers.'"

Bud glanced at her and paused. Then, thoughtfully, he said, "I don't want to talk about it anymore. Let's have a nice dinner and talk about your day."

"There's not much I can do in weather like this. I did go the Junior League meeting. It isn't as much fun as it used to be. The causes are so revolutionary now." Missy said.

"We both have to adjust to modern times it seems."

"You're so understanding. I don't know what I'd do without your kindness."

"You'd do just fine. Here we are." He pulled up in front of their favorite Chinese restaurant. The food was always interesting and the waiters pretended not to understand English. They could be cozy and say whatever they wanted in privacy.

Bud and Missy had built a little world of their own. She invited him to all the social events. He enjoyed the exposure and she liked having such an easy escort. Bud took her out to dinner and the theater on weekends. They had been considerate of each other's needs. Their intimacies had always been discreet and proper.

The waiter took their order and left. Missy said, "Tell me what's upsetting you."

"I don't think I can take any more of the political arena. I am going to have to get away. Get back to nature and try to find myself."

"That's a cop-out. You don't have to go away to find yourself. You're right here with me," she said.

"I'm okay with you, but I find the office repulsive. I'm just another warm body. I have to do something I can believe in. I've been thinking about the grass roots."

"Daddy says, 'Crabgrass is the root of all evil.' I don't know much about grass roots."

"It means rural voters. Down to earth people. I mean I have to get back to nature. Back to basics."

" You're not going to drop out? What about your career?"

"I don't know. That's why I have to take some time off."

"Have you considered running one of Daddy's plants in the Midwest?"

"I wouldn't be of any use to him, the way I am," Bud noted. "I've got to get away for a little while."

"Sounds like running away from the problem. Where will you go?"

"May be true." Bud paused pensively and then stated, "I don't know where I'll go, but I do know I'm going."

"When will I see you again?" she asked.

"You'll be lucky if you don't see me again. I'll never be able to take care of you properly. Don't know if I'll be able to take care of myself the way things are going. It isn't you, Missy. It's me. You must be able to understand that I need this."

"I'm trying."

"Let's not spoil our dinner with all this talk. Let's just have a pleasant evening together."

"How am I supposed to do that with you leaving?"

"It's not the end of the world," he said with a warm smile. "Come on. Let's celebrate a new beginning. A better way to go."

"I'll try, but it is so uncertain." Missy said, holding back a tear.

"You can be sure the sun will rise, the birds will sing, and you and I will be happier," he said, with gusto.

"You are such a dreamer."

They were distracted by the waiter bringing their food. It looked good and they were both hungry. They dove into the meal, chatting pleasantly, and forgetting that it was the last supper. Missy sat quietly as Bud drove her home. As he pulled up in front of her house, she said, "That was so much fun. I can't believe you are going to go away."

"I won't have a job here and I wouldn't be able to do good work at anything until I get myself straight."

"You seem to be straight enough to me."

"I do very well when I'm not at work, thanks to you. Thank you for being there."

"Do you have to go?"

"Yes. I just keep getting crankier. I don't know myself anymore."

"Daddy gets cranky and Mummy just says, 'He'll get over it. He's had a bad day.'"

"It isn't fair to you. I can't live this way."

"Why not?" she asked.

"It's not how you are, it's where you're going. I've been getting worse. I won't be any good for you or anybody else until I start getting better."

"I don't understand."

"It's hard for me to explain," Bud said. "I'm not sure I understand it either, but I know I have to do it. You'll just have to take my word for it."

"Where did I go wrong?"

"Taking up with a young idealist in politician's clothing instead of a businessman, I guess," he said. "You didn't do anything wrong. It isn't you, it's me. This isn't easy, but the easy way out won't help either of us. You have been the best part of the last few months, but I can't go on leaning on you."

"I don't mind."

"Yes, but, I do. I'm the bad guy here. Let's just say good night and remember all the wonderful times we've had together."

Missy started to cry and Bud put his arm around her, saying, "I don't want to make you unhappy. If I thought I could make you happy, I would do it in a minute, but I can't go on kidding myself. I will never be able to take care of you properly.

Missy sobbed harder, so he said, softly, "It's better this way. I can't go on with this charade at work. I'm trying to be honest." They just sat there in the car, hugging each other for a long time.

As Missy's sobs quieted, Bud said, "I'll never forget the good times we've had," as he turned and opened the car door. He went around and opened the door for her and she stepped out. He took her arm and walked her slowly to the door. At the door, he took her in his arms, kissed her, and said, "Thank you."

She said, "Oh, Bud." She kissed him farewell, having given up. "Will I see you again?"

"Maybe someday," he said as they turned toward the door.

She wiped the tears from her eyes, straightened her dress, and opened the door, saying, "Will you come in?"

"No. I'd better be going. Good night, Missy."

She just looked at him as he turned and started down the walk to his car. In the car, he felt miserable. He'd tried to break off their relationship gently. . . not like a rejection, but it ripped at the fibers of his heart. Missy had made these last days bearable for him, but he had to get away by himself.

It wasn't until the next morning that he started thinking of his alternatives. What would he do? Where would he go, when he quit politics?

The November elections settled the problem. When the grass roots votes were in, the senator lost his bid for reelection. Bud was the only cheerful person in the staff room. He didn't have to quit, because they had all lost the jobs.

He drove home, excited about his new beginning. Now he could sort out the options. At home, he threw his coat on the bed and sat down. It seemed like a long time since he was free to do what he wanted to.

His mind wandered back to the last time he had some time off and he reached for his book of phone numbers. He picked up the phone and dialed long distance.

It rang four times before a voice said, "Hello?"

"That you, Rose?"

"Yes, who's this?"

"Bud Green."

"Thought it sounded like you. Just didn't expect to hear from you at this time of year."

"This is the most important time of the year in Washington."

"Why is that?"

"It's the day after election day and my senator lost."

"Oh, dear. I'm sorry to hear that."

" Don't be sorry. I've had enough of politics to last me for a long, long time."

"And that's what you called me to tell me?"

"Yes. Who's living in the farmhouse?"

"Nobody this time of year."

"Well, you said I could fix it up and stay there if I was so smart."

"Well, I didn't mean it that way, but you are welcome to it if you really want to. It's mighty cold."

"You better ask the rest of the family, because I'm serious. I have to get out of this town and get my head back together."

"Hold on. I'll ask." There was a silence and some mumbling in the background. Bud smiled at his impulsive daring do. "They say you're welcome to it, if you can stand it."

"I may show up within a week."

"Suit yourself."

RICHARD C. HARRISON

"See you soon, Rose."
"Nice to talk to you again. Bye."

SOLO JOURNEY

Bud began to gather his things together for the big move. Everything that he sorted out for packing reminded him of home. Thinking back to a happy, carefree childhood, the pangs of home-sickness were overshadowed by a need to find himself. It was time to grow up. He had to do it alone. He needed time to sort out his innermost feelings. . .get them straight. . . and then, start over.

He called his grandfather and explained the situation. The mature wisdom, understanding, and kindness came over the phone and into his heart. "Are you sure you want to do this, Bud?"

"Have to, Gramp. May take a little time, but I'll let you know how I'm doing, as soon as I sort out a few things."

"You're always welcome here."

"Thanks, I needed that," Bud said. "But this time, I have to do this on my own. Have to do it myself. Just let everybody know I'm okay and I feel good about what I'm doing."

"I'll pass the word, but you have to call your mother."

" I'm not sure where I'm going and there may not be a phone."

"I know, but you have to tell her your plans."

"She is happy with her new family. I don't want to upset her with my problems"

"I understand, but you still have to call her and let her know what you're doing."

"Okay, Gramp, I will. And I'll let you know how I'm doing. Bye."

"Take care of yourself."

He hung up the phone. His grandfather's kind words had made his eyes water. He wiped his eyes, looking over his meager belongings. Didn't want to bother his mother with his problems. She had enough to worry about without adding more to her load.

He reluctantly dialed his mother's number thinking, maybe's she's not home. Suddenly her sweet voice came over the phone.

"Hi, Mom. This is Bud."

"What a nice surprise." She sounded preoccupied and said, "Hold on while I go in the other room." He heard her say, "Hang up the phone, when I pick up the other one." There was heavy breathing that became muffled and then a click, as his mother picked up the extension in her bedroom, saying, "Where are you?"

"I'm in Washington, DC, but I won't be here much longer."

"Where are you going? Are they sending you out on the campaign trail?"

"No, Mom, my Senator lost the election."

"Oh, I'm so sorry to hear that."

"Don't be sorry, Mom. I'm glad he lost. I've had enough of politics."

"Then you're coming home?"

"Not yet, Mom, I'm going to Rehoboth Beach for a while."

"You're not going to become a beachcomber, are you?"

"Aw, Mom, you know better than that."

"You're always welcome here."

"I know, Mom, but I have to do something first, then I'll come. I'll see you. Gotta go. I'll be all right. I'll let you know how I'm doing, when I get settled. It may take a little while to get set up, but just want you to know that I'm in good shape."

"When will you be coming home?"

"I don't know, yet, but Mom, I have to go now. Take care of yourself and say hello to Justin, Tiny, and Nancy for me."

"Oh, Bud, I miss you."

"Me, too, Mom. Gotta go. Bye," he said hanging up.

It was hard to explain to his mother. He couldn't lie and say he was being sent on the campaign trail. He looked around at his things spread all over the room. It felt good to clean out the closet, but now he had to pack it all in his car.

GRASS ROOTS

Each thing he packed was taking on a new meaning. He had come to Washington as a starry-eyed idealist to save the world from the ravages of war.

He liked the idea of the grass roots, working from the bottom up. If each person took the time, the world would be a better place for everyone and he decided to start with himself.

He had to climb another mountain. He had climbed a mountain with his grandfather. When they reached the top, there was nothing there until his grandfather pointed out the panoramic view. "Once in a while, you need the big picture. When you have seen the overall view, our little area takes on new meaning."

Bud knew he had to start over from the ground up. He knew he had to find himself, first. . .to lay a solid foundation for the future. He had to do it himself, alone. He had come to the moment of truth.

Bud paid his last rent check, bundled his belonging together and left town. The beltway was roaring as usual with people rushing around like bumper cars. The Annapolis highway was less hetic. Once over the Bay Bridge, traffic really thinned out.

The flat countryside of Delaware was a welcome sight. It was the slower pace and quiet little towns that looked so good to him. He wasn't sure where he was going, but he knew it was time.

He nearly drove off the road, staring enviously at a man on a tractor with his tiny son on his lap. Bud was wondering if his father would have taken him for a ride like that if he'd had the chance. When his tires hit the gravel shoulder, he snapped out of his trance and eased back on to the pavement.

The farm fields with brown stubble were frozen stiff. Some of the farmhouse windows had plastic sheets stapled over them. One farmer had piled bales of straw all around the crawl space, looking like a dead hedge.

There was no activity outside. The people must be huddled around a warm fire reading the *Farmer's Almanac.* As he neared his destination, the excitement of the adventure exhilarated him

When he pulled into Rose's lane, Roamer came out barking at him. "Hey, Roamer. How have you been?" Bud asked. He held out his hand, gave the dog a friendly pat and Roamer wagged his tail.

The stately old farmhouse stood prominent and dignified, surrounded by bare trees. The leaves had turned and fallen in the November wind. The afternoon sun broke through the high, wispy clouds.

Bud walked over to the trailer and knocked. A young man with a pleasant smile came to the door. His hands were callused from rural labor. His eyes had a twinkle and his clothes could pass for resort wear.

"Hello, I'm Bud Green. Is Rose here?"

"Hi, I'm Rose's brother, Thorn," he said. "She's gone out, but you must be the nut that's going to live in the farmhouse."

"That's me," Bud beamed.

"Help yourself," Thorn said, motioning toward the farmhouse,"It's unlocked."

"Thanks. I'll let you know how I make out," Bud said as he turned toward the old farmhouse.

THE OLD FARMHOUSE

With a feeling of confidence, Bud strode across the lane to explore the old farmhouse. He looked at it in a different way this time. It was as if he was exploring himself from outside of himself.

One of the porch steps was rotten. Stepping over it, he went to the door. It opened into a hall, with a door on each side and the upstairs steps in front of him. It smelled musty. The closed-up house held the cold and chilled him to his bones.

Opening the door to the left, he found an empty room with a fireplace that was full of cobwebs. The fireplace mantle was ornate, but the paint was peeling. Going from room to room, he discovered the water was turned off in the bathroom and kitchen. There was a wooden table and two wooden chairs in the kitchen. There were odd bits of abandoned furniture scattered through the rooms. He decided to start in one room with a primitive setup. Just do enough for the night at this point.

He went back outside to inspect the crawl space. The pipes were exposed and the weather felt like it was freezing. He would have to enclose the crawl space before he could get any water.

Getting back in his car, he drove to the nearest store to buy a kerosene heater. He could at least have a warm night. He took a space heater and a can of kerosene back to the farmhouse and fired it up by the fireplace in the front-room.

He'd bought a broom. While waiting for the place to warm up, he swept out the room. As the room began to feel warmer, icy air from the fireplace whirled around his ankles. There didn't seem to be a damper in the fireplace to stop the draft. He brought the table in from the kitchen. Tipping it up on its side, he propped it up in front of the fireplace with a kitchen chair to stop the draft.

When the one room was clean enough, he brought his things in from the car. Fortunately, he had kept the sleeping bag from his college days. He had decided to start in just one room at first.

Putting his toothbrush and toothpaste in his pocket, he left for something to eat. He found a MacDonald's with a clean men's room. After he had eaten, he went to the men's room to make his ablutions for the night. It would be dark soon and his flash-light wasn't much good for reading.

Back at the farmhouse, he unrolled his sleeping bag before it turned dark. He checked the kerosene heater and crawled into the sleeping bag. As darkness came, the heater gave off a bright glow, tinting the room with a warm, rosy hue.

"Well, I did it and I'm glad," he said to himself. Pleased with himself, he crawled into his sleeping bag and fell into a deep and happy sleep. He didn't even hear Rose come over to see if he was all right.

Rising early the next morning, he was a little stiff. He grabbed his shaving kit, threw in the toothbrush and paste, and headed for MacDonald's. He went straight to the men's room and came out shaved and smiling.

The breakfast looked good. It was fast and tasty. Things were looking up. Out in the morning air, geese flew across the sky, honking good morning to each other. A man waved to him as he drove off and Bud waved back, smiling.

He went back to inspect his new home. After refilling the heater he went outside to look around the yard. He needed some way to enclose the crawl space so he could turn on the water. He remembered that he had seen a farmhouse with the bales of straw stacked around the outside of the crawl space.

"Well, look who's here," Rose said. "Want some breakfast?"

"Hello, Rose," he said, surprised to see her all dressed up so early in the morning. She was prettier than ever, he noticed. "Thanks, but I've just had a lovely breakfast at MacDonald's"

"Sounds awful," she said, making a face. "Was it any good?"

"Very tasty, but I'd love a rain check."

"I"ll ask you again. Can't believe you'd want to spend the night in that house."

"It's cozy. And there are no politicians in there."

"Suit yourself. I'm off to work. I'll talk to you this evening, unless you go to sleep before I get home."

"I'll stay up and wait for you."

Rose drove off in one direction and Bud drove off in the other to find some bales of straw. He spoke to the salesman in the hardware store about enclosing the crawl space. "Straw bales might be cheaper, if you can find them. I"ll ask around."

Bud looked over the hardware, while the clerk went to ask the others. The clerk found him browsing by the toaster ovens and gave him a farmer's name and address, saying, "Try this man and see if he has any bales left."

Bud found the farmer's house. There were some bales in an outbuilding behind his house. Bud went up to the front door and knocked. A dog barked from the back yard. An inside door opened and shut.

The front door swung open, revealing a sullen old man. Bud scanned his work shoes, khaki pants with suspenders, and flannel shirt, open at the neck, revealing the top of his tee shirt. He looked at Bud inquisitively.

"Good morning," Bud said cheerfully. "I'd like to buy some bales of straw."

"How many you need?"

"Don't know. How many will you sell me?"

"All there are in that shed out back, three dollars each."

"Could you deliver them, just half a mile down the road?"

"When you need 'em?"

"Today, if possible."

"Well, when you find out how many you need, let me know."

"Thanks. May I look at them?"

"Help yourself to a look."

"I will. Be back soon."

The farmer just looked at him and closed the door to the cold. Bud went back to the shed. The dog was penned up in a chain link dog run. Bud measured the length of the bales with his shoe and estimated the height. There were a lot of bales.

Back at his farmhouse, he paced the parameter of the house. He estimated twenty-five feet by twenty-five feet or ninety feet all the way around. The bales looked to be three feet each. Thirty bales would go around once. Ninety dollars for thirty bales.

He drove back to the farmer's house and wrote a check for ninety dollars. Bud gave him the address, asking if he needed any help.

"Could use a hand," the farmer said, going back for his coat. Bud and the farmer stacked thirty-five bales (five for good measure) on a rubber-tired hay wagon hitched to a tractor. Bud led the way to Rose's place and they unloaded them.

Bud spent the rest of the day stacking the bales around the crawl space. He wondered if enough heat would go down through the floor. Crawling under the house, it was considerably warmer. He found a water faucet in a hole and turned it a little. He could hear the water start to run.

Dashing inside, he checked the kitchen sink and then the bathroom. The toilet was slowly filling. He tried the faucets in the sinks. They dripped water, so he turned them off. Back out in the cold, he turned the faucet all the way on. The water made more noise as it gushed to fill the pipes.

Back in the kitchen, he turned on the faucet in the kitchen sink. The faucet sputtered and pipes clanked as the pipes filled with water. He let each faucet cough the air out of the pipes.

"Have to keep the kerosene heater going all the time," he said to himself. The heater would go for twelve hours on one filling. "Like a cow milking schedule. I'll fill it at 6a.m.and 6p.m.. If I don't wake up, the cold will wake me." He had begun to talk to himself, but it helped him get things organized.

Going in for a break, he brought the other kitchen chair into the front room. The kitchen and the bathroom doors had to be left open to let in the heat, because of the plumbing. It had become too warm in the front room with the doors shut, but now it was a little cool. It would be better for sleeping. Good temperature for physical work.

Thinking about the pipes freezing, he realized he couldn't go home for Christmas. Bud had always gone to his grandfather's for Christmas. It was time to write a letter to explain to his grandfather where he was and why he couldn't come back this year. It took a long time finding the right words and then he had to copy it over.

He wasn't sure how to drain the pipes if he had to go away in the cold weather. But it wasn't just the water and the heater that was keeping him away. It was a desperate attempt to find a meaning in his life.

He had to make peace with the outside world. It was time to look inside himself. It was difficult to put his circumstances in perspective. Each new thought needed a careful explanation. As he rewrote the in-depth descriptions of the conditions, trying to make it clear and concise, he was putting his priorities in order for his future. When it was right, he put it in an envelope and put it aside to mail the next time he went to town.

Bud's brain was active and wandering. Suddenly he thought about electricity. He walked through the house looking for the fixtures and outlets. "Tomorrow I'll sweep the whole place out." He went outside to see if the wires were still connected to the house. They looked as if they were still there.

Going back inside, he looked at his watch. Rose would be home soon. He would ask her about the water and electricity when she came home. He sat down on a wooden chair and surveyed the room. It needed a lot of work. Maybe if he found a construction job, he could learn some know-how and make enough to buy some supplies.

He heard Rose's car pull into the lane. Looking out the dirty window, he saw Rose coming up to the front steps. Rushing to the door, he called out, "Watch out for the second step! It feels like it's rotten."

"You are crazy! How are you making out?" she asked.

"Just fine. Come in and look. I want to talk to you about something."

She came in feeling the warmth. "Oh, you have been busy."

"Still primitive, but quite comfortable. I put straw bales around the crawl space and turned on the water."

"Won't the pipes freeze?" she asked.

"Don't believe so, long as I keep the kerosene heater going. Think the electricity is still hooked up?" he asked.

"Why don't you check with Delmarva Power. You could set up an account in your name and see what they say."

" I'll do that tomorrow. Where is the water company?"

"We have a well and septic. We're the water company."

" Do you mind if I use some water?"

" Long as the pipes don't freeze, nobody cares. Well, you look settled in. Would you like to come over for a warm dinner?"

" Thought I'd ask you out to dinner," Bud said.

"Won't be necessary. I'm going to fix dinner for my brother and me. One more won't be any problem. Walk over about six."

"Don't want to be in the way."

"No problem. See you at six."

Rose stepped carefully over the rotten step and Bud watched her through the dirty window. *"I'll get some Windex and paper towels tomorrow,"* he said to himself. He refilled the heater for the night, washed up in cold water, and combed his hair.

WARM DINNER

At exactly six o'clock, Bud knocked on the trailer door. He heard footsteps and Thorn opened the door with the newspaper in one hand and the glossy advertisements under his arm. "I see you're still alive and well. Come in. I'm just taking the guts out of the paper, as we say in chicken country," Thorn explained.

"Thank you," Bud replied. The door opened to a comfortable looking living room. Inside, it was a cozy home. The trailer was warm and toasty. Three places were set on the dining table. The sounds of cooking came from the kitchen.

"Let's sit down until Rose is ready," Thorn suggested. "The kitchen is too small for more than one cook." Thorn waived graciously toward the comfortable living room chairs and they each selected a chair."

"How's it going in the old house?" Thorn asked.

"It's fine. A kerosene heater warmed it up. I've turned on the water."

"I hope the pipes don't freeze."

"I put straw bales around the crawl space. It feels warm under there now."

"Now all you need is a cook like Rose."

"I heard that," Rose said, coming out of the kitchen. "I see you've met Thornton."

"We've spoken several times," Bud said. "Last summer, when I came to pick you up early, before you were ready."

"I'm ready now and so is your dinner," Rose announced. They sat down to a fancy dinner. Rose had outdone herself.

"This is delicious," Bud said.

"You should come more often," Thorn said. "Rose is a good cook, but this is like a holiday feast."

"I'm glad you noticed, Thorn," Rose said.

The friendly sibling rivalry reminded Bud of a poem that was hung on his grandmother's kitchen wall, when he was younger:

> This world that we are living in
> Is mighty hard to beat.
> You get a thorn with every rose
> But ain't the roses sweet.

He decided not to mention it.

"What I can't understand is why you bother to work on that falling down house?" Thorn asked.

"It isn't falling down, it's just abandoned," Bud explained.

"I guess I started it," Rose said, "when Bud stuck up his nose at the mobile home and said we should fix up the farmhouse. I told him to try living in it, if he was so smart."

"It is a classic structure. It's beauty and charm should be restored and used," Bud chimed in.

"Tisn't worth it," Thorn objected.

"Yes it is! With a little tender loving care, that house will increase in value, but this trailer will depreciate, the way a car does, until it has to be replaced," Bud said.

"That's right. We studied that in my real estate courses," Rose said. "But we couldn't do it at the time."

"Dad and Mom bought this place four years ago," Thorn said. "When Dad came home from the hospital after his heart attack, he needed a warm place to recuperate. The house was chilly and he was in no shape to fix it, so he got a mobile home."

"Thorn took over the chickens. Dad and Mom go to Florida in the winter when it gets too cold for him."

"I stayed home to see to the chickens. This year, Rose started her career, so she stayed home, too. It's been nice. Her cooking's much better than mine," Thorn admitted.

"She is a beautiful cook and she cooks beautifully," Bud said jokingly.

"So that's how Rose lured you down here in the middle of the winter," Thorn teased.

"Thorn!" Rose reprimanded sounding annoyed.

"Well, why did you come down here this time of year?" Thorn said, ignoring his sister.

"I joined a senator's staff to work for World Peace and it turned out to be a lot of mudslinging. I was ready to quit, when the senator lost his reelection bid," Bud explained.

"Sorry to hear that," Thorn replied.

"It's a new beginning for me. I remembered the stately farmhouse and Rose's challenge, so I took her up on it."

"Dad said it'd cost too much and take too long," Thorn said.

"I've got time. I've saved up a little money, but I'll have to get a job. It'll take money to fix it properly," Bud said.

"Our real estate office needs someone to fix things in our rental houses. Do you think you could do that?" Rose asked.

"Anybody can fix most anything, if they just take the time. I'll try to fix anything the office needs to have fixed. I'll learn on the job as I go along," Bud said, accepting the offer. "Just let me know. You know where I'll be."

"Let you know tomorrow when I get home," Rose replied.

"I've heard of some crazy arrangements, but this has to be the craziest I've ever heard," Thorn said.

"This may sound strange, but as I restore the farmhouse, I restore myself. My faith in humanity. As the doctor cures the, the patient cures the doctor," Bud theorized.

"You're right," Thorn said, "it does sound strange!"

Bud didn't mind Thorn's teasing. He was thrilled to be part of this family group. But he looked serious, instead of reacting to Thorn's remark. Rose said, "Thorn, You shouldn't say things like that to our guest."

"That's all right," Bud said, "I was just thinking about the holidays. Always gone to my grandfather's farm for Christmas. This is the first time I won't be going home."

"You always mention your grandfather," Rose pointed out, "but you never mention your father."

"My father died overseas in the army about the time that I was born. I never knew him," Bud explained.

"Oh, I'm sorry to hear that," Rose said, with sympathy. "Must be hard growing up without a father."

"My grandfather's been a father to me. I was lucky to have such a wonderful time with him," Bud said proudly.

"Would you like to come over here for Christmas? We'd love to have you, wouldn't we, Thorn," Rose exclaimed.

"We could use the company. Mom and Dad will be in Florida," Thorn noted.

"That's very kind of you, but I need to use the time to get my life in order. I came here to find my way and I have to do this on my own," Bud said.

"Suit yourself," Thorn said. "You're welcome to stay in the old farmhouse as long as you want."

"If you get lonely," Rose said, "come over anytime."

"Don't worry about me. I'll be fine," he said.

After a delightful dinner, Bud offered to clear the table and wash the dishes. "You may clear the table, but I do the dishes," Thorn said. "It's a one-butt kitchen and I know where to put things away."

When the table was cleared, Bud found Rose reading the paper in the living room. "Thank you for the exquisite dinner."

Looking up from the paper, she said, "It's better for you than fast food."

"Do you get that paper delivered to your door?"

"Yes. The only paper they deliver now is the *Journal* in the morning edition."

"Is that a daily paper?"

"Yes. It's the *Wilmington News Journal*. It's yesterday's news. They use the same wire services as the *Washington Post*. It's too close to the Philadelphia Inquirer, so they have to wait twenty-four hours to use the wire-service news," Rose explained.

"That's good enough for me. I read the entire cereal box in the morning. How can I subscribe?"

"Here's the phone number," Rose said, handing him a slip of paper.

"Thanks It's past my bedtime. Hate to eat and run, but I have a lot to do tomorrow. Say good night to Thorn for me."

"Thank you for coming. Thorn and I get tired of looking at each other. Sleep well."

"Good night."

Bud let himself out into the night air. A cold wind whipped across the lane. A bright winter moon shone through high wisps of clouds. The farmhouse was washed in pale shadows. An orange glow filtered through the front window.

Bud felt the steps with his shoe as he stepped over the rotten step. The warmth of his front room welcomed him. He took his shaving kit into the bathroom cleaning his teeth in the dark.

Rummaging in the kitchen, he felt around for a galvanized bucket. Lighting a match to see if it was clean enough, he looked too long, burning his finger. He filled the bucket with water, feeling with his finger so it didn't overflow. Heaving the bucket out of the sink, he set it on the kerosene heater. "That'll help the humidity in here and give me hot shaving water in the morning," he said to himself, stripping off his clothes.

He crawled into his sleeping bag. His full stomach had made him drowsy. Listening to the wind rattle the window, his mind went blank and he drifted off to a peaceful sleep.

RICHARD C. HARRISON

MENIAL TASKS

The winter sun woke him. He looked around. His clothes were thrown over a chair. He'd seen an old dresser around the house somewhere. The water on the heater was steaming.

The hot water and his own bathroom were more comfortable. After shaving, he filled the heater with kerosene and fired it up. He filled the water bucket and put it back on the heater.

He fished out clean jeans, a shirt, fresh underwear, and socks and put them on. Reveling in the luxury of warm water and clean clothes, he set out on a new day.

Sweeping and washing gave Bud a new feeling of independence and inspiration. Gandhi devoted part of each day to menial tasks as a meditation. Bud sang to himself as he worked, *'Tain't hacha, it's the way hacha do it.* Bud was careful to avoid being too compulsive and loosing himself in the job. His mind was free to soar to great heights. While sweeping the floor, he wondered about people all over the world. Everyone sweeps their own dust and cleans their own place. He wasn't alone, but sharing a universal activity. He had found meaning in something that had been going on since the beginning of time. He discovered a universal truth of nature, while cleaning a toilet. Domestic work brings you face to face with life. If you do natural work, you live longer. Wives usually outlast their husbands, because they do all the domestic work. He was inspired to write down his discovery as a fable or fantasy.

GRASS ROOTS

In primitive times, men dressed up to attract women. When the women had babies, the men went hunting. Stuck at home with the children, the women gathered berries, planted gardens and did all the domestic work.

Today, men are expected to go to work, losing sight of nature. They either do other people's drudgery or they live in a make-believe world of paper pushers and they shrivel up and die.

Mother Earth and Mother Nature produce the natural wonders of life. Father Time is a clock watcher, counting the seconds to the end of the year, like the grim reaper of death.

Bud was surprised to find such deep and lasting meaning in menial tasks. He wanted to share his discovery with someone, but it would be hard to explain it to Rose. How could you explain the beauties of housework to a member of the opposite sex? One person's joy is another person's drudgery.

The joy of menial tasks was an inspiration to him. The challenge of putting the house back together stimulated his mind. He was free to make things right again.

Outside in the morning air, the wind had died down and the sun gave a little warmth. The fields were frozen stiff. Looking up, he watched the Canada geese overhead, honking at each other to line up for the next leg of their long trip north to Canada.

Breakfast at MacDonald's was the same. He wrote out a list of what he needed to do.

Delmarva Power
Find laundromat
Cheapest microwave oven
Food store
Juice, Milk, and Cereal
Bread and Peanut Butter
Oatmeal cookies
Canned pears
Laundry soap, Dish soap, and
Bath soap
Windex and Paper towels

Pleased with his list, he dumped his breakfast tray in the trash bin and set out on his errands. Delmarva Power made him fill out a lot of forms and put down a tenant's deposit. He added light bulbs to his list

He asked directions. "The Bay Mart Shopping Center is just over the high-rise bridge on Route 1," the clerk said, pointing east. "The laundromat and food store are right there."

The decision to go up and down every aisle in the food store was the only way to go. Look it all over and don't be impulsive. Next the laundromat.

Looking over the rows of shiny white boxes, he selected an unoccupied washing machine. There were three young women and one man. "You come here often?" he said to the man.

"More often than I like," the man answered.

"Where can I get a cheap microwave in this town," Bud asked.

"Try Ames, just down the highway," the man said, pointing west.

With his laundry in and the washing machine going, he drove off looking for Ames. The enormous discount store was a flurry of activity. No one paid any attention to him. He waited to catch the eye of a cashier while she checked out a customer.

"Excuse me? Where are the microwave ovens?" he asked.

"Way in the back!" she said, starting on the next customer in line.

He wandered to the back of the cavernous store, gawking at clothes, lawn and auto supplies, athletic goods, stereos, patio furniture, and God knows what all. Finally he found the kitchen appliances. Reading all the blurbs on the microwaves, he found one for under a hundred dollars.

Looking around to survey the situation, he saw a man with a hand truck helping a customer. "Excuse me? May I just take the display model?" he asked.

"I'll be right with you," he said. He was a nicely dressed black man in his thirties with a slight limp. Bud wondered what he did for work before Ames came to town.

"Now, have you found what you want?"

"Yes. This microwave."

"That's been on sale. I think they are all gone. I'll look in the warehouse. You wait right here."

So this is how you shop for bargains, he mumbled aloud. The store was set up like a warehouse. Piles of all kinds of merchandise stacked up aisle after aisle. Bud studied the other shoppers' body language and clothes. Most of them looked as if they were caught in a web, trying to survive. They are the ones who read the glossy ads that make the newspaper so bulky.

Waiting dutifully in front of his selection, he felt trapped as he eyed other options. I should have locked the car with all the groceries in it, he chided to himself. What seemed like an eternity, was not that long.

The clerk appeared with a cardboard box labeled "MICROWAVE OVEN" on his hand cart.

"This was the last one. Meet you at the check-out counter."

"That's great! I'll be there!"

Hurrying back to the front of the store, Bud picked out the shortest check-out line. Rows of cash registers beeped out each item. It was the finish line. Lines of irritated customers, waiting to be processed, were anxious to be freed. Travelers wondering if they could get through customs safely. Checkpoint Charlie.

When his turn came, Bud's credit card was accepted, and the clerk wheeled his purchase out to his car. Driving back to the laundromat, he marveled at the discount merchandising tactics.

Throwing his wet clothes in a canvas bag, he started home. He had found a clothes line and plastic clothes pins in the food store. He rigged up the clothes line in the warm kitchen and hung up his laundry to dry.

He set the groceries on the kitchen counter and put the milk on the cold back porch. He couldn't wait to start washing the windows. The insides of the front room windows were clean, but the outside dirt showed through. When he cleaned the outside, he found places he had missed inside. "If I get to compulsive, I'll never get to the other windows," he instructed himself.

He noticed the rotten front step. He dug out a tape measure and wrote down the dimensions. He walked back and forth on each step and across each board on the porch floor. They felt solid enough.

It was time to replace the step. The man in the lumberyard cut a step board to his dimensions. He bought a hammer and some nails and went back to fix the step.

Removing the rotten step was the worst part, but soon the new step was in place. It needed paint, but that could wait for better weather. Standing back to look at his handy work, he was pleased with himself.

One thing at a time, the old place was coming around. It was beginning to restore the dignity of the house and himself.

MR. FIXIT

When Rose came home from work at lunchtime, she brought a list. "Here are the jobs we need done. The names and addresses are listed. You can pick up the keys at the real estate office."

"Thank you, Rose Let me look them over," Bud replied, taking the list from her.

"Lemme know whacha think about 'em," Rose said, going in.

"Can I take you out to dinner?" Bud asked.

"Not tonight. I have to call a bunch of people tonight. Do you want to come to dinner here?"

"No, thanks. Want to get ready to do these jobs."

Bud eagerly took the list into the warm farmhouse. Sitting down to scan the list, he made notes. "Torn screening on porch, outside light out, broken step (there's one I know I can do), put trash cans away, check house for heat, squirrels, and vandals."

"I can buy the tools I need as I go along. Keep records for reimbursement. This is going to be fun!" he said, out loud. "How much do I charge. I'll ask Rose what is the going rate. Make a note to ask Rose. Also, ask Rose for a map from the real estate office and drive around and find these places."

It was lunchtime. He made a sandwich and poured a glass of milk. Taking it into the front room, he watched out the window for Rose to come out. He'd almost finished when she came out.

Rushing out to catch her, he called, "Hey, Rose."

"I have to get back to the office."

"May I follow you over there. Maybe you can give me a map of the area, so I can get started."

"Okay. Follow me."

They drove in tandem toward Rehoboth Beach. Rose pulled into a parking lot and Bud pulled in beside her car. "Come with me and I'll introduce you to the others," Rose motioned.

"I just need a map," he said, following her in. The girl on the front desk looked up.

"Hello, Denise," Rose said. "This is Bud Green. He's going to be Mr. Fixit for us."

"Hello, Bud. We need you."

"Thanks. Going to try to keep things running," Bud said.

Rose walked back to her office. She walked around her desk and sat behind it facing the door. "Have a seat, Bud. I'll try to find you a map."

"I don't know what to charge. Do you know the going rates?"

"I can look up what we've paid to have things fixed, when I get time."

"No hurry. Just want to get an idea.

"Here's a map of Rehoboth. And here's a map of the county with every county road on it," Rose said, handing them to him.

"That's perfect. I'll be on my way."

"Happy hunting."

Bud drove into Rehoboth Beach the route he had taken last summer. The crowds had left and he found a quiet little town.

Many of the shops were closed. All the parking meters had been taken off their metal posts and put away for the winter. Crazy Eddy had decorated the parking meter posts with all kinds of junk Nearer the ocean, he used drift wood and inland he used whatever had been left lying around. The "NO LEFT TURN" signs had been replaced with the "KEEP RIGHT" signs. Everything was neat and orderly. Most people waved to him as he went by. The resort community had taken on a local look, an off-season air.

Driving around exploring the area was an adventure. Looking over a house, told a lot about the owners. Some people took care of their properties and some neglected them. Bud decided to make notes.

The house with the outside light out looked well cared for. He parked and figured out how to open the outside light fixture. He unscrewed the light bulb. It was sixty watts.

He went home to pick up his new hammer, nails, measuring tape, and a sixty-watt light bulb. Then back to the real estate office for the keys. He'd have to learn how to plan these trips.

He drove to the house with the rotting outside shower floor. He had the key, so he went inside to look it over. There was a list of repair people the owner had posted for the tenants. The list read like a list of characters in a romantic novel.

Plumber- Mr. Hazard

Electrician-Mr. Blizzard

Appliances-Mr. Thoroughgood

He copied down the names for future reference. He could call them and ask about the warranties. The outside shower would call for a carpenter. It was easy work that he could do, if he had the time. He measured the rotten wood, made a sketch, and locked up the house.

In the car, he looked over his list and went on to the house the burned-out light bulb. When he replaced the light bulb, the light came on, giving him instant gratification.

He made a quick note. The light bulbs were two for $1.20. Had he worked efficiently, it would have taken an hour. Twenty-five dollars to change a light bulb seemed high.

He drove to the house with the broken step and measured it. The lumber yard cut it for him. He went back and took the rotten step off and hammered on the new one. Going to measure, back to the lumber yard. Cost of new step. Back to house and repairing step. Three hours plus materials. It would have to be painted.

If he couldn't find matching paint, he would have to paint all the steps. He went to the paint store and looked at the paint samples. They gave him a folder of deck paint samples. He went back to the steps and matched the color. One little can, a brush, and an hour would finish it up.

He bought a paint brush, turpentine to clean the brush and enough to paint the steps on his farmhouse. Thinking of it as a fringe benefit pleased him.

He stopped by Rose's office to report on the work done. She was delighted with his activity. "I need to estimate the cost of painting the step."

"I found these old bills from contractors," Rose said, as she handed him copies.

"May I keep these?"

"Yes. I made those copies for you."

"Let me go home and work this out."

"You've made a good start."

"I'm all excited about this new venture."

Bud went home to look over the copies of the contractor's bills. Sitting in a kitchen chair by the window, he perused them carefully. He liked the ones that were itemized as time and material. He started writing a breakdown for each of his jobs.

Realizing he needed a desk, he looked around. The kitchen table, propped against the fireplace to stop the draft, would be perfect. In a stroke of inspiration, he went out and bought a roll of insulation.

Setting the table upright, he tore off a large piece of insulation and jammed it up the chimney in the fireplace. He held his hand in each corner of the fireplace, to see if he could feel a draft. The air was still and the draft was blocked.

He put the table in front of the window, pulled up a kitchen chair, and sat down. "Now, we're getting somewhere," he said out loud, feeling much more comfortable.

When he had finished itemizing each job on a separate piece of paper, he piled them alphabetically. Sitting back and looking over his work, he thought about keeping up with many more jobs in the future. He would need three piles: One: Jobs to be done, Two: Completed jobs to be billed, and Three: The completed jobs that were paid in full.

With the electricity working, he dug out his bedside radio. Scanning the local stations, he found some soothing music. He flopped in bed and drifted off to a peaceful sleep.

The next morning, Bud looked out the front window and saw two morning papers, in clear plastic bags, lying on the lane. He threw on his clothes and dashed out to recover yesterday's news.

He glanced at the headlines as he fixed breakfast. Reading every page, he took time for a leisurely breakfast. The *Wilmington News Journal* was a compact version of the *Washington Post*. It had one page of comics instead of three. A financial page instead of a whole section with redundant articles.

GRASS ROOTS

He made a smooth transition from the *Washington Post* to the *Wilmington News Journal.* He could never read all of the Post in one sitting, but the News Journal gave the important news to him. It was short and sweet.

After breakfast, he took his itemized bills of completed jobs to the real estate office. "If you can wait a few minutes, I'll give you a check," the secretary said.

"I always have time for a check," Bud said with a smile.

It was the beginning of a new venture. Taking his first check to the nearest Delaware bank was an exhilarating big step. Opening a business checking account made him feel that Mr. Fixit had become a legitimate member of the grass roots. He'd planted a seed that he could nurture.

Every day of the following week, Rose brought home a pile of job orders for Bud. He was thrilled with the amount of work he had to do.

Whenever a job called for a tool he didn't have, he made a game of buying the right tool. He researched the quality and longevity of each tool and made a selection.

He kept the tools in the other front room, laid out on the floor. There was plenty of room to reorganize them as they were needed. His final decision was a tool box. He decided on two boxes, one for the back of his car and one for special jobs.

He had to go to the real estate office to make his phone calls. His last call was to order a phone for himself. He put a jack in the front room and another in the room off the kitchen. This room was where he planned to have his bedroom when he had rewired, insulated, and paneled it.

The first call he made, once the phone was installed and the telephone man had left, was to his grandfather and the second to his mother. He missed being in touch with home. He gave them his new phone number with pride. It was a symbol of his success and a celebration at his new-earned freedom.

It wasn't long before he bought a box of file folders. Used cardboard boxes had become his fine cabinets. He made a game of keeping records by hand. He had never run a business before and if he wrote everything down, he could learn how business works.

As the new venture blossomed into a full-time job, Bud found very little time for his restoration of the old farmhouse. He was much in demand as Mr. Fixit. He made enough money to subcontract some of the restoration of the old farmhouse, including new wiring and insulation. The outside work had put color in his cheeks and there was a spring in his step.

Having seen repairmen's signs in front of houses they were working on, he called Rose to ask about getting a sign. "We have a couple of old real estate signs you could paint. They are as large as the law allows," she indicated.

"That would be perfect," Bud said enthusiastically.

"I'll bring a couple of them home when I come," she said.

Bud met her when her car pulled up and he unloaded the metal signs. He scrubbed the rust off of them and gave them a coat of paint. He designed a "Mr. Fixit" logo and blocked out his phone number on the financial page of an old newspaper.

When the sign was dry, he carefully painted his new logo and phone number in large block letters. Standing back to admire his artistic endeavors, he nearly spilled the open paint can. It unnerved him enough to close up the paint can and put everything away. He planned to paint the other sign another day.

One morning the milk was frozen on the back porch. It was time to check out the refrigerator. The electricity was working, so he wrestled the refrigerator out from the wall. He found the plug and plugged it in. Hearing a hum coming from the box, he filled the ice trays and decided to wait and see what happened.

The stove used propane gas. There was a tank out back. He decided to call the propane company and have them look at it. He made a note to call them and fixed coffee in the microwave.

The pioneer feeling of finding his way on his own gave him pride in his work. As things began to fall in place, he found a new happiness in his accomplishments.

WINTER FREEZE

By February, the work orders began to pile up. Bud felt a pressing need for a helper. Whenever he went to the hardware store or lumber supply, the other contractors always asked if anybody knew of any good workers.

Bud asked everyone he met if they knew of any good workers. He got a couple of names. When he came back to the farmhouse that evening, he called them. One of them, Doug Rhodes, was available to come to work the next morning.

"I'll be looking for you first thing in the morning," Bud told him. "Do you know where I am?"

"Yeah," Doug said, "I'll see you tomorrow."

After a hasty dinner, Bud went into the front room to make a list of jobs for the helper. He put his new "Mr. Fixit" sign in his car, straightened up the front room, and went to bed.

The next morning, Bud hurried to dress so he could catch Rose before she left for work. He grabbed the same clothes off the chair. "Got to start hanging things up at night."

He picked up his reports and went out to look for Rose. Roamer wagged his tail and trotted over to bid him good morning. Giving him a pat, he said, "It's a nice day, Roamer." The air was fresh and crisp. The bright sun looked warm, but the chilly wind tweaked his nose.

Roamer turned his head, pricking up his ears, as Rose came out to her car saying, "Good morning, Bud."

"Morning. I have the property reports for you," he offered.

"Good. I'll take them with me," Rose said, smiling.

Picking up the newspaper, Bud went in to fix his breakfast and wait for the helper. After reading the paper over breakfast, he went into the front room to look over the jobs he had set up for the new helper. He glanced out the front window frequently, looking for a strange pickup.

By ten o'clock, he began to worry. *"Maybe the helper lost his way,"* he mumbled. Bud would have done the first job that he had set up for the helper, but he was trapped. He had to stay and wait for him. Bud didn't even want to leave the window.

He reviewed all of his paperwork. It was almost eleven when he got through to the helper. The phone rang several times and finally someone answered.

"Yeah!" a voice answered.

"Is Doug Rhodes there?" Bud asked.

"This is Doug Rhodes," he replied.

"This is Bud Green. I talked to you yesterday about a job and you said you'd be here this morning," Bud reminded him.

"I'm cleaning ducks!" Doug exclaimed. The shock of this remark caught Bud off guard. His tone of voice implied that Bud had interrupted him. Also, there was a subtile suggestion that anyone from the big city didn't have their priorities straight.

Bud's interest in the grass roots had led him to this serene and tranquil area. He was about to learn why lower Delaware was called "slower Delaware." The seasons of migration of ducks, geese, and tourists make the priorities.

In the Federal City, the same work goes on day after day, oblivious of the weather, in central air conditioning and heating. In Slower, Lower Delaware, however, no one in their right mind does odd jobs in the good weather, especially off-season.

"Oh," Bud said, a little taken aback "I was counting on you this morning."

"I'm right in the middle of these ducks. Can't get there before twelve," Doug explained.

"I see." Bud was baffled and wanted to get to the bottom of this face to face. "I have to start on these jobs. I'll try to be back here for lunch at noon. If I'm not here, wait a little while for me."

"Okay. I'll be there between twelve and one," Doug stated.

"You remember where I am?" Bud asked.

"Yeah, yeah. I know where it is," he said as he hung up.

Bud put down the phone, a little confused. He had come down here to get away from the pressures of the big city, but how laid back can you get? He didn't want to be irresponsible. Doug Rhodes had been a shock Bud didn't know that this cold shoulder was just the tip of the iceberg.

Mumbling to himself, Bud left to start his first job.

Arriving back at the farmhouse at twelve sharp, he didn't find a strange pickup in the lane. He went in to fix lunch.

Everything had been going so well when he did all the repair work himself. This Lower Delaware attitude seemed so bizarre. The feeling of freedom he found as his own boss was dissolving into the stress of being the boss. Learning to fix things was logical, but trying to organize the grass roots workers was becoming a mystery.

As he was eating in the front room, a pickup drove into the lane. Bud jumped up and ran out. "Doug Rhodes?" he asked, as he approached the pickup.

"Yeah," the driver said. A young, short man with two days beard growth, looking serious, got out of the truck He was wearing camouflage hunting clothes. "Guess you're Bud Green."

"Yes, I'm Bud Green," Bud said, shaking hands. "Let's go in and talk a minute. You caught me in the middle of my lunch."

As Doug stepped into the warm farmhouse, he pealed off his jacket and tossed it over a chair. His sweatshirt said it all,"A bad day hunting is better than a good day working."

They went into the front room. Bud offered him a chair and sat back down to lunch. "Have you eaten?" Bud asked.

"Yeah," he said. "I ate before I came."

"Waited for you to show up instead of getting my work done. Wish you'd call me, when you're going to be late."

"We don't have a phone in our duck blind. It's the end of the hunting season and we we didn't expect to see so many ducks."

"Well, I have an answering machine. You could have called before you went duck hunting and left a message on my machine."

"You big city people have all the latest gadgets."

"Don't live in Washington. I live here," Bud said proudly, looking at Doug Rhodes. "I have a lot of jobs to be done."

"Sounds like you're taking over the work around here.

"Bud ignored the resentment in his voice. "I don't think so, but I was looking for some help with these jobs."

"That's what I'm here for."

"Do you think you could help me out? The pay is good and I pay by the job. The work seems regular."

"We'll see what you need done."

Bud went over the list he had made out for the helper. Doug just sat there and listened. "What do you think?" Bud asked.

Doug looked at Bud, then looked out the window. Then he looked as though he was about to speak After a pregnant pause, he said, "Let's get started."

Bud took him to the first job and put him to work, saying, "I'll be back in an hour. I've got to fix a toilet over on Wilmington Avenue. I'll be back before you're through."

Bud pulled his new sign out of the car and planted it in the front yard where his helper was working and drove off. When Bud returned to Doug's job, he inspected the work and Doug had done a good job. "Looks real good," Bud said. "Ready for the next job?"

"Sure, but the police left this for you." Doug handed Bud a form made out to Mr. Fixit, reading, "You must have a business license to do business in Rehoboth Beach. The license fee is eighty dollars."

In frustration, Bud read it again. "But my office isn't in Rehoboth Beach," he mumbled. "Can't expect me to buy a license!"

"The good old boys in city hall can do whatever they like," Doug said. "Can't fight city hall."

"We'll see about that. Ready for the next job?"

"Lead the way."

Bud took Doug to the next job. "I'll go to city hall to get this straightened out. Should be back before you're through."

At city hall, Bud explained that his business address was not in Rehoboth Beach. The clerk said, "You come into town to do your work"

"Just fix things."

"Then you have to have a business license."

GRASS ROOTS

Bud tried to explain that the oceanfront area east of the inland waterway was divided into five towns" North Shores, Henlopen Acres, Rehoboth Beach, Dewey Beach and Indian Beach Does this license cover the other towns?"

"No, but you can't put up a sign in Henlopen Acres or North Shores. They also have a sign ordinance," the clerk pointed out.

Reluctantly, he filled out the forms and paid the eighty dollars, feeling victimized by the good old boys as well as the local workers. The new kid on the block was at the mercy of the established community.

Doug was a good worker once he got started. Bud learned a lot about grass roots attitudes. It took a lot of diplomacy to get along with Doug Rhodes.

He hired another helper and his diplomatic skills were tested to the limit. He found himself in the roll of referee.

As he hired more helpers, he became more selective. He only called the ones that did the best work He realized that he had to check the jobs first, then assign a helper to it, and, finally, go back and check to see that it was done properly.

Trying to organize a crew of rugged individuals was getting him down. For his own sanity, he made a major decision. He was going to mind his business and let them mind theirs. "I'm leaving for the first job at eight thirty. If you're here then, I'll give you a job."

The odds of workers showing up showed a dramatic drop when the weather was good for outside work. The spring weather brought more tourists and fewer workers. The shopkeepers, anxious to get open, all called Mr. Fixit. In desperation, Bud called all the helpers who had worked for him and asked them to round up anybody they could, Doug Rhodes brought his father, Doug Rhodes, Senior along to help.

Doug Rhodes, Senior, was taller and leaner than his son. He was easy going and strong as a bull. In his fifties, he worked harder than the younger men. The other workers all liked him and his gentle persuasion inspired them to work harder. He soon became Bud's number one crew chief and could get the best work out of Doug Rhodes, Junior.

They were both called Doug Rhodes. When Doug Rhodes, Junior was a child, they called him Dusty. This suited everyone except Dusty.

When Dusty came of drinking age, he wanted to be called Doug, like his dad. The problem was, when you called their name, they watched your eyes to see which one you were looking at. Bud was learning that grass roots was not about a group, but it was about a lot of individuals.

At the end of a bright spring day, Bud pulled into the lane. There was a strange car parked by the trailer. "Rose or Thorn must have visitors," he puzzled. Bud had never seen another car in the yard. He parked by the farmhouse and went in.

There was a knock on his door and Bud found Rose smiling at him. "Can you come over and meet Mom and Dad?"

"Oh, they must be back from Florida."

"Yes, just come as you are."

"First, let me put these things down."

PART FOUR
SPRING THAW

"Dad and Mom, this is my friend, Bud Green. Bud, these are my parents, Thornton and Lily Gardener."

Going in the mobile home with Rose, he found a middle-aged couple settling in. A short, dumpy man sitting in an easy chair resting after his long drive from Florida. He scrambled to his feet, stuck out his hand, and smiled, "Nice to meet you, Bud."

"Rose has said good things about you, sir," Bud said.

Rose's mother had been adjusting things on table tops, back to the way she liked them. She was a wiry, short woman with a simple house dress. Her hair was cut in an athletic bob and her eyes twinkled, deepening her smile lines. She turned and came toward them.

"You the young man Rose met last summer?"

"Met Rose last summer."

"Well, I'm pleased to meet you. What are you doing down here this time of year?"

"It's a long story. Guess I just needed to get away from the big city."

"Bud's been fixing up the old farmhouse," Rose said.

"Thought it looked different. More solid, somehow," Mrs. Gardner remarked.

"Wouldn't let me do that kind of work after my heart attack," Thornton said, "so we put in the mobile home."

"Won't you sit down?" Lily said. "How about a cup of tea."

"Or a drink," Rose's father said.

"Now, Thorny," Lily reprimanded, "you know what the doctor

137

said." Bud noticed that Lily made Thorny the head of the house, in the grand housewife tradition, as long as he ran it to suit her. Bud felt, "He ruled the roost, and she ruled the rooster."

"Doctor didn't say anything about Bud," Thorny said. "Here, sit here."

"Thanks," Bud said, sitting where he was told.

"Now, how'd you get interested in fixing up the farmhouse?"

"Just thought it looked sort of classic-worth fixing up."

"So did I. It reminded me of the good old days, the way the gingerbread set off the roof line. Lily found a lot of things that needed fixing. We had to give it up when I got sick and the bad weather set in."

"Then you don't mind if I stay and keep on fixing it up?"

"Stay as long as you want to. It seems to be agreeable to Thorn and Rose. Besides, it's nice to have it occupied, far as I'm concerned."

"I've settled in for the time being. Had the electricity put in my name as a tenant and put in a phone. I'm doing odd jobs for Rose's real estate office."

"Well, you seem to have a good start."

"Fixing up the old house is helping me get myself back on track. I had big ideas about World Peace up in Washington, but the mud-slinging in the election was too much for me. I had to get back to what I believe in. Restoring the old house helps me restore some of my dignity."

"Know what you mean. I envy you."

Here's your tea, Thorny," Lily said "Now what can I get, Bud?"

"I'm happy just talking. Thank you just the same."

"What have you two been talking about?" Lily asked.

"Bud's setting up a business in the old farmhouse. He's helping Rose with her career."

"Glad it's being used for something. I just hope you don't freeze to death over there."

"I keep it warm with a kerosene heater."

"That place was impossible," Lily said . "I found so many things that needed fixing, a family couldn't live there."

"I started out very primitively, but it keeps on getting better all the time."

As Bud was talking, Rose's brother, young Thorn, came in the front door. "See you made it through the winter, Bud," he said.

"Best winter I've ever had," Bud replied.

"Say, where'd you get that little sports car?" Thorn asked.

"Worked in a gas station when I was in high school," Bud explained. "Bought it second- hand and the mechanic helped me fix it up."

"Looks like it'd be fun to drive," Thorn said.

"It is, but I need a pickup truck now," Bud said.

"Any time you want to trade cars, for a day or so, you can drive my pickup and I'll drive your car," Thorn offered.

"I'll take you up on your offer Let me know when you want to do it," Bud replied quickly.

"How about Saturday night?" Thorn asked. "I have a date with Mary and I want to impress her. She's the girl for me and I need all the help I can get."

"I'll clean it out and have it ready for you," Bud said.

"You'll stay for supper, won't you?" Lily asked.

"Maybe another time. I have to make out my reports and send out my bills. I'm having trouble hiring a helper and I have to have the work ready for him," Bud answered.

"You can do that after supper," Lily said.

"Now don't push him, Lily. He knows what he has to do," Thornton noted.

"Thank you both. It sure is a pleasure to meet nice folks like you." Bud stood up, saying, "Now don't get up. I know how to let myself out. I'll take a rain check, Mrs. Gardner."

Rose appeared from the back of the mobile home. "I'll see you in the morning Bud," she called out.

"I'll have a report for you to take to work tomorrow. Good night," he said, heading for the farmhouse.

The next morning, Bud hurried to dress so he could catch Rose before she left for work He grabbed the same clothes off the chair, mumbling, "Got to start hanging things up at night."

He found his reports and went out to look for Rose. Roamer wagged his tail and trotted over to bid him good morning. Giving him a pat, he said, "Beautiful day, Roamer."

The sun had taken over the clear blue sky and was steadily warming the fresh, crisp air. The trees had a light dusting of chartreuse. The weather was perfect for an outdoor activity.

Roamer turned his head, pricking up his ears, as Rose came out to her car saying, "Good morning, Bud."

"Good morning. I have the property reports for you."

"Good. I'll take them with me."

"Now that your mother's back in the kitchen, how about my taking you out to dinner this weekend?"

"I have to work Saturday and Sunday, but I have Monday and Tuesday off."

"Will you be too tired Sunday evening, or should we wait till Monday?"

"Sunday would be perfect," Rose replied. "I'll be ready to relax by then. I get home about six."

"Just let me know Sunday evening, when you're ready."

"It's a date. I'll be looking forward to it," Rose said as she drove off to work. Picking up the newspaper, Bud went in to fix his breakfast.

Bud had plenty to do, fixing up the farmhouse. He was learning to rewire the house in his free time. When he had a job that he couldn't do, he hired a subcontractor. He offered to be the helper for the subcontractors' jobs, as a good will gesture. Bud was becoming a brain-picker, watching how the job was done and asking pointed questions.

When he hired an electrician to help him find a short circuit in a rental house, he got him to come by and look at the farmhouse. The electrician told him how to rewire one room. "When you get the wiring in place, call me. I'll come by and hook it up, if it looks okay," he offered.

The electrician had replaced the old fuse panel with a new circuit breaker panel and hitched up the old wiring to it. Bud planned to go one room at a time, tearing out the old beaver board paneling and putting new wiring beside the old. In the cold weather, he could work inside a little bit at a time.

Bud rewired the room just off the kitchen and called the electrician to come out and check his work Satisfied with Bud's wiring, the electrician connected Bud's new wiring to the new breaker panel.

When the new wiring was working, Bud insulated the walls and paneled the room. As soon as he could move all his belongings into his new bedroom, he could start rewiring the front room.

The week went by quickly. As he worked to finish his new bedroom, he was thinking about his upcoming date with Rose. He worked Sunday morning, putting the final touches on his new bedroom. He had picked up a queen-sized box spring and mattress, when an investor decided to replace the beds in a house he had just bought. He rewired a phone jack next to the bed.

After lunch he cleaned up the room and flopped into the bed to catch a nap. He wanted to be rested and ready to go when he took Rose out for the evening. He drifted off to sleep.

. . .As a small boy, he roamed the fields around Gramp's farm. From the top of a hill, he saw a beautiful valley. Lured toward this magical paradise, he came to a barbed wire fence. The barbs were long and sharp. The fence seemed to stretch endlessly in both directions, blocking his way. Determined to explore this land of enchantment, he tried to carefully climb over the barbed wire fence. When a barb tore his pants, he panicked, grabbed the wires, and cut his fingers. When the frustration of the pain and the blood became overwhelming, he woke up with a start.

He looked around the room. Spying the clock, he thought, Must have needed the rest. There was time to get dressed for his date. The bucket was full of hot water. He lugged it into the bathroom, shaved, and took a marine bath, a sort of stand-up sponging off. It wasn't his favorite way to bathe, but it sure beat sitting in a cold tub of water.

He had laid out his clothes on a chair and he dressed in no time. Ready to go, he sat on the edge of his new bed, waiting for Rose, as he admired his handy work. He was pleased with the progress on the house and he had made enough money to fix up one room. Also, he had saved enough to take Rose out.

"Hey, Bud, are you in there?" Rose called out.

"All set to go. Be right there," he called out to her as he rushed to the door.

Seeing Rose standing on the porch, he said, "Boy, you're a sight for sore eyes." He admired her trim figure in her dressy outfit. Since she had been dressing for the office, she had a whole new wardrobe.

"Thank you, kind sir," she said, imitating his teasing manner with a courtesy. "I hope I'm not overdressed."

"You're perfect. Shall we go?" he said, opening the car door for her.

"I'm not used to such courtesy."

Closing her door, he went around to the driver's side and took his seat. "Where would you like to go?"

"I chose the place last time. Why don't you say where you want to go?"

"That was last summer. After a new year, you start over."

"Oh, is that how it works?"

"Well, if you don't pick a place, I'll return to the scene of our first date." He put the car in gear and drove off.

Parking at the Lamp Post restaurant, he said, "Here we are." The hostess asked about reservations. Bud put their name on the list and led Rose into the bar.

She immediately recognized a couple from the office. They greeted each other gaily and she introduced Bud to them. "Bud, I want you to meet John and Carolyn Goodwin from the real estate office. This is my old friend, Bud Green. You may know him as Mr. Fixit."

"Well, I'm delighted to meet you," John said. "You've been a great help to us. I hope you keep up the good work. We can't get along without you," Carolyn said.

"I try to be helpful. I really enjoy fixing things myself, but Lower Delaware workers are a ystery to me," Bud replied.

"That's why they call it Slower Delaware," John laughed. "That's why we need you."

"If you don't like the way we are around here," Rose spoke up, "why don't you go back to where you came from?"

"I was enjoying living here," Bud said, "till I tried to hire a helper."

Ignoring Rose's remark, John said, "We were going to order a drink and it's no fun drinking alone. Why don't you join us?"

Bud looked at Rose, waiting for her to say yes or no. "That would be fun," she said. "Okay, Bud?"

"Any friend of Rose's is a friend of mine," Bud said as he pulled out a chair for Rose and pushed her in. Rose and Carolyn fell into a discussion of a mutual friend as they all sat down, while the men looked around for a waitress. John caught her eye and waved her over to the table.

"Can I get you something from the bar?"

John said, "We'll have two whiskey sours."

Bud looked at Rose and waited.

Rose said, "I'd like a glass of white wine."

"Make that two white wines," Bud said and the waitress went over to the bar to fill the order.

"How did you get into this Mr. Fixit business?" John asked.

"That's a long story. I came down here from Washington to fix myself and it flowed over into fixing other things."

"Bud has been restoring Dad's old farmhouse," Rose said with enthusiasm, "and he's doing a wonderful job."

"Have you always done this sort of work?" Carolyn asked.

"No, I was on Senator Blassforth's staff working for World Peace. He was up for reelection and he got into a mudslinging campaign. I didn't like his politics and when he lost, I came down here to start over," Bud replied.

"That's fascinating," Carolyn said. "Tell us more."

"That's all there is to it. Have you always lived here?"

"No, Carolyn and I were selling real estate in a little town in Pennsylvania," John said. "We always came here in the summer. Business was too slow up there. When we had an opportunity to move down here where the action is, we jumped at it. We've been happy ever since."

"Mr. Goodwin, your table's ready," the hostess said. "It'll just be a minute, Rose."

The Goodwins got to their feet, saying, "So nice to meet you. Keep up the good work."

At last, Bud and Rose were alone. Rose said, "I hope you don't mind having a drink with them. We work together and I have to be friendly."

"I liked meeting them," he said. "Rose, this is my treat to you and if you don't do what you want to do, I won't be happy."

"I'd forgotten that you are Mr. Nice Guy. You've worked so hard, I think you ought to have a good time, too."

"Every day's a holiday when I'm with you."

"Mr. Green," the hostess said, "your table's ready."

They picked up their half-full wine glasses and followed the hostess. As they came to the table, Rose put down her glass and said, "Excuse me a minute. I see a client I talked to today."

"Go get 'em, tiger," Bud said, playfully.

"Do you mind?"

"Not at all. Please speak to them."

Rose went to say hello to her client and Bud sat down. He looked around at the people. The off-season crowd was different from the in-season crowd. They were mostly locals that knew each other. It was a good crowd for Sunday night.

The waitress brought the menus, saying, "I'll give you a little time to look over the menu."

Bud opened the menu and read all the entrees, trying to make up his mind.

"Sorry about that," Rose said, returning to the table, "but I just had to speak to them. They came down to look for a place to buy and they don't know anybody here."

"Don't be sorry, Rose. I'm glad you feel comfortable enough to do what you want to do and I know you'll be back," Bud said.

"I'll try to keep the business contacts to a minimum."

"It's nice to see you so active in your new career. You're very impressive."

"Tell me. How are you doing?"

"With what?"

"With yourself. You said you came down here to get yourself straightened out."

"I'm getting better, but it's a slow, ongoing process. I'm beginning to see what I really want."

"What do you want?"

"When we talked about democracy working from the bottom up, I began to get the idea. Finding you has turned the tide."

"Never mind me. What're you going to do now? You gonna fly off to the big city to build your home and seek your fortune?"

"Slower Delaware has made me look at life as part of nature. I'm beginning to get a handle on it, a new lease on life. The more I stay in Sussex County, the more I like it. This is God's country," he said, skipping his problem with the locals.

"Well, I think so, but you just complained to John about the people around here."

"Everything was going so well till I tried to hire a helper. He didn't show up and when I called him, he acted like that's the way it is around here. I guess some of the big city has rubbed off on me."

GRASS ROOTS

"What about World Peace?"

"I'm getting a handle on it. It's a personal matter. I'm beginning to see what made me so fanatical about World Peace. I've been thinking about my father and grandfather. I want to be around to help my children grow up."

Rose started to comment, when the waitress interrupted, "Can I get you something from the bar, or are you ready to order?"

"Would you like another glass of wine?" Bud asked.

"This is terrible, but I really would like another glass."

"Why don't you bring a small carafe of white wine?"

"A small carafe is about four glasses."

"That's perfect. We'll have one, please."

As the waitress went away to get the wine, Bud looked at Rose, raised his glass, and said, "Here's to a successful career for a lovely lady."

"Here's to your happiness, Bud," she said, holding up her glass and clinking it against his. They took a sip, looking deep into each other's eyes.

"I'm celebrating the start of a brave new world," Bud said. "I'm proud of what you're doing. And I'm proud of the amount I've been able to accomplish. Also, I'm indebted to you for your hospitality."

"Let's just have a nice evening together," Rose said. "You deserve it and I think I have earned an evening out. I'm proud of what you've done, but I think we've thrown enough bouquets at each other. Let's just have a good time."

"I'll go for that," Bud said. He loved the way Rose lived for the moment. Bud reckoned, most people aren't doing what they're doing, they're doing something else. When he swept the floor, he was settling the affairs of the world. When he was fixing the old farmhouse, he was fixing himself. But, when Rose goes out to dinner, her mind is on having a good time. She doesn't worry, if she has left the car lights on, or if she has forgotten to unplug the coffee pot. She had a way of doing what she was doing at the time she was doing it.

"Now, what are you going to eat?" Rose said, picking up her menu and interrupting his thoughts.

"I'm not going to tell you, but I know what I want. You hav to order first, because you're the guest of honor."

"Let me see," she said, perusing the menu.

The waitress appeared, asking, "Are you ready to order."

"Yes, I think so. Are the soft shells fresh?" Rose asked.

"Not this time of year," she reminded Rose.

"Then I'll have the broiled flounder," she responded.

"Good choice. And you sir?" the waitress asked.

"New York strip, medium rare."

"What type of salad dressing?"

"Blue cheese," Rose said.

"I want my salad undressed," Bud said, feeling devilish.

The waitress blushed. Recovering, she asked, "Would you like lemon on it?"

"No, thank you," instead of bare, Bud said, "just plain."

She gathered the menus and went away.

Bud poured some wine in Rose's glass and a little in his. They took another sip. Alone for the moment, they looked into each other's eyes again and broke out into wide grins.

"Did you see much of Missy Mannerly in Washington?"

"Yes, she invited me to some fancy social functions. I felt it was only proper to repay the social obligations, so I took her to a few shows and dinners. She was a little upset when I left, but there are a lot of fish in the Washington scene."

"Do you miss her?"

"Not really. We just were convenient escorts for each other. Do you have someone you go out with?"

"No. I've been too busy trying to get started in the real estate business. This is the first time I've had a real date since we went out last summer."

"Well, maybe we should go out more often."

"Be nice, but we both have a lot of work to do first."

"Yes, but, all work and no play makes Jack a dull boy."

"That's the way it is when you're just getting started in a new field."

"I'm just getting started, too. I've got quite a way to go before I can relax."

The waitress brought their dinners and they were hungry for the food. They ate with interest, poking the salad and cutting up their entrees. As they finished, the band was setting up.

It wasn't Bunky Eye, it was the Little Big Band. There was a lot to set up. It was an eight-piece dance orchestra. When they were ready, the leader counted off slowly and the saxes wheezed out an intro. It wasn't like the bright businessman's bounce of the Washington society orchestras.

They played in a slow drag, not too coordinated. They were retired senior citizens trying to relive their youth with some nostalgic old tunes.

Bud and Rose didn't have a spontaneous reaction. It was more of a delayed response. "Would you like to dance?" he asked.

"Don't want to be the first one on the dance floor."

"They'll be warmed up in another couple of tunes."

"How about some dessert and coffee?"

"Mm. Sounds good."

As the waitress cleared their dinner plates, Bud asked,"What do you have for dessert?"

"I'll bring you a dessert menu."

"And two coffees, when you come."

The band tried a peppier number but the bass and drums were the weak links. The rhythm section didn't have a good beat. It was too bad, because no one was dancing.

Rose chose ice cream and Bud agreed. That was one thing he didn't fix at home. When they had finished their dessert and coffee, Bud called for the check.

"If you want to dance, I'll give it a whirl," Rose offered.

"The band didn't inspire anybody to dance. Let's just drive down to the Henlopen and look at the ocean."

"Sounds good to me."

Bud drove into town and pulled up at the Henlopen parking lot and parked facing the ocean. There were other cars with people in them parked on both sides of them.

"The ocean seems to fascinate people. They just sit and watch it," Bud said, as he put his arm around Rose.

He bent to kiss her, but she said, "There are too many people here." He couldn't argue with that. They sat in an uncomfortable silence for a short while. Then Rose said, "Let's go somewhere else."

Bud started the car and drove slowly through the Pines. As soon as they left the parking lot, Rose moved closer to him. She slipped her arm through his and laid her head on his shoulder.

"Put your head. . .on my shoul. . .der," Bud sang softly.

"Never forgotten that night, Bud. Everything was so right. It was magic."

"I remember the magic. Think we'll ever find it again?"

"I've learned to wait and give it time. Guess it's like riding a bicycle. If you try too hard, you fall on your face."

He pulled over to the side of the road and said, "Rose, you're very special to me. I don't want to do anything to offend you, but I can't express it very well in words." He leaned down and kissed her cheek.

"You're very special to me, too, but I'm not ready for a commitment right now."

"Neither am I. I just enjoy being with you."

Rose hung on tight to his arm. "I don't want to let you go, but I'm not ready to keep you either."

"You don't have to talk about it if you don't want to. May we stay right here another minute?"

She didn't say anything. She just held his arm tightly. After a long silence, Bud started the car again and drove home. He pulled into the lane and stopped. She turned to him, saying, "Thank you for a nice dinner and a lovely evening."

"It's my pleasure, Rose. Maybe we can do it again."

"That would be nice, but let's not rush it."

"I have a lot to do, but I'll take time off whenever you say the word."

She gave him a tender, warm kiss, opened the door, and started for the trailer. He jumped out and walked her to the door. "Thank you for making it a lovely evening," Bud said.

"Good night, my dear," she said, with a kind smile.

She went into her trailer and he went to the farmhouse. The glow of the kerosene heater made angular shadows from the kitchen where it had been moved. Bud was used to going to bed in the dark. He didn't turn on the lights. He dropped his clothes on the chair and crawled into bed.

It was such a different kind of mood this time. As he lay there in the dark, he hummed a slow halting tune, Put your head on my shoulder." Contented, he drifted off to sleep.

Coming back from the bathroom to dress, the early morning sun cast a sparkling beam through the window of his new bedroom, highlighting tiny dancing particles of dust. The brilliant ray brought him a message: Time to buy a vacuum cleaner.

He made a note to call the Electrolux man and fixed breakfast before the crews came. Bud had been rewiring, insulating, and paneling between Mr. Fixit jobs.

He had a list of work orders almost every day. If it kept on like this, he would have to hire a regular helper. Working long hours had made him conservative. He didn't want to hire anyone regularly until he was sure he could keep them busy.

Hiring part-time workers in Lower, Slower Delaware strained his patience, tested his nervous system and shook the very ground where he had put his faith.

When he found a good worker, he tried to keep him, but the good ones move on to better opportunities. In an effort to hold onto the better workers, he formed a crew and made the best worker crew chief. Knowing this would only hold the good men a little while, he formed another crew as soon as he had enough work for them. Jobs were coming in and his business was growing.

After taking his crews to their jobs and telling them what to do, he went back to the farmhouse. He called the electrician to come and inspect his front room.

He had removed the old beaver board paneling in the front room and rewired the walls. A stack of rolls of insulation sat in the middle of the floor. While waiting for the electrician, he stripped the old paint off the ornate mantle around the fireplace. It was tedious work, scraping each little groove, but necessary before it could be repainted properly.

He admired the design but his fingers were getting tired. He had finished about half of it when the electrician came to check the wiring. When the electrician approved the wiring and hooked it up, Bud put up the paneling. He ducked out to check on his jobs and give the crews their final instructions for the day.

He loved the independent feeling of the grass roots until he tried to hire helpers who had grown up with this independent feeling. Their irreverence tried his patience. It was every man for himself. Putting together a crew became a balancing act of faith and perseverance.

He needed to get back to simpler things like stripping the ornate fireplace mantle. One man's drudgery is another man's occupational therapy.

ICE BREAKER

Back at the farmhouse, Bud had nearly finished stripping the ornate fireplace mantle when Rose came bursting in the door.

"Sold my first house!" she yelled. "We have to celebrate and I'm paying for dinner!"

"Congratulations!"

"I'm so excited. I want to take you out to dinner tonight and celebrate."

"Easy come, easy go. Are you sure you want to do this?"

"Sure do. Stop fooling with that while I'm talking to you." Rose said impatiently. "How soon can you be ready?"

"Fifteen minutes."

"Be out in front in fifteen minutes and I'm driving. I'm just going to tell my family the good news, wash my face, and come right out."

Bud stood up, a little shocked as she ran out of the old farmhouse, giving a war whoop as she danced down the front steps.

Bud hastily cleaned up and put on fresh clothes. Rose had hit a home run, but he hadn't had time to take it all in. He was still in the part about, "Crack! The ball is sailing. It's going, going, going, gone! It's over the fence! It's a home run!" The roar of the crowd drowns out the exhilarated raving of the radio sportscaster.

Throwing on his clothes, Bud hurried out. Roamer was wagging his tail listening to Rose's excited explanation of the sale through the trailer walls. Bud knocked on the trailer door.

RICHARD C. HARRISON

Rose yanked the door open, while talking to her family, "See you later. Bud and I are going to celebrate my success."

Rose hopped in the driver's side of her car, so Bud got in the passenger side. She started the car, her sparkling eyes beaming at him, and planted a big kiss on his surprised lips. "Okay, let's go!" she said to herself, driving out of the lane.

She went straight to the Lamp Post and parked. She gave the hostess her name and led Bud into the bar. She spotted John and Carolyn Goodwin and went brazenly up to their table.

"We're celebrating my first sale!"

"Well congratulations, Rose, hello, Bud," John said. "You have to sit down and tell us all about it over a drink."

"What do you think of Rose, now?" Carolyn asked Bud.

"Knew she'd be a success. She's a very special person."

John flagged the waitress and they ordered their usual. Bud let Rose handle the conversation this time. It was her day in the sun and she was loving every minute of it.

Another couple spotted Rose and stopped by to congratulate her. Every other person seemed to be in real estate and had heard about her good fortune. The exciting celebration drowned out the TV news program and Bud was caught up in the enthusiasm.

The hostess said, "Miss Gardner, your table's ready," with a tongue in cheek formality fitting the occasion.

"Oh, good!" Rose said to the hostess. Rose was beaming as she took Bud's arm and followed the hostess to the table. Bud pulled out Rose's chair with a flourish as the hostess laid the menus on the table, saying, "Your wait person will be Jane tonight. She'll be right with you."

A few more people stopped by the table to congratulate Rose before Jane came to take their order.

"Small carafe of white wine while we look over the menu," Rose said, with savoir-faire. She glowed with self-confidence as she smiled at Bud.

"You're something else," he said, delighted with her new spirit of triumph. "Nothing succeeds like success."

"Hope I didn't sound like a top sergeant," Rose explained, "when I asked you to help me celebrate. I was so excited, I had to let off a little steam."

"Why not? You've earned it."

"Thanks for being so nice about it."

"Let's just enjoy the evening together."

She was hearing her words coming back to her. Bud added the trigger word, "together" and it thrilled her. "I'd love it," she cooed, looking at him as she picked up her menu.

As they finished their festive dinner, an electronic trio was setting up their equipment. Rose ordered, "Two coffees and a dessert menu, when you have time." She was enjoying her new role and taking charge.

"I'll have vanilla ice cream with chocolate sauce. I'm going back on my diet tomorrow," Rose said with reckless abandon.

"Sounds good. We could share one. When you eat from someone else's dish, the calories don't count," Bud joked.

"All right! One sundae and two spoons. Hold the whipped cream and cherry," Rose said to Jane.

The idea was fun and they giggled as they ate. The trio was a surprise. They sounded like a larger group. The man at the keyboard burst forth with the latest pop tune, with an up-tempo twist. The driving bass line synchronized with delicate drumming as the singer moved to the microphone under a blue spotlight.

Bud and Rose pushed back their chairs, moving to the rhythm. Walking toward the filling dance floor, he took her in his arms and then spun her out, giving her the reins. She made some new moves he had never seen before, effortlessly responding to the lilting pulse of the music.

She was celebrating and he was glad to be in on it. As they invented new steps, others watched in amazement. Bud tried to downplay his part, giving all the glory to the queen of the ball.

After a long set, the musicians took a break. Bud and Rose walked back to the table, laughing and frazzled from all the physical activity. She flopped down in the chair he held for her, saying, "That's more fun. It's a good band."

"I really enjoyed that. You came up with some new steps or you've been practicing."

"I don't know how I learned to dance. I just move with the music and the mood. The music's marvelous," Rose said.

"I could dance all night."

"So could I. Let's have another cup of coffee. Or another glass of wine?"

"Let's stick with the coffee," Bud said.

When the trio came back, they danced again. Each tune they played had a stimulating arrangement. Rose's movements were a lighthearted spectacle of sheer joy. She inspired the feeling of festivity in all the other dancers, building to a fever pitch. When the singer announced a short break, the crowd groaned their displeasure in a friendly manner.

Sitting down again, Rose sighed, "I suppose we should stop while it's still fun. I do have to work tomorrow and I'm afraid I've run you ragged."

"Your wish is my command. You're the boss tonight."

"I don't think I can make any more decisions tonight. You'll have to help me here."

"Let's quit while it's fun. Are you ready to go?"

"I think so," she answered.

"Check, please," Bud said as the waitress passed the table.

"Hey! This is my treat. Don't you dare pick up the check!"

"Wouldn't think of it," he said jokingly.

Rose paid the check and they went out to the car. As Rose started the car, Bud said, "Thank you for including me in your celebration."

"You're a good sport. You made it the time of my life."

She drove into the lane and parked. "Congratulations, Rose you"re on your way to success and happiness."

"Oh, Bud," she said, throwing her arms around him, "I'm so happy!" They hugged each other with exuberance. Then she kissed him tenderly and moved toward the door.

Bud jumped out and walked her to the trailer. He kissed her gently and said, "See you tomorrow."

"Good night," Rose said as she went in.

"What an evening!" Bud said to himself, bouncing up the front steps. Admiring his elegant new bedroom, he carefully hung up his clothes and hopped in bed. His toes tapped out a rhythm under the sheets, as he lay there remembering the tunes and Rose's graceful dancing movements.

When his leg started to cramp from too much toe tapping, he jumped out of bed. Walking off the cramp, he picked up a cookie in the kitchen and went back to bed. Relaxing this time, he drifted off to sleep.

As spring brought warmer weather, the old house was ready to be painted on the outside. Having rewired, insulated, and paneled the inside on the first floor, Bud needed a change. He wanted to get out in the air for a while.

He closed all the upstairs doors except the bathroom. The bedrooms would serve as insulation with the milder weather.

Bud picked up a color chart of exterior paint samples and called on Thornton Gardner. "Come in, Bud, and sit down."

"I'm planning on taking a week off and painting the outside of the farmhouse. I brought a color chart of the paint samples to see if I can match the old paint."

"Don't need my permission. If you want to paint the old house, you can paint it any color you like."

"Maybe Mrs. Gardner has a preference. Wouldn't want to paint it twice."

"Lily, can you come in here for a minute," he called out.

Lily Gardner appeared with an apron over pastel slacks. "Oh, hello Bud. I didn't hear you come in."

"Bud, here, is going to start painting the outside of the old farmhouse and he brought some color samples. Show her what you want to do."

"I liked the original colors, gray with white trim," Bud said, showing her the color chart. "I think a little darker gray, because the old color has faded, and this off-white. Maybe an even darker gray for the accent, like the shutters and front door. What would you suggest?"

"Sounds perfect to me, but you're not planning on doing it, climbing up on ladders and all that?"

"Yes, ma'am, I was. I may need to hire a helper or two when I get started painting, but first I have to pick out the paint."

"Like your colors, but I think we ought to hire a painter."

"We'll see," Bud said. "That's all I need to know for now. Thank you for your time."

"Any time, Bud. You know where we are."

Having chosen the colors, he tried to estimate the amount of paint it would take. He only had one extension ladder, but if he needed another, he could rent one.

Taking his figures to the paint store, he wasn't too far off from the store's estimate. He asked for the painter's discount and took a couple of cans and brushes to get started. He figured he could cover the cost of the paint if it only took one coat.

He decided to take a week off and get started. He started in the back, where it wouldn't show. After one day of painting he hired a helper. Bud had to do little emergency jobs that came up for Mr. Fixit, leaving the helper to do most of the painting.

It took more than a week just to paint the siding. When the siding was finished, he had the helper paint the high trim. Bud could paint the lower trim between odd jobs. After three weeks, he called the Gardners out to admire the new farmhouse.

The stately lines were embellished by the reborn gingerbread along the roof line and the front porch. The accent color on the front shutters set it off. The house posed, as if it was all dressed up in its Sunday best.

"Oh, doesn't it look strong and proper," Lily said.

"No house has ever fallen down for lack of paint," said Mr. Gardner, "but it makes me proud to have such a fine-looking house across the lane. Wait till Rose sees it!"

"Glad you like it," Bud said proudly. "Well, I just wanted to show you how it's coming along. I have to run into town and help a shopowner fix up for the summer season."

"Oh Bud," Mrs. Gardner said. "We're going to have a little engagement party for young Thorn and Mary, at the country club. Wouldn't you like to bring Rose?"

"Sure would. When is it?"

"Friday evening about six, upstairs at the club."

"I'll ask her when she comes home. Thank you very much."

"The house is beautiful," Lily said. "You run along and help the man get his store open."

Bud drove into town, thinking about the improvement, not only in the house, but in himself. He really loved what he was doing and he was at peace with the world.

The more he learned how to fix things, the more enthusiastic he became. One thing led to another until he became completely engrossed in the projects. The thrill of watching the house grow more serviceable was one thing. Starting a thriving business was exciting, he couldn't resist it. Working long, hard hours for himself was the best experience he had ever had.

When he returned home, he waited for Rose. Dashing out to meet her when she drove in, Bud called out, "Hey, Rose, You didn't tell me Thorn was getting engaged?"

"Isn't engaged yet," Rose replied.

"Your mother asked me to come to the engagement party at the country club. Let's go together."

"That would be nice."

"Friday night about six. I'll be ready whenever you say."

"We can leave here about a quarter of six, but no later."

"Be waiting for you."

"Hey! The farmhouse looks great! Is it all finished?"

"Outside paint is finished. Next time I'll hire a painter."

"You should be proud of what you've done," Rose said, and turning to go in, "no later than a quarter of six."

"I'll be ready before that on Friday."

Bud dug out his Washington "uniform" and looked it over. He had time to get it cleaned and pressed.

The next morning he drove into Rehoboth Beach, pulling up in front of the combination Glamorama Cleaners and Trailways Bus station. As he went in, Brenda greeted him with, "You drive back and forth a lot. Was wondering when you're gonna come in."

Brenda was a large woman in her forties. Her friendly smile and easy manner would disarm the meanest man in town. She would make a perfect barmaid.

Her turtleneck sweater and corduroy slacks gave the impression of a country gentleperson. Maybe it was the makeup around her large, round eyes. She used a natural tone of lipstick

"I'm Bud Green," he said, introducing himself.

"I know. My name is Brenda. Everybody tells me what's going on in town. You're also Mr. Fixit."

"Well, news travels fast in this town."

"There are two ways to get the real news," Brenda began. "You can stop at the Captain's Table for a cup of coffee or stop by here to get your cleaning. That stuff in the local paper has been edited, but our news is unvarnished."

"Must remember that, Brenda."

"You're the one who took Rose to the Lamp Post to celebrate her first house sale."

"You do keep up on things," Bud said with a nod. "I have to have these clothes by Friday or before."

"Cost you more on special, but they'll be ready tomorrow."

"Can I give you one shirt to be done at the same time?"

"Yes, indeed. Where you going in these city clothes?"

"Don't know if I'm supposed to tell you, but I might get my clothes quicker if I do. Thorn Gardner and Mary Thoroughgood are getting engaged."

"You still haven't told me where."

"It's at the country club. Private party, I think."

"Now I owe you one. The gay nightclub burned down last night. At first they thought it was some rednecks, but it turned out to be two gays fighting with each other. One of them tried to set the other on fire."

"Now, how do you know that's the way it is?"

"You'll see. Wait till the next paper comes out. It'll be in the Whale and the Delaware Coast Press."

"When do they come out?"

"Every Wednesday. What else would you like to know?"

"That's enough for me. Thanks for the news. Better get going."

"Have your clothes ready for you, tomorrow after three."

"See you then," Bud said, going out the door.

As Bud started on his jobs for the day, he kept thinking about taking Rose to Thorn and Mary's engagement party. Does it have any special significance? Why did Lily Gardner invite him? He was thrilled that Thorn was becoming engaged and happy to be taking Rose. Just felt as though things were closing in on him.

The next day, he picked up his clothes at the Glamorama Cleaners. Brenda was full of new stories. She handed him his clothes after he had paid her. He was on his way home and he didn't want to talk too long with her.

"Thanks for the special. See you," he said as he left.

Friday, Bud cut his day a little short and went home to get ready for the engagement party. At five-fifteen, he dressed in blue blazer and gray flannel slacks.

GRASS ROOTS

He felt comfortable in his city clothes. He was ready for the party, so he went outside to wait. Roamer came over to see him. "Don't get too close, Roamer. I've got on my city clothes. We can't get dog hairs all over them." He bent over and patted Roamer's head at arm's length. Rose came out as he was trying to avoid the dog hairs.

"Well, don't you look nice," Rose said.

"Shall we go in my car?" Bud asked, opening the passenger door for Rose and she slid in.

When he was settled and ready to drive, he said, "Tell me the best way to get to the country club." He didn't want to say that he didn't know where it was.

"Just go out to Route 1 and head for Rehoboth," she said. "I'll tell you when to turn."

"Have your parents always belonged to the country club?"

"Yes, Daddy joined when he lived in Rehoboth. He could walk to the old club, when it was in town. The golfers wanted to enlarge the course, so they sold the golf course land in town to a developer and built a new club out on the north point of the bay. The builder wanted to develop the old club land with a cluster plan, but the good old boys didn't approve it in time. Now it's a development, full of prefabs on narrow lots, called Country Club Estates. Turn right here," she explained as they approached the turnoff.

Bud eased into the right lane and turned by the Sports Complex. "That's easy. Just this side of the purple dinosaur."

"Yes, it's become a gaudy landmark."

The road made a sharp left turn around a horse barn and then headed south. They soon came to a sign, reading, REHOBOTH BEACH YATCH AND COUNTRY CLUB.

"Is there a yacht basin?"

"There will be when it's finished. The land in town became so valuable that they could buy the whole point of the bay. They have tennis courts, swimming pools, and a good golf course. When the houses are all built, there will be more people living here than in the city limits of Rehoboth Beach."

The road curved to the right as substantial houses loomed up on each side of the road. The bay was behind the houses on one side and the golf course was behind the houses on the other side.

A rambling, two-story, masonry building spread across the panoramic view of Rehoboth Bay. Bud pulled up and parked. As he got out of the car, a brisk breeze off the bay messed up his hair. Combing his hair with his fingers, he looked over the pastoral scene of the golf course with it's manicured grass and majestic trees.

He opened the car door for Rose. She took his arm and led him in the front door. The decor was all new and modern. "This is quite a pleasant club," Bud said..

"We lost the picturesque charm of the old club, but the new club has better equipment and facilities," Rose said, as she led him through the dining room. The large room was half-full of club members eating dinner.

They walked through to another large room with comfortable chairs around a large fireplace. The entire back wall was floor ceiling glass revealing a magnificent view of the bay. It was the cocktail hour and several people sat in comfortable chairs, scattered around tables.

"We go up here," Rose said, starting up the stairs. At the head of the stairs, there was a receiving line with Thornton and Lilly Gardner, young Thorn and Mary, and Mary's parents, Simon and Bea Thoroughgood. Rose went through the line first, saying, "This is my friend, Bud Green," to the Thoroughgoods.

Bud congratulated them as Rose admired Mary's engagement ring. Bud had been looking forward to meeting Thorn's fiancee.

Mary's bright smile had caught Bud's eye as he went through the receiving line. Her brown hair shone in shoulder length waves. When he noticed her tasteful cocktail dress, he wondered what she usually wore. He liked the classic lines and the modest over-the-knee style. Her high heels put her almost at eye level with Bud. *She must be five-ten barefoot*," he thought.

He didn't recognize Thorn. He had never seen him in his dress-up clothes and something was different about his hair. His hair-styling made him look more like a tourist than a native.

At the end of the line they joined the happy crowd. The room was a duplicate of the room below, but the second floor view was better. The furniture was arranged on the perimeter of the room, leaving a large area for tables of finger food in the middle. There was a bar along the wall opposite the windows, with busy bartenders providing the lubrication.

The club members seemed to be successful trades people. Bud

GRASS ROOTS

liked the idea of regular people belonging to a club. The old Washington clubs seemed to be full of stuffy professional people and third generation, inbred, peculiar heirs. It was refreshing to meet some down-to-earth members. It was the high life in the grass roots.

Bud and Rose talked to everyone there. The conversations were engrossing and they were excited about the engagement. They didn't notice the time slipping by, until people started leaving.

Lily Gardner was greeting people in the center of the room as they were leaving. Rose stood beside her, so Bud hovered near Rose. Lily said to Bud, "You stay, because we're going to have dinner downstairs as soon as the guests have left."

"I'll stick with Rose," Bud said.

When the last of the hangers-on left, Rose and Bud followed Thorn and Mary, the Gardners, and the Thoroughgoods down to the dining room. The Thoroughgoods were shy and quiet. They were the guests of the Gardners and they were visibly apprehensive about giving away their daughter.

Mrs. Gardner led the way to the dining room. The hostess greeted them as their guests of honor, leading the way to their table, and casually removing the RESERVED sign.

Bud held Rose's chair for her and Mr. Thoroughgood followed suit with his wife's chair. Looking over the polished silverware and cloth napkins, the men sat down together. Rose admired the small bouquet in the center of the table.

The waiter explained the specials for the evening as they all looked over the menu. The cocktail waitress appeared and offered to bring drinks, but everyone said they had enough.

Bud chatted with the Thoroughgoods, trying to put them at ease. He tried to avoid questions about how he fitted into the family. It was too complicated to explain.

The dinner was good, for a club dining room, Bud observed. Club food never seems as good as the food in a place that is open to the public.

When everyone had their fill, Mr. Gardner called for the check. When Mr. Gardner signed for the dinner, everyone thanked him and stood up to leave. They all congratulated Mary and Thorn and said words of encouragement to the Thoroughgoods. The happy group walked out to the parking lot together.

"I'll bring the car around for you?" Bud whispered to Rose.

"No. I'll walk with you."

They bid a cheery goodbye to each other heading for their cars. Rose caught Bud's arm as they walked off alone together.

"Thank you, for being so kind to the Thoroughgoods," she said. "You're a big help."

"Big event for Thorn and Mary. I was delighted to be there. Least I could do."

"Made me very nostalgic," Rose said, climbing into the car.

Bud thought about her remark as he walked around the car to the driver's side. As they started back down the road, Rose slid over and snuggled up close.

"Should make you happy to see your brother setting out on a big adventure with such a nice girl," Bud said.

"Thorn and I have grown up together. In one way, I'm happy for him. In another way, it's breaking up our family."

"Can't stay young forever. Life goes on and we all grow up and move on. You'll probably be next."

"Don't plan my future for me!" Rose said indignantly. "You sound like my mother."

They drove along quietly, each thinking about Rose's future. The lights twinkled across the bay as they followed the little caravan down the country club road. The lead car slowed for each speed bump in the road. The homes looked different at night with their lights on. The families had come home and their households were lit up with inside activity.

Back to Route 1, Bud followed the flow as it turned east. There didn't seem to be an access road across the divided highway. The Friday night traffic was building up. He followed the other cars into Rehoboth Beach.

"I've never been in Rehoboth on Friday night in the spring. Seems to be quite a few people for this time of year."

"They come out to see what's happening," Rose said, sitting up and looking around. She had been snuggled close to him, lost in her thoughts. "Let's drive down around the U and see what's going on near the ocean."

There were people bundled up in jackets walking on the sidewalks. There were plenty of parking spaces. An occasional bicycle wove through the traffic. A few shops were open and most of the restaurants were busy.

"Didn't know so many shops would be open," Bud said.

"They're open on weekends this time of year. Most of the people from Washington won't be here till tomorrow. Many of them rent their cottages all summer and come down off season. They'll all be in the real estate office tomorrow."

The traffic moved right along. They went down around the U easily, gawking at the sights. As they started back up the main drag, Bud turned north, to get away from the traffic.

As they drove through the quiet residential section, most of the cottages were dark and the streets deserted.

"I've been wondering where Thorn and Mary are going to set up housekeeping."

"Not getting married till June. Why'd you think of that?"

"May want to take over the farmhouse," Bud replied.

"Oh, I don't think Thorn would want to live there. I'll ask him about his plans next time I see him."

"Well, it's fixed up enough so they could use it. It'll soon be time for me to find a place of my own."

"The family likes the idea of you living there. I'm sure we want you to stay as long as you want to."

"I love that old farmhouse, but it isn't mine. I'll need to find my own place soon."

"Don't worry about it now. You've fixed it up and you might as well use it."

"Well, ask Thorn about their plans."

"I will. I always have such a good time when I'm with you. I never want to go home, but I have to get up early tomorrow and work all weekend."

"So do I. We better go home and get a good night's rest."

"It's so quiet here. This must be the way it used to be when Daddy lived here."

"Isn't like this in the summer."

Out on the highway, the weekend crowd was on their way to a party or fun and games. Bud drove back to the Gardner's place, thinking about the future. As he pulled into the lane, he said, "Well, here we are. Back at the old homestead."

Rose stayed in the car and leaned toward him. He took her in his arms and hugged her. She softly cuddled into him so they fit together, molding into one. Each of them had changed the other without meaning to.

He broke away just enough to kiss her. She turned toward the door, saying, "I'd better go in."

Bud walked her to her door, saying, ""Thank your mother for including me."

"Good night, my dear."

As Bud went into the farmhouse, he looked at it differently. He just went methodically to bed. The puzzlements were too much to sort out at night. He just remembered Rose, as they hugged in the car, and drifted off to sleep.

The summer merchants were beginning to fix up their shops in anticipation of the coming season. This created more work than Bud could handle.

Mr. Fixit took on more temporary crews to get all the shops open on time. Bud was run ragged, just checking on the jobs and acting as the "go-for".

Learning his way around, and meeting the owners of the local businesses was an exciting adventure. When he came across a job at Fifty Park Avenue, he remembered Missy's cottage. He drove down Surf Avenue by the ocean and turned on Pennsylvania Avenue.

Pennsylvania Avenue was a wide macadam street with room for diagonal parking on both sides near the ocean. As he drove past Missy's house, he looked over the new screen panel he had fixed on her porch the week before.

At First Street, he turned right. Turning away from the ocean on Park Avenue, he headed into the woods on a narrow sandy lane. On his right, there were large summer houses. On his left, a broad median full of mature trees. As he crept along the bumpy lane, the trees in the median thinned out into a parking area. There was a large brown shingled cottage with faded pink shutters across the parking area. Bud spotted a small wooden hanging sign, reading, THE COR-NER CUPBOARD.

At the end of the block, he came out on Second Street. It was as if he had come out of the woods to a paved road again; as if he had been in a time warp to an earlier era. Across Second Street, Park Avenue had two paved lanes and a wide grassy median with well chosen plantings.

Making a U-turn on Second Street, he turned back into the woods on the sandy lane going the other way. He pulled over at the third house, the one with the sign. Stepping out of the car, he looked around in wonder.

The Corner Cupboard was an old inn tucked away in the middle of a residential area. All the cottages on Park Avenue were substantial, two-story homes on large lots. As he went to the door, he was wondering about the zoning. A business-like woman in her thirties opened the door, saying, "May I help you?"

"I'm Mr. Fixit," Bud replied.

"I'm Mrs. Hooper's secretary," she said. "Come in and I'll see if I can find her." She led him through an inviting living room. There was a fire in the fireplace, magazines and newspapers neatly laid out on a table, and a bowl of mints.

Through the door to the left, they came to a kitchen that was used as an office, with a couple of people sitting on chairs. Bud said to the man who had smiled at him, "That's some road."

"That street is like old times," the man said. He was an older man, dressed like a tourist on vacation. The season is set by the weather and the school schedules. He had reached grandfather age and didn't have to worry about school schedules anymore. When you are too old to swim in the ocean or get up out of a beach chair, the off-season becomes the in-season.

"Only street in Rehoboth Beach that isn't paved," he said in a deep baritone voice. He was a thin old man, but he must have been a public speaker. "The people on this block don't want it paved. You have to drive slowly with nature's caution bumps."

"It's like being in the woods," Bud suggested.

"That's why they call it 'the Pines.' Now, everything north of Rehoboth Avenue is called 'the Pines.' The people who come to the Pines year after year are mostly from Chevy Chase or Old Town, Alexandria, and remind you every chance they get."

Bud smiled and the old man rambled on. "South of Rehoboth Avenue was called "the Heights". Mostly Delaware people rent there, from Wilmington, New Castle, and Dover. The ex-governor has a house here."

"Yes, I've explored the Heights," Bud said. "They also have trees, but Dewey Beach is more barren."

"South of the city limits is a barrier reef, all the way to Bethany Beach. Dewey Beach and Indian Beach had grown up on the barrier reef that separates the Atlantic Ocean and the Rehoboth Bay. Route 1 turns south at Dewey Beach and runs down the middle of the barrier reef for twenty miles to Bethany Beach. There are state parks along the way," the man continued to explain.

"The barren barrier reef allows one city block on each side of the highway, the ocean side and the bay side. As Dewey and Indian Beach developed, the drinking water on the barrier reef was intolerable. The tourists drank whiskey all the time and whooped and hollered like Indians. They say that's why they call it Indian Beach."

Bud acknowledged the elderly tourist's running commentary with nods, grunts, and a friendly smile. The old gentleman was just getting warmed up.

"Now that the county has put in water pipes all the way to Dewey and Indian Beach, the area has gone big time. The Rusty Rudder complex takes up over two blocks of what used to be little summer shacks," the man rambled on.

"Rehoboth Beach is a peninsula, not a barrier reef, because it is protected from the ocean currents by lower New Jersey. The cottages sit back in the trees on streets that run inland from the beach. Inside the cottages you feel more like you are in the mountains than on a barren beach."

Bud had mentioned a trigger word and his lecturer was either lonely or he had been vaccinated by a record player needle. In either case, the conversation came to a screaming halt as Mrs. Hooper came staggering in, out of breath. She was an older lady, nicely dressed, but scowling as if harassed.

She looked around at the people waiting. Bud said, "I'm Mr. Fixit."

Her scowl changed to a relieved grin and she said, "Let me show you what I need done. I used to have a Moor who did these jobs for me, but I can't find him this time of year."

"What do you mean by a Moor?" Bud asked.

"The Moors are the best workers. There's a colony of them over by Lewes," she pointed out.

GRASS ROOTS

Puzzled by this, Bud just went on with his job. He thought A group of Moors had come across the ocean and settled in Lewes.

After that, he made it a point to ask around about the Moors. Every time he asked someone, he got a different story.

The blacks said the Moors were half-breeds, half-Indian and half-white or half-black. The whites said the Moors had olive-colored skin and were diligent, clean, and efficient - the best workers. They were also good tradesmen, like plumbers and electricians. Bud never did get a clear idea of what they meant by "Moors." He made a mental note to try to hire one if he could.

"I'll bring a crew in here tomorrow morning," Bud said to Mrs. Hooper. "They should be finished before noon."

"I'll be here to check on them," she said. "We're switching over from bed and breakfast to our summer dining room."

"This is an unusual place," Bud mentioned, "in the middle of a residential area."

"Been here over forty years. We're allowed to go on running this place because it's still in the family. There's a 'grandfather clause' in the zoning records."

The job was easy and Bud enjoyed the history lesson. The more he learned about the area, the more he liked it. Bud's car crept down the bumpy sand lane and came out of the woods on First Street. His next stop was a little shop that sold lemon ice in the ocean block of Rehoboth Avenue. The contrast between the quite retreat and glitter of the main drag impressed him as he found the little shop.

Wedged between two stores was a small counter at the sidewalk. An agile man in his forties was busily working on getting the counter ready for summer. "Hello. I'm Mr. Fixit."

"Oh, hello," he said, as his dark eyes twinkled under a clump of curly dark hair, "I'm George Moliere." He spoke with a soft, friendly accent that sounded European. "Come around here," he said, opening part of the counter, "and I'll show you what I need to have done."

As Bud climbed into the shop, he noticed it had been closed up all winter. "Where do you spend your winters?" Bud asked.

"Oh, I go back to France, sometimes. Or Morocco or Spain."

"How did you happen to come to Delaware?"

"Came here with a friend one year and liked it. The local people here are very provincial. They say, 'Why would you want to travel, when we have everything you could ever want right here in Delaware?' I guess I've always traveled." He showed Bud what he needed done and Bud assigned a crew to do the job tomorrow.

Bud stopped by the year 'round book store, Browseabout, to check on a crew. The owner, Mr. Crane, was a roly-poly man in his late thirties. He had been a school teacher and worked during the summer in Rehoboth before opening the store. He enjoyed an interesting conversation and was a provocative speaker on many subjects.

"How are things coming along?" Bud asked.

"Your crew is finishing up," he said. "I see your crews all over town."

"Wanted to start out small but I've had so many calls I had to hire a few crews to do the work."

"If you just go to work, there's more than enough to do. My neighbor started enclosing his screen porch with clear plastic panels. When his neighbors saw what he was doing, they asked him if he'd do the same to their porch. He agreed and now he has orders for the next six months."

"Know how that is. It happened that way to me."

Bud gathered up the crew to take them to their next job. As he complimented the crew chief on the good work, he couldn't keep from thinking back to his first encounter with Doug Rhodes, when he was shocked by the laid back ways of Lower, Slower Delaware.

Standing in front of the Browseabout, Bud said to his number 1 crew chief, "I've found a man who comes to work on time and finishes the work on schedule."

Doug Rhodes, Senior, broke into a friendly grin. In a gentle aside to Bud, he said, "He isn't from around here, is he?"

Bud grinned back. The grass roots of Lower, Slower Delaware were growing on him.

Memorial Day was his deadline. He had hired more crews to handle the seasonal rush. His crews were still working when the migration of early visitors started coming in droves. He had first seen the town as a tourist in the summer. This was like working back stage, getting ready for the big performance, and he was playing to a full house.

"Just came down Route 1. The tourist traffic has turned it into a drag race!" a busy shop-keeper yelled to Bud. "It's a combination of bumper cars and a demolition derby. Stay away Route 1. The crazies are coming!"

PART FIVE
JUNE

The first weekend after Memorial day, Bud found himself bogged down in paperwork. His mind was beginning to drift away from the big city ways, as he spent long hours processing the work orders for Mr. Fixit at his desk in the front room.

With a pile of job orders on the desk, he glanced at the cardboard boxes full of filed papers on the floor. He was thrilled with the booming success of his business venture, but he had learned more about running a business than he had bargained for. Gazing out the window at the bright sunshine, his mind had drifted back to his frist trip to the beach.

"Living here year 'round, I should go to the beach when the weather is nice and the sun shines," he said aloud. *"When the cookies are passed, pause and take one."*

Bud dug out his bathing suit. He pulled on a sweater and long khaki slacks over his swimming trunks and drove into the middle of town to take in the summer sights and relax.

The parking meters were back in action and most of them full of cars. Turning north, he looked for a street with no parking meters. Finding a place past the end of the boardwalk, he parked, pulled off his sweater, slacks and shoes, and walked down to the sandy beach.

The morning breeze was too strong for sunbathers. There was no one braving the cold water. The bright sun warmed his shoulders, so he walked along the wet sand near the water. The waves lapping the sand made the beach scene a pleasant distraction.

There was very little tourist activity on the beach. Bud found most of the visitors, gathered on the boardwalk, bundled up in sweat suits, sweaters, and jackets. The boardwalk merchants had opened for business while they put the finishing touches on their summer setups.

The seagulls flocked around a man on the boardwalk. He was tossing caramel corn up in the air over the beach. The quickest seagulls caught the kernels in the air. A crowd had gathered to watch the activity. It reminded Bud of J. Livingston Seagull.

A young man in corduroys and a sweater was flying a colorful kite on the beach for his girlfriend. They were young, maybe in their twenties. Her long hair trailed behind her in the wind as she watched the kite. Bud wondered about their relationship. She looked at her friend as much as she looked at the kite.

Bud bent down to look at an interesting shell. It was shaped like a Shell gas station sign. It was brown and white and was a perfect specimen. He put it in his pocket and walked on.

Funland was open, but not busy yet. There were a few young people hanging around. No one was playing Whack-a-Mole. He thought about Rose working diligently at the real estate office.

She has a running start on her career. What if she makes too much money, buys a big house, and marries a wealthy Realtor. He'd have to wish her well and hope she lived happily ever after.

It was time to settle down and raise a family. How could he ask her to make a commitment, when he was just getting his little business started? How could he tell Rose how he felt about her?

At the south end of the boardwalk, he stopped to turn around and go back. The deserted beach south of him stretched as far as he could see. Dewey Beach was just around a bend in the shore.

He had left the commercial area back nearer the center of town. Stately old beach houses sat back from the boardwalk. The owners had resisted cashing in on their valuable property. Now they were sitting in the catbird seat.

Scanning the beach, he was surprised to see two nuns, in black habits, sitting in reclining beach chairs in the sand. Their chairs were turned toward the sun with their black clothing trailing in the breeze, looking like Zoro.

He looked at the horizon. The ocean showed a slight curve. He knew the earth was round, but he'd never seen it curve before now. Wondering if the curve was visible from a ship out in the middle of the ocean, he thought, Columbus and his peers must have discussed this gentle arc. It was a wondrous sight.

Marveling at the natural beauty, he felt he had come home. This was where he belonged. Why work fifty weeks a year, for two weeks here, when you could stay right here and enjoy it all year?

He started back with his shoulders erect, drinking in the sights. Mother nature put on a grand display. Walking back up the beach, he enjoyed the warm sand under his bare feet. The sun warmed the other side of his body as a fragrant ocean breeze filled his lungs with an intoxicating bouquet of sea air.

Glancing at the busy shopkeepers, he fantasized. They had to work back-breaking hours for three months, tapered off for three months, rested for three months and then started getting ready for another season. It was a good way of life. They played on the bay and went duck hunting. They had so many different things to do that they didn't have time to work all year.

A small camp of bathers had rigged up a windbreak by tipping their umbrellas against the wind. Colorful beach towels filled the gaps between the umbrellas. The breeze would die down soon and they had claimed their space in the sun.

The sun passed the high point of its daily arc over the sandy beach, warming the air, as he approached the center of boardwalk activity. Almost everyone on the boardwalk was eating something, mostly ice cream cones. He turned away from the water, lured to the ice cream counter on the boardwalk.

Standing in line, reading the list of flavors posted on the wall, he couldn't help but overhear the couple in front of him as they talked enthusiastically.

"They select the best flavor from each brand and order from all the wholesalers." Soon he was confronted with a series of decisions.

"Do you have chocolate with nuts in it?" he asked.

"Swiss chocolate almond."

"That's it."

"One scoop or two?"

"One."

"Sugar cone or cake cone?" the clerk asked, pointing to the cone dispenser.

"Sugar cone."

Bud fumbled for the folded bills in the little button pocket of his swim trunks. Holding the cone in one hand, he funneled the change back into the tiny pocket. He grabbed an extra napkin and headed for a bench.

Carefully shaping his ice cream with expert licks as he caught each melting droplet, he sat down on a bench on the boardwalk. Looking around between glances at his ice cream cone, he became intrigued with the compatibility of an unusual group of people. Two teenagers, a middle-aged woman and an older woman sat on a bench across from him.

Being so relaxed and congenial together implied that they had lived together comfortably as a family. Comparing their facial features for clues and bloodlines, he found variations of hair and eye color, but their noses were all cast from the same common mold.

The teenagers talked playfully among the group. They were too far away to make out exactly what they were saying but their facial expressions and body movements said enough to hold his attention.

The teenage boy sprawled almost horizontal with his knees casually crossed. He was gently kicking his sister's sneaker in a secretive, teasing manner.

The grandmother ignored them as she raised both feet up in front of her, stiff-legged, to admire her new white padded walking shoes, the way a lady admires her new high heel pumps. They were all wearing substantially new athletic shoes.

To get back at her brother's teasing, the girl sat up and gave him a knee chop. She held her hand stiff, the way a doctor would test for a reflex action. The boy's knee didn't respond.

She crossed her legs and tried it on her knee but got no response. The boy tried it on his mother's knee, with no response, as the grandmother and mother watched in amusement.

Then the grandmother was drawn into the game. She felt around the mother's knee, below the knee cap, with the tips of her fingers. Everyone watched with interest as she stiffened her hand and tried a knee chop on the mother. The mother's sneaker bobbed up with the proper response.

Bud was tempted to test his reflex action as he watched the people on the next bench testing theirs. He remembered the first time a doctor picked up a rubber-tipped hammer, told him to relax, and hit him just below the knee cap.

"What do you think you're doing?" Bud had asked the doctor.

"Testing your reflex action," the doctor said as Bud's foot bobbed up. The new aspect of reflex actions needed more exploration. He went home to tell what the doctor had done to him. The next day at recess, he tested all his playmates' reflex actions.

Bud noticed two other people down the boardwalk, testing their reflex action. It might have contagiously spread further, but the sound of an inspired religious fanatic pierced the air, "REPENT!"

Everyone turned to see a young black man, dressed in his Sunday best, striding determinedly toward the boardwalk. At thirty second intervals like the siren, he called out at the top of his powerful voice, "REPENT!" Scantily clad bathers stared in amazement as he started striding down the boardwalk, yelling, "REPENT!" As he walked on, the sound grew fainter.

Bud finished his ice cream cone and wiped his hands and face with the napkin. He spied a young mother washing her daughter's tiny face and hands in the drinking fountain. His fingers were still sticky. Even an ice cream expert can't get the stickiness off his hands and face with just a napkin. He stepped over to the drinking fountain, as the mother led her daughter away.

The drinking fountain was an impressive stone monument. The stones formed an arch over the fountain. Fresh, cool water ran continuously. A bronze plaque, set into the stone, announced, *Erected by the Women's Christian Temperance Union 1929*. This little monument, in the center of activity, seemed to mark a time between Rehoboth's inception as a Methodist camp meeting ground and the Nation's Summer Capital. It stood proudly in the midst of the revelry, trying to point the way to health and happiness.

Refreshed by the cool, clear water so near the briny sea, Bud glanced at his watch and walked on up the boardwalk. A happy stride took him back to his parked car. He put on his khaki slacks over his swimming trunks, having decided to stop at the real estate office on the way home.

He whistled a happy tune as he drove along. "*I should go to the beach more often,*" he thought as he parked the car and walked into the real estate office.

He picked up a work order and peeked into Rose's office to see if she was there. She looked up from her desk and said, "Hi, Bud. Come in."

"I've been to the beach. The sun is shining and there are a lot of tourists already."

"Must be nice."

"Oh! Rose, who handles your bookkeeping for the office?"

"Jane does it on the computer. Why do you ask?"

"Oh, nothing. I just seem to get bogged down in paperwork and I thought I might find out how the experts do it. You know, pick the expert's brain."

"We'd have to hire a big staff of people to do what the computer does automatically. It's a lifesaver."

"Well, I won't keep you from your work. See you later."

At the front desk, Bud asked, "Is Jane here?"

"Yes, the second door," the receptionist said, pointing down the hall, "you may go right in."

Bud found the door and looked in. As the lady looked up at, Bud asked, "Jane?"

"Yes, Bud, were you looking for me?" she asked. It was always amazing that everyone seemed to know his name.

"Yes, I was. I'm bogged down in paperwork. I asked Rose who keeps the books."

"The computer keeps the books. I just pretend I do."

"What do you mean."

"I'm about to make out the reports for your work orders," she said, typing on the keyboard. "Watch this."

The printer started up and paper rolled out the back. As one report was finished, she tore it off as the printer went busily on to the next one. She handed Bud the itemized report.

"Well, this is amazing. How does it do it?"

"I put in the data and it processes it, like my food processor. It just does the drudgery superfast, while I do my nails."

"I've seen enough. Thank you for the demonstration."

Bud went home, still marveling at the efficiency of Jane's little computer and the ease with which she handled it. *It sure would be nice to keep his records that way*, he thought.

RICHARD C. HARRISON

He pulled into the familiar lane. Bounding up the front steps, he went to look at his backlog of paperwork.

Keeping records by hand had taught him a lot about pricing a job, when he was just getting started. With four crews helping the shop-keepers get set up for the summer season, the paperwork became monotonous and was piling up. Also, he missed the word processor he used to write his reports in the senator's office.

It was time to do something about the paperwork. He had inquired about the price of a computer and found they were over two thousand dollars for 'your basic business setup.' He called Midway Office Supply to ask about a used computer.

"What are your requirements?" the salesperson asked.

He was afraid they would ask something like that. Stalling for time he said, "I'm just keeping work orders. Job orders, itemizing time and materials, and word processing would be nice."

"We have a customer who needs to become IBM compatible. He has an old CP/M machine that he needs to sell, with all the software. I'm sure he has WordStar, SuperCalc, CP/M, Microsoft Basic, and dBASE II," they informed him. Bud was getting confused, but it sure sounded impressive. "I think you could get it all for about six hundred dollars."

"Only six hundred dollars! Will it do what I need it do?"

"It will if you buy a printer."

Bud knew there would be a catch to it. "How much is the cheapest printer?"

"A couple of hundred dollars. I'll give you the man's name and telephone number. You can take a look at it."

Bud wrote down the man's name and telephone number, saying, "Thanks, I'll get back to you," and hung up. He called the man, got his address, and went to look at the computer.

He drove into Rehoboth Beach and found the house just a few blocks south of Rehoboth Avenue. It was a well cared for, two-story house with modern additions. He turned into the driveway, got out of his car, and went to the side door. When he knocked on the kitchen door, it opened almost immediately. "Hi, I'm Harry Hazzard. You must be Bud Green," he said, holding the door open. "Come in."

"Nice to meet you," Bud said, stepping into a large kitchen. It was neat and clean and his desk was set up just inside the door.

"I do all my bookkeeping on this little computer, but now I have to buy a new one. I resisted Big Blue as long as I could but Big Blue won."

"Big Blue?"

"IBM. I do a lot of work at home, and take it to the office when I go in. The office is changing over to an IBM compatible setup. I can reformat my homework to run on their machine, but it's a pain. I'm being forced to switch over, too. Here, I'll show you how I keep my records."

He flipped on the power. The machine whirred and groaned as a menu came up on the screen. He moved the highlight down until it came to SuperCalc and entered it. The machine groaned some more as copyright messages flashed by, until a spread sheet came up on the screen.

"Now watch this," he said, typing in a file name. The spread sheet was filled with several itemized work orders, with a column for "Debit", "Credit", and "Balance."

"There are formulas that do all the bookkeeping," he said, typing a command. Most of the numbers instantly changed to formulas. Bud was surprised at the speed and efficiency of the little electronic marvel.

"Don't go so fast," he said, bending to read the screen.

"If you change the cost of any part of the job, the numbers change all the way down," Harry said enthusiastically. "Watch this," he said, flipping back to the numbers. "You can play, 'What if?'" He changed one number near the top and each number changed down through the page as Bud watched in awe.

"Wow! That's amazing!" Bud exclaimed. He knew that would save him a lot of time and trouble.

"That's just the spread sheet. I have a data-based program that's dynamite, once you learn to use it. The word processing program is easy because all the help is on the screen. Or you take it off if you need more room on the screen. There's a basic program for writing your own programs but I don't think you want to go into that for a while.

"I paid twenty-six hundred dollars for it new and that was a bargain," Harry explained. "The manufacturer has gone bankrupt, but it has standard parts, so anyone can repair it for you.

That's why I'm only asking six hundred dollars for it all"

"Understand I'll need a printer, too," Bud said, trying to resist getting caught up in the excitement.

"Have an old dot matrix printer that I'll sell you for a couple of hundred. Works like a charm. I'll even give you some tractor-feed paper, since I'll be changing to sheet feeder when I get my new computer."

"Hate to spend that much money on used equipment. There's no warranty and it might break down."

"Midway Office Supply knows where to take it if it ever needs fixing, and they're very reliable."

"I only have seven hundred dollars in my account. If you can wait a month or two, I think I'll buy it."

"Time is money. I need to settle this now. If you write me a check today, you can have them both for seven hundred."

Well, that did it, Bud thought to himself. He heard himself saying. "You've got a deal, if you'll help me set it up."

"You drive a hard bargain, but you seem to be a nice guy. If you'll help me pack it up, we'll take it right now and set it up for you. When you have a problem, you can call me anytime and I'll help you get started."

"It's a deal."

"Here, you can sit down at the kitchen table and write out a check while I go find the boxes. You have to keep the boxes in case you ever need to get it fixed. '

He returned with boxes and started packing it up. Watching him carefully fit the stiff polyfoam forms into place on the computer and then the printer, Bud was impressed with how easy it seemed to be.

"You carry the printer box and I'll take the computer box. I'll follow you out in my car."

Bud picked up the bulky box and they went out to their cars. Bud led the way back to the farmhouse. They carried the boxes into the front room and set up the computer on the table. There wasn't much room left on the table for his papers, so he laid them on the floor for the time being.

When it was all plugged together, Harry turned it on. As it whirred and groaned, Bud watched the copyright notice flash by again until the menu came up. Reading the directions on the screen, Bud found the down arrow key, moved the highlight down to SuperCalc, and pressed ENTER and the spread sheet popped up.

"How do I find that spread sheet file you showed me?"

"There's a lot of help on the screen. Look at the top of the screen. Just move the highlight over to 'directory' and push the ENTER key."

Bud tried it and a list of files popped up on the screen, in a little box overlaid like a sheet of paper. "Which one of these files is the one you showed me?"

"I've made copies of these for my new computer, so I left these for you to look at. You can make your own when you get the hang of it. I showed you 'JOBS.CAL.'"

Bud moved the highlight to JOBS.CAL and pushed the enter key. Miraculously, the spread sheet filled with numbers.

"It's working perfectly," Harry said. "Now, just move the highlight to 'print' and push ENTER. When Bud did this, the printer started up printing what he had seen on the screen. "You ought to read the user's manuals. It'll tell you all you need to know. There's an index in the back," Harry said, getting up to go. "I'll leave you to play with it. It's easy when you get used to it. Just call me when you get stumped."

"Thanks for helping me set it up."

"Have fun," he said, going out to his car.

Bud just stared at his complicated new equipment. It had all happened so quickly, he didn't know where to start. It was a daring move and it made him uneasy. The fear of the unknown was getting to him.

He knew it was going to be a help to him, but it seemed to be so complicated at first. The word processor in the senator's office had been set up for him. One of the secretaries had helped him learn to run it. This time he was on his own.

He turned it off and put the plastic dust cover over it. He picked up the user's manual as he went out to check his crews.

After dinner, he took the manual to bed. After a few chapters, he dropped off to sleep and the manual fell to the floor.

The next day, Bud rearranged the papers on the table. He found a small space to finish up the paperwork he had been working on. When he was satisfied with the paperwork, he turned on the power switch to the computer.

He pulled up the spread sheet. Opening the manual to the chapter entitled, "Getting Started," he tried out the training procedures. He was delighted with the way it worked and was itching to process a work order on it.

After several mistakes and corrections, he finished a work order and printed it out. It was beautiful. He was so excited, he turned the computer off before he had saved it. As soon as he realized he had lost his hard work, he called Harry.

Harry laughed and said, "That's how you learn to always save, before you turn it off. It's gone. You have to save it on a disk or else do it over again."

It was a painful lesson. Bud said, "Never do that again."

"See, you've learned the most important thing already. Call me anytime."

"Thank you," Bud said as he hung up.

"That's enough for today," Bud mumbled, flipping off the power. He went out to check his work crews. He planned on learning to run this new toy by setting aside an hour a day. He felt he had learned enough about doing odd jobs, now he had to learn how to keep his work organized.

After a week or two, he had worked out a system. He kept double records, in the computer and handwritten, until he could be sure it was working safely. He made a printout of each day's entries and found he didn't need the handwritten copies.

He'd picked up the strange vocabulary of politics and power struggle talk. He learned to "do lunch." Then, construction and odd jobs talk, and now he had to learn computer talk. Always make a backup. Garbage in, garbage out, was becoming a catch phrase. A printout was called a hard copy. There's nothing wrong with the computer. It's the nut behind the keyboard.

Bud became so engrossed with his new toy that he spent long hours interfacing with a smart terminal. With each new discovery, he found he was lured on to the next. He was able to do things that he had never been able to do before.

He set up a cut-off time for going to bed. Having put in long hours, burning the midnight oil, and falling exhausted into bed, he was having trouble getting up in the morning.

He processed the work orders for the day on the computer. Looking at his watch, he snapped off the power, and dutifully went to bed.

"What is so rare as a day in June?" Bud's grandfather liked to quote in late spring. Bud had turned off the kerosene heater. Opening the windows, the fresh morning air had inspired him to go to the real estate office to check the work orders. He dressed in khaki pants and a knit shirt. As he went out to the car, Rose came out to greet him.

"Where are you off to this beautiful morning?"

"I don't know, yet. I thought I'd check in at your real estate office to see what they need and look in my folder."

"Checked your folder before I came home last night. It's empty. Let's go to the beach. It looks like a nice day for it."

"Okay, if I can bring my beeper," Bud said, thinking about enjoying the good life, as long as he was living there, anyway. "I'll put on my bathing suit."

He rushed back inside and slipped out of his pants and boxer shorts together and threw them across the bed. As he pulled on his bathing trunks, his beeper went off and he grabbed the phone.

The real estate office had a job for him. "I'm on my way to the beach with Rose," he explained.

They said, "No problem. Stop by and pick up the work order on your way." He grabbed his khaki pants and pulled them on over his bathing suit.

He rushed out, saying, "Your office called and I said I'd stop on the way to the beach."

"Okay, Let's go."

"I'll drive," Bud said as she got into Bud's car and they took off. I'll just see what they want and be right back," he said as he parked at the real estate office.

He rushed in and the receptionist introduced him to a client who was waiting for the head broker. They greeted each other and Bud checked his folder. As he was pulling out a work order, the receptionist called him over to her desk.

She pointed toward the floor, asking, "Are these yours?"

His boxer shorts were lying on the carpet.

Must have been in my pant leg and slid out on the floor. "Never seen those before in my life," he lied, blushing.

"Would you mind picking them up?"

"Not at all," he said, bending and hastily picking them up.

He started to throw them in the receptionist's wastebasket, but she said, "No! Not in here! Over there," she said, pointing toward the copier wastebasket.

Bud dumped them in the basket by the copier and rushed out.

He yanked the car door open and sped off so quickly that Rose said, "We're not in that big a hurry."

"Had a catastrophe in there and I have to get away."

"What happened?"

"It's hard to explain. My boxer shorts must have still been inside my khaki pants when I pulled them on over my bathing suit. Anyway, the boxer shorts fell out of my pant leg on the floor, in front of the receptionist and a client. When I picked them up, it was very embarrassing."

Rose laughed.

"Isn't very funny."

This made her laugh harder. "You're the sort of character who could pull it off with a flair."

"I was rushing to go to the beach with you. They must think I'm a weirdo."

"They can't get along without you. I'm beginning to feel the same way. What was the work order about?"

"I don't know. I didn't have time to read it," he said. He handed the work order to Rose as he drove.

"This is no emergency. You can fix this later on today."

Bud found a place to park near Fisherman's Beach. They took up their beach gear and walked down to the beach. The bright sun had brought out a few early bathers. They found a place and Rose spread out a towel, took off her cover-up, and sat down.

Bud stood looking at the fishermen. One had hip boots and bathing shorts. It looked strange, as though he didn't need the boots. He could wade out as far as the boots would go and not get his bathing shorts wet.

"Look at that fisherman with the boots and bikini brief."

"Maybe there are jellyfish today, but it's too early for them to come out of the bay."

"He looks as though he's trying to catch his dinner. He's serious about it."

GRASS ROOTS

Bud sat down and looked at the sea. The gentle breeze was not noticeable sitting down, so he pulled off his shirt and long pants as the sun warmed him. Lying back on a towel that Rose had spread for him, he said, "If I fall asleep, stick a fork in me to see if I'm done."

"Put on sun block and you won't burn."

"I'll do it in a minute. I feel too exotic to move now. Put some on my back for me."

"Well, all right, but it could make us look like an item. This isn't a trick, is it?"

"Come on, Rose. It was your idea."

She squirted cold sun block on his back and giggled when he flinched. She rubbed it all over his muscular back with gentle strokes, enjoying the game. "That feels delicious," he murmured.

"I don't want to create a precedent, but I'll expect you to spread some on my back when I turn over."

"Gladly."

They had both worked hard at their jobs and it was pleasant to just daydream on the beach for a change. They got along like two peas in a pod. Neither of them was ready for a commitment, but everything was pointed toward their being together. It was as though Mother Nature was slyly taking charge of their lives.

Rose stirred and Bud looked up. "Is it my turn to spread the suntan lotion?"

"It's sun block. We don't use lotion anymore."

"Let's not get technical, when I'm offering my services."

"Sorry about that. Yes, I'd like some sun block on my back, if you don't mind," she said.

"It'll be my pleasure."

"Don't get carried away. Just spread it around a little."

He carefully put some in his hands and warmed it up so as not to shock her with cold sun block. He was hesitant to touch her firm body at first, but he was soon into the swing of it. He didn't want to stop.

"Okay. That ought to do it," she said.

"Just a few more places. I wouldn't want you to get burned and blame it on me."

He couldn't resist grabbing both sides of her ribs and giving them a squeeze. She jumped up giggling, saying, "I was afraid I couldn't trust you."

"You're right. Couldn't resist that. Won't do it again."

"Don't make promises you can't keep."

"I'm just a man, doing the best I can," he sang a popular song refrain.

They settled back on their towels, content in their own thoughts. Little children ran by, spraying sand on Bud. He sat up and looked around at them. The sun was almost straight overhead "Almost noon. May I take your lunch order?" he asked.

"Brought a couple of apples in my bag. I'll get one for you, if you are hungry."

"I'm not used to health food, but it sounds good."

She dug out an apple and handed it to him. "This is the life," he was saying to himself. "Doesn't get any better than this." Then he asked Rose, "What was that work order?"

"Just a light bulb that the tenants were too lazy to change. You can do it before dark and everyone will be happy."

" Think I'll take a stroll down the beach. Want to come?"

"No. You go ahead. I'll be right here till you get back."

Bud walked over to the jetty. Climbing over gracefully, he headed for the water's edge. The beaches were full of fun-loving bathers. As he walked along, he studied each character, forming little fantasies about where they were from and how they lived.

The people were so distracting, he didn't notice the ocean. The tide was out and the gentle waves made the swimming ideal. Near the middle of the boardwalk, the crowds were congested. There were too many people to single out individual characters, just a blur of activity. Turning around, he headed back to the serenity of Fisherman's Beach.

Rose was still lying on her stomach, just the way he had left her. When she looked up, out of the corner of her eye, he said, "Ready for a dip?"

" Been lying here thinking about it." She rose up on her knees, adjusting her bra straps. As she stood up, she pulled the corners of the back of her bikini pants down and out. It was a standard maneuver with the new styles for women.

They walked down to the shore and stood ankle deep to get used to the water. Soon they were knee deep; and then they took the plunge together as a large wave broke in front of them. Their bodies relaxed and the ocean's cooling system took over. They bobbed in the waves a while and then started for shore.

Bud caught a wave and body surfed in. He wiped out at the end and came up dripping and looking disoriented. Rose let the waves ease her to shore and they came out of the water laughing. They staggered up the beach together, refreshed and smiling. They found their towels and dried off.

Rose sat down, took out a comb, and started fixing her hair. Bud spread out his towel in the sand and laid down. "Boy, this is the life!" he said, feeling content.

Rose found the sun block and read the label. "I think this sun block is waterproof," she said, scanning the claims.

"How are you supposed to wash it off?" Bud asked.

"Oh, I don't think it's that waterproof," she said, with the plastic bottle still in her hand. "At least, I don't think it's soap-proof."

Bud sat up with a big grin, saying, "Maybe I should put some more on your back."

"Too late," she smiled. "Sun's getting lower in the west. Maximum rays are between eleven and two. Be going home soon."

"This has been such a wonderful day, I hate to leave."

Rose got up and started folding her towel and gathering her things into her beach bag. "All good things come to an end sometime," she said. "I want to get to the shower before Thorn comes home. He takes a long shower, using up all the hot water."

"I don't have a shower," Bud said admitting his shortcoming.

"Why not turn on the outside shower, back of the farmhouse?"

"That's right. Hadn't thought of that." He got up, folding his towel Rose put on her cover-up. He decided to carry his pants and towel over his arm to the car.

They collected their gear and headed for the car. Bud drove Rose home feeling warm and contented. When he pulled into the lane, Rose said, "Thank you for coming with me. It was a perfect beach day."

"Glad you asked me to the beach. I really enjoyed it."

Rose went in and Bud walked around back of the farmhouse to inspect the outside shower. The pipes came out from the kitchen wall and went up about six feet. They were joined at the top and arched away from the farmhouse. There was a rusted shower head pointing at him.

He went into the kitchen. The pipes seemed to be coming from under the sink. He found the turn-off valves under the sink and he cracked them open. Back outside, the shower head was dripping and water was running out the bottom of the pipes. He quickly tightened the plugs on the bottom, closed the handles, and went back in. He opened the valves under the sink and heard the water fill the pipes and stop.

He went out and hung his towel on a nail where it wouldn't get wet. As he turned on the shower, he flinched as the cold water hit his warm skin. He missed the warm shower he had used in Washington.

Turning it off, he dried himself. He wasn't used to taking an exposed shower wearing a swim suit. A cold shower was better than no shower at all. He went back to the car for his pants and went in to dress. He found a new pair of underpants, reminding him of the embarrassing scene at the real estate office. Remembering the work order, he went out to the car to look for it.

The work order was on the front seat. It had to be done before dark, so he went reluctantly out to fix the light. Under normal conditions, he would have checked his folder at the real estate office, but he was too embarrassed to go there.

Feeling tired and hungry, he decided to catch a quick bite to eat at a fast food restaurant. When he got home, he took the user's manual for the computer to bed. The fresh air and sunburn had him sleeping like a baby before he had read a page.

GRASS ROOTS

MARY AND THORN

Mr. Fixit was deluged with work when the season started. The summer crowd was hard on the rental properties, with too many house guests, spring break, and endless summer parties.

Bud was busier than a bikini-clad teenager in a land-breeze with a swarm of horse flies. Little nit-picking problems tried his patience, like a stopped-up toilet, a jammed disposal, a septic tank overflowing, torn screens, and Lord knows what all.

Near the end of a hectic day, he stopped by the real estate office to drop off his reports. When he found Rose's office door opened, he stood there watching her frantically shuffling papers at her desk.

"Looks like you're drowning in paperwork," he said. "You need a computer."

Rose glanced up looking frazzled. "I'm trying to get all my work done, so I can take the weekend off."

"What's the big occasion?"

"Have you forgotten that Thorn and Mary are getting married Saturday afternoon?"

"That's right! But you have till Saturday afternoon."

"There's the rehearsal dinner on Friday evening at the Sea Horse Restaurant. You and I are invited," Rose said.

"Glad you told me," he said, sounding a little annoyed.

"We've both been so busy lately, I haven't had a chance to tell you. There's more. I volunteered you to be an usher. The rehearsal is at the church Saturday morning at ten o'clock."

"I offered to help, but I didn't know you were going to offer my services without telling me."

"Don't tell me you won't do it!" Rose snapped.

"Of course I'll do it, but let me know ahead of time."

"Sorry. Been working so hard, I never see you anymore."

"You're busy and I better get going if I'm taking off this weekend. See you this evening, when you get home."

"Like to talk it over with you tonight."

"See you then," Bud said, rushing off.

He was able to prevail upon his best crew chief to take the beeper and cover for him on the weekend. Then, he concentrated on finishing up all the current jobs.

That evening, when Rose drove into the lane, Bud went out to meet her. Getting out of her car, she said, "Oh, Bud. Do you have the time to come in with me and talk a minute?"

"Sure," he said, following her in.

"Thorn!" she called out, "can you come here a minute!"

"Just a minute," echoed from a back room.

"Sit down," Rose said to Bud, glancing at the mail. Having scanned the letters, she called out, "We're waiting for you, Thorn!"

"Don't bug me, Rose. I'm coming!" Thorn said as he stormed into the room. Seeing Bud, he composed himself. "Hello, Bud. How've you been?"

"I've been run ragged, fixing up after the summer renters. How are you holding up? It's not too late to change your mind."

"Now, don't even mention such a thing," Rose said, taking over the conversation. "I asked Bud to be an usher and he said he would."

"That's great, Bud," Thorn said, looking pleased.

"I've been thinking about this wedding," Bud said. "I have a vision of you and the bride driving off in a pickup. How are you getting to the church for the wedding?"

"I'm riding with Dad and Mom in their car," Thorn answered.

"I'll park my car in the church driveway and leave the keys in it for you. Maybe Rose will drive me back."

"Oh, Bud," Rose bubbled, "that's perfect! I'm going to be a bridesmaid and you can escort me from the church, but we're not coming right back. There will be a reception at the country club after the wedding. I'll drive you there."

"Where are you going for your honeymoon?" Bud asked.

"We're flying to a resort for a week of marital bliss."

"Where are you going to live when you come back? The farm-house is all fixed up and I can find another place to live."

"No way. We're renting a little house down the road, till we can buy a place. Besides, Dad is planning on giving the farm-house to Rose, when she gets married."

Bud and Rose looked at each other as though they were being manipulated. "Let's get back to Thorn and Mary's wedding," Rose said quickly, breaking the spell.

"If it's all settled, I have a lot to do," Bud said, going toward the door.

"Thanks again, Bud," Thorn said.

Rose walked him out the door. When they were outside in the dark, she said, "Thank you. You're always so helpful," as she gave him a tender kiss. "I don't know what we'd do without you."

"It's the least I could do. You all have treated me like one of the family. I don't know what I'd have done without you."

"You always seem to do just fine," she said, as she turned to go in. "Thank you, again."

"See you tomorrow," Bud said.

Friday, Bud took off from work early. When he had bathed and dressed for the rehearsal dinner, he went out and stood on the porch . The evening sun cast long shadows across the yard. The air was still and serene. In a trance, he stood there, in the still of the evening, admiring the rural view.

Roamer looked at him quietly standing there and seemed to sense Bud's pensive mood because his tail thumped the ground as he wagged it without getting up. Roamer's ears pricked up as he turned to watch Rose come out, looking like Cinderella as she stepped out of her coach.

"Here she is," Bud sang, trying to sound like Bert Parks, "Miss America." Rose smiled and bowed to the audience. "Your car or mine?" Bud quipped.

"I'd love to ride with you, kind sir," she said with a Cinderella curtsy.

He opened the car door for her and waited until she gathered her skirt around her. He drove into Rehoboth Beach, looking over the main drag. The Sea Horse restaurant's parking lot was nearly full. He found a place at the far end and they walked happily into the restaurant.

"Do you have a reservation?" the host asked.

"The Gardner party," Bud said.

"That would be the Thoroughgood party," he said, scanning his list of reservations. "Follow me, please." Bud and Rose followed him to a private dining room in the back.

Bud had never been to a rehearsal dinner, so he had the idea that they were going to rehearse something. It turned out to be a get together to meet all the other members of the wedding.

"This is our dear friend, Bud Green," Rose said, introducing him to the others. It was a friendly family affair. Mary's sister and her best friend were the other bridesmaids. Her brother was the other usher. Each family's idiosyncrasies provided the entertainment for a spontaneous good time.

Since the day of the engagement party, each member of the two families found themselves getting edgy. Their home life was being torn apart with the new union. Their personalities changed, as if there was a death in the family.

They used logical explanations in an effort to solve their emotional problems. Mr. Thoroughgood kept repeating, "We're not losing a daughter, we're gaining a son." The tension built as the hours grew shorter. Closing in on the fateful day, things were getting out of hand.

As if by magic, everyone spontaneously shed their worries at the door and joined into the festivities. The characteristics of each family became uproariously funny. Bud overheard one of them saying, "They're finding out how crazy his family is." And the other said, "They're a straight bunch, but a good bunch, as the old saying goes."

After a couple of drinks, the Thoroughgood children gathered together and sang some funny parodies. In the age of television, this live performance was a new twist in home entertainment.

This bit of innocent fun was the icebreaker that ignited the festivities. Everybody joined in the fun, feeling relaxed and comfortable.

GRASS ROOTS

By the time they all sat down to dinner, they were a new combined family. They had been rehearsing how they were going to put up with each other for the rest of their lives.

Sitting next to Rose, Bud watched her anxieties fall away and her old personality come back. *So that's why they have the rehearsal dinners,*" he thought to himself.

The group was having such a good time, they looked as if they would have stayed, all night. Mr. Thoroughgood stood up, dinged his glass and said, "I want to thank you all for helping to make this such a good party for Thorn and Mary. May they find joy and happiness in the days ahead. Thank you all for coming."

Everyone stood up, cheered the speaker and jovially talked enthusiastically to each other at the same time. As they moved away from the table, last minute quips were tossed back and forth to each other.

When they had said their congratulations and good-byes to each of the others, Bud and Rose went out to the parking lot. He found the car at the far end of the lot. "That was a nice party and the people were charming," he said.

Climbing into the car, Rose said, "I enjoyed each one of them." Rose was feeling good and snuggled up to Bud on the way home. "Nice to have a good friend like you at a time like this."

"Feel the same. You think good friends could fall in love?"

"Why not? It's just the biological clock isn't synchronized with the economic clock."

"They're getting closer," Bud said. "We should leave some of it up to serendipity."

"I know, but I'm having too good a time to worry about deep thoughts tonight. Let's get Thorn and Mary married first."

"We'll do it up properly," Bud said, as they drove home in silence, lost in their own thoughts. Pulling into the lane, Bud said, "The good part of having a good friend like you, is we can have some quiet time together. Don't have to talk all the time."

"That's a comforting thought," she said, kissing him good night. As she went toward her door, she said, "We should leave about nine thirty for the rehearsal at the church."

"What do I wear?"

"Anything. It's not a dress rehearsal. See you tomorrow."

RICHARD C. HARRISON

Saturday morning Bud dressed leisurely. He dawdled over his breakfast reading the paper. A holiday was a welcome change.

Finally, he got up and looked over his dress clothes for the wedding. He laid them out on the bed and sat down for a second cup of coffee. He wasn't used to having time on his hands. It was a day of rest.

He thought about his grandfather and decided to call him to see how he was doing. Looking at his watch, he decided to wait until he returned from the rehearsal.

He looked over his desk work without sitting down. He had complete confidence that his crew chief would handle any new work orders.

Going out to the porch, he decided he should get some porch furniture, at least something to sit on, maybe a bench. The sky was promising a beautiful day for the wedding. One wispy cloud floated in an enormous deep blue umbrella. The birds in the trees were discussing their plans.

When Rose came out with her father and brother, he greeted them with, "It looks like a perfect day for a wedding."

"Somebody up there is taking care of us," Thorn said.

"Let's all ride in Dad's car," Rose said, getting in the back seat. Thorn sat in front with his Dad, so Bud climbed in the other side by Rose. It had been so long since Bud had ridden in the back seat, it felt strange.

Bud looked out the window at the countryside. Rose jabbered with Thorn in front as their father drove into Rehoboth Beach.

Bud watched to see which way they would go. They went into town. Going straight down Rehoboth Avenue, around the U-turn at the ocean, they turned north on First Street. Three blocks up First Street they turned toward the ocean.

Bud glanced up at the street sign, reading, "Olive Avenue." They parked in front of a quaint little church and got out of the car. Across the front of the church, in tasteful gold letters, Bud was pleased to see, "All Saints Episcopal Church."

It was like an omen. It resembled the church Bud had gone to in Elmira. Bud looked at the steep roof with the familiar cross at the top. He pictured it standing as a proud landmark near the ocean for a hundred years, as the resort had grown up around it.

GRASS ROOTS

They were the first ones to arrive, and the doors were locked. While Mr. Gardner tried the parish hall doors, Rose went to the church office doors. As they were returning to say they couldn't get in, the minister came from the rectory next door, saying "You're early."

"The others will be here soon," Mr. Gardner said.

"We have to lock the church these days, to protect it from vandalism," the minister said, apologetically. He unlocked the doors and led them in, saying, "Make yourselves comfortable. I'll be back in a minute."

"What a charming little church," Bud whispered to Rose as she sat down in the back pew. Bud slid in beside her.

"Look at the exquisite kneeling cushions," Bud whispered.

"Aren't they unusual. The ladies of the parish have worked hard making different needlepoint beach scenes for each one."

The sun streamed through the stained glass windows, painting bright, dazzling colors across the powder blue carpet running up the center aisle. The vibrant reds and delicate purples blended with the deep blues in an inspiring array.

The traditional lamps hung from a majestic cathedral ceiling and gave Bud a familiar, lofty feeling. "I'm glad you're a member of this church," he whispered.

"Dad went here as a boy," she whispered, "and we always came here as children. I have been working on Sundays, lately."

"When you have a Sunday off, maybe we could take time to go to church."

"That would be nice."

Mary and her family arrived, igniting the spirit of the night before. The members of the two families greeted each other like kissing cousins. The minister came back, calling out over the babble, "If you'll all follow me up the aisle to the front of the church, we'll get started."

It was like staging a play. He told each one where to stand and told them their cues, as they walked through the movements, with only two mishaps. "Are there any questions?" the minister asked. After a brief pause, he said, "We'll see you back here this evening. Thank you all for coming."

The babble rose again and they all filed out of the church. Bathers, carrying folding beach chairs and towels as they walked down the middle of the street, gawked at the crowd coming out of the church. There were friendly good-byes, as they all drove off.

Back at the house, Bud asked, "Anything I can do to help?"

"No, thanks," Rose said. "Just be on time ready to usher."

"Going to wash my car for Thorn. See you at the church."

Bud changed into work clothes and started cleaning the car. He was too compulsive and took a long time making everything neat and shiny. It was a labor of love and Bud really got into it.

By the time he grabbed a bite to eat, it was time to dress for the wedding. Time flies when you're not doing anything. He dressed and hastily drove to the church.

He backed his car into the church driveway and parked just past the sidewalk, so no one could block him. He went into the church office to wait for Thorn. A man from the florist came in and gave Bud the bouquets and boutonnieres in a big box.

Bud pinned on his boutonniere and went around to the front of the church to greet any early arrivals. It seemed as though he stood there a long time, but soon, Thorn arrived with Rose and his parents. Bud explained about the flowers and sent them in.

Mary's brother arrived and Bud pinned his boutonniere on his lapel. People drifted in and they seated them. Bud saw Mary and her parents drive up. Bud sent them in the parish house to get their flowers. Soon the church was nearly filled and ready.

While it was the first time that Bud had been a member of a wedding, he felt at home. He had escorted some familiar faces up the aisle. The church felt familiar, and the Gardners had made him feel like part of the family. He was proud to be a part of this small community.

The ceremony went smoothly. Thorn spoke his vows loud and clear. Mary recited hers softly, so they were barely audible, but everyone knew what she was saying. At long last, the bride and groom kissed to uproarious applause that startled Bud and they came smiling down the aisle.

Bud waited until Rose turned to walk and he offered her his arm. They walked the aisle, smiling at their friends in the pews and feeling on top of the world. Rose threw rice on the bride and groom as they drove off in Bud's sparkling clean car.

Together, they greeted the members of the congregation as they filed out into the sunshine. When most of the others had left, Rose said, "My car is way down the street." They walked down and drove off.

"That was a lovely wedding. I hope Thorn and Mary will find happiness together," Bud said.

"Dad says I'm not losing a brother. I'm gaining a sister. But I'm not used to it, yet. It went so fast."

"Beginning of a new family, a major event So exciting."

"It's overwhelming! A new beginning for Thorn and Mary is the end of an era for me. I need more time to get used to it."

"You'll be the next one."

"Let's not talk about that now. Let's have a good time at the reception."

"Suits me. One thing at a time."

The band was playing and the crowd was celebrating when they walked in. It was like New Year's Eve in Times Square. The deed is done and the time had come. The best man stopped the band to toast the bride and groom. There were the usual eulogies to the bride and groom. One of Thorn's friends, who had enough to drink, finished them off with,

"Friends may come and friends may go
And friends may peter out, you know,
But we'll be friends through thick and thin
Peter out or peter in."

Titters crept through the gathering, building into knee-slapping guffaws. The band took advantage of the moment and burst into a lively tune, as the revelry resumed.

The drinks were flowing and the food was delicious, in spite of the balancing act of holding a plate on your knee when you are all dressed up, and with revelers jostling you. The rest of the evening was a happy blur.

When the party was over, Bud and Rose found their way to the car. On the way home, Bud said, "That was some blowout!"

"Must have been a good party, because I don't remember what went on. So many people having such a good time, made it a gala celebration."

RICHARD C. HARRISON

"Is it always this exciting around here?"
"Once in a lifetime."

THE NATION'S SUMMER CAPITAL

Bud took on all the work orders that came his way. Figuring it was seasonal work, he took on too much. He worked seven days a week, like the shopowners, and sat up every night entering the jobs in his data processor.

As the days went by, he began to realize that Mr. Fixit was not a seasonal job. It hadn't let up since Memorial Day. Near the end of June, he decided he needed a day off. He scheduled only the emergency jobs for the day and called the others to tell them their schedule for two days ahead.

The next morning, he spent an hour doing desk work in his swimsuit. Then, tossing his long pants and a towel in the car passenger seat, he drove to the beach. In Rehoboth, the main drag was congested with traffic. Tourists were all over the place. Half-bare vacationers danced between the stalled cars on their way to the beach or shopping.

Remembering the quiet little town he had driven through on his first Mr. Fixit trip, he smiled at the contagious festivity. As the traffic started moving slowly forward, he realized he couldn't turn left this time of year.

Creeping toward the U-turn at the boardwalk, he felt like he was caught in a cattle drive and heading for the corral. The cars all wedged toward the dead end and U-turn at the ocean. "Tilly was right.

Everyone has to do this at least once every summer."

He felt like mooing as he crept around the U-turn. Pedal cabs, parked by the Women's Christian Temperance Union drinking fountain, were ready to take you on a sight-seeing tour.

When he finally came back to First Street, he turned right and looked for a parking space. All the parking meters were full of cars. He drove north, just past the end of the boardwalk, where he had parked before. There were no meters and no spaces. Driving away from the beach, he found an empty space in front of a cottage.

He parked, grabbed his towel and started for the beach on foot. At the end of the street there was a path over the dunes. He took the little boardwalk over the fenced-off dunes to the ocean. Sitting down in the sand, he took off his shoes. He flung the shoes and towel around his neck and headed for the water's edge.

He started walking up the beach feeling on top of the world . He was in a mood to count his blessings. Feeling like one of the lucky few, his faith in mankind had been restored.

The bright sun spread little sparkles over the ocean's waves as they pulsated rhythmically. Near the shore, the waves burst forth with dancing fireworks of white foam. The sand had been washed by the high tide. Seagulls screamed with excitement over head as they circled freely over the playground. Bud felt confident that God would be pleased as he looked down from the blue expanse of Heaven.

"Well, look who's here?" a familiar voice broke his mood.

Looking up, he was confronted by Missy's stern expression. She stood stiff-legged with her hands on her hips. She had taken him by surprise, but he chose to ignore her intense look. He said, "Hello, Missy. How have you been?"

"I'm doing all right," she said, "but where have you been?"

"I've been right here in Rehoboth Beach."

"You mean you're a dropout, a beachcomber!"

"No, I've been putting the pieces back together. I feel almost whole again."

"Well, I think you owe me an explanation," she said, looking furious. "Just what do you think you're doing?"

"Why don't we sit down somewhere and I'll try to tell you?"

"Better be good," she said, turning and walking up to her pink umbrella. Bud followed her through the loose sand and they both sat down.

"Where have you been staying?" Missy asked.

"Been living in the Gardner's old farmhouse."

"Living with Rose?"

"No, no. The Gardners don't live there. I'm the only one who lives there."

"Well, where do they live?"

"In a mobile home across the lane. You see. . ."

"In a trailer!" she broke into his explanation.

"Now calm down and let me tell you," he said "After they bought the farm, Mr. Gardner had a heart attack. When he came home from the hospital, the weather turned cold and the farmhouse was too drafty for his recuperation. Mr. Gardner bought a mobile home that was warm and comfortable and put it on his property. I've been restoring the farmhouse for him and restoring myself."

"Sounds like a handyman."

"I've started a little business called Mr. Fixit. I fix up rentals houses for the out-of-town investors."

"You've become a tradesman?"

"Guess you could say that. I replaced part of the screen on your porch. Usually have a crew do it, but wanted it to be done right, so I did it myself. Now tell me what you've been up to?"

"Now don't try to change the subject. What about Rose?"

"She has started her career in real estate and she's been quite successful."

"I mean you and Rose!"

"We're just old friends."

"You've said that before."

"I know. Well, we've been out to dinner a couple of times and we went to the beach together once. Just a good friend. What's this all about?"

"Well, look what the cat dragged in," Betty Brass said as she walked up to them. "Am I interrupting something?"

"Certainly hope so," Bud said cheerfully as he stood up, "It's good to see you, Betty. Is Geoffrey in town?"

"No, he's working, but he'll be down on the weekend."

"Where have you been, Bud? I haven't seen you around."

"We were just talking about that. It's a long story, and I don't think I can tell it again. You can get Missy's version of it later."

"Won't believe what he has been telling me. Sounds crazy!"

"Well, tell me," Betty said with a craving for information.

"Tell you later, when I have the straight scoop. I'm trying to piece it together. He keeps talking in riddles. Every time he tells me something, I have to start over."

"Nice to see you again, Bud," Betty said, waving good-bye.

"Be good," Bud said, casually.

"I don't ask things like that of you," Betty joked as she walked back down to the water.

"You can be so nice," Missy said "It's so frustrating. I didn't know what to tell people, and you act as though nothing has happened."

"Something wonderful has happened to me. I enjoy the work I'm doing and I feel like a human being again."

"What did I do wrong?"

"You didn't do anything wrong. I told you it wasn't you. I needed to get back to reality. Let's be friends. We could walk to Obie's and I'll buy you lunch."

"That will just start tongues wagging again. I didn't know what to say to people after you went away."

"I'm sorry if I caused a problem for you, but you knew how unhappy I was working in politics."

"Yes, and what about World Peace?"

"I've decided it starts in the grass roots. If each of us tries to vote intelligently, we can make democracy work. I'm working on World Peace, one person at a time."

"Sorry I asked. What about your career?"

"I'm learning how to run a business and I really like what I'm doing. I have so much work, I had to hire four crews to help me. I'm keeping the records on a computer. And the farmhouse is looking better every day."

"You like being a big fish in a little pond."

"I haven't thought of it that way. Perhaps you're right. A busy fish is a happy fish."

"You seem so content just to do your busy work. What about your plans for the future?"

"I like to live and let live. What's wrong with doing a good job at something you like? I've met a lot of nice people down here."

"Mr. Nice Guy. Did you know that nice guys finish last?"

"Don't think of life as a race to the finish. When you get to the finish line, they bury you. If you didn't enjoy the trip, you missed the best part. You should stop and smell the roses."

"You're such a dreamer."

"Well, look who's here," Mr. Mannerly said, coming to the beach, with a robe over his swimsuit.

Bud stood up and shook hands, saying, "It's nice to see you again, Mr. Mannerly." For the first time, Bud didn't feel obliged to perform. It was nice to talk to him man to man.

"Good to see you again, Bud. We're having a little party on the Fourth of July at the house about six. Why don't you drop by and join us?"

"That's kind of you, but we'd better see what Missy says about it," Bud said, looking at Missy.

"We'll be expecting you," Missy said with a deceptively sweet tone of voice.

"Well, thank you. I better be running along. You have a beautiful day for the beach," Bud said to them as he turned and walked back to the water's edge.

"*How do I get myself into these situations*?" he pondered as he trodded up the beach. He wondered if he could ask Rose to go with him again. He'd tried to tell it like it is, but he didn't feel that he had gotten the message through to Missy.

A young girl in a bikini walked out of the water in front of him, heading for her towel. As Bud watched her graceful stride, he caught a glimpse of a familiar face out of the corner of his eye. It was Tilly, sitting with a group of younger girls.

Curiosity drew him up to the group. "Hello, Tilly," he said as he drew near.

"Well, if it isn't Bud Green. You look healthy and happy. How's the world treating you?" Tilly asked.

Been on top of the world. How are you doing these days?"

"Doing fine. I'm working for Senator Youngbloom, the young man who beat Senator Blassforth. He wanted to carry on the continuity. I'm the only one who stayed on."

"He's smart to keep you on. You know all the ropes."

"How are you doing with World Peace?"

"I've been distracted by a new venture. I've started a new business down here and having the time of my life."

"What kind of business?"

"Mr. Fixit. I take care of the cottages and shops for the absentee owners and some of them when they're here. I've got more business than I can handle."

"Mr. Fixit must have fixed you. You look a lot better."

"Thank you. I just wanted to say hello.

"You better not walk past without speaking. Have you seen Missy Mannerly?"

"Yes. Mr. Mannerly invited me to his Fourth of July party. Would you like to go with me?"

"No, thank you. I came down here to get away from all that. stuff."

"I'm not sure I want to get involved either at this point, now that I'm out of politics," he said, turning to go.

The party might not be such a bad idea after all. It was not as though he had any political obligations. He might drum up a little business. Maybe Rose would pick up a client. What did he have to lose? he thought.

He walked up to North Shores. When he saw the towers, he was tempted to walk on and investigate them again, but the sun was hot and a dip would be refreshing. There didn't seem to be lifeguards after North Shores. He sat down on the beach by the last lifeguard, put his shoes on his towel, and dropped his beeper and watch into a shoe.

He inched his way into the water. It was that or take a daring plunge. Each time the cool water hit a new high on his body, he flinched. "Should have run down and dove in."

A large wave settled that and he dove into the buoyant surf. He floated around, recounting his blessings. His mood had gone full circle. Bud was beginning to understand what was meant by the pursuit of happiness.

When he came out of the ocean and dried off, he headed for the road beyond the dunes. He had decided to avoid the people on the beach. He didn't understand why Missy was so upset. Anyway, he didn't want to brood about it anymore.

He planned to go home and ask Rose to go to Missy's party with him. He drove home whistling a happy tune. Turning into the lane, he noticed that Rose wasn't home yet. He went around back to take a shower. A splash of cold water was enough and reminded him to look for the water heater.

When he had dried off, he went in to search for the hot water heater. He traced the pipes under the house. They went to the kitchen closet. Inside the kitchen closet, he found signs of a water heater having been there at one time, a long time ago.

Then he noticed the pipes going through the ceiling. He ran upstairs to the bedroom over the kitchen. There were two closet doors, one plain and one with louvers. He yanked open the door with the louvers and there it was.

He brushed aside the dust and read all the labels on the tank. It was an electric thirty-gallon water heater. He took off the plates with a screwdriver. Inside the top plate, there was a thermostat and inside the bottom, he found a red button.

He pushed the red button and heard a click. Looking up, he spotted a water valve. He opened the valve and the water started filling the tank. "Thank God, I found that," he said out loud, "might have burned out the heating element without the water."

When the tank was full, the heater just sat there. He felt around the tank and imagined it was slightly warmer. Deciding to wait and see what happened, he went down stairs and got dressed.

He was checking out his jobs that he had scheduled for the next day, when Rose drove in. He ran out to catch her.

"Hi, Rose."

"Hello, Bud. You look like you've been to the beach. You have a little color in your cheeks."

"I have. Also, I have an invitation for you. The Mannerlys have asked us to their Fourth of July party."

"Oh, dear. I won't be able to go. I have floor duty that day and I won't be home in time."

"Can't you get someone else to cover for you?"

"Not on the Fourth of July. Besides, that's when the best customers are in town. I don't want to miss this opportunity."

"Well, I guess you know what's best for you."

"That was very kind of them to ask me to come. Do you think they will be upset if I don't show up?"

"Not at all. We'll do it next time."

"Thanks, Bud," she said, carrying her briefcase as she went in her front door.

Bud went back into the farmhouse, thinking he could go by himself. He had some new business cards that he could give away.

Going into the kitchen, he cracked the hot water tap. It coughed and spit a little bit as it dribbled brown water. Bud felt the water and it was cold. He turned on the tap full force and let it run a minute or two.

Beautiful steam started to rise from the sink. He carefully felt the water and jumped back, shaking his finger. "Ow! That's hot!" He turned off the tap, grabbed a screwdriver, and bounded up the stairs. Taking off the plates again, he reset the thermostats a little lower. As he put the plates back, he said, "No use in overheating the water for just one person."

That evening, he drew a tubful of warm water and reveled in his new luxury. In bed, the comfort of a bath, together with the fresh air and sunburn, lulled him easily into a deep sleep.

The next morning, the luxury of hot water surprised Bud as he was about to shave. He had forgotten about this new amenity. "Ah ha! The time has come to put a modesty skirt on the outside shower." It hadn't occurred to him to build an enclosure around the outside shower before this.

Having worked on several outside showers, his preference was the screen-lined lattice. He sat down at the table and sketched a four by four stall. The door would be the hard part. He made a list of materials: 4 - 8' 4X4 posts, 3 - 4'X4' sections of lattice, 4 - 4' 2X4 studs, and 1 - 4'X8' piece of screen.

Eating breakfast quickly, he took his job orders and the new shower specifications and left. He dropped the lumber order at the lumberyard and asked them to deliver it to the back of the farmhouse. He had established charge accounts at all the supply places in the area.

When he had finished his jobs, he rushed home to see if the lumber had come. There was a beautiful pile of lumber and screen behind the farmhouse.

Not bothering with concrete footings, he dug post holes and put up the posts. When he tried to nail the lattice to the post, the post gave way and the nail flew in the air. He realized he had to pull the posts out of the ground, lay them down, and nail the lattice to them on the ground. He built the second side, on top of the first side, to make it true.

The assembled sides were awkward for one man to handle and it took more digging to get the posts in the ground. It looked great, until he tried to make a door. The door didn't hang right, but it would open and close. He decided to try out the new shower. Taking off his clothes in the enclosure, he threw his clothes over the side and turned on the water.

Standing in the shower, he went into a happy trance as the warm water soothed him. A strange feeling rose up from his toes. Slowly casting his gaze down toward his feet, he began to realize there was a flaw in his plan. Feeling the sandy mud oozing between his toes, it wasn't necessary to look down to tell what was wrong. He needed decking to stand on to keep his feet clean.

Turning off the water, he tried to hook his toe into the nearest piece of clothing he could reach without exposing himself. He could just barely reach the knit shirt. Holding it like an olive leaf, he made a dash for the back door, scooping up his pants on the way. It was a hair-raising experience. Next time, he'd hang a towel on a nail on the door, after he built some decking to stand on.

He made a list of supplies for the next morning's trip to the lumberyard. His stomach clock went off. Nothing in the kitchen looked appetizing, so he headed out to dinner.

On the evening of the Fourth of July, Bud dressed carefully, having taken a refreshing outside shower. He drove to the Pines and spent a long time finding a place to park. The summer crowd had parked in every imaginable space. He settled for a spot in the third block from the ocean and set out walking to the party.

Groups of tourists were walking around in the middle of the streets. Once they found a place to park, they were afraid to move their car. Everybody seemed to be walking this weekend.

"Good evening, Mrs. Mannerly," Bud said as he stepped onto the porch. "It's nice to see you again."

"Well, Bud Green," she said. "It's been a long time. Missy, look who's here."

Missy had been watching him walk in alone with interest. "Yes, I know," Missy said, looking at Bud, but talking to her mother. "Daddy saw him on the beach and invited him."

"Good evening, Missy," Bud said properly.

"I'm glad you came," Missy said. "Didn't Rose come?"

"It's a busy weekend for her," Bud said. "All work and no play makes Jack and plenty of it."

"Well, Missy," Mrs. Mannerly said, "aren't you going to introduce Bud to the other guests."

Come along, Bud," Missy said, yanking him by the arm. She led him through a group of ladies and gentlemen standing with drinks in their hands and talking in a holiday spirit. A piano player was providing background music for the tinkling of glasses and the mummer of conversation.

There was a bar set up in the den. They had placed a table across the kitchen doorway, covered it with a white cloth, and piled bottles and glasses on it. A bartender in a white jacket, standing on the kitchen side of the table, was busily fixing drinks for a line of thirsty party goers.

"This calls for a drink," Missy said as they stood in line. "I feel we should at least look happy tonight."

Bud felt that Missy was caught in a festive web by her hospitable parents. "I'll drink to that," Bud quipped, trying to put her at ease and be non-committal.

"Hello, Missy," Betty Brass called out, sweeping into the room with Geoffrey right behind her. "Hello, Bud. Geoffrey, you remember Bud."

"Yes, of course," Geoffrey said. "How have you been, Bud?"

"Fine. How have you been?"

"Working myself to death."

Betty said, "Missy, we've been in such a rush. Let's go powder our noses. The boys can take care of themselves, now that they've found the bar." Betty was eager to hear all about where Bud had been and what he had been up to. She took Missy's arm, wheeled her around, and said, "If you'll excuse us for just a minute," as she whisked Missy away.

"Betty made me be on time," Geoffrey said. "I worked myself to a frazzle in town, drove down here, and she won't give me a chance to catch my breath."

"Better than having time on your hands," Bud said, making con-versation.

The man in front of them picked up two drinks and walked off as the bartender looked up at them Geoffrey said, "Scotch and soda." The bartender looked at Bud, so he said, "White wine."

They watched him fix the drinks When he handed them their drinks, they turned to join the party. Geoffrey said, "Let's go out on the porch and sit down I'm exhausted."

They threaded their way through the guests to the porch and Geoffrey found the wicker sofa where Bud and Missy had sat last year. As they sat down, Geoffrey said, "We've been busy at the office and everyone dumps the dirty work on me. Then I come home and find my neighbor is ruining the neighborhood."

"What's he doing."

"He carries the garbage out to the curb!" Geoffrey said, looking shocked, "and then chats with the garbage man!"

Bud laughed, thinking, "Geoffrey's acid tongue is amusing."

"We lost our power," Geoffrey went on, with perfect timing, "when we stopped carrying riding crops." Geoffrey's humor was especially funny, because it implied he had a sheltered life as a little boy under the careful guidance of an aristocratic and domineering mother. "Look at old Smedley in the green blazer with his young wife on his arm. She was his secretary, before the real Mrs. Smedley died. The old fool thinks everybody doesn't know."

Bud looked up at Mr. and Mrs. Smedley. Geoffrey's anecdotes were helpful to Bud. He had wondered about who the guests were and what they do. Most of the guests were still fighting the good fight in the Federal City, climbing the social ladder, and lured into power struggles. Having escaped the rat race to get back to nature, Bud was shocked to see them scampering after rewards like rats in a maze.

They had been sitting there as Geoffrey pointed out other charac-ters and sketched their plots, when Missy and Betty found them. "You shouldn't be sitting here," Missy reprimanded them, "you should be mingling with the guests."

"But many of these people are in trade!" Geoffrey sneered, in his best form. They all laughed and Bud and Geoff stood up, ready to face the music.

"Really, Geoff! Are you going to be like this all evening?" Betty said. "These are Missy's guests and I want you to behave."

"They're the same people who were here last year," Geoff said. "Also, they're mostly friends of Missy's Mummy and Daddy."

"Watch it!" Betty warned him.

"Oh, that's all right," Missy said, "I think Geoff puts a little spice in the conversation."

"The hostess and I agree on one thing," Bud said. "Geoff adds a little sparkle to the party. Let's mix with the guests."

"Just as long as I'm not expected to dance," Geoff said.

"This is a lovely party, Missy," Bud said. "You always look so pretty. Is that a new dress?"

"Well, thank you, Bud. I leave this dress at the beach cottage to wear to parties down here," Missy explained.

"Here come those nasty Welches," Betty said to Geoffrey.

As the Welches came along, Mrs. Welch said, "Hello, Betty and Geoff."

"Nice to see you," Betty smiled a push-button smile and they embraced while the men shook hands. "Want you to meet Bud Green. The senate staffer."

Bud smiled and shook hands.

"You're in the senate, huh?" Mr. Welch asked.

"I was, but I've started a little business down here and I'm enjoying it so much, I may never go back," Bud replied.

"I envy you." Then, taking his wife's arm, "What do you want to drink, dear?"

"I'll come with you and tell the bartender myself. Nice to see you all," Mrs. Welch said, waving as Mr. Welch nodded.

"She isn't so bad, but he is boooor-ing," Geoff said, with a sing-song ending to his sentence.

Bud couldn't believe they dislike them so much and could still greet them with such phony compliments. He wondered if any of the conversation was honest. At least Geoff's remarks were to the point.

"Come with me," Missy said, catching Bud's arm, "want you to meet someone." There was a group around a tall, smiling man. Missy wedged through the crowd and said, "Mayor Hughes, I'd like you to meet Bud Green. He seems to have moved to your area."

"Hello, Missy .Lovely party. Hello, Bud. I'm John Hughes. Welcome to the Nation's Summer Capital," he said, reaching out to shake hands.

"Thank you. This is God's country," Bud said shaking hands.

"You bet it is," the mayor said, "do you play volleyball?"

"Played some in college."

"We have a pick-up game on Deauville Beach on the weekends. Why don't you come out and play with us? If you like the way we play, we always need more players."

"Thank you .I'll look for the game on the beach."

Other people interrupted the mayor, so Missy and Bud floated away. "He's quite young for a mayor," Bud said, "but very nice. You have dignitaries here."

"Thought you ought to meet the mayor while he's here."

"Thank you, Missy. That's very thoughtful of you."

"There's one more person you should meet," she said, leading him by the hand through the throng of people to another group of people surrounding an older, shorter man. Missy wedged through the group pulling Bud with her.

"Bud, I'd like you to meet our congressman, Tom Evans. Tom,want you to meet Bud Green, a friend of mine, who seems to be a new Delawarean," Missy said.

"Hello, Missy. Lovely party. How do you do, Bud? Welcome to the First State. Small Wonder."

"Pleasure to meet you," Bud said. "It is a small wonder." The congressman was warm and congenial. His handshake was firm as his gentle eyes smiled under brown wavy hair. Bud had never met a congressman socially, before. It was a small wonder. Making conversation, Bud asked, "Do you live in Washington?"

"No, I commute from Wilmington, but I spend my summers here in Rehoboth Beach."

"I've found that Delaware is God's country."

"Couldn't agree more. I'd like to talk to you some more. I hope I see you on the beach," he said as they shook hands and smiled. As others came up to talk to the congressman, Bud left.

The thrill of chatting with Delaware's only congressman, one-on-one, was new to Bud. In Washington and the suburbs, the representatives can't physically know all the people they are representing. But here he was chatting with his own congressman.

Bud felt that he had become a local when he applied for a Delaware driver's license. Talking to his own representative in Congress inspired him to join the grass roots by registering to vote in Sussex County.

As the congressman turned to answer a question, Missy said, "Let's find Betty and Geoff. They were here a minute ago."

They found them at the food table, trying out all the finger food. "Mm, this is scrumptious," Betty said "What is it?"

"Mummy's crab dip," Missy said "She learned the recipe from a caterer. She had to buy the recipe. Isn't it good?"

"Delicious!" Betty agreed.

"Try the beef, Bud," Geoff said. "Melts in your mouth."

Bud tried the beef and it was delicious. He had another and then went methodically around the table, trying everything. He stayed too long in front of the fresh shrimp. As people tried to reach around him, he moved on.

He hadn't planned to stay so long, but he had been having a good time mingling with the crowd. He recognized some names he had done work for. "Oh, I replaced your outside shower door."

"Are you Mr. Fixit? Good job."

"Yes. Do you want a card, for when something goes wrong?"

"Yes, I would. Thank you."

As the last people were leaving, he found Missy. "Thank you for the delightful party, Missy. I had a wonderful time."

"Don't go yet Wait till the others go. I'd like to see you when things quiet down."

"All right," Bud said as couples came up to Missy to thank her for the party as they were leaving.

Bud fixed himself a little plate of the delicious food and sat down in a wicker chair. He made himself right at home, but a little out of the way of the leaving guests.

As the last guests were leaving, Missy joined him in the next chair. As Mr. and Mrs. Mannerly came in through the front door, Bud stood up and said, "Thank you for inviting me to your lovely party."

"Glad you enjoyed it, Bud," Mr. Mannerly said.

"Bud and I will help straighten up," Missy offered.

"Oh, don't bother," Mrs. Mannerly said, "let the caterers do it. That's what we're paying them for."

"We're tired," Mr. Mannerly said, "if you'll excuse us, we are going to our room to put our feet up."

"Sounds like a good idea," Bud said. "Thank you, again."

As they left, Missy looked at Bud with a searching look in her eye. He looked in her eyes, wondering what was on her mind.

"Penny for your thoughts?" he said.

"Are you really going to stay here year 'round and fix things for people?"

"I'm not ready to leave yet. I'm going to stay here for a while. Want to give it a fair trial."

"Are you happy down here all winter?"

"In seventh heaven. Best thing that's ever happened to me."

"What do you do down here all winter?"

"The same thing you do in Washington."

"But there are so few cultural things to do here. There's no theater, no art galleries like they have in Washington. Don't you find it a little barren?"

"Not at all. The Canada geese flying over, the fresh aroma of the ocean, and the open countryside are much preferable to the carbon monoxide of the beltway. There are too many people in Washington and they don't ever leave. Down here, I get enough of the social life in the summer to last all year."

"Don't you get bored in the winter down here?"

"If I ever do, I can go to Washington. I found that it's no farther from Rehoboth to Washington than it is from Washington to Rehoboth. I don't feel stranded at all."

"I've been coming here all my life. The streets used to be sandy roads. You could walk to movies when they used to be in town. There have been so many changes, the T-shirt stores and the gays, that I don't want to stay here anymore."

"Guess we have different views. A tale of two cities."

"I missed you, Bud."

"So did I, but I wasn't much to miss, always complaining and out of sorts. I had to get away and it's done me a world of good. I just wish I could make you understand."

"I've tried, but we keep getting farther and farther apart."

"Noticed that, too, but it has nothing to do with you or me. I'm okay and you're okay, but we're just drifting apart. Nice to be with you this evening, however. I really enjoyed the party."

"Glad you enjoyed it."

Bud stood up and Missy got up, too. He looked at her in her pretty dress. "You know, you are so pretty, the men will be flocking around you like bees around the honey." He leaned forward and kissed her nicely.

"Oh, Bud," she said, wrapping her arms around him in a warm embrace, "I missed your arms."

He put his arms around her in a comforting way and softly sang, "Can't we be friends?"

"Yes," she whispered. She let go, straightened her dress and dried the corners of her eyes.

"I better be going along. Your parents are tired and the caterers want to finish picking up," Bud said, turning to leave.

She walked him to the door and asked, "When will I see you again?"

"When I get a break and go to the beach. I'm still very busy keeping up with all these cottages. Take good care of your-self. You're a wonderful person," he said, kissing her good night with a friendly hug.

"Thank you for staying and talking."

"It was my pleasure," he said, starting out on the long walk back to where he had parked.

People were still walking around in the middle of the street in the moonlight. The stars peeked out between the trees. There were some parties still going strong in a cottage or two. It was the playground for the great nation's capital in all its glory.

He found his car right where he'd left it. Driving out of the revelry into the quiet countryside, he was content to go straight home to bed.

LOVE LETTERS IN THE SAND

On a bright, sunny July morning, Bud headed down Route 1 to estimate a couple of work orders, just south of Dewey Beach. One was in Indian Beach and the other in the Sailing and Tennis Club. The car radio was playing *Love Letters in the Sand* and it looked like a perfect beach day for the tourists.

As he drove through Dewey Beach, he slowed for the bathers walking across the highway on their way to the beach. They were loaded down with beach gear, carrying everything but the kitchen sink. As their bare feet hit the gravel, they did an ungainly dance. In a desperate effort to keep their balance, elbows and knees jagged at awkward angles. As one of them stubbed his toe, he performed a breathtaking solo.

As the song ended on the radio, a commercial caught his ear. Chubby Checker was coming to the Rusty Rudder on Saturday night.

A large, rustic wooden sign on the bay side caught his eye. The sign stood just above the parking lot foliage. Carefully landscaped with scruffy Loblolly pines, Bayberry bushes, and tall wavy beach grass, made it look as if they had naturally taken root around the perimeter of the parking lot.

A large, weathered rudder stood out on the sign as an illiterate symbol and subliminal suggestion above the lettering, THE RUSTY RUDDER. The looks of the place intrigued Bud as he drove by. He had never seen Chubby Checker live. Maybe he could get Rose to go with him.

After Dewey Beach, he looked across the highway, driving south past about ten blocks of large summer homes on the oceanside of the barrier reef. Each street had a chain that connected to two white posts each side of the street, with a little sign, PRIVATE PROPERTY. Some of the chains were down.

After the last street, an empty stretch of sand ran between the highway and the ocean as far as he could see. Bud made a U-Turn and drove back slowly, looking at each street sign. Turning into a street that went down to the ocean dunes, he looked over the large sandy lots.

Wind blown pines, stubborn bushes, and some sea grass had survived the oceanfront storms and the blazing sun. The newer summer houses were three-story mansions built on pilings. The pilings provided room to park in the shelter and some of them were enclosed, displaying two or three stately garage doors.

Bud found the address and wrote an estimate for the work. It was a small job, but it should be done right. He decided to put his best crew on the job.

He left, heading for the Sailing and Tennis Club, across the highway on the bay side, he drove back to Dewey Beach and made a U-turn. Pulling into the Sailing Club, he drove past the tennis courts and parked by the clubhouse overlooking the bay.

The steady breeze was just right for sailing, strong enough to fill the sails, but not strong enough to produce white caps. Three or four tiny sailboats were tacking back and forth in front of the clubhouse. About two dozen sailfish and sunfish were pulled up on the beach.

The bay stretched three miles to the horizon. Scanning the bay, a clam digger caught Bud's eye. A pretty girl in cut-off jeans was wading thigh-deep. A wicker basket, floating in an inflated inner tube, was tied to her belt loop with a rope. This delightful sight gave him the impression that you could wade all the way across the bay.

Halfway across the bay, Bud spotted a typical comic scene. A Sunday sailor was standing knee-deep in his Bermuda shorts, trying to push his powerboat off a sand bar, while, in the boat, his furious woman was trying to calm their hysterical child. These days, affluent landlubbers can buy a motorboat with a boat-trailer and head for the bay, bringing their families along to experience the joys of running aground.

He walked around the clubhouse looking for the office. On the bay side there was a deck high above the sandy beach. He was tempted to climb the wide wooden steps and take in the view, but he put it off till later.

When he came to the office door, he looked in. A clean-cut man looked up from behind an orderly desk. He reminded Bud of a typical school counselor. His preppie clothes and boyish smile smoothed the way for him. Soothing words, delegation and passing the buck had kept his face from wrinkling.

"Come in," he said "What can I do for you?"

"I'm Mr. Fixit," Bud said, stepping in.

"Oh, yes, we have some little problems with the clubhouse."

"It looks quite new. It's a substantial building."

"The club started twenty-five years ago with a college boy from Indian Beach, two rental sailfish, and a pup-tent."

He looked to be in his thirties. "You couldn't have been here then?" Bud asked.

"I was a little boy, They let me hang around. Learned to sail these little boats by watching and asking questions."

"And what can I do for you?" Bud asked, jovially copying his first remark.

"Come with me and I'll show you," he said, jumping up. "Just little things, but I'm not handy with tools."

They were little things and Bud fixed them himself as the manager pointed them out: a loose door knob, a stuck window – just little things. The two men carried on a conversation as the manager pointed out the problems and Bud fixed them.

"Chubby Checker is coming to the Rusty Rudder," Bud said.

"Yes. It's a large place. They have to hire name acts to attract a large enough crowd to fill the place," the man said.

"All I saw was a parking lot as I drove by. What's it like? How big is it?"

"Takes up the whole block. They started buying up little cottages, one at a time, till they bought out the whole block. Then, they tore down the little cottages and built a large, year' round restaurant with three dining rooms, a disco bar room, and a large deck overlooking the water. The restaurant was so successful, they bought up all the little cottages in the next block and put in a charming shopping complex called, 'Ruddertowne.'"

"Sounds very fancy for this area!"

"Well, it is. You know, when Dewey Beach developed on this barrier reef, the water was terrible. On Indian Beach they drank wine and whiskey all day and acted like wild Indians."

"That's what I hear," Bud said, nodding in the affirmative.

"But when the county ran the water lines out here, the area went big time."

"Certainly sounds that way."

"You ought to stop in for a sandwich and look it over."

"About lunchtime," Bud replied "I'll try it." Bud finished the handyman chores and wrote out a bill. "Nice chatting with you," he said as he left and headed back up the highway.

Turning into the street, running down to the bay between the Rusty Rudder and Ruddertowne, he looked over the parking lots on each side. A cluster of quaint shops, huddled together, gave Ruddertowne an intriguing ambience. Actually, it was a large modern building with a clever facade. The octagonal lighthouse that rose from the beach would have been the focal point, but the building code's restrictions limited it's height.

Cars were parked at an angle, head in, along the side of the Rusty Rudder. Bud pulled into an empty space and got out. There were wooden steps leading up to the open deck near the bay end of the street. An elaborate turn-around had been freshly paved as the street met the beach. A circular garden was wrapped with a curved sidewalk for the passengers of the Ruddertowne Trolley, as though the street between the two properties belonged to them.

Just past the turn-around, young men and women in bathing suits were engaged in a frolicking game of volleyball on the beach. Bud watched the game as he went up the steps to the deck.

Young adults in bathing suits were in a holiday mood as they ate and drank on the deck. The loud laughing and enthusiastic conversations gave the feeling that the joint was jumping.

Bud found a table and ordered a sandwich. Colorful sails of a sunfish animated the bay. A couple of powerboats had parked at the long pier jutting out to the channel. Lights ran along the pier, so you could come by water, day or night, to refresh your crew. Everything looked new and beachy.

He sat on the deck just inside an enclosed, air-conditioned deck area. Down a couple of steps, like a sunken living room, was a larger deck full of tables of young adults at play. There was an outdoor bar up a few steps at each end of the deck.

He looked next door at the Ruddertowne deck. Next to the light-house, there was an enclosed cocktail lounge with a deck over the water. A couple of empty tables on the deck were a contrast to the noontime action where he was.

After lunch, he went in and walked through the dining rooms. In the center of the first dining room, there was a white gazebo around the salad bar. Floor to ceiling picture windows gave a view of the bay. Another room was like a ship's mess hall. Old, wooden signs added to the atmosphere.

The disco bar had a group of easy chairs around a cozy fireplace. The brick wall had an occasional bottle substituted for a brick. A long bar ran down the whole side of the building and ended in a disco with a sunken dance floor. There were tables separated by a brass railing from the dance floor.

The main entrance was at the end facing the highway. A long ramp led up from the parking lot. There was an occasional bottle in the brick walls here, also. The tasteful design gave a casual flair to the holiday feeling. It had taken a lot of planning and a lot of front money.

He decided to look around Ruddertowne. Walking down the steps, past the volleyball game, and up the Ruddertowne steps, he found an ice cream store. On the bay side, he came to another restaurant called Crabber's Cove. There was an air-conditioned, cathedral ceiling din-ing room with rest rooms off the upstairs balcony.

The restaurant overflowed on to a large deck built over the water. Each redwood table was covered with a paper spread that had dia-grams and an explanation about how to pick crabs. There were some happy people banging crabs with wooden mallets. The sign adver-tised the best sunset on the bay.

Walking around the building, Bud came to the water sports rent-als on the beach, just south of Crabber's Cove. There were surf boards, sunfish sailboats, and power skis. The bright-colored sails on the bay waters were like butterflies swarming around the deck.

Bud walked all the way around Ruddertowne. He looked in the kite shop, Rudder T-shirt shop, the tobacco and gift shop, and all the rest. He was surprised to find a seafood carry-out on the highway side.

He went on to check on his other jobs, thrilled with his new discovery. He couldn't wait until evening to tell Rose. As he worked his way near the real estate office, he stopped to see if Rose was there.

He went in, checked his folder, and peeked in Rose's office.

"Hi, Bud. Come in."

"Hello, Rose. Have a minute?"

"Yes. This morning was busy here, but now the visitors have all gone to the beach in the sunshine."

"Chubby Checker is coming to the Rusty Rudder Saturday night and I hope you'll go with me. The size of the place is amazing. We could have dinner there, too, if you like, my treat."

"What time do you want to go?"

"Then, you will? Anytime you say."

"I can't be ready to go till seven."

"I'll be ready and wait till you're free. Don't want to hurry you. Want you to enjoy it."

"Sounds great! I can be ready by seven without rushing. Just you and me, this time, I promise."

"Then it's all set. I won't keep you from your work. I've got two more jobs to check on."

"Bye and thank you, Bud."

Bud finished up his jobs early Saturday afternoon. He had been thinking about his date with Rose all day. He went home and washed his car. When it was sparkling, he flopped on the bed and stared at the ceiling. A cool breeze was drifting across the room, from the window. The old farmhouse was cool in the summer. He relaxed and fell sound asleep.

He awoke with a start, when he heard a car pulling into the lane. Thinking it was Rose, he jumped up to get himself ready. Looking out the front window, he saw that it was Rose's mother coming back from shopping.

He found his robe and a towel and went out to take a shower. He loved the outside shower in the fresh air. Going in to get dressed, he knew he had plenty of time. When he was ready, he took a chair out on the porch and sat down to read the paper. He had left in a hurry that morning and had only scanned the news.

He read the syndicated columnists' clever renditions of the news. He was sitting back, admiring the bucolic view, when Rose pulled into the lane. "Be out in a minute," she called out as she went in the house.

"No hurry," Bud called back to her, without moving. "We've got plenty of time."

Scanning the clouds on the horizon trying to distinguish any recognizable shapes, he was at peace with the world. It seemed like no time at all when Rose came out in a pretty dress, saying, "I'm sorry I kept you waiting."

"You're ahead of schedule," Bud said. "My, don't you look beautiful." He opened the car door for her with a flourish. She sat down, pulling her skirt in, as he closed the door. In the car, Bud asked, "Shall we eat at the Rusty Rudder?"

"Like to try it."

When they arrived, the parking lot was full, so Bud drove into the Ruddertowne lot and found a place. "Long as we're here, let's walk around Ruddertowne and look it over," Bud suggested.

"That would be fun," she said, hopping out before he could open the door for her. When they came to Crabber's Cove, Rose said, "Let's sit out on the deck and pound crabs."

"That's what I like to hear," he said "I'll see if I can get a table by the water."

They were escorted to a table on the deck with a panoramic view of the bay. Rose said that beer goes with crabs, so they each ordered a beer. Bud studied the table top instructions that told how to pound crabs.

"I'll show you how I do it when our crabs come," Rose said, getting into the swing of things.

"I'm a landlubber," Bud confessed, "I'll need all the help I can get."

Little puffs of cotton, high in the sky, were beginning to turn pink as the sunset painted the heavens with golden shafts. "You pick the nicest places, Bud," she said "Look at that beautiful view."

"Reminds me of a lake back home," Bud said "You ever been to

New York state?"

"No. I've been to Dover and Wilmington. Once we went up to Philadelphia to see the Liberty Bell with the crack."

"It's 'The Empire State, the state that has everything.'"

"That's the way we feel about Delaware."

"I was just quoting the chamber of commerce slogan. I want to go to see my grandfather. I'd like to take you with me."

"You never mention your mother."

"Mom became a widow and a mother at the same time. We went to live with my grandparents in Elmira. Mother went to work and Gramp and Gram looked after me. When Mother married again, and moved out, I was allowed to stay on with Gramp. He's like a father to me. I guess I think of his place as home."

"Don't you miss your mother?"

"Yes, but she has a new family; my half-brother and half-sister. I sort of feel out of place with them. They're nice to me, but I feel more at home with Gramp."

"Do you get along with your stepfather?"

"He's nice to me and my mother is very happy with him, but they have a life of their own that I don't fit into very well."

"Must be hard for you, feeling like an orphan?"

"Don't know any other way. Had a wonderful time, so far. Let's go up for a short visit. I want you to come with me."

"Meeting your family sounds serious."

"Look! I have to go and I want you to go with me. We could have a wonderful time."

"Well, I don't know."

"Just want to see how they're doing. You'd enjoy the trip."

"Ready to order?" the waiter asked. He was a young man with a summer job. The servers' uniform seemed to be khaki shorts and a navy-blue knit shirt.

"Rose," Bud said, "Why don't you order for us?"

"We'll start with a half a dozen crabs," she said.

"All right!" the young man said, picking up the menus. "I'll bring them right out."

As the waiter left, Bud said. "Rose, you're my best friend. I enjoy your parents and I'd like you to meet my grandfather."

"I've never taken a trip with a man."

"Neither have I. I mean, with a woman. I've never had a good friend of the opposite sex before."

"It would look questionable. What would people think?"

"We're always seen together and no one has said anything. I know what we could do. I'll buy you an engagement ring. Will you marry me?"

"Are you proposing marriage to me?"

"Yes, I am."

"Thought you are supposed to get down on one knee."

"Want me to do that here?" he said, sliding his chair back.

"Not really. But I'm not ready to make a commitment. I've just started my career."

"So have I, but we can't wait forever. You're the one for me. We could have a long engagement. And, you can always break off the engagement, whenever you want to. It isn't etched in stone till you are married," Bud rambled.

"Let me think about it some more," she said.

"Take all the time you want. I'll try not to mention it again till it's time for me to go to New York."

"Thank you for asking me. I like the idea, but I want to be sure I'm doing the right thing."

"That's fine with me. Now let's enjoy the evening."

"You're stealing my line and I love it," Rose said.

"Here we are," the waiter said, setting down a tray full of steaming crabs, mallets, forks, sharp knives, and a roll of paper towels. Rose took a crab, put it on the paper-covered table in front of her and went to work on it. Bud watched her and then picked out a crab for himself. He started looking it over. It looked scrawny and complicated. They had given him a wooden hammer and a sharp knife.

Rose broke off the legs and set them aside, so Bud followed. As she went to work on the main body of the crab, Bud looked over the utensils. He thought the knife would be less conspicuous, but he had no idea where to find the meat.

"Here, let me show you," Rose said. Turning his crab over, she said, "See this little apron. Watch me as I pull it off and break the crab in two. There's the crab meat and you throw this part away."

"Thank you. I think I've got it now."

Rose put her crab meat in the melted butter, so Bud did the same.

Then she dug it out with a fork and ate it with a smile of satisfaction. Bud tried it *"Butter would make anything taste good,"* he thought to himself.

When Rose had finished the meat from the body, she took a claw and pounded it with her mallet. Bud found himself in a sea of tables of crab pounders. It was fun trying fresh seafood with the locals. Eating outside also makes everything taste Better.

Rose demonstrated one more crab for him. Bud was beginning to feel like a native. The early Indians had caught their dinner in the sea. Rose said the local tribes were Nanticoke Indians.

Rose picked the crabs quickly, but Bud took a long time. It was a new game for him. Rose sipped her beer and watched him pick the last crab. "You're getting to be an expert."

"Feel like I'm rowing upstream, working like a madman for a little taste. I don't have the hang of it yet."

"You're doing very well for a beginner."

"It's like a one-legged race. The newcomers always get the booby prize. I feel like a pea-picker who's all thumbs."

"Don't let me rush you. Those crabs were good."

"Would you like some more?"

"No, thank you. Maybe some coffee and dessert in a while."

"Now you're talking my language."

The waiter appeared as Bud was finishing his last crab. He picked up the trayful of discarded crab shells, asking, "Would you like some more?"

"No, just some dessert and coffee," Bud said.

"I'll bring you a menu," the waiter said.

As the waiter left, Bud said, "That's a lot of fun, but I'm afraid I held you up."

"Every day's a holiday when I'm with you," she said with a sweet smile, quoting an old song.

The band started playing next door at the Rusty Rudder as the waiter served their dessert. The music came across the water in the moonlight "What we need is a check," Bud said to the waiter.

"No hurry," Rose said. "We'll have plenty of time. It's just the warm-up music for Chubby Checker."

When they had finished, and Bud had paid, they strolled hand in hand around the deck toward the music. As they rounded the corner of the Ruddertowne deck, they looked across at the Rusty Rudder's enormous deck. It was jammed with a noisy crowd.

"Oh, dear," Rose said, "looks like a group grope."

"They're all packed in like sardines!" Bud observed.

They looked over the scene from the vantage point of the Ruddertowne deck. The parking lots were full and a large bus was parked near the turnaround. Big block letters on the side of the bus spelled out CHUBBY CHECKER.

There was a table and four chairs beside them on the quiet deck. "Let's sit here and watch the show in comfort," Bud said.

"That's a great idea," Rose said. They were facing the back of the band, but they had something like a box seat.

A Mercedes sedan drove up beside the bus and Chubby Checker jumped out. He climbed up the back of the bandstand deck..He swung his leg over the railing, like a boxer entering the ring, and a roar went up from the crowd.

He stepped quickly to the microphone in the spotlight and sang, "Come on, baby. Let's do the twist." The crowd went wild and pandemonium set in. The crowd tried to sway with the music, but they were packed too tight.

"This is like a George Washington's birthday sale in a DC department store," Bud recalled.

"Is that how the nation's capital celebrates the father of our country's birthday?" Rose asked.

"Yes. I was surprised, because in Elmira, we used to have a patriotic parade and speeches. In DC, the bureaucrats have fixed incomes and spend their holidays looking for bargains."

Chubby Checker's song ended in a round of applause, as the band made a fast segue into the next number. Chubby Checker made a few dramatic moves that could be considered a bow and came in singing the next song right on the beat. It was a polished act and a nostalgia trip for the crowd.

After several songs, Chubby Checker took several bows, all around in each direction, to a raucous ovation of applause, yelling, and shrill whistles. When the band started an easy dance tune, Chubby Checker started climbing over the back of the bandstand. Bud said, "We can slip out of here before the crowd jams up the parking lot."

"I'm ready to go," Rose said "Lead the way."

It was clear sailing back to the car and they were out on the highway in no time. As they started up the highway, Bud said, "Looks like an accident up ahead."

Rose soon figured it out. "It's a state police roadblock. You may have to take an alcohol breath test."

"That's all I need, another first."

"There's nothing to it. You just blow in a little tube."

"They cart me off, toss me in jail, and throw away the key."

"You'll pass. You only had one beer because you were so busy picking crabs."

She was right. Bud took the breath test and passed. "I've never run into anything like that," Bud said.

"It's MADD, Mothers Against Drunk Drivers. They pressured the courts and police till they enforced the new drunk driving laws," Rose explained.

"From the looks of the crowd back there, the police should reap a bonanza tonight."

"They set up the roadblock between the bay and the ocean. To avoid it, you'd have to drive several miles, all the way around the bay, or take the Ruddertowne Trolley."

"Well, this has been an exciting evening. We got to see how the other half of the world lives."

"The most exciting part for me was your proposal."

"I really meant it, but I promised not to bring it up."

"I'll let you know soon," she promised.

They drove on in silence. Rose snuggled close to him and hooked her arm around his arm and put her head on his shoulder.

PART SIX
THE RING

A work order came in for Ye Olde Jewel Shoppe on Route 1. Having driven past the sign many times, Bud wondered what it was like. He had been looking for an excuse to drop in and size it up. He went there first, looking around with curiosity.

Glass showcases full of jewelry formed a U-shaped counter surrounding the customers with enticing trinkets. Clerks moving around behind the counters showed selected items while the customers were corralled by low display cases.

Behind the counter, display cases sat on chests against the side walls. Two jewelers sat on a glass-enclosed platform in the back corner repairing jewelry and watches. On the back wall, a curtain covered the door to the storeroom and safe.

An older woman behind the counter, asked, "May I help you?"

"I'm Mr. Fixit," Bud said.

"You should talk to my husband," she said as she went to speak to a man on the stool at the repair desk. The contraption he had on his head made him look like a welder. It was a wide magnifying lens that covered his forehead, held on by a band set deep in his wavy, gray hair. He flipped up the lens, looked over at Bud, and smiled.

He came over to Bud with his lens sticking up at a rakish angle like an outfielder's sunglasses. After a warm greeting, he explained why he had called Mr. Fixit, as Bud listened.

The shop had a glass front door to encourage people to come in to the shop. He also had a wrought iron door that he closed and locked at night, to keep people out. The iron door was so heavy that it was beginning to sag on it's hinges. Bud looked it over and suggested his best carpenter could fix it tomorrow, if that would be soon enough.

"That'll be fine. I can open it myself, but it's too heavy for my wife or daughter to open the way it is," the man stated.

With a stroke of inspiration, Bud said, "I have a problem. Perhaps we can help each other. Do you sell engagement rings?"

"Congratulations!" the man quickly responded.

"That may be a little premature. I just want to be ready with a ring, in case she says yes," Bud replied.

"What size does she wear?" the man asked.

"I have no idea and I don't want to ask her. Let's say it will be a surprise," Bud said.

"Why don't you ask her mother?" the man suggested.

"That's a good idea. I'll do it," Bud said.

"We have quite a variety. My wife will show them to you," he said, glancing over at the older woman standing behind the counter. She beckoned Bud over to take a look at the rings.

"Can you give me a price range? I don't know much about this. I don't want the most expensive ring, but I don't want the cheapest one either," Bud said cautiously.

"Least expensive," she corrected. "We carry rings from a hundred dollars to a thousand dollars in stock. We will be glad to order any ring you want."

"What does a five hundred dollar ring look like?"

She showed him several rings that looked good to him.

"I'll find the size and come back and try to pick one out."

"She can exchange it, if she prefers a different one."

"Thank you. I'll be back soon."

Bud checked out the other work orders, assigned the crews to their jobs for the day, and went home to see if he could find the Gardners. When he knocked on the door, Rose's father opened the door. "Hi, Bud. Won't you come in?"

"Hello, Mr. Gardner Is Mrs. Gardner home?"

"She sure is," he said to Bud. He called out, "Lily, Bud is here to see you."

Lily Gardner came out quickly, saying, "Hi, Bud. It's nice of you to stop by and see us."

"Do you have a minute to talk? There is something I'd like to ask both of you," he said quite seriously.

"All the time in the world," Mrs. Gardner said. "Sit down, Bud, and let's talk."

They all sat down and waited for the other to start talking. Bud was trying to compose his thoughts, but he felt uncomfortable and wondered how he had gotten into in such an awkward situation. As he started squirming, he blurted out, "I've been so busy and I haven't had a chance to talk to you for a while."

"Is anything wrong?" Lily asked.

"That depends on how you feel about what I am going to say."

"Well," Thornton said, "let's have it."

"Rose and I are just starting our careers," Bud pointed out.

"We both know that," Lilly said.

"Okay. Here it is. I would like to ask for your daughter's hand in marriage," Bud said, feeling he was hyperventilating.

"Oh, that's wonderful," Lily said.

"But you first said you are starting out on new careers," Thornton said. "What does that have to do with getting married?"

"Well, Rose isn't ready for a commitment just yet," Bud said "You see, I want to go up to New York state and visit my grandfather. I want Rose to go with me to meet him. I thought she would feel more comfortable traveling with me after we were engaged. Does any of this make any sense to you so far?"

"Yes, I think it does," Lily said. "The two of you have been seen together a lot of places around here. I think it's time you thought about a commitment."

"I am serious about getting married, but I should wait until I'm sure about my income," Bud said.

"You seem to be doing all right so far," Thornton said.

"Well, Rose hasn't said yes yet. She's thinking about it. I thought I'd buy a ring, just in case she decided to say yes."

"That's a good idea," Lily said enthusiastically.

"But I don't know her ring size," he said.

"I'll get you a ring that fits Rose's finger. You can take it for size, if you bring it back," Lily said happily.

"I'll guard it with my life. Don't want to push Rose into this; just want to be ready when, and if, she makes up her mind."

Lily went to get the ring. Thornton said, "I appreciate your coming to us about this, Bud. So many young people run off and get married and spring it on their parents."

"We may have to have a long engagement. We both want to get our careers together," he said.

"Oh, don't worry about that. You are young and you both are hard workers. You can build your careers together. Also, I am going to put the farmhouse in Rose's name, anyway. You'll have a place to live right from the start," Thornton said.

Lily came back with the ring and said, "This has been handed down in my family. It was my great grandmother's ring and I don't want anything to happen to it."

"I'll bring it back this evening," Bud said, getting up to go. "Thank you for your time."

"Anytime, Bud."

He drove straight back to Ye Olde Jewel Shoppe. When he had picked out a ring, he went back home to show it to Lily and give back her ring.

Lily was thrilled to see the ring he had picked out. "Let's keep this a secret until Rose makes up her mind," Bud said.

"I'll try," Lily said.

Bud looked at the old farmhouse in a whole new light. He was seeing it the way Rose would see it. He would have to put in year round heat and finish the upstairs. Going upstairs to see about which room could be the master bedroom, he heard a strange noise. He stopped on the stairs to listen.

"Bud Green! Are you in there?"

It was Rose's voice, but she sounded irate. He had never heard such a tone of voice from her. "Hello!" Bud answered, "I'm up here." He turned and started down the stairs as Rose burst in the door.

"I want to talk to you!" she said most emphatically.

"Come in, Rose," he stammered.

"I am in," she stated, standing stiff legged with her arms akimbo, looking like an old sea captain braced against the storm. It was obvious that she meant business.

"What's the matter?" he stammered, standing in shock, frozen halfway down the stairs.

"You've been talking to my mother about our being engaged."

"Oh, I'm glad you brought that up," he said, trying to sound calm. "I want to talk to you about that."

"You better start talking and it better be good!"

"I promised not to mention it to you again, but now that you have brought the subject up. . ."

"What are you talking about?" Rose broke in impatiently.

"Your mother offered to help me with a problem. When the subject came up about our being engaged, I told her we were just starting our careers and you hadn't made up your mind."

"You told my mother about it behind my back?"

"I needed your mother's help," Bud said, carefully. "We got to talking and when the engagement came up, I had to tell her we're just starting our careers and we hadn't made up our minds."

"Look, it's hard enough being a liberated woman starting out on a career. Now you're asking me to be a housewife."

"I don't want you to change. I like you just the way you are. You can just keep on with your career."

"Marriage is a serious move for me," Rose tried to explain, under duress. "I'm an old-fashioned girl!"

"Make up your mind, Rose," Bud snapped "You're either a modern liberated woman or an old-fashioned girl. Which is it?"

"Don't yell at me," she warned. "I'm trying to tell you my problem. If I marry you, I want to take care of you properly. Is that so bad?"

"I don't want a clinging vine to mother me, who is always agreeing with me, playing a role." Bud said firmly, "I want a real live girl, for better or for worse, warts and all."

"Warts?" she screamed.

"You know what I mean! I just want you to be yourself and do whatever you want. Is that so bad?"

"But you don't know me!" She was becoming exasperated. "What if you don't like me when you get to know me better?"

"I just want you to be yourself. Just act naturally."

"I'm naturally quite outspoken!"

"I want you to speak up and say what's bothering you," Bud scolded. "You're too polite."

"But you always get mad when I speak up!" she yelled.

"Of course I do, but you still have to speak up!"

In the stairwell of the old farmhouse, they stumbled on the secret of a sound relationship. The anxiety and frustration of their quarrel pushed Rose to the end of her rope. Belligerently Rose said, "If you don't like the way I am, you can fuck off!"

The F-word stunned Bud momentarily. The unvarnished expression shocked him, but Rose's declaration of independence delighted him. Smiling, he blurted out, "Hold that thought."

As Rose turned to storm out, Bud quickly collected his wits and said, "You're right." He came down the rest of the stairs saying, "Why don't we sit down in the front room and talk about it calmly? I have something I want to show you." Rose turned to look at him, as he nervously led her to the front room. There were two chairs, one on each side of the restored fireplace. He motioned her to one and sat down in the other. She sat down, trying to be quiet, curious to find out what this was all about.

"I had a problem that only your mother could help me solve."

"Our engagement was between you and me," she insisted. "You had no right to talk to mother behind my back."

"Had a problem that only your mother could help me with," he said, sliding off the chair onto his knees toward Rose. "It's about a friend of mine. I should have come to you, but we have both been so busy lately." He reached in his pocket and pulled out the ring case. "Would you like to help me with the problem?"

"What are you talking about?" she asked.

He came nearer, walking on his knees. "This is what I'm talking about," he said handing her the ring case.

As she opened the case, her eyes widened with surprise. "It's a ring!" she exclaimed.

"Yes, try it on and let me know what you think of it?"

She slipped the ring on her finger. "It just fits!" she said in amazement. "What friend is it for?"

"Will you marry me?" he said, quite softly and tenderly. "I am on my knees this time."

"Oh, Bud. You are such a big nut, but I love it," she said with a sparkle in her eyes.

"You mean you will?" he asked.

GRASS ROOTS

"I hadn't decided. Wait a minute! How did you know my ring size?" Rose said, quickly recovering her poise.

"Your mother told me," Bud said "I asked her not to tell you and she said she would try. I just wanted to be ready, in case you said yes."

"What about my career?"

"You can just keep on going with it. We both are trying to get established. I've been able to turn my life around down here. Your father said we should go ahead and get married and build our careers together."

"You told my father, too!"

"He happened to be there. I told them I had asked you to go to New York with me to visit my grandfather. I thought you would be more comfortable traveling with me, if we were engaged. I do not want to rush you into this, but the timing is important."

"I don't believe this!" Rose said, throwing both hands in the air.

"Your mother said that we had been a lot of places together and it was time to make a commitment."

"This is so sudden," she said, softly, as she considered the matter before her.

"I know it isn't fair to ask you to marry me, when I'm just getting started. I am serious. I am ready to make a commitment to you. That's why I want you to go to New York with me."

"Well, if Mom and Dad think it's all right, I could try to rearrange my schedule," Rose said, beginning to accept the idea.

"Look, I want you to wear this ring up there. I want you to decide for yourself when the time comes. If you change your mind about me later, I'll understand."

"It's not that," she tried to explain. "I don't want to take on more than I can handle. You are a very special person in my life. I don't want to let you down."

"Don't worry. We'll talk about it some more, when you've had a chance to mull it over. In the mean time, you keep the ring," he said handing her the box. "The jeweler said that you may exchange it, if it doesn't suit you."

"Oh, Bud. What will I say when people ask me about it," she mused, looking fondly at the ring on her finger.

"Don't have to wear it till you're ready. Okay?" he said.

"This isn't the way I thought it would be. . .the way it is in story books."

"You can tell your own special story to our grandchildren."

"I'm not ready to start a family."

"I'm not ready to start a family, yet, either. I'm sure that when I do start a family, I want to do it with you. That's why I want you to meet my family."

"I do want to meet your family. I just have so much to do that I feel overwhelmed."

"Don't worry about it now. I've said my piece and I will understand if you don't go along with my plans. Let's not talk anymore about it now," Bud said.

"I'm used to being in control of my life. I'll have to learn to rely on your judgment. I want to do the right thing."

"Everything is going to be all right," he said, standing up and pulling her to her feet. He put his arms around her. They just stood there, letting osmosis do the communicating.

"Your parents are going to be wondering what we're doing in the old farmhouse," he said, making a move toward the door.

"They seem to be throwing us together in this old house, as if they are reliving their youth. We ought to be giving them their money's worth, but don't get any funny ideas, just yet." she smiled at Bud and turned toward the door, glancing down at the ring.

"I'm always full of funny ideas when I'm with you," he said, following her out. He walked her back to her mobile home. At the door, he kissed her gently and said, "Don't worry. It'll all work out."

"Thank you, Bud," she said as she went in.

When the door closed, he spun around jumping with joy as he quietly lip-synced an Indian war whoop. Dancing across the lane, he was so full of himself, he danced all the way home.

LABOR DAY

Late in August Bud was working long hours, as the summer season built up to a frenzied climax of the Labor Day revelry. The merchants were hoping for a record crowd, while the locals' jargon humorously drawled the word "tourists" until it sounded more like "terrorists." When he finally arrived home, he was tired and hungry. His telephone answering machine was blinking at him. "Must have missed a call."

He pushed the "MESSAGES" button and flopped down in a chair to listen. "This is for Bud Green, so Mr. Fixit can relax. It's Betty Brass calling. Geoffrey and I are having a little Labor Day party and we request the pleasure of your company at 12 Oak Avenue around sixish, on Labor Day. Regrets only, 227-2277. We do hope you and Rose can come. Bye."

Bud pulled out his appointment book and wrote in the square marked Labor Day, "Party, Betty Brass, sixish - bring Rose." He planned to leave for New York two days after Labor Day for a one-week trip. A few early business close-ups had been scheduled for his crews. Most of the summer businesses planned to stay open in September with limited hours. Some of the shops try to stay open all the way to Christmas.

He heard a car pull into the lane. Jumping up, he called through the open front window to Rose, "Can you come in here for just a minute." Rose came in and he played the telephone message for her. He watched her as the message repeated again.

"Oh, dear," Rose said. "That's very nice of her. I won't be home until six on Labor Day. Do you think sixish means we can come at seven?"

"I think so. I'll call Betty," Bud replied. He picked up the phone and thanked Betty. When he said they might not be able to get there until seven, she said that would be perfect and thanked him for calling. He said to Rose, "She's thrilled. It's all set."

"I'll try to sneak out a little early."

"You won't have to rush. I'll be ready and I have plenty of things to do while I'm waiting for you."

"Looks like we're an item in the social set," she said, getting up to go. "Better get going." Bud stood up and kissed her quickly and she rushed off.

Everything was set for the trip. Too tired to fix a dinner, he pulled out a TV dinner and popped it in the microwave.

Labor Day was just that for Bud . He had to fight his way through a holiday mob to handle the emergencies. He quit at noon to go home and get ready for Betty's party. When he put away all the tools and job orders, washed the car, and had taken a shower, he lay down to a well-earned rest.

Laying there, mulling over the events of the last year, his mind wandered back to the early days. He remembered working for World Peace. There seemed to be little peace in the political power struggles. He could hear Tilly saying, "Politics is local. As they say, it's the grass roots that count." Genuine peace had come to him in the grass roots.

He seemed to have found the secret down deep inside himself. Once he was at peace with himself, everything else seemed to fall in place. Rose had said, "Democracy works from the bottom up, not from the top down." Her simple statement seemed to take on new meaning with each new project he took on. He drifted off to sleep, counting his blessings.

. . .Bud and Rose were taking part in a drama twenty-five years earlier. Rose was taking the part of his mother and Bud realized he was acting the part of his father. Bud was saying, "I want to settle down here and raise a family." Rose said, "Women raise the families." Bud insisted, "I want to be around and raise my children myself. . ."

The afternoon sun dropped low enough to shine across the bed where Bud was napping. Bud woke enough to estimate the time from the sun. He lay there thinking about his grandfather. It was a nostalgic rest period. Taking time to review the drastic steps he had taken, he was pleased with the results. Things were going so well, but this is no time to let down.

Dressing for Betty's party, he worried that Mr. Fixit would not keep going while he was away. He was giving his beeper to his number one crew chief and asked him to take charge of the emergencies while he was gone.

When he was dressed, he went in to his desk in front room. He typed his proposed travel schedule, with his grandfather's and mother's name, address, and phone number. He printed five copies: one each for the crew chief, the Gardners, Rose's real estate office, Rose, and himself. Tearing off the pin-feed edges and pulling the pages apart, he made a neat pile on the corner of his desk. Then settled back and waited for Rose to come home.

At six-fifteen, he heard Rose's car pull into the lane. Going to the door he called out, "There is no need to rush, Rose. We have plenty of time. The party's just getting started."

"I'll be right out."

Roamer observed their conversation from a comfortable spot under a tree. When Bud looked in his direction, Roamer thumped his tail against the ground. Lush September foliage edged the sandy path leading to the porch. Bud's rehabilitation had worn a path to success as a symbol of his pursuit of happiness.

A gentle summer breeze rustled the leaves in the tall trees lining the old lane, causing the birds to complain. The sun was sinking lower toward the horizon, shooting golden rays through puffs of cumulus clouds. Bud was delighted with the magnificent display, feeling that God was in his heaven.

Maybe it was the magic of the moment. Rose came out looking radiant. There was a glow that seemed to shine through from deep down inside her.

"It's a beautiful night for a party," she said.

"Not half as beautiful as you," Bud said, trying to express how he felt. He was moved by her loveliness, but his feet didn't seem to be moving.

"Shall we go?" Rose asked, walking toward his car.

"Oh, yes," he said, feeling clumsy, "I'm coming." Bumbling toward her, he opened the car door for her. She slid in and pulled her skirt out of the way for him to close the door. He waltzed around to his side of the car and drove off. There were a lot of cars parked around Betty Brass's house. I'll let you off at the door and go find a parking space?"

"No," she said gently. "I'd rather go in with you."

A car pulled out a half a block up the street and Bud zipped in before anyone else came along. They walked hand in hand down to Betty's house.

"Bud and Rose!" Betty called from the porch door. "So glad you could come."

As they greeted Betty and Geoffrey, Betty exclaimed, "Let me see your ring, Rose." Rose proudly held out her left hand. "Is it what I think it is?"

Bud hadn't noticed that she was wearing his engagement ring. He was pleasantly surprised and speechless.

"Its still unofficial. Bud and I haven't announced that we're engaged, as yet."

"Well, you have now," Geoffrey said.

"Let's wait till later," Bud said, "let's not make a fuss."

"Come with me," Geoffrey said, linking arms with both of them. He found Missy and called out, "Missy and Will, I want you to meet some friends of mine."

Missy turned and smiled. "Hello, Bud - Rose. I want you to meet Will Wadsworth. Will, these are old friends of mine, Rose Gardner and Bud Green." Everyone shook hands and greeted each other cordially. Both Bud and Rose wondered if Missy was quoting them when she said, "old friends," but neither of them let on.

"Where there's a will, there's always a way," Geoffrey said in his teasing manner.

"It's Willard W. Wadsworth, III," Missy said.

"What does the W. stand for?" Geoffrey went on.

Will said, "Willard Wright Wadsworth. They're all family names."

Bud said in an aside to Missy, "Looks like you've found Mr. Right."

"Almost as nice as you," she whispered to Bud.

Geoffrey announced, "Rose and Bud are engaged!"

Missy turned to Rose and asked, with a big smile, "May I see your ring?" Rose held out her hand. Missy exclaimed, "Oh, Rose, it's beautiful."

Will looked with mixed feelings at the ring. As more people gathered around to see what was going on, Geoffrey stood on a chair, saying, "Ladies and gentlemen, may I have your attention. I have an exciting announcement. The Realtor Princess is merging with Mr. Fixit. I want to propose a toast to our two dear friends, Rose Gardner and Bud Green, who have announced their engagement. May all their troubles be little ones!"

There was a round of applause. The group around them formed a line to congratulate the future bride and groom. After the last well-wisher wandered away, Bud said, "Guess we've made Betty and Geoffrey's party a success."

"Geoffrey's talking about little ones, when we're just getting started on our careers," Rose pointed out.

"Don't pay any attention to Geoffrey's flippant remarks."

A balding, heavy set man rushed up to them, saying, "I'm Bob Welch. My wife and I met you at the Mannerlys."

"Oh, yes Like you to meet my fiancee, Rose Gardner."

"Congratulations, my dear," he said, pulling her to him to give her a peck on the cheek. Then, turning to Bud, "What I want to talk to you about is this. We're fixing up our house for sale and we need to do some cosmetic fix-up."

"Rose is an expert on that. She knows what you need to do to sell it in this real estate market. We'll both take a look at it and give you an estimate."

"That will be a big help. How soon could you look it over?"

"We're leaving town right after Labor Day for a week," Bud said, looking at Rose. "Will you be down here in September?"

"That would be better for us," the man replied. "We live here year 'round. It'll give us a little breathing room. I'll give you the address and phone number and you can call me when you return."

"We'll make a point of it," Bud said, handing him his card. Rose pulled a card out of her purse and handed it to him, while Bud wrote down Mr. Welch's address and phone number.

"I'll expect to hear from you in a week or two," he said, going back to the bar.

"Maybe we should postpone our trip," Rose said. "Mr. Welsh might go to someone else while we're gone."

"I don't think so. He came to me, because I am low key. I don't solicit business, but when someone comes to me, I try to do a good job. My business has grown by word of mouth."

"I like to follow up on my contacts right away," Rose said," to let them know I'm working for them."

"All work and no play makes Rose a workaholic. When you get too compulsive, it turns into a dog-eat-dog scenario. You used to take life easier, one day at a time," Bud reminded Rose.

"Is this about moderation?" she asked.

"I say, moderation's all right, if you don't overdo it."

"Very funny," she said sarcastically. "Let's go mingle."

Bud was thrilled to introduce Rose to the mayor of Rehoboth Beach, John Hughes. She was really impressed when he introduced her to Delaware's only congressman, Tom Evans. Bud told him how the grass roots businessmen felt about the economy.

Two other people asked Rose for her card. Neither Rose nor Bud had come to the party to make business connections, but the quests asked, "What do you do?" Betty's guests had learned the art of drawing new people into a polite conversation.

When they had nibbled and drunk their way past most of the guests, they looked around for Betty and Geoffrey. "We've had a wonderful time," Bud said when he found Betty near the door.

"You made the party for us," Betty said as Geoffrey came up.

"Thank you again for asking us," Rose said. "We've been having the time of our lives."

"Now, be good," Geoffrey said, with a devilish smile.

"Yes, Daddy," Bud joked with him. Feeling devilish himself, he curtsied to Betty, saying, "Mama said I had a good time."

Betty laughed and curtsied back to him, as Rose and Bud left, Betty called after them, "Thank you for coming."

"Thank you," Bud called out over his shoulder. When they were alone, Bud said, "Want to walk down to the beach?"

GRASS ROOTS

"That depends," Rose said, "on when we leave for New York. I have to pack and do a few things."

"I want to leave early Wednesday morning. It's a long drive," he replied.

"The day after tomorrow? I don't know what to pack to go to a place I've never been. I feel like bringing everything I own," Rose said in a panicked tone.

"You may bring everything, if you can fit it in the car. If you find you have forgotten something, we can buy it there."

"We both have a lot to do if we're leaving for New York the day after tomorrow. We better get home," Rose said.

"You're so right," Bud said. It was the first time that she finely agreed to go. "I was so proud when I saw my ring on your finger. I'm glad you wore it tonight."

"Thought I'd try it on a bunch of strangers first. Bet you didn't even notice it until Betty pointed it out."

"I'm new at the ring game. Guess I'm quite naive."

"That's what I like about you," she smiled.

Driving home in silence, they contemplated their plans for the future. Rose snuggled up to Bud, wrapt in quiet contemplation.

RICHARD C. HARRISON

GRAMP

Bud leapt out of bed as the first rays of the sunrise began subtly to paint the morning sky. Aroused by the excitement of an adventure on the open road with Rose, Bud dressed quickly in the clothes laid out the night before, glancing at his packed bags. Impatiently, he ate the hearty breakfast that he'd planned the night before. Had to last through the first leg of their trip.

He cleaned up the kitchen in record time, grabbed his bags and went out to pack the car. It seemed a sacrilege to disturb the solitude of the fresh, new day, so early in the morning. He opened the trunk quietly and slid his bags in place.

The day after Labor Day had been spent in a frantic effort to wrap up unfinished business and pack for their trip. Bud and Rose had not seen each other all day. At the end of the day, Bud caught her as she drove in. "I'll be ready to go early tomorrow morning, as soon as you're ready."

"I'm as ready as I'm going to be," she had said with a kiss and a quick hug. "I'll see you first thing in the morning."

Bud left the trunk of the car open for Rose's bags. Looking around the familiar surroundings, he searched for words to try to describe his new life to the folks back home. He was feeling on top of the world, like the seagull who caught the caramel corn in midair. The freshly painted farmhouse stood proudly in the yard. He had taken several pictures and sent them home with letters. However, the pictures didn't cover the mystery of his personal renaissance..

Rose came to the door lugging a big suitcase. Bud dashed over to help. Lugging her bag to the car, he put it in the trunk. "That all you're bringing?"

"Should I bring more?"

"No. I just thought that if there was more, I'd carry it out for you. That's what fiances are for."

"I should take advantage of it during the courtship," she said, hopping in the car. Bud jumped in and drove down the lane waving good-bye to the Gardners, who had come out in their robes to see them off.

The exhilaration of setting out on their own together, made their trip a bright and happy adventure. Rose was thrilled with a fresh start with Bud. She was looking forward to exploring his mysterious unknown world. Bud was eager to show Rose his roots. At last, he was going home, proud of getting himself straight and thrilled to have Rose with him.

"I plan to drive right on through to Gramp's," Bud said, "with just a couple of stops to eat. Tell me when your hungry."

"How long will it take to get there,"

"If I don't get lost, we should be in Elmira in eight hours of driving time. Add a couple of hours for eating and rest stops and we can hope for ten hours. We should get in around eight."

As they settled down for the long drive ahead of them, Rose said, "Tell me about your grandfather."

"Let's see," Bud began. "I'll tell you what people have told me. When Gramp was born, he was named Archibald Worthington Greene. He married Mary Elizabeth Hartington, when he joined the army reserve as a second lieutenant. Soon Mary produced a son, Archibald Worthington Green, Jr., that's my father. They called him Archie. He had bright red hair. As an army brat, he learned to make friends and to get along with strangers. He was a likable achiever. To identify him from other redheads, friends called him the unique and unmistakable name of "Red Green.""

"Oh, come on! You're making this up."

"I'm just telling it the way I've overheard it."

"Well, go on then."

"Gramp left active duty as a captain in the reserves when Archie was four. They moved to the family farm outside Elmira, New York. When Archie (that's my dad) was old enough for college, he signed up for the ROTC program. He graduated from college as an ROTC second lieutenant in the army reserve. Archie went on active duty, so he could afford to marry his college sweetheart, Gloria Wellington Lipschidts, from Michigan. That's my mother. She was glad to change her name to Green."

"Don't stop now."

"I was born on the farm as Archibald Worthington Green, III. They all called me Bud. Soon after I was born, word came that my father, Archie, had been killed in the line of duty. When I was old enough to walk, Mom found a job, while grandma took care of me on the farm."

"How do you know so much about your father if you were so tiny when he died?"

"Just telling you what I've heard all my life."

"Well, go on, I want to know more."

"In time, Gloria met a nice gentleman named Justin Tyme. She invited him to dinner at the farm. Justin and I liked each other from the start. They went on a honeymoon, leaving me on the farm with Gramp and Grandma. Justin had a house in Elmira, but when they came to pick me up, I didn't want to leave the farm. They all agreed that I could stay on the farm for a little while. Soon, Gloria was pregnant again, starting a new family. Now, I get along well with my half-brother and half-sister."

"Are you sure you're not making this up? You told it as if you were out of yourself watching the characters in a play."

"I just told you what I have heard all my life. I heard it in bits and pieces, but that's how I have put it all together."

"Well, you tell interesting stories. You have never spoken of your grandmother before today."

"She died when I was in college. She had made our old farmhouse into a home. Together Gramp and I had to learn how to care for the old place ourselves. We didn't appreciate all the work she'd done until she was gone."

"Well, what about your other grandparents, your mother's father and mother?"

"I don't know them. They haven't acted like grandparents to me.

I wouldn't know them if I saw them."

"I find that strange. Haven't you ever asked about them?"

"Yes, but Mom and Gramp never mention them when I'm around. When I ask, they just change the subject and pretend they aren't upset. They look like they were responding to a sales pitch at a funeral. You can ask them if you like."

They had wedged into the heavy traffic driving north after Labor Day. Station wagons and vans loaded with beach gear rolled along as little sports cars darted in and out between lanes.

"Where are all these people going?" Bud wondered aloud.

"This is the main highway to and from the beach for Dover and Wilmington. The Delaware vacationers are heading home."

Bud and Rose drove north, up Route 1, through the flat country-side. The wide median, between the double lanes, was lush with the summer growth. They passed a large riding mower keeping it trim and neat. Farms and little stores gave way to small towns as they headed for Dover.

As they neared Dover, huge cargo airplanes seemed to hover in the sky. "Dover air base must be close by," Bud said.

"They fly troops into battle in those big planes and fly the corpses back here. It's the army's morgue for the war dead."

"That morbid thought ought to tell us something."

"It's a big installation! Dover's the state capital, but there are more air force people than real people there."

The highway wound through a congested area with stoplights, right by the air base. There was a lot of local traffic, as the highway wove through the metropolis. It was a different part of Delaware that Bud had never seen.

Fast food places and shopping malls were beginning to take over the landscape. As they continued north, Bud was surprised to see so much activity going on. "This is where I used to turn to go to the University of Delaware in Newark," Rose remarked.

"I didn't know it was in Newark," Bud said. "Is it in New Jersey?" pronouncing it as if it were one syllable, "New'rk."

"Not 'New'rk,'" Rose corrected, "New-ark, Delaware."

They had been on the road almost two hours when a little clump of skyscrapers loomed on the horizon across the river. He knew he must be nearing Wilmington and had to watch the road signs for the turn-off .

When he took the bypass road around Wilmington, Rose said, "We are going a new way for me. I've always gone downtown."

"They say Wilmington is a suburb of Philadelphia."

"Largest city in Delaware."

"Looks about like Elmira to me."

"Can't wait to get there and see for myself."

Bud turned inland into the hilly section of Pennsylvania. They passed through Amish farms with hex signs on the barns. She eyed the rolling hills and scenic farms, saying, "This country is so beautiful. I've seen pictures of this area, but I thought the artist added the rolling hills to make a pretty scene."

"I grew up in a hilly section. Just looks like home to me."

Rose was so interested in the passing scene that she forgot that she was hungry. About one o'clock, Bud said, "Mind eating fast food for lunch, if we stop for a nice dinner later on?"

"Now that you mention it, I am hungry. Any place you pick will be fine."

Bud found a fast food restaurant on the highway. They both got out, stretched their legs, and headed for the rest rooms. It was a new experience for them both, traveling together. They had to wait and see how things worked out on a trial and error basis. Bud insisted on paying for the lunch. Rose offered to pay, but he said, "This is my trip. Thank you for coming."

"Then I'll pay for the gas."

"I asked you to come as my guest."

"If we're a team, maybe I should do some of the driving."

"I'll let you know when I get tired. I really enjoy setting out on the open road with you. I feel we are starting our lives. It's an adventure."

Rose's contented smile said more than the words, "We've come a long way together."

They finished their lunch. Bud dumped the trays in a trash bin and they drove off again. Bud pointed out landmarks as they went deeper into Bud's territory. By six o'clock they were near Elmira. Bud pulled into a gas station and made a phone call while the attendant filled the tank.

Coming back to the car, he said, "I called Gramp to tell him we're going to stop for dinner. He insisted that we press on and have dinner with him."

"Fine with me."

"I had planned to stop to give you a break before you had to deal with strangers."

"That's sweet of you, but I'm as ready as I'm ever going to be. Just let me use the rearview mirror."

As they pulled up to Gramp's house, Rose said, "Looks a lot like the old farmhouse in Delaware."

"I guess it does," Bud said, jumping out, when he saw Gramp marching toward the car. Rose watched as they greeted each other with a warm hug and a hearty handshake.

As she stepped out of the car, Gramp said, "You must be Rose. Come in, my dear. We'll get the bags in a minute."

Gramp took her by the arm and led her into the front parlor, while Bud lugged the bags into the hall. "Let me look at you. I see Bud has good taste."

"Thank you, Captain Green," she said with a shy smile.

"Please call me Gramp. May I call you Rose?"

"Yes, please do."

"Can I get you some refreshment after your long trip?"

"I'll wait for Bud, but you have what you usually have."

"This is not a usual occasion. Before I bore you with a lot of questions, I thought we ought to get to know each other."

Bud came staggering in and flopped in a chair beside Rose. "Put our stuff in the hall. You look great, Gramp."

"You look better than I remember, Bud. I guess I should thank Rose for that. How about a little refreshment, Bud? Rose said she'd wait for your decision."

"Have any white wine?"

"Sure do. Want to see if it's drinkable? As long as you're up, bring me a beer. I haven't been waited on in a long time."

Bud went to get the drinks. "Now, Rose, if you don't make yourself at home here and relax, it will be your own fault. You can do whatever you and Bud want to do while you're here."

"I want to know all about Bud's family. All he talks about is you. Tell me about his mother."

"She's a fine woman. She has a fine family and a wonderful husband. You'll most likely visit them tomorrow."

Bud came back with a glass of beer and two glasses of wine. "Old place looks the same to me," Bud said. "Good to be home."

"You two have made this old place come alive," Gramp said, raising his glass. "Here's to a happy reunion for Bud and a warm welcome to his beautiful Rose."

They sipped and talked together as though Rose had known them forever. Soon, Gramp said, "I'll put the dinner on, if you're ready."

"May I help," Rose asked, starting to stand up.

"Next time," Gramp said. "I'm doing this dinner. You two can just bring your glasses into the dining room."

The table was set for three. Bud remembered that Gramp sat at the head of the table. He seated Rose on one side of Gramp, where his mother used to sit and sat down in his old place on the other side. Gramp brought in roast beef with potatoes and gravy, vegetables, and salad. He sat down and said, "You remember that grace we used to say, Bud?"

They all bowed their heads, as Bud tried to remember

> "God, give us a bit of sun,
> A bit of work and a bit of fun.
> Help us through the mess and clutter,
> With our daily bread and a bit of butter."

They all smiled, saying, "Amen," together. As they raised their heads, Gramp served the plates. Gramp gave each of them a generous helping, enough for a farm hand.

"That's a lot to eat," Bud said. "Can't eat that much."

"You have to have your fill," Gramp said. "Just eat what you want and I'll give the rest to the animals. You used to come back for seconds."

They chatted over dinner, getting to know each other. Gramp had been eating alone in the kitchen. He was thrilled to be back in the dining room with the young visitors. When it was dark, he said, "Let me show you to your rooms."

Gramp picked up the smallest bag and led the way up the stairs as Rose followed him and Bud struggled with the other two bags. "This is your room, Rose, next to the bath. Bud will be right across the hall. There are fresh towels and things laid out. If you need anything else, just holler."

Rose was relieved to have a separate bedroom. Bud hadn't thought about it before this moment, but he went along with the idea. He wanted it to be comfortable and proper. Gramp figured that they could tiptoe across the hall if they had to be in the same bed.

Bud set up Rose's suitcase on a low table, so she could go through her things. He threw his bags on the floor in his room and went down to clear the table. When Gramp and Rose came down, Gramp complained, "Here, what's going on here. I do the dishes."

Well, you're too late," Bud said. "I've already started them. You and Rose can sit down and talk a minute. Just don't talk about me while I'm gone."

Gramp took Rose's arm and led her back to the parlor with a knowing smile. "We wouldn't do anything like that, would we," he said, facetiously. They sat down again in the front parlor. The furniture was "country antique" with a comfortable lived-in look. It was the room that was always kept neat and clean, in case the preacher dropped in.

"Last year was the first time that Bud didn't come home for Christmas. I couldn't understand it until I met you."

"It wasn't me. It was our old farmhouse that kept him from coming home. He'd turned on the water and he didn't know how to drain the pipes. He was heating it with a kerosene heater and it had to be filled twice a day," Rose explained.

"He was living with you?" Gramp asked.

"No. We bought a small chicken farm with a charming old farmhouse like yours. Just as the cold weather set in, Daddy had a heart attack. The old farmhouse was drafty and cold, so we put a mobile home next to it and moved in. Bud thought we should have fixed up the old farmhouse, but Daddy wasn't well enough to do it."

"How's your father doing?"

"He's in great shape now. Mom and Dad go to Florida every winter and my brother and I stay home and keep things going .But my brother was married this year."

"Congratulations are in order there. Then, you and Bud got together."

"No. I had met Bud the previous summer," Rose said. "He was not happy with the politics in Washington and he was almost ready to quit. When Senator Blassforth lost the election, Bud called me and asked if he could stay in the old farmhouse."

"He could have come here."

"He was too depressed. He had to get himself straightened out and he had to do it himself. He moved into the old farmhouse and started restoring it. He said he was restoring himself by doing it. I thought it sounded crazy, but it seemed to work. 'He's running a business out of the restored old farmhouse."

"Bud has to do some things himself. He is a nice guy, but he needs to be independent."

"He's a wonderful man. We are just starting our careers. I wasn't ready for a commitment, but Bud wanted me to meet his family, so he gave me a ring to wear. Also, my family thought it was time I met you."

"Well, I'm glad you came."

"So am I. There's one thing I don't understand."

"Maybe I can help."

"It's Bud's other grandparents, his mother's father and mother?" Rose asked.

"I was afraid you were going to ask me that. It's a long story. When you and I have more time, I'll tell you about them."

Bud had finished the dishes and appeared, saying, "How are things going in the front parlor?"

"We're getting along in high style," Gramp said.

"I want to unpack a few things," Bud suggested. "How about you, Rose?" Gramp and Rose stood up.

Gramp said, "I have a couple of things to do. I'll see you in the morning for breakfast. It's so nice to have you here. Sleep well."

"Good night, Gramp," Bud said.

"Nice to be here," Rose added, heading for the stairs. As Rose unpacked, Bud looked in on her. "Find everything you need?"

"I'll be quite comfortable here. Oh, Bud, I've fallen in love with your grandfather. Also, I'd love to visit your mother tomorrow," Rose said with a newfound excitement.

"So would I We'll talk about it in the morning," Bud replied. He bent to kiss her good night, looking for any sign of an invitation..

GRASS ROOTS

"Good night, my darling," she said, kissing him.

He went back to his room, put away some clothes, and hopped into bed. It had been a long day and sleep came easily.

RICHARD C. HARRISON

GLORIA

The coffee's ready," Rose said when Gramp and Bud came into the kitchen, saying, "Good morning," in unison.

"What else may I fix for your breakfast?" Rose asked.

"Hope you found something to eat for yourself," Gramp said to Rose, "Bud and I are used to fixing our own breakfast."

"I'll just fix myself a bowl of cereal," Bud said. "We'll check in the refrigerator and hit the grocery store this morning. What do you want for dinner, Gramp?"

"Gloria and Justin have invited all of us to dinner at their house, this evening," Gramp announced. "That's Bud's mother and stepfather, Rose."

"Been looking forward to meeting them . We should phone them. Maybe I can bring something for dinner," Rose said

"I'll call them," Bud said, "after breakfast."

They all sat around the sturdy kitchen table. The aroma, of brewed coffee and fresh fruit mixed with the clean country air. The hand-built counters and cabinets had worn well over the years where countless meals had been prepared. The modern refrigerator and stove seemed to fit in with the friendly decor. A bunch of fresh vegetables lay on a counter beside a large bowl of fresh eggs.

After breakfast, Bud called his mother "Hi, Mom. I want to bring my friend, Rose, to see you."

GRASS ROOTS

"I want you, Rose, and Gramp to all come for supper tonight. 'We'll eat at six, but why don't you and Rose come earlier and we can talk," she suggested.

"Rose wanted to help with supper or bring something," Bud replied.

"Thank her, but that won't be necessary," she answered. "I've fixed most everything ahead of time. It's all ready. All you have to do is come."

"Thanks, Mom," Bud said appreciatively. "We'll be over sometime this afternoon. Bye"

"Gramp," Bud said, "I want to show Rose where I grew up. We can start with the farm. Then drive in to Elmira to visit Mom. Dinner is at six, but you may come earlier and listen to us gab."

"I'll be there before six. You two run along," Gramp said.

Bud and Rose walked around Gramp's farm. The farmhouse looked like Rose's, but the similarity stopped there. Instead of long chicken houses, there was a large red barn built into a steep bank. The sliding front doors led to the first floor, while the back door led to the second floor.

Gramp's field of corn curled over a rolling hill, looking like a green blanket covering Mother Earth. A stand of trees, scaled the steep rise, reaching skyward. They climbed up to the tree line. Standing arm in arm, Bud pointed out the boundaries of Gramp's farm, tucked away in the quiet countryside. Rose wasn't used to climbing hills, but once up high, she was enchanted with the view.

A dry, cool breeze felt good on their faces as a gentle sun emphasized the deep September colors. Rich soil of the valleys and low lands had washed down from the hills. Gramp had planted his vegetable garden in the hollow behind the house. "This is where I grew up," Bud said. "I've always loved this place."

"You're very fortunate. It's really beautiful," Rose said.

"Let's go tell Gramp we're leaving. I'll show you Elmira and buy you lunch," Bud said, leading the way.

As they walked, hand in hand, down to the house, Rose watched black crows soaring in wide circles over the cornfield. Back at the house, Bud told his grandfather they were leaving and drove off to town.

The winding road to town curled around each little rise and gully.

RICHARD C. HARRISON

It had grown into the topography over the years from an old Indian trail or a cow path. As they approached the lowlands of the valley, little stores and gas stations began to crop up.

Driving into the business district, Rose was impressed with the old buildings. It was not like the updated shops of Rehoboth Beach. Each year there seemed to be new shops and restaurants in the resort town, with its extensive remodeling. In Elmira, most of the buildings hadn't been remodeled for fifty years.

The narrow streets had been widened as much as the buildings would allow. The sidewalks were wedged between the curbs and the buildings. Funny old stop lights swayed overhead at each intersection midst the wires and utility poles. Half the parking meters were empty. In her resort town, the parking meters were full during the season or removed during the off season.

Bud parked and they walked around his old home town. Bud showed her a few of his old haunts on the way to a restaurant. The facade of the restaurant had been remodeled in blue glass, back when that was the rage in the thirties. Stepping in on a worn linoleum floor, Bud picked out a booth. Vinyl seats had been in vogue and had held up well. They ordered a sandwich while Bud told her about the things he'd done when he was young.

After lunch, Bud drove to his mother's house. They left the business district and turned into a residential area. Each house was different. Through the years, each house had sprouted out of the ground, one at a time, like the volunteer trees in a mature forest. Most of them had wide porches. Large shade trees lined the streets.

Bud parked in front of a two-story, brown shingle house with a porch across the width of the front. Two enormous maple trees were crowded between the side walk and the curb. A teenage boy sitting on the porch, jumped up, calling out, "Bud's here!" He ran down to the sidewalk as Bud came around the car.

"Hi, Tinny," Bud said, going around to the passenger side of the car. "There's someone I want you to meet." He opened the door for Rose and said, "Rose, say hello to Justin, Junior, my half-brother. Tinny, this is Rose Gardner, my fiancee."

Rose said, "Hello, Justin," as he smiled and awkwardly nodded his head, digging his toe into the ground. The front door burst open as Bud's mother ran down the porch steps with her arms outstretched.

"Oh, Bud, is it really you?" she cried out.

"Hi, Mom," Bud said. There was great comfort in his mother's arms and they stood there too long, leaving Tinny and Rose knowing what to do with their hands. "Oh, I almost forget the most important part," Bud said, turning to Rose. "Mom, I want you to meet Rose Gardner."

"Welcome, Rose," she said. "Come on in. Bud's been gone so long, and I've been worrying about him, but I see that he's in good hands." Rose couldn't get a word in edgewise as the others followed into the house. "Do you have time to sit and talk for a little while?"

Bud broke in, "Mom, we've come to see you, especially. For you, we have all the time in the world."

"It's so good to meet you, Mrs. Tyme," Rose said.

"Why don't you call me Gloria and I'll call you Rose?"

"I'd like that. I've been taught to address my elders with a respectful Mr. or Mrs. It's a hard habit to change, but I'd like a special name for you," Rose said sincerely.

"Well, that's settled," Gloria said. "Let's take a cool drink out to the garden and sit a while."

"Sounds good to me," Bud said, leading the way to the kitchen. They all went for a tall, cold lemonade and carried it out, down the back steps. A cement walk wound around the house. A two-car detached garage sat on the back of the lot. A stockade fence from the back of the garage to the neighbor's garage made the yard private. Flowers were blooming between the garages.

Bud stepped out on the manicured grass to the lawn chairs at the garden end of the lot. They all took chairs and sat down.

"Where is your sister?" Bud asked Tinny.

"Nancy went shopping with another girl," Tinny said. "She'll be back soon."

"I worried about you, Bud, when you didn't come home last year," Gloria said to Bud. "Seemed as if you had just dropped out of sight."

"I did," he stated.

"I guess you and Rose had better things to do. I've been hearing about your engagement," Gloria added.

"It wasn't me," Rose spoke up. "It was an old farmhouse like Gramp's."

"I don't understand," Gloria said.

"I had to find myself," Bud said. "It's a long story."

"Will you tell me about it, Bud?" Gloria asked.

"I was fed up with the shenanigans and hoopla of politics in Washington," he attempted to explain.

"What do you mean?" she asked.

"I went there to work for World Peace. They used me as a status symbol for a while, to make it look like they're doing good things. They pretended to be interested in World Peace, but didn't even read my report on it. The election year turned into a war of negative advertising and mudslinging. When I handed in my lengthy report on World Peace, they switched me to the abortion issue. I was very disillusioned by the political power struggles. I was about ready to quit, when my senator lost the election."

"I was sorry to hear that," Gloria said.

"Don't be sorry. It's the best thing that ever happened to me. When Gramp suggested I work within the system, I was a wide-eyed fanatic. My work wasn't really wasted, because I learned something about the system," Bud said.

"What system?" she asked.

"Politics is local. It's the grass roots that count. This country isn't run from the top down. Democracy works from the bottom up. Had to take the time to look inside myself. I'm working on World Peace, one person at a time, starting with myself," he said.

"You just dropped out of society?" Gloria exclaimed. "We were so proud of you working on the senate staff. And now you've run away to the boondocks! You left the nation's capital for the grass roots? What's so important about the grass roots?"

"Grass roots are the rural voters," Bud replied. "Most of them are rugged individualists who think for themselves and live their lives the way they believe is right. Many fundamental ideas start there. A good idea grows up like an oak tree. It starts as a tiny acorn, rooting in the local soil. As a shoot grows up toward the sun, it adjusts to the environment. As it grows stronger, it branches out in all directions, reaching for the sky. All these refinements bloom into an elaborate filigree of ideas blended together. There is no room in a big city for this type of growth. The sophisticated hi-tech media call this 'local color,' but it's the main part of the show."

"You sound like a fanatic about the grass roots. Are you happy in

GRASS ROOTS

Rehoboth Beach?" Gloria wondered.

"I sure am," he assured her. "You see, the migrating birds are lured by the grain left in the farm fields by the mechanized reapers. The ocean lures the tourists. We have both kinds of wildlife. The flyways bring the water fowl and the highways bring the beach towels."

Tinny broke in, asking, "What about the old farmhouse?"

Rose said, "Maybe I can tell you about that. Last summer, Bud and I went to dinner. When he came to pick me up, he saw our mobile home across the lane from our old farmhouse. He said we should fix up the old farmhouse and live there. I told him it was too cold and drafty and he could live there if he's so smart. Well he came down, in the dead of winter, moved in and started to fix up the old farmhouse. He said it was helping him fix himself up. Now he's running a business from the old farmhouse and he's still living there."

"It's hard to explain," Bud said, "but I had to get back to basics."

"Why didn't you just come home, Bud?" Gloria asked. "Justin and I have told you, you're always welcome here."

"Mom, I had to do this myself. I didn't want to bring my troubles home and dump them on you. I had to get away by myself and start over the right way."

"I know you want to have a life of your own, but you don't have to return as a big success. You can always come home. Home is the place you can go when you need help," Gloria reminded him.

"This time I had to do it myself. The best medicine for me, at that time, was fixing up that old farmhouse," Bud replied.

"Sounds crazy, but it worked," Rose added. "The old place looks better than ever and Bud's business is doing well."

"What kind of business is it?" Gloria asked.

Bud said, "It's called Mr. Fixit. I fix anything that goes wrong around the house. Our slogan is, 'The better homes you see, have our TLC,' Most of my jobs are referrals from real estate offices."

"Is <u>that</u> what you want to do for a living?" Gloria asked.

"I've found happiness with my new way of life. Some homes look better than others, only because they are well cared for. I don't believe in trashing everything when it's broken. It's easy to fix most things, if you just take the time to do it. I took the time to fix myself. I like my new way of life."

"Maybe you could fix my bike," Tinny said.

"Okay, Tinny," Bud said. "If you ladies will excuse us, I'll take a look at it."

"I'm beginning to get the idea," Gloria said. "Go right ahead and let's see what you can do."

" He can do anything," Rose said.

"He has always been able to do anything, if he puts his mind to it," Gloria said.

"I know."

"He looks so much like his father. I worry about Bud a lot. He never knew his father, but he adores his grandfather. It's wonderful to see him looking so well. Thank you for taking such good care of him," Gloria said, firmly squeezing Rose's hand.

"He's been taking care of himself. We're just starting our lives together."

"Oh, Rose, here I am talking about myself. May I see your ring?" Rose got up and held out her hand. "It's lovely. Have you set a date?"

"No, we haven't," Rose said "I'm starting my career in real estate and I'm not ready to make a commitment, but Bud wanted me to come home with him to meet you. He gave me the ring to wear on the trip. Bud is the dearest person I've ever known and I wanted to meet you too, so, here we are."

"Thanks for bringing him home. I don't see much of Bud anymore," Gloria said, looking wistful ."How long can you stay?"

"We've been working so hard, that we haven't had much time together. We've taken a week off. We wanted to do this right, but I feel as if we're rushing into it."

"There never seems to be enough time for the things we want to do. I guess I can't complain when Bud takes the time to do what he wanted to do."

"Hey, Mom!" Tinny called out, "Bud fixed my bike." He was riding in circles in the driveway as Bud studied the mechanism.

"That will do for a while," Bud said "When I'm in town, I'll try to pick up a new pedal."

" Thank you, Bud," Gloria said, "for fixing Tinny's bike."

"That was fun," Bud said. "Now, what can I fix for you."

"You'll be sorry if I give you the list of things that need to be fixed around here," Gloria chuckled.

GRASS ROOTS

"Well, you better get out your list. Mr. Fixit is here now."

Gramp appeared, striding across the lawn, "Who's Mr. Fixit?"

"Hello, Gramp," Rose said. "Bud is Mr. Fixit. That's what his business is called."

"Well, Mr. Fixit, do you think you could fix me a lemonade? Gramp asked.

"Coming right up, Gramp," Bud said, jogging into the house.

"Well, Tinny, that's some bike," Gramp said.

"It's not new. Bud just fixed it for me," Tinny said.

"Better put it in the garage, so Dad doesn't run over it, Gloria said. Gramp kissed Gloria hello and sat down, as Bud brought his lemonade. Rose watched her new family with delight.

A car drove in the driveway and Justin waved out the window as he drove into the garage. He soon came out smiling at the company. A tall, slender man walked meekly toward the little group on the lawn. "Hello, everybody," Justin said, shyly. "This is a real treat having Bud here."

Bud jumped up and shook his hand, saying, "It's so good to see you again. May I present my fiancee, Rose Gardner? Rose, this is Justin Tyme, my stepfather."

"How do you do, Mr. Tyme," Rose said, standing up.

As Rose stood up, Justin offered her his hand. "It's a pleasure to meet you, Miss Gardner."

Gloria broke into their conversation, "Justin. We call him Justin."

"All right, Justin," Rose said, "Please call me Rose."

Justin, being too shy to kiss his wife in front of the guests, put his hand on her shoulder. "If you'll excuse me," he said, "I'll freshen up before dinner."

"We'll eat when your daughter gets home," Gloria said. "She's been shopping with a girl friend all afternoon."

"That's fine," he said, going in.

"She is her daddy's little girl," Gloria said. "She can get away with murder with him. Justin loves her too much. Spoils her rotten."

"There's a fine line between spoiled and loved," Gramp spoke up. "I think she is a lovely young lady."

"Oh, Gramp," Gloria said, "You just like anything that wears a skirt. You men are all the same."

"Now, I won't interfere with the way you bring up your children.

You do a wonderful job. But all men aren't the same. Archie was quite unusual, but he was nothing like Justin. I don't know how we could have gotten along without Justin."

"You're so right, Gramp," Gloria said. "I don't know how we could ever get along without you. You've been a pillar of wisdom for all of us." Gloria stood up as she said this and as she started for the door, "I'll see about dinner."

"Can I help," Rose said.

"No, dear. Thank you, but we have to wait for her royal highness to wander home," she said, imitating a lollygagging stroll into the house as everybody laughed.

As Nancy came lollygagging up the driveway, Gramp said, "Well, have you bought out the town."

Nancy's face beamed, when she saw Gramp and Bud sitting out in the lawn chairs. "Hi, Gramp! And Bud!" She rushed up to Gramp and threw her arms around him.

"Your big brother has come to see you," Gramp said.

"I missed you, Bud," she said shyly. "Where have you been for so long?"

"I've been to Washington, DC and told them how to run the country. Then, I went to the Nation's Summer Capital and decided that I like it so well I am going to make my home there. When you get a little older, you can come and visit us," Bud said.

"Us?" Nancy asked.

"Oh, sorry, Rose," Bud said. "Nancy, I want you to meet a special friend of mine, Rose Gardner. Rose, this is the famous Nancy Tyme."

"Hello, Nancy," Rose said, "I know we'll be good friends, if you're half as nice as your big brother."

"That's swell," Nancy said.

"I'll tell your mother you're home," Rose said, going in to help Gloria. She liked the easy way Bud's relatives got along with each other and she loved what Bud had told them. Something special had happened to her in the Tyme garden.

Rose found Gloria in the kitchen holding a large silver tray full of crystal stemware filled with ice water. "Here, let me do that," Rose said, "I'll put one at each place on the table." Rose carefully took the tray, adding, "Nancy's home."

Carrying the tray into the dining room, she was surprised to see so many elegant things. The ornate sideboard was covered with lovely silver pieces: a large coffee urn with a sugar bowl and creamer, tall candlesticks matching the ones on the table, candy dishes and other embellishments. There was a florid L on each one, for Gloria's family name, Lipschidts.

Gloria had dutifully polished them herself .They had come from a grander house that must have had servants. Rose carefully placed a glass at each place. She paused to admire the room for a brief moment and took the silver tray back to the kitchen.

"You have a beautiful dining room," Rose said, "with so many nice things."

"Mother and father have given us some of the things I grew with. Justin loves having them all set out."

"They are so beautiful. Bud never mentions your mother and father," Rose blurted out. "I want to get their address?"

"I know, dear," Gloria said softly. "Mother didn't approve of my marriage to Bud's father. When Archie died, as Bud was born, mother couldn't stand it. She's never gotten over it to this day." Gloria's eyes watered as she went back over her life.

"I'm sorry," Rose said "I didn't mean to upset you."

"I wanted to tell you," Gloria said, wiping her eyes on her apron.

"Where do they live?" Rose again asked.

"Michigan. Daddy died in a boating accident four years ago. '"I'll get you mother's address. You should have it."

"That's thoughtful of you."

"Well, I think the dinner's ready."

"I'll call everyone in," Rose said as Justin appeared at the kitchen door.

"You ladies are busy in the kitchen," Justin said. "Let me tell them you are ready." He went out the back door and everyone came trooping in to the dining room. In the dining room, Justin stood behind Gloria's chair, waiting for her to be seated. When she was ready, he pulled out her chair for her and pushed her chair up to the table. Gramp pulled out Nancy's chair, while Bud seated Rose. Tinny waited until Justin was ready to sit down and they sat down simultaneously. It was a natural ritual that just seemed to happen.

Gloria put her napkin in her lap and looked at Justin. He bowed his head and said, in rich theatrical tones,

"Bless this food to our use,
And bless us to thy service.
We thank you for our guests,
Rose and Bud. Amen."

Gloria immediately picked up her fork and put a bite of food in her mouth, signaling everyone else to start eating. Nancy and Tinny dove into their dinner as everyone took a bite of food.

Justin said, in his regular, soft voice, "Bud, what are you doing these days?"

"I maintain vacation cottages and businesses. My company is Mr. Fixit. I fixed Tinny's bike and I understand Mom has a list of things I can fix for you while I'm here."

"I was just teasing you, Bud," Gloria said. "Rose doesn't want to stand around and watch you fix things while you're here."

"Rose is off to a flying start in a real estate career," Bud said.

"Do you like living in a resort area?" Justin went on.

"Rehoboth Beach reminds me of Elmira for nine months of the year and Washington, DC for the other three months. Our work and play schedule is dictated by the weather, the migration of geese, and tourists. It's Mother Nature's wonderland."

"Glad you like it. You both you look healthy and happy."

"How are things going for you, Justin?" Bud asked .

"Very nicely, thank you. I enjoy my work. Gloria is a joy to be with and Nancy and Tinny are keeping me young."

The dinner went well with Justin quietly presiding at the head of the table, and Gloria supervising at the other end. Gramp sat between the youngsters, across from Rose and Bud. Tinny said, "Nancy says my haircut makes me look like a nerd."

Gramp spoke up, "We all have an idea inside our head about what we are like." Gramp was a good story teller, so they all listened quietly. "I think of myself as being young and virile, until I try to do something strenuous, like stand up." They all laughed. "Then I'm rudely reminded of my age."

Rose and Bud enjoyed the pleasant formalities. The Tyme family had taken Rose into the family with a warm welcome. After dinner, Gramp said, "I think I'll mosey along. I've got young company to see to."

"We'll follow you out to the farm," Bud said.

"Thank you for the lovely dinner and warm hospitality," Rose said to Gloria and Justin. "Nice to meet you, Tinny and Nancy."

"Thanks for coming," Gloria said. "Hope we see more of you while you are here."

"Get out that list for Mr. Fixit," Bud said, heading for the door.

"Go on with you," Gloria laughed.

Bud and Rose followed Gramp's big car as he drove over the dark, winding road back to the farm. When they were back at the farm, Gramp said, "Good night, sleep well and I'll see you in the morning at breakfast." Bud and Rose went upstairs together. Bud turned to kiss her good night.

"You have a lovely family, darling," she said, giving him a warm kiss and a hug. "It's been a wonderful day for me," she, closing her door.

Bud went to the bathroom to clean his teeth. It was good to be home, but he missed the old farmhouse. He went back to his room, alone, as usual. He hung up his clothes, put on the new pajamas he had bought for the trip, and hopped in bed.

Lying there, he reviewed the events of the day. His mother was happy with her family. Justin was a good provider and a loving father. Tinny and Nancy were neat kids.

He was startled by the squeak of a door knob. His bedroom door quietly opened and closed, as he peered at the darkness. A soft voice whispered, "Bud, may I come in and talk?"

It's Rose! He sat up in bed, whispering, "I'm over here."

He held out his hand and her soft touch sent a thrill of excitement through his veins. She sat down beside him on the bed, "Something's happened. I want to tell you about it."

"Please do," he whispered.

There was an endless pause. Finally she cleared her throat squeezed his hand, resettled herself, and whispered, "I have made a monumental decision."

"And what's that?"

"I love what you told your family. I love your family for being so kind. Oh, Bud, I love you." She threw her arms around him and they fell back on the bed in a warm embrace.

Bud was so happy he was beside himself. He didn't know what to say. He blurted out, "You are the girl of my dreams. I hope I'm not dreaming now."

"A long time ago, on the beach, you asked me if I wanted to go out with you. I said I'd let you know, when you make your move. Well, I've come to a decision. I've decided that I want to spend the rest of my life with you."

"Oh, Rose, don't wake me up. That's the best news I have ever heard."

"You're not dreaming, darling, and neither am I," she said, as they snuggled, tenderly together. "I rumpled up my bed, so Gramp will think I slept there."

HARDSCRABBLE

The next morning Gramp was fixing pancakes and sausage as Bud and Rose came down together, wearing enormous grins.

"What have you two been up to?" Gramp said. "First you sleep late and when you finally come down, you are grinning like a couple of silly jack-o'-lanterns."

"We're on vacation," Bud explained, "and we are so happy to be here with you."

"See how he is, Rose," Gramp said. "He should run for office. He could dodge any question and charm the pants off the voters at the same time."

"He's been campaigning against negative advertising," Rose said. "What are you fixing on the stove?"

"A hearty breakfast for all three of us, something that'll stick to your ribs," Gramp replied.

"Smells great," Bud said as he pulled out a kitchen chair for Rose.

Gramp had the table all set. As he served Rose and Bud a short stack and some sausage, he said, "Our government has led me to believe that food causes cancer. I think they're trying to make us paranoid. They don't know what farm-fresh food tastes like. There's more in this covered platter in the middle of the table. Go easy on the maple syrup. It is the real thing. Not the watered down concoction they sell in stores." Sitting down, he asked, "What are your plans for today?"

"Like to hang around here today," Bud said. "Maybe we can help you around the farm."

"Sounds good to me," Rose added.

"Don't need anything done, but you're welcome to do whatever you like around here," Gramp said.

"I'd like to take Rose up to Hardscrabble," Bud said.

"I left it open. I just came back when I heard you were coming. I may go back again for a short stay after you've gone, before I close it down for the winter."

"What's Hardscrabble?" Rose asked.

"Name of Gramp's camp in the Adirondacks. It's not like any-place else. You'd have to go there to see what it's like."

"Is it far from here?"

Gramp said, "Day's drive from here if you poke along the way I do. Limekiln Lake is near Fourth Lake in the Fulton Chain."

"Fulton Chain's a series of lakes numbered from First Lake through Eighth Lake. The Boy Scouts have canoe trips there, following the old guide paths. There are short portages between some of the lakes," Bud explained.

""When do you want to go?" Rose asked.

"Any time you want to, but I didn't leave any food there, Gramp said. "When you get there, guess you'll have to rough it."

"Let's go tomorrow morning," Bud said. "We can stay over-night in open-camp and come back the next day."

"Sounds like fun," Rose said. "I'd love to see Gramp's camp, where you used to go in the summer."

"I'll fix you a good breakfast," Gramp said. "Don't want you driving on an empty stomach. Now run along and let me get my kitchen cleaned up the way I like it."

Bud and Rose went out for a walk in Gramp's fields. The air was invigorating and they walked along a path around a field that was ready to harvest. On the far side they stopped to rest by the fence.

"Lets go back a day or two early," Bud said, "so you can tell me how you want the upstairs of the old farmhouse fixed up?"

"I'd forgotten about the old farmhouse."

"It's your new home. It's easy to fix when I'm there alone. Now, you have to decide how you want your home to be, as the lady of the house."

"I don't know about that!" Rose said indignantly.

"Did I say something wrong?"

"Just the terminology. I'm not sure I want the privilege of the title, Lady of the House. The privilege of cleaning the toilets goes with the title."

"I plan to do my share of the housework. If we just take our time and keep trying, I know it will work."

Rose became moody and walked off by herself. Bud found her staring off into space. When he spoke to her, she ignored him and didn't answer. When he tried to comfort her with an embrace, she turned away.

"Something's bothering you!" he insisted. "We have to talk about it!" His tone of voice showed anger and worry.

Softly, she said, "I don't know how to say it."

"That's better," he said. "Thought you'd lost your voice."

After a pregnant pause, she began to ramble, "I feel lost. I didn't want to give up my career for wifely duties. "I'm not ready to stay home and take care of you."

" I'm not asking you to take care of me," Bud said "I've always been able to take care of myself. You can go on with your career. We can work on our careers together."

"Marriage is a serious move for me," Rose explained. "I'm an old-fashioned girl."

"Thought you were a modern liberated career woman," he said.

"I'm a liberated woman when it comes to my career, but I'm an old-fashioned girl when it comes to raising a family. I just don't know what to do."

"When the cookies are passed, pause and take one," Bud said.

"What's that supposed to mean?"

"It's just a funny saying that grandma used to tell me, when I didn't know what to do. I think it means you only go around once. Don't pass up an opportunity."

"Seeing you with your family has changed my view of life and messed up my goals. I don't know if marriage is an opportunity or a dead end."

"You're afraid a family will interfere with your career and I'm afraid my career will interfere with my being there for my children. Now that we have it out in the open, I'm sure we can work it out."

"Well, I do like your family," she said, beginning to smile.

"And I like an old-fashioned girl with modern ideas. It won't be a dead end for either of us, if we both keep trying."

Making up with an embrace, the warmth of each other's arms united their conflicting dreams in a fusion of love. The embrace after the conflict was the icing on the cookies.

Early the next morning, they set out to see the summer scene of New York state. Bud drove north on rural back roads toward the Finger Lakes. Rose was delighted with the picturesque little towns and rolling hills. The finger lakes were civilized, with road houses offering food, drinks, and entertainment. There were still some tourists in the off-season, but nothing like the ocean crowd. There were cozy cottages set in the woods around each lake. Swimming, boating, and camping were still going on. Water sports and relaxing seemed to be the top priorities.

It was a long drive, so they just rubber-necked through the resort areas. As they finally approached the larger mountains of the Adirondacks, the scenery was even more spectacular. The early September weather was invigoratingly chilly.

Bud stopped in Old Forge to buy food for breakfast. "When we get there, we have to carry our things on our backs for about a mile, unless we can rent a canoe. Maybe we should eat an early dinner first, while we are in civilization," Bud suggested.

"Might be an interesting restaurant over there. Looks like an old trading post," Rose said, motioning towards the building.

They went into the barn-like rustic building. The chairs and tables were made of bent tree branches. In the Adirondack style of bentwood furniture, the branches still had the bark on them. They found a table and ordered the special.

Rose loved the camping atmosphere. "This is where they come to get back to nature," Rose said. "You should have come here to get back to basics."

"Thought about it, but it's too far to go. It's too close to home. I had to get away somewhere by myself."

"Glad you came to Delaware."

"So am I."

After dinner, they stopped in a little grocery and picked up enough food for a simple breakfast and headed up the road. Just after Fourth Lake, Bud turned off on a road that went up a large mountain. Bud shifted to a lower gear to climb the steep winding road. He left the car in low gear as they started down the steep road on the other side. As they rounded a sharp curve, the large lake lay dead ahead, framed by the trees on each side of the dirt road. Coming down a steep slope, it looked as if they were going to drive right down into the lake. Bud turned sharply the last minute and parked in a parking lot behind a cottage that served as a store and canoe rental for the lake people.

"Thought you were going to drive into the lake," Rose said.

"Yes. The first time I came here as a child, I felt the same way. When Gramp first came here there was no road. He had to walk over the mountain."

"That's what people mean when they talk about wilderness,"

"That's what Gramp liked about it. Leave our things in the car and I'll show you the lake and see about renting a canoe."

Bud led the way around the building, down a path toward the lake. The well-worn path was covered with pine needles and led through a grove of evergreens. Rose cried out, "Ouch!" as she stubbed her toe on a tree root that had grown across the path.

Bud turned and caught her as she stumbled. "Every time I came up here, I tripped on a tree root growing across the path. It's nature's way of getting my attention. I'd stop and inspect the root, rubbing my sore toe. Then my gaze would follow the root to the trunk of the tree and up to its majestic branches raised to the heavens. As I looked around for blueberries, a contentment settled over me."

Safe in Bud's arms, Rose examined the tree root and the tall pole of the tree trunk. Gazing at the high branches reaching out for the sun, she gave his arm a gentle squeeze. "You're my pail of blueberries," she said with a contented smile.

As he led her to the lake, the path dissolved into a narrow, sandy beach. Gentle waves lapped along the shore, as they walked out on the dock. "The water is so clear, I can see the bottom," Rose said.

"Limekiln Lake is spring fed. You can drink the water, but I'll get a bottle of well water for you."

"Thank you."

"Here I'll show you where we're going," he said. "See the sandy beach? Well, Gramp's camp is on the point at the far end of the beach.

RICHARD C. HARRISON

The sandy beach curved in a gentle arc from the parking lot to Gramp's camp on the point. Rustic cabins nestled back in the trees along the beach. The rest of the shore line was irregular and uninhabited. Miles of crystal-clear water stretched to tree-lined banks. Lush foliage rose from the deep lake, up steep mountains to the sky. Little ripples of blue water on the lake reflected the trees with a wavy mirror image. White, paper birch trees punctuated the virgin timber here and It reminded her of a picture in her schoolbook about Indians in a canoe, covered with birch bark, held together and sealed with pine tar.

Bud came out, saying, "They are bringing out our canoe. Let's get our things out of the car." As they walked back up the path, Bud said, "Watch out for tree roots in the path." By the time they had gathered their things, the canoe was at the dock. Bud stepped into the canoe and Rose handed him the gear.

As the rental man handed Rose a paddle, she said, "You'll have to teach me how to paddle a canoe."

"I'll teach you tomorrow," he said. "Just lay the paddle near the front of the canoe. We used to say, 'I'll sit in back, was the stern reply.' I'll do all the paddling for now. This canoe is very tippy, so when you step in, put your foot in the middle. I'll steady the canoe for you until you are seated."

Rose climbed in with apprehension. Each little tip sent her adrenaline rushing to her nervous system. "Be careful back there. I don't want to turn turtle," she said nervously.

"Hadn't planned on turning over. Sit back and relax. We're just going down the beach to Gramp's camp. Better than walking," Bud said, pushing off from the dock and waving good-bye to the rental agent. He paddled quietly out into the tranquil lake.

"When I was young, we used to go around that far point in the evening, to watch the deer come down for a drink. We had to be very quiet and paddle softly, so as not to scare the deer." Bud easily paddled the length of the beach and pulled up at the last dock. "I'll steady the canoe while you get out," he said. When Rose was on the dock, he handed her the gear.

He got out, pulled the canoe up on the sand and turned it over for the night. They picked up their things and Bud led the way up a path between granite boulders and sturdy trees. The point rose about ten feet above the beach.

Bud went up on the porch of a barn-like building. A rustic sign, fashioned of sticks with the bark still on them, spelled HARDSCRABBLE.

Rose said, "In Delaware, there is a crossroads called 'Hardscrabble.' I never knew what it meant."

"Never looked it up, but the name says it," Bud said as he fished through as little hole by the door.

What are you doing?"

"Fishing for the latch string," he said, as he pulled a string through the hole "Remember when friendly invitations used to say, 'The latch string is out.'" He pulled the string and the door opened. Rose looked at the latch. A board, worn smooth with use, was raised on one end by the string, lifting it out of its wooden latch.

They went in and looked around. The exposed rafters of the mansard roof gave an airy effect of a cathedral ceiling. Rose looked in wonder at the wood burning, iron cook stove. Nearby was Gramp's rocking chair. There was a little table, between the chair and the stove, with wooden "stick" matches and a large metal ash tray. On the other side of the stove there was a dining table with chairs and a hanging kerosene lamp. Kerosene lamps with concave, mirror reflectors and sparkling clean globes were hung on the walls between the windows. The single beds against the wall had studio couch type covers with cushions against the wall for back rest.

"Shall we light the lamps before it gets dark?" Rose asked.

"Gramp never wanted lamps lit until after twilight. If we light them, we'll have to wash the globes. Let's sleep in the open-camp. I'll build a campfire and I brought two flashlights."

Bud led the way out the back door. "This pump on the back porch has to be primed to pump lake water. We don't need to use it for such a short stay."

"Gramp said we would have to rough it," Rose said, looking at the carefully stacked stove wood.

"Speaking of roughing it, there're two paths from the porch. The one, going up the hill, leads to the privy. It's a two-holer. The other path, leading down by the lake, leads to open-camp. Let's go down and settle in," Bud said, leading the way.

Rose stubbed her toe on another root, because she was full of curiosity about the open-camp down by the lake. She caught her balance and pretended her toe didn't hurt. *When you're hit by the pitcher, you trot easily to first base, pretending it didn't hurt*, she thought.

Open-camp was an Adirondack lean-to, with the sides and back made of large logs. The front was open, facing the lake. The roof rose from three feet in the back to seven feet at the front, with a three-foot overhang tapering down in front. There was an enormous log across the base of the front, to climb over or sit on. In front of the log structure there was a circular clearing with a mound of old wood ashes in the center.

Bud collected some kindling wood, while Rose went into the open-camp to inspect their quarters. There were balsam boughs for a mattress and room for a row of sleeping bags. Through the years there had been initials, names, and dates carved in the logs. She spread out their sleeping bags and arranged their supplies. When Bud reappeared with a load of firewood, she asked, "What are these names and initials carved in the logs?"

"Mostly deer hunters," Bud said. "They come through here in the winter when nobody's here. Open-camp is what they call an Adirondack shelter. It's a welcome sight when you've been tracking through the snow all day. Gramp can always tell if they've been here, when he opens the camp in the spring. Gramp's been here in the winter and he doesn't mind if they use it."

"People come up here in the winter?"

"Gramp tells a story about a man who brought his son up here to rough it. The boy rolled a snowball for a pillow and settled down for the night. The father kicked the snowball away, saying, 'I said we were roughing it.'"

Rose laughed and said, "We don't have to go out of our way to be uncomfortable. Our shelter is really cozy and the view of the lake through the trees is enchanting. The air is fresh and stimulating," she said, pulling on her sweater.

Bud built a campfire as Rose sat on a log and stared at the flames. The fire climbed through the twigs and licked the thin kindling sticks. The smoke curled up through the enormously tall pine trees. She watched the sparks swirl up through the smoke, to the highest branches and fade out. "Don't set the woods on fire while we're here," she said.

"I'm an old hand at this," Bud said. "Gramp likes to put cedar bows on the fire to make a fireworks display. It's like a bunch of fire flies, swirling up into the trees, doing a dazzling dance. It's spectacular, but you'll have to settle for an ordinary campfire to-night."

The sun was setting on the farthest mountain and the dancing flames began to light their little area. Bud came over and sat beside her. "We used to come up here every summer. The peaceful isolation has always been precious to me. It's never lonely in these woods. Beavers and chipmunks are busy enjoying nature's wonderland. The deer stop by and stare, before hightailing it through the trees. An occasional bear looks you over before you both run off."

"Are there any bears around here?"

"You'll never see one. They're more afraid of you than you are of them."

"The fresh air has put roses in your cheeks."

"I've been active, gathering the wood. Every spring, Gramp walked through his three acres and selected a tree for the year's stove wood. He and I'd cut it down with a two-man, voom-pah saw, one on each side of the tree. It was hard work, but I was lured by the chance to yell timbeeeeer! Then we trimmed off the limbs with an axe and propped it up for sawing. Gramp measured the lengths with a stick and we sawed the logs with the two-man saw, Bud remembered fondly. "After we rolled the sawed logs down to the chopping area, we split them with a splitting wedge and an axe. Then we piled them up to dry in what Gramp called cob houses. We worked every morning till we were tired and then took off for a swim."

"Sounds like a lot of hard labor."

"It's a labor of love, because Grandma could cook cookies, pies, and cakes in the wood stove and I loved that. I wanted her to have all the firewood she needed. It was a hardscrabble, but we knew she was taking care of the kitchen, while we labored."

"I won't have much time to work in the kitchen and work in the real estate office."

"I've been doing my own house work and working. If we share the housework, it will be easy. I don't want you to do anything differ-ently. You just have to be yourself."

She snuggled close to him, watching the magic of the fire. They sat there, in silence listening to the gentle waves lapping on the shore and the crackling of the campfire. In time, they took the quiet tranquility to bed with them.

Lying in his arms, Rose jumped, as an eerie, "Oohoohoohoo," came through the darkness. It was a plaintive wail.

"What's that?" she asked, with alarm.

"That's just a loon out on the lake. They call out to their mates at night."

"It sounds so spooky."

"Yes. They used to frighten me when I was very young."

As the gentle sounds of nature sang their little songs, they drifted off to a sound sleep in their cozy retreat.

The morning sun woke Rose. She looked around at her strange surroundings, wondering where she was. Sitting up, the sight of the lake through the trees comforted her. The campfire was just a pile of ashes. The morning air was crisp and still. The woods stood silently as tiny birds fluttered through the branches. A little mouselike creature with stripes down his back popped up on the front log. "Well, good morning," she said to the little creature as he sat up on his haunches, looking at her.

She was sitting there in her sleeping bag, marveling in the natural wonders, when Bud came around the corner. "Breakfast will be ready soon," he said "Did you sleep well?"

"I slept like a log. This place is divine. You scared away my little visitor."

"Just a chipmunk. Grandma had them eating out of her hand."

"He was wondering when I was going to get up. You were up, but I feel so lazy."

"Privy will clear your sinuses. I have some hot water up at Hardscrabble to wash with. We can have a swim after breakfast."

"Do I have to get up right now?" Rose asked. "I've been sitting here, drinking in nature's wonder."

"Don't have to do anything until we're ready."

Bud had slipped out of bed at the first rays of sunshine. After a trip to the smelly privy, he built a fire in the wood stove, got a pot of water from the lake, and put it on the stove. When it was hot, he shaved and washed up.

When Rose climbed up the path to the privy, he pulled the sleeping bags out to air in the sunshine and straightened up the open-camp. He was happy to be back in Gramp's camp, but it was beyond his wildest fantasies that he would be sharing it with the girl of his dreams.

When Rose appeared at Hardscrabble, Bud had the table set and the food ready. "Sit down and I'll give you some breakfast."

"This is a pleasant surprise," she said, pulling out a chair and settling down. "How did Gramp find this place?"

"He was in Old Forge as a young man when he saw an ad for acreage for sale in the mountains. There was a government topographical map of the area, with wavy lines for elevations. He looked at the map and picked out a point on the lake. They were selling the land for three dollars an acre, so he bought an acre, but he wanted to see the land. They sent him with a guide who carried his boat on his shoulders over the mountain on the other side of the lake. The guide rowed him three miles across the lake. Gramp liked what he saw, so they went back and he bought two more adjacent acres, for a total of nine dollars."

"How could he get back here?"

"He bought a guideboat and carried it over the mountain and rowed across. The guideboat is out in the boathouse. I'll show it to you after breakfast."

"Must have been really isolated in those days."

"Must have been. Gramp asked the guide to come back here and build him a shelter. The guide came back here with an ax and chopped down trees, notched them, and built open-camp with just an ax, all by himself. It was the first shelter on the lake. When they built the road and the cottages sprang up, Gramp liked the company, until someone brought in a motor boat. Gramp was furious. He said they would scare the deer away."

"What did he do?"

"He just pontificated quietly in his rocking chair. He told anyone who'd listen how he disliked labor-saving devices. His standard line was, 'The hardest work people do is breathing. When they invent a portable iron lung you can carry on your back, we won't even have to go to all the trouble of breathing.'"

"He is a marvelous philosopher and a delightful gentleman."

"He has been more than a father to me," Bud said seriously.

"You've been a wonderful son to him," Rose added.

Bud had never thought about that aspect before. They ate in silence, each wrapped up in their own thoughts. After breakfast, Bud took the dishes out on the back porch and washed and rinsed them, while Rose straightened up the table and the stove.

When she came out, Bud was feeding the table scraps to the chipmunk. "I see my friend followed us up here."

"Let's go look in the boathouse," Bud said, when the dishes were set out to dry. A long, narrow house, sided with vertical saplings, sat just to the side of Hardscrabble. Bud unlocked the door and they went in. There was a canoe, a rowboat, and the guideboat.

"I've never seen anything like that before," Rose said, as she looked over the guide boat.

It was longer and wider than a canoe. It was all handmade of wood and varnished to a high luster. The sides curved in and then down to a narrow flat bottom, wide enough for a shoe. "Look at all the little ribs."

"They're handmade from roots that have grown in that shape, so the grain will follow the curve," Bud reported. "It's very strong and light, so it'll hold a lot of supplies. Bud took a hand-carved wooden yoke from its hook on the wall. This is the yoke for portage over the mountains. It fits in these notches and is carved to fit the neck and shoulders of the guide. This is a real Adirondacks guideboat. The oars are like a racing scull. The curved blades and oar locks let you feather the oars on the back stroke."

"It is beautiful. . .A work of art."

"Glad you think so. I've learned about nature by studying the growth in the grain of the wood. What say we have a swim?"

"Sounds good to me."

They put on their swim suits and walked down to the beach. Rose stuck her toe in the water and flinched. "Oh, it's so cold. When does it warm up?"

"It doesn't. It's spring fed, but it is invigorating when you get in. I have to take a breathtaking dive off the dock, or it takes all day to wade out."

Bud went out and dove in as Rose stood with both ankles in the water, trying to get used to the cold water. Bud swam around as Rose inched her way out.

"Gramp used to tease the women about their swimming. They say they like to swim, but when they get in the water, they yell, 'Don't touch me!'"

"I can see what they mean." Rose had waded out above her waist and leaned forward into the water to swim. "It is nice once you get used to it."

After a good swim, they sat on the sandy beach in the morning sun. When they were dry, Bud said, "I hate to break the spell, but we better get started back soon."

"Oh, Bud, I'd stay here forever with you," Rose said. She stood up and they went to gather their things together. When they were ready, Bud checked all the doors and pushed the latch string back inside.

On the beach, he lined up their things on the side of the dock, flipped over the canoe, and pulled it into the water. When he was in the canoe, Rose handed him the gear. He steadied the canoe while she stepped in carefully. They felt like old hands.

"When are you going to teach me to paddle?"

"Next time. Just relax and I'll give you a scenic ride," he replied. Bud maneuvered the canoe with expert strokes. They slipped easily along and docked back at the rental dock. Rose hopped out and they unloaded the gear. Bud was pulling the canoe up on the sand, when the man came out, saying, "You can just leave it right there. Did you have a good trip?"

"Smooth as glass," Bud said. "We'll be heading back."

"Give my regards to your grandfather," he called out as they retraced their steps to the parking lot.

Bud drove straight back to the farm, except for a stop for lunch. As Rose surveyed the scenery, everything had a new but familiar meaning to her, after their camping experience. She had a new appreciation for the modern conveniences, but she would always remember the quiet of the wilderness.

RICHARD C. HARRISON

PART SEVEN
BACK TO WORK

When they told Gramp that they were going back a day early, he wanted to have the rest of the family out to dinner. "We can have everybody come out after church on Sunday, for a day on the farm," Gramp suggested, "and have an afternoon Sunday dinner."

"What can I do to help," Rose asked, "and don't say you have it all ready, because we're planning it now."

"All right, young lady," Gramp said, "Bud and I will be the kitchen help and you can give us instructions."

"She's an outstanding cook," Bud said. "This ought to work our well."

"Well, show me what you have to work with," Rose said, going to the kitchen. "Bud and I can go to the store and pick up whatever we will need. Gramp, you can handle the invitations."

"I'll call Gloria right now to make sure they are coming."

Gramp called and got an enthusiastic response, while Rose looked over the raw materials. Rose planned a banquet and made a list for the store. She loved to cook and welcomed the chance to display her talents to her new family. It gave her something to do and she took the challenge with gusto.

"Bud, will you drive me to the food store, I want to pick up a couple of things," she asked.

That gave Bud a chance to participate. He came out saying, "It will be my pleasure." They hopped in the car and drove off. Bud went with her while she made careful selections like an old pro. When they pushed the cart up to the check out counter, Bud reached for his wallet.

"Oh, no, you don't!" Rose said. "I'm paying for this."

"Yes, ma'am," Bud said, letting her have her way. He was allowed to wheel the groceries to the car, and when they got home, he was allowed to carry in the bags. Rose unpacked the bags while Bud went back for the others.

"Now, what can I help you with in the kitchen?" Bud asked after he had carried in all the grocery bags.

"I'll let you know when I need some help," Rose said, busy with the groceries. "Why don't you and Gramp just relax until I need you? I promise to put you both to work as soon as I get it straight in my mind."

Bud went into the front parlor and sat down, looking around at all the mementos from his childhood. He pulled a photo album off the book shelf and lost himself in memories. Drifting off to sleep, he dreamed of his childhood.

. . .He heard his grandmother in the kitchen, as he played with his toys in the parlor. . .

Gramp came into the kitchen, saying, "Rose, what can I do for you?"

"There is one thing I want you to do before I leave," Rose said. "Why don't you come over here and sit by me while I work? You said, when there was time, you'd tell me about Gloria's mother, Bud's other grandmother."

"Oh, dear. Well, all right. I try to be civil to Regina Lipschidts, because she's my in-law, or is she an outlaw?"

"She is Bud's other grandmother," Rose reminded Gramp.

"She's never acted like a grandmother to Bud," he snapped. "She didn't approve of Archie and refused to come to her daughter's wedding. Archie brought Gloria out to stay at the farm, when he was sent overseas. The Lipschidts were not happy when Bud went overseas, leaving Gloria on the farm and pregnant."

"Pregnant with Bud?" Rose asked.

"Yes," Gramp went on, trying to keep his cool. "Bud was born on the farm about the time his father died overseas. This finished off

Regina Lipschidts for good. We haven't seen her since. My wife, Liz, helped Gloria with the baby. As time went on, Liz sort of took over. Gloria wanted a place of her own, but the meager subsistence from the army wasn't enough to support her and the baby. Gloria found a job, while Liz took care of Bud.

"Oh dear," Rose sighed "And what happened then?"

"Gloria found a nice man named Justin Tyme. She invited him to the farm for dinner. Bud and Justin liked each other from the start. It wasn't long before Justin and Gloria left to visit her parents in Michigan. The Lipschidts approved of Justin and offered to foot the bills for the wedding. When they were married, they left Bud on the farm with us and went on a honeymoon.

"What a story," Rose said "Tell me more."

"Justin had purchased a house in Elmira, but when they came to pick up Bud, he didn't want to leave the farm. We all agreed that Bud could stay for a while. Soon, Gloria was pregnant and starting a new family. Regina visits the Tymes, but makes some excuse to leave when Bud comes to visit."

"That's awful! She doesn't know what she has missed."

"We never mention his other grandmother in front of Bud. Told you it was a long story, but I don't like the aftertaste. Let's change the subject. Talk about something nicer."

...Bud, asleep in the parlor, was dreaming that Gramp had come home and was talking to his grandmother in the kitchen. He slowly woke up to the sound of voices in the kitchen. ..

Rose was asking, "What time is church tomorrow?"

"If we go to the church in Elmira, the service is at eleven. I like the one with the choir and the sermon," Gramp said.

Bud got up and went into the kitchen. "We could all ride together in your big car," Bud suggested.

"I'll be leaving about ten-thirty," Gramp said, "so I can find a place to park. You both are welcome to come with me."

"We'll be ready," Rose said, speaking for Bud. She was full of her new roll of running the house from the kitchen.

After breakfast the next morning, they all rode in Gramp's big car into Elmira and parked near the church. As they got out, Rose admired the church. "It looks a lot like our old church in Rehoboth

Beach. It has a nice, familiar feel to it."

"Yes, it does, like the Rehoboth church where Thorn and Mary were married," Bud agreed.

Rose still wasn't used to the word "married," so she paused.

Gramp strode up to the church door to greet some friends. He turned and waited for Bud and Rose to join him, so he could proudly introduce the young couple to his old friends.

After several introductions, they started to go in, just as the Tymes came walking up. "Well, look who's here. Don't you look fine in your Sunday clothes this morning," Gramp called out and they all went in together. Sliding into an empty pew, they said a little prayer, each one taking a moment to themselves.

As they settled back in their seats, Rose whispered to Bud, "I feel right at home in this church."

"I felt that way in your church," Bud said, looking over the congregation in front of him. One man had on his Sunday clothes, but he hadn't finished combing his hair. His wife, anxious to be on time, had probably yelled at him, so he had rushed out.

The organ started the processional hymn and they rummaged for a hymnal. When the choir burst forth, Gramp's booming voice gave them a run for their money. To him, it wasn't a performance for an audience, they were all singing to God. Gloria looked embarrassed, but the children liked it and sang as loud as they could. Justin maintained his disciplined participation.

The church was small enough to hear the sermon without the boost of modern electronic amplification. Each person got the feeling that the preacher was chatting with them personally. The time went quickly and they found themselves, back out in the sunshine, feeling holy and proper.

The Tymes had to go home and change, but would be right out to the farm. Bud, Rose, and Gramp waved goodbye to them, calling out, "See you soon."

They greeted a few more of Gramp's friends and went back to the farm. Rose went to the kitchen and put on an apron. Bud and Gramp followed her in and asked what their assignments were.

"You can go change out of your Sunday best. Then you can set the table before the guests arrive."

They went off to change, while Rose got herself organized. She had put the turkey in to roast when she got up and it would be done soon. She decided to have the men take it out to cool on the sideboard when it was done. Gramp and Bud had fun setting the table and had time to check with Rose about their further duties before the company arrived.

The Tyme car pulled up to the farmhouse and the children burst forth at a gleeful run. Gloria called after them, "Now try not to get too dirty before dinner." Justin had dressed as casually as he ever does with a tweed jacket and a knit tie. Gramp and Bud welcomed Justin and Gloria into the parlor.

Rose popped in to say hello. Gloria asked, "What can I do to help?"

"Not a thing," Rose said proudly. "I have two assistants who are very capable. Besides, they know where everything is."

"May I come out and talk to you while you're working in the kitchen?" Gloria asked as she got up and started toward the door. Justin picked up the Sunday paper and Bud and Gramp went out to see what the children were up to.

They found Tinny and Nancy peeking into the barn, too timid to go in without an escort. Gramp caught up with them and took them in to show them around as Bud joined them. Nancy asked about everything, while Tinny tried to get into everything he should't have.

Bud said, "Tinny, want to shoot a few baskets?"

"Yeah," Tinny said enthusiastically.

Bud found the basketball and Tinny grabbed it out of his hand and ran out. Tinny ran around to the side of the barn where the hoop was, and started to shoot a basket. Bud ran in front of him, waving his arms and showing his best blocking form. "That's not fair," Tinny said.

"Come on," Bud teased, "dribble around until you find a chance to shoot."

"I can't."

"Okay. I'll give you a free shot." Tinny shot and the ball hit the rim. Bud grabbed the rebound and dribbled out to take a shot. "You have to try to block me."

"I don't know how."

"Okay I'll show you." They spent a long time rehearsing and practicing dodging, feigning, and fancy moves. They were still at it when Gloria called Tinny in to wash up for dinner.

Bud rushed upstairs to wash up and report for kitchen duty. "You can take these in and put them on the table," Rose said. The banquet was taking shape. Rose had outdone herself again.

As the guests drifted into the dining room, the men helped the ladies into their chairs and waited for Rose. As she took off her apron and sat down, Gloria said, "Isn't this a splendid display of delicacies. It's grand to have the whole family together. Especially with our new American beauty, Rose."

"Thank you, but let's not throw too many bouquets at each other," Rose said. "The food will get cold."

"The ball's in your court, Gramp," Bud said.

Gramp bowed his head and everyone followed suit. With his dramatic, booming voice, he said,

> "As our bodies receive thy food,
> May our minds be open to thy wisdom,
> And our hearts receive thy love. Amen."

"That's beautiful," Rose said. "Where did it come from?"

"Oh, I made it up for Thanksgiving a long time ago when we were having a big dinner with a lot of friends. The dinner was slow, everybody got drunk, and I never got to say it. I've never forgotten that Thanksgiving."

"This is like Thanksgiving," Bud said, "and I like your way of giving thanks."

As Gramp served the plates and passed them, everyone passed around the side dishes.

"Yuck, what's this?" Nancy said.

"Now, Nancy!" Gloria said.

"That's scrambled monkey glands," Bud said.

"Bud!" Rose reprimanded.

"Oh, goodie," Nancy said.

"You can put it on your potatoes, if you like," Rose said.

There was a long silence as they settled down to tasting the deliciuos repast. Finally, Gramp said, "Rose, this is the best dinner I've had in years."

Justin spoke up, "Rose, everything is utterly delicious."

Rose looked shy. She had enjoyed cooking it, and was glad to have this chance to participate in the festivities. She knew her efforts were a success when the Gloria spoke up.

"May I have the recipe for this dish," Gloria asked.

"Learned it from my mother. I'd love to share it with you. I'll write it out for you after dinner," Rose said proudly.

Like Thanksgiving, everyone ate too much. Even Nancy had cleaned her plate. Bud struggled to his feet to clear the dirty dishes, saying, "How about some dessert?"

"Maybe later," Justin said, and they all followed suit. "Do you have any coffee?" he added.

"Coming right up," Bud said, carrying the plates to the kitchen. Rose had made a fresh pot of coffee and laid out the cups on a wooden tray with the cream and sugar. Bud carried the coffee in and put it in front of Gloria to serve as he finished clearing the table. He was so thrilled with Rose's culinary demonstration, he rinsed the dishes, put them in the dishwasher, and cleaned up the kitchen. Rose was a neat cook, who cleaned as she went along.

The others were talking about the good old days when Bud returned to the dining room and sat down.

"Coffee, Bud?" Gloria asked.

"Thanks, Mom," he replied.

"Where've you been?" Gramp asked "We've been talking about old times."

Hope I didn't hold you up. I was just putting a few things away. I can take my coffee into the parlor," Bud said.

They all got up and moved to the parlor. Gramp settled into a comfortable chair, saying, "I ate too much. I'll have to wait till the bloat goes down."

"I've been trying to teach the children to say, 'I've had a sufficiency,' but now they will be quoting your farm talk," Gloria said.

"Sorry about that, Gloria," Gramp said, "but once in a while the unvarnished expressions won't hurt them."

They sat around, chatting, until Tinny asked, "What's for dessert?"

"May I bring it into the parlor?" Rose asked.

"Sure," Gramp boomed, "we'll never be able to get up and go back to the dining room today."

GRASS ROOTS

Rose served everyone dessert and more coffee. Bud cleared the empty dessert dishes when they were through. When he had added them to the dishwasher and returned, Justin stood up.

"We've had a delightful time. Think we'd better be running along home."

Everyone stood up and walked out to the car. There were big hugs and tearful goodbyes, as each one embraced each of the others. When the cycle was complete, Justin held the car door for Gloria and the children jumped in the back seat. He drove off with a lot of waving out the window.

"Rose, you and Bud made the day a gala event," Gramp said,"thank you."

"It was your idea," Rose said, giving Gramp a friendly kiss and a hug, "thank you!"

"We have to put our things together," Bud said, "if we're leaving early tomorrow morning."

"You better get cracking," Gramp said. "I'll have a good breakfast ready for you when you get up, something that'll stick to your ribs."

Bud and Rose went up to pack. They were relieved that the visit had gone so well. When they had packed, ready for the next day, they flopped into Bud's bed.

"Nice to feel that I'm a part of your wonderful family," Rose said.

"They all feel the same way. You're a charmer and I'm so proud of you," Bud replied.

"Thank you, dear We better get to sleep if we're going to get up and go in the morning," Rose said. They fell into a contented sleep in each other's arms.

They woke up to the aroma of Gramp's breakfast. Rose threw on her clothes and went to see what Gramp had fixed while Bud wrestled the heavy bags out to the car.

"Something smells good," she said. "Good morning, Gramp."

"Sit down. If you don't see what you want, just holler and'll get it for you. It' my turn to put out the grub," Gramp said, taking charge.

When Bud came in, Rose was already eating her breakfast. "Sit down, Bud, and I'll bring you a plate," Gramp offered.

"This is like old times, Gramp," Bud reminisced.

"It's better, with Rose here," Gramp pointed out.

"Thank you, Gramp," Rose said, politely. "We've had the time of our life. You all have made me feel right at home."

"We want you to come back," Gramp said sincerely.

"Maybe you can come down and visit us," Rose said.

"I'll come to your wedding," Gramp replied.

There was that word again. Rose looked up and paused, then said, "You can come visit us before that. We haven't set the date. It may be some time before we get married. We're just starting our careers."

"You don't need to worry about your careers," Gramp advised. "You can do that when you're married. Bud will inherit the farm one day. You'll always have a place to live."

"We have a lot to do. We don't want to rush into it. I'll let you know when and if we're going to get married. In the mean time, why don't you come down for a Delaware vacation?"

"I have a lot to do, keeping Hardscrabble going by myself, but maybe you will come up when I'm there in the summer."

"It's your turn to visit us," Bud chided, as they finished eating. "Thank you, Gramp, for everything. We better get on the road." They walked out to the car with happy hugs, handshakes and goodbyes. As they waved out the car window, Gramp called, "Keep in touch! Let me know how things are going!"

They drove happily home, excited with their adventure. Back at the old farmhouse, Rose thanked Bud for the wonderful trip. When she started toward the mobile home, he carried her bag to the door. At the door, she said, "Here, I'll take that." She gave him a tender kiss and said, "I'll come over tomorrow. We can look at the old farmhouse together."

"I'll be waiting for you," he said. "Thank you for being so kind to my mixed up family."

"They were delightful. I'll drop them a note tomorrow. Get some sleep and I'll see you tomorrow," she said as she went in and closed the door.

Bud lugged his bag into the old farmhouse and threw it down on the bedroom floor. Looking around at familiar surroundings, he worried about how his business had been doing without him.

He dropped in bed, delighted that Rose had been embraced by his family with so much kindness and warmth. Happy to be back in his new home, he fell into a peaceful sleep.

OFF SEASON

Bud awoke early from a peaceful sleep. He was alone, back in the old farmhouse. His packed bag lay on the floor with hisclothes thrown on the top of it. Remembering that Rose was coming over that morning, he jumped out of bed.

After a hasty breakfast, he cleaned up the kitchen, unpacked his bag, and put the clothes away. When he went into the front room, Mr Welch's card was waiting for him in the middle of the desk. Looking at his watch, he saw it was too early to call him.

He called Doug Rhodes, Sr., his number one crew chief, who had been running Mr. Fixit for him while he was away. "Hello, this is Doug Rhodes."

"Senior?" Never sure of which Doug Rhodes he was talking to on the phone, he had to ask.

"Yes?" he replied.

Bud Green, back from New York. How has it been going?"

"Didn't expect you back so soon. Everything seems to be going along okay."

"In that case, why don't you come by here tomorrow and we can see where we are."

"I'll be out to see you first thing tomorrow morning."

He hung up, noticing the dust that had collected on the desk. He found a dust cloth and wiped off the desk and chairs. With Rose coming, he decided to vacuum the floors.

At nine o'clock, he called Mr Welch. "Mr Welch, this is Mr. Fixit, back in town. We can drop by to see you today, if It'll be convenient for you."

"Well, you came back early. I'll check with my wife."

After a pause, he came back on. "What time?"

"We could be there this morning, any time you say."

"How about this afternoon?" Mr. Welsh suggested.

"Don't have to clean up the house for us," Bud reminded him.

"We have an appointment this morning."

"Okay. We'll be there after lunch."

Bud wondered about the appointment. Mr. Welch sounded as if something was bothering him. Rose hadn't appeared, so he took the vacuum upstairs with him. The upstairs had not been cleaned in a long time, so he just went from room to room. He was just finishing up when he heard Rose calling to him.

Running downstairs, he flung open the door. "Good morning, my dear. You must have slept in."

"I was up early, but Mom and Dad wanted to hear all about my trip. They became so excited about each thing I told them, I got carried away."

"I called Mr. Welch and we have an appointment at his house after lunch."

"Oh, good."

"I've been vacuuming upstairs, so we can look it over."

"I would like to talk to you, before we get into that. Have you made coffee?" Rose asked.

"Sure have. Come out to the kitchen," he said He found two cups and poured them each a cup of coffee. Sitting at the kitchen table, Bud waited for Rose to start talking. She took a sip and said, "Mm, that's good coffee."

"Thank you," Bud said and looked at her as he waited for her to speak.

After another sip and a look around, she said, "Remember when you gave me this ring, you said you wanted me to wear it in York?"

"Yes?"

"You said you thought I'd be more comfortable if we were traveling together as an engaged couple."

"Yes?"

"Well, I came home wearing it and now my parents are pushing me toward the altar. They're pressing me to set a date."

"Yes?"

"Can't you say anything but yes?" Rose asked.

"No," he said, smiling.

"Look, this is serious. It's hard enough to be a liberated woman. I'm afraid you'll want me to give up my career and be a housewife!"

"Never asked you to give up your career! Just because you get married, you don't have to give up your career."

"I may be liberated, but I'm still an old-fashioned girl. If I'm going to be a housewife, I take family matters seriously."

"I'm not asking you to change," Bud insisted "I like you just the way you are."

"Oh, no! First, I set a date. Then, I have to go through with the wedding. You take me on a honeymoon and sweet talk me into starting a family. Next thing you know, I'm married to a broom and a pile of dirty diapers and you expect me to keep on with my career!"

"Damn it! You don't have to do any of that stuff I don't give a damn what you do!"

"Now the truth comes out! You don't care."

"I care a whole Hell of a lot! I don't want to change you. If you don't want to get married, we could just live together."

"No way! I'm too old-fashioned for that."

"Just make up your mind to be a modern liberated woman or an old-fashioned housewife. The bottom line is you can be both."

"Speaking of bottoms, the bottom line is dirty diapers and I can't take them to the office with me."

Just because women are the only ones who can give birth, doesn't mean that men can't change diapers. I want to be around to help bring up my children."

"They all say that. Just look at the young husbands around here. They say they want children. Their wife stretches her body all out of shape having children. Do they stay home and help with the children? No, they still want to go out hunting, fishing, and drinking with the boys."

"Well, I'm not like that," Bud snapped. "I could work my schedule around a baby's needs, like those newfangled liberated househusbands."

"That's crazy," Rose said, in exasperation. "My father went to work and my mother stayed home and took care of me."

"My father didn't have the opportunity."

"Oh, that's right," Rose said, thinking twice before she again. "I'm supposed to be a loving fiancee in New York and then suddenly back into a career woman when I get back. And, now, my mother is on my back to set a date. I'm not sure I'm ready to wear this ring around here," Rose said, arms waving.

"But Geoffrey made that big announcement. This is a small town and everybody must know by now."

"That's just it. I'm the one who decides, not them. I want to be sure I'm doing the right thing."

"It's a woman's privilege to change her mind. I told you I'd understand if you didn't want to go through with it."

"I didn't say I didn't want to go through with it. I just don't want to be rushed into it."

"Good for you. I like it when you stand up for what you believe in. You don't have to do anything that you don't want to. I don't want you to say, 'I do,' when you don't."

"Don't be so agreeable. Thought you'd be upset with me."

"One thing at a time," Bud said. "Let's go look at the rooms upstairs. After all, your father is putting this house in your name and I'm going to fix up the rooms to your liking, no matter how we turn out. It's your house and I'm just fixing it."

"I never can figure you out," she said, standing up and taking one last sip of coffee. "Well, we've gone this far. . ."

They went upstairs and looked over the rooms. Rose picked out the front room over the living room, because it had a fire-place. "Floors look pretty good. With a flowery wallpaper and white woodwork, it ought to be cheerful."

"We can pick out the wallpaper on the way back from our appointment."

"I want to check in at the real estate office, but I'll be back home for lunch. I want to take a listing agreement with me, in case Mr. Welch is ready to sell," she said.

They went down stairs and Rose said, "I'll see you about twelve-thirty, ready to go," as she went out the door.

"See you then." Bud had dressed in such a hurry that morning that he decided to start over, so he would be fresh for his appointment. He took a shower and put on clean clothes. He puttered around the house until lunchtime. He ate right at noon, so he'd be ready to go when Rose came out.

After lunch, he went out to wait for Rose. Roamer came over wagging his tail "Hello, Roamer. Where were you last night when we came home?" He gave him a pat on the head, wondering about a dog's life. Roamer just seemed to always be around, like the trees and bushes.

Rose came out carrying a briefcase and they hopped into Bud's car and headed for town. The off-season traffic rolled along at an easy pace, now that the hustle-bustle of the summer rat race was over. Bud drove straight to Mr. Welch's house. As they came to the house, there was a car parked in front with a sign stuck on the door, reading, PHEEVER REAL ESTATE.

"Oh, no! What's he doing here?" Rose gasped.

"Whose car is it?" Bud asked.

"We don't make derogatory remarks about other Realtors, but in his case, everybody badmouths him, because he never returns their phone calls. He propositions everybody and seems to take all comers. He gets away with it, because he is a local boy whose father owns the real estate company," Rose explained.

Just then, Mr. Welch came out on the front porch with Mr. Pheever. Bud saw a slender, agile young man dressed in florid slacks and a white dress shirt, open at the neck and the sleeves carefully rolled past the wrists. His body movements and hand gestures made him look like a volleyball player.

"Do you mean he is a womanizer?" Bud asked.

"He doesn't limit himself to females, so I've heard."

"Well, let's see what he's up to," Bud said getting out of the car. Rose followed him up to the porch, as Mr. Welch looked nervously at them.

The real estate agent turned and called out, "Hello, Rose." As Bud came up to them, he turned to Bud, "I'm Buck Pheever."

"Mr. Fixit," Bud said. "Hope we aren't interrupting any important business."

"We're just talking about the election," Mr. Welch said,"The homeowners' candidates won. The business people formed their own group called, 'Citizens for a Better Government,' but their candidates lost. We feel parking is a problem, but they want all the business they can get."

"Well, I didn't vote," Buck said, "because my one vote doesn't make any difference. It's like peeing in the ocean."

"We would have voted, but we were out of town," Bud spoke up. "Your vote could make the difference."

"I've got to run along, Mr. Welch," Mr Pheever said. "The lottery changes numbers today and I feel lucky. Nice to see you, Rose, Mr. Fixit."

"Your odds are better voting in the election than playing the lottery," Bud said, feeling annoyed with him.

Mr. Pheever just smiled and waved as he jumped in his car and sped off.

"He called my wife," Mr. Welch explained, nervously "and she thought he was with your company. She didn't know."

"He's a piece of work. That's all right. We're here now," Rose assured him.

"Well, come in." he motioned.

They went in and Mr. Welch showed Bud what ought to be fixed up to sell the house. Rose followed along, taking notes.

"This is easy to spruce up," Bud said. "The way I see it,won't take more than a week. What do you think, Rose?"

"The front door sticks. It's hard to show a house when you can't get the customers in the front door," she pointed out.

"I figured on fixing that," Bud said.

"I have a list of comparables for you. Is there someplace where we can all sit down?" Rose said "I want to show you what has sold in this area and what is for sale now."

They all sat down at the kitchen table and Rose held court. They settled on a price and Rose filled in a listing agreement dated one week ahead. Mr. Welch hesitated and called to his wife to join them After a rehash of the comparables, they both signed it, with a feeling of relief for everyone.

Rose and Bud thanked them and left. In the car, Bud said,"We should celebrate our success."

"Not yet," Rose said, "Take me home, because I have a lot of work to do now."

"You have another job to do," Bud said "First you have to pick out a wallpaper pattern on the way home."

"Well, I'll look at them, but let's not make a big project out of it. I have my work cut out for me. You have to watch out for people like Buck. We almost lost this job by being away."

"Don't get caught up in the contagious dog-eat-dog routine. Don't have to be that way, just because he is. Plenty of work for everybody," Bud said, trying to keep things in perspective.

They went in and looked at the wallpaper samples. While Rose was looking them over, Bud ordered a gallon of off-white semi-gloss, a brush, turpentine, and some supplies for the Welch house. "We can take some of the samples home to try out."

"I like this, this, and this," Rose said. The clerk gave them samples to take home. Gathering the supplies and they left.

He drove her home and went in to type out the work orders he had sketched out at the Welch house. Satisfied with the work, he printed two copies, one for his foreman.

Then he went upstairs to clean a window sash, so he could paint a color sample for Rose to approve of when it dried. When the painting was done, he washed out the brush and tidied up.

After dinner, he lay in bed listening to the radio, thinking about Rose. Her indecision was unsettling, but he had tried not to show it. Now it was bothering him.

He was back to work as Mr. Fixit and he had a meeting with his foreman in the morning. *Better get to sleep*, he thought.

The next morning, he heard a truck pull into the lane as he was finishing his breakfast. He went to the door and led Doug Rhodes in to the front room. Doug gave him a good report on what he had been doing. Doug took great pleasure in giving the beeper back to Bud, saying, "This beeper doesn't fit in around here in Lower Delaware."

"Thanks for covering for me, Doug. You up for a new job?"

"You bet. I'd like to get back to regular work."

Doug talked over the Welch job and gave him the work order. "Told the man we'd do it in a week. Have some supplies for you."

"I'll get started on it today."

Watching Doug drive out of the lane, Bud couldn't help going back over his experiences in the grass roots. He had come to the grass roots to find himself. The old farmhouse and Mr. Fixit helped, but as Mr. Fixit grew, he tried to hire local workers. They didn't trust outsiders meddling with their way of life.When he decided to mind his own business and let them mind theirs, things got better.

The workers noticed that he worked along with them. He preferred doing the work himself to hiring someone else to do it. Besides, he wanted it done right. In time, the word got around that, he was fair and paid well when the work was done right. They soon discovered that he hadn't come down here to make a killing .He liked their way of life and just wanted to be part of the grass roots.

If Rose would just make up her mind!

Bud tried to lose himself in his work, but Rose's refusal to make up her mind loomed like a dark cloud over his work. His grass roots hopes and dreams were being stunted by a dark shadow, untill bad times in the economy cast a ray of hope.

When the housing crunch came to Rehoboth Beach, contractors found their speck houses overbuilt. They tightened up their payrolls and let several people go. Nobody was buying, so people started fixing up what they owned and building additions.

One contractor's assistant came to Bud with a proposition."I know the construction business, but I can't handle the paper-work. We could form a new company with you keeping records while I handle the building. You have a good credit rating and I will work hard and establish good credit ratings for our new company."

His name was Du Wright, Du was short for Duval. He looked like a guard on a pro football team. His stocky build was all muscle. His curly hair looked good uncombed and windblown. His face and arms had a ruddy complexion from working outside.

"I'll need some advice and references," Bud said, trying to hide his enthusiasm. "Let me think about it and get back to you.It sounds interesting."

"I brought all the references with me that you will need. Check them out and talk to your advisors. I also have a printout of the old building schedules that will help with estimates and get the jobs done on time. Call me back, either way."

"Look. I am interested. I just don't want to get myself overextended. Planning on getting married soon."

"So I've heard, congratulations. Be waiting for your call."

"You'll hear from me within a week," Bud assured him.

Bud called all the references and got good reports. He also asked what they thought about his potential business venture.

"If you're keeping all the records, then you should be the only one to sign all the checks," one suggested.

Another contractor said, "Have him submit a budget for each job and hold him to it."

And another said, "Make him president of the corporation, but you should be the secretary. The secretary signs all the contracts and checks."

"You'll be the contractor, and he's the builder."

"Don't keep any inventory and try to hire temporary help, unless you have a large, presold project."

"Check out each customer's credit references."

Bud called his accountant. He had learned to ask the accountant how to do it, not if he should do it. He told him the suggestions that other contractors made. The accountant said,"I'll prepare a set of books and the records I want you to keep."

The thorough building schedules Du had left impressed Bud. He'd set it up with a spread sheet and a database to keep up with the progress of the construction and ride herd on the budget.

In five days, he was ready. He called Du Wright and said,"Let's get together and talk."

"I can come to your place right now," Du said, excitedly.

"Be waiting for you," Bud replied.

Du arrived in fifteen minutes and Bud went over all of his specifications. Du went along with all of them except signing the checks. "I want to be able to write a check when I need supplies," he said.

"Charge it to the company. You said you want to be the builder and me keep the books and payroll," Bud reminded him.

"Well, I'll try it that way and see how it works," Du said.

"It's a deal. I'll set up a Delaware corporation with you as president and me as secretary. Bea and Rose can be treasurer and vice-president, but we have to decide on a name," Bud said.

"The name ought to say we build additions the right way."

"How about Bildrite, Inc.?" Bud asked, spelling the name.

"It isn't spelled correctly. I think it should be called The Build Right Corporation," Du replied.

"How about Ritebild, Inc.?" Bud continued still spelling.

"Or Wright Built, Inc.," Du added, spelling aloud.

"Okay, let's go with that for now. I'll start processing the paper work. All we need now is a job," Bud concluded.

"I may be able to come up with one and you may run across a remodeling job in your work," Du said.

"While you're waiting for the paperwork to be processed, why don't you work out the lowest estimate on winterizing this old farm-house," Bud said "I have insulated the walls on the first floor. I stacked hay bales around the foundation last year, but we want something more permanent."

If you're not in a hurry, we can do it very economically between other jobs. There is a new insulated plastic product that looks like brick on the outside. It's easier and cheaper than enclosing the crawl space with cinder block," Du reported.

"Well, look it over and let me know," Bud said.

Du went out to look over the old farmhouse. Bud sat at his desk wondering if he was doing the right thing. There wouldn't be much expense, except filing the corporation papers, until they got a job. Then he would have to be thorough in his estimates.

He called his lawyer and made an appointment to get started on the paperwork. When Du came back in, Bud asked him to go with him to see the lawyer. "I'll meet you at the lawyer's office," Du said "I want to go home and work out this estimate."

"See you there," Bud called out to him as he left.

Mr. Fixit was turning out to be a year 'round business and the new construction business would fit in with it. Thinking back to why he had come to the grass roots of Delaware in the first place, he decided to try to keep the good attitude he had worked so hard to achieve. He would have to take time each day to start his mornings right.

If this project takes off and Rose sells a few more houses, it would have removed the blocks to marriage before winter. When he came back from the lawyer's office, he waited around for Rose to come home. He felt he should discuss it with her.

When he heard Rose's car pull into the lane, he ran out on the porch and called her in to talk. They settled in the chairs each side of the fireplace. "You know Du Wright?" Bud asked.

"Yes   He was the foreman for a building contractor who's in finnancial trouble. His spec. houses aren't selling. We're in a real estate slump, but I've just sold another house," she said.

"Homeowners can't get top dollar for their homes, so a lot of them are remodeling, instead of moving. Du and I are setting up a company to remodel homes. He's going to be in charge of the construction and I'll do the paperwork. What do you think?"

"Mr. Fixit is expanding?"

"No. Mr. Fixit will be separate. This is a joint venture between Du and me, called, 'Wright Built, Inc.'"

"I wouldn't put a lot of money into construction in the middle of a slump."

"All I'm spending is the cost of incorporation, which isn't very much. Du is going to give me an estimate about winterizing the old farmhouse. We are going to try to do it wholesale when there is time between other jobs."

"Have you looked into the costs and procedures?"

"Thoroughly. I sign all the checks and contracts, when I have investigated the customer's credit rating and have a large deposit. We have to cover our costs as we go along."

"Sounds like you know what you are getting into," Rose said.

"That's what I wanted to hear you say. I want to put you down as vice president. You don't have to do anything yet, but we may have to have a corporate meeting when the papers come. Du's wife will be the treasurer. Do you know Bea?"

"Yes, we meet in the grocery store quite often. I've never been an officer of a corporation. I won't know what to do, but if I hear of any remodeling jobs, I'll let you know."

"Du is looking for a job for us, now. When we start a job, I plan to put four percent into advertising. Until then, I don't have to invest anything more."

"It'll cost something to winterize the old farmhouse," Rose said. "But it would be nice to be cozy and warm."

"I've already winterized the first floor. My next project is to winterize the master bedroom walls, so I can get on with the painting and papering."

"Sounds like a lot of work. What can I do to help?"

"Nothing, except go out to dinner with me to celebrate the new venture."

"I think we should celebrate, when you have your first job. I'd better help Mom with the dinner. Would you like to join us tonight for some real food?"

"Thank you, but I have some more work to do on this new project. May I have a rain check?"

Rose stood up to go, saying, "You can always come to dinner. Don't have to wait until you are a success, as your mother says."

He kissed her goodbye, "Yes, I know."

When Bud received the papers of incorporation, he called Du. They had to have a meeting with Du, his wife, Rose and Bud Du came right over and asked Bud to look over a remodeling job with him. They had to prepare an estimate. Going to look at the job, they both took copious notes. Then they each went home to put together separate estimates.

The next day they compared notes and Bud typed up a formal estimate for submission, with a financial statement for the cleint to fill out. Bud was trying to build-in the necessary safeguards. They went together to meet with the client, a Mr. Jones, who wanted to add a room to his house.

Mr. Jones said he'd fill out the financial statement so they could get started as quickly as possible. They said they'd put his project at the top of their list, once everything was signed.

Mr. Jones brought his financial statement to Bud the next day. "This looks good to me," Bud told him. "Do you mind if I make a couple of phone calls and we can get started."

"Go right ahead," he said, smiling reassuringly.

Bud went into the bedroom and called Mr. Jones' mortgage company, bank, and employer. They all gave him their approval.

Bud anxiously went back to the front room, saying, "Well, Thank you for waiting. If you'll sign this contract and give me a check for the cost of the materials, we'll start right away."

Mr. Jones signed the contract and wrote out a large check.They exchanged a warm handshake and friendly good will. When he left,

Bud put in a call to Du. "We got the Jones contract. I told him we'd start ASAP. We also have to set up a corporate meeting with you, Bea, Rose, and I, when you have time."

"That's great! I'll pick up some more supplies and a helper and get started," Du exclaimed with excitement.

Bud set up a schedule for the building project and then went down to the bank to open a new account for Wright Built, Inc. and deposit the check. The feeling of euphoria was overwhelming as he drove to town. At the bank he tried to act more composed with a business-as-usual expression, but he drove home feeling on top of the world.

When Rose came home that evening, he met her in the lane. "I have two important things for you to do," he said.

"Well, give me a chance to get out of the car. Can't you say hello and how was you day, first?" she remarked.

"No! This is too important! I can't wait."

"Let me set down my briefcase. Now, what is it that is so important that it can't wait?"

"We are going out to dinner to celebrate Wright Built, Inc.'s first job."

"You said there were two things."

"As a corporate officer, I have a job for you. We have to have a corporate meeting and sign the papers. Will you call Bea Wright and set a time we can all get together?"

"I don't know her that well, but I guess I'm going to get to know her now. I'll see what I can do, tomorrow."

"What about dinner tonight?"

"Let me check with Mom. She may have it on the stove by now." She went in and came right out again. "Okay, you can have your way this time. When do you want to go?"

"Fifteen minutes?"

"I'll be ready."

Bud ran in and washed up and changed clothes with the speed of an actor getting ready for the next scene. By the time he ran outside, Rose was standing there, with an I got here first grin.

"You're a quick change artist," she said. "I forgot to say congradulations. I'm really proud of you," she said as she threw her arms around his neck and gave him a big kiss.

Bud was taken by surprise, but went along with the act. He opened the car door for her and she hopped in. As he drove off, he asked, "Where would you like to go?"

"This is your celebration. I've made enough decisions for one day. I'll be happy long as I'm with you."

He drove into Rehoboth and parked on Wilmington Avenue and led her into a restaurant called, La La Land. She looked the place over with interest and curiosity. Bud led her to a narrow deck between two matching old cottages. Looking through the windows, she saw tables set up in the rooms on both sides. He went straight back to an open court in the back yard, surrounded by bamboo on each side. A little shed across the back, housed the bar. The tables in the open courtyard were set up with silverware on the same white table clothes A colorful bouquet of flowers adorned each table. Waiters hurried back and forth.

When a waiter stopped to help them, Bud said, "Two. May we sit out here?"

"Of course," the waiter said, pulling out a chair for Rose.

"Where did you hear about this place?" Rose said to Bud "I've never been to La La Land before."

"Want you to be in the mood for what I'm going to ask you," Bud said.

The waiter interrupted him with, "My name is Nigel, and I'll be your waiter tonight," with an effeminate swish. "May I bring something from the bar?"

"A bottle of white wine and two glasses," Bud answered.

"What had you started to say, before the wait person came and interrupted you?" Rose asked.

"He has very graceful moves. He should make a magnificent waiter," Bud noted.

"Yes, I noticed that, but you left me hanging," Rose said.

Fortunately, Bud saw the waiter returning with the wine. He looked up at the waiter in appreciation. The waiter placed the bottle on a neatly folded towel laying on his arm, so Bud could read the label. "That's fine," Bud said. The waiter removed the cork with a flourish and poured a little in Bud's glass.

Bud picked up the glass and looked at the color, sniffed the aroma, and tasted the bouquet. "That'll do very nicely," he said and the waiter filled Rose's glass and then his. Bud raised his glass and said, "Here's looking at you, kid." Rose enjoyed his performance. She had seen the same old movie.

They each took a sip. As Rose put her glass down, she said,"I give up. You're full of yourself tonight. I'll wait till you remember whatever it was you wanted to say."

"All right, here it is. I'm ready to set a date and I think Thanksgiving will be a perfect time for a double family reunion."

"Oh, dear I don't know what to say."

"I'll give you three choices: yes, no, or maybe," Bud said.

"Will you be serious? I'm trying to think," she said.

"I have said what I wanted to say. You don't have to answer right now. Let's just enjoy this unusual place. You may order whatever you find interesting," he said.

"Not so fast I think I'll just sip a little wine and celebrate your new success. By the way, what's La La Land mean?"

"To me, it means a dream world. It's what people from the's nation's capital are looking for on a holiday."

"Maybe we should ask where the name comes from."

"I did. The etymology falls into two categories. First,Los Angeles is popularly known as La La Land, and second, there is a book by that name."

"I like your meaning better. It is like dining in a fairy tale and I love it."

"I've been in La La Land ever since I signed a contract for our first job for Wright Built, Inc.," Bud said. He raised his glass and they clinked glasses, "Here's to our future together."

"I'll drink to that," Rose said.

The dinner was unusually tasty and intriguing. The magic of the decor, the service, and the food lived up to the name. They celebrated in La La Land.

When Rose finished her coffee, she said, "I'll talk it over with Mom and Dad. Maybe Thanksgiving would be a good time for a double family reunion."

"You mean you agree to the date?" Bud said with surprise.

"I said maybe. Don't get carried away just because we're in La La Land. I'll talk it over with Mom and Dad and see what they say," Rose replied.

GRASS ROOTS

Rose told her parents that Bud had suggested Thanksgiving as a good time for a wedding and double family reunion. They loved the idea, but they would have to postpone their trip to Florida.

Lily said, "Oh, Rose, we'll change our plans. We could leave for Florida when you leave on your honeymoon, can't we Thorny,?"

"I'll see what I can do, tomorrow," Thorny said.

Lily took this to mean it was all set. She immediately made extensive plans for the wedding, starting with ordering engraved invitations and making endless lists. She invited Bud's family and relatives to the rehearsal dinner at a private dining room at the Sea Horse Restaurant.

Rose took this to mean everything was on hold until her father could make the arrangements for a later Florida trip. She thought the date was still not settled, until Bud mentioned the reception. He said, "Gramp wants me to find a proper place for the wedding reception. I thought of the country club where Thorn and Mary announced their engagement."

"Isn't he jumping the gun?" she snapped, sounding indignant.

"Your mother invited him to the rehearsal dinner and he just wanted to do his part," Bud tried to explain.

"Well, I didn't know the date was set!"

"Gramp said it was Thanksgiving."

"Well, I'm the one who has the last word!" Rose said, as she stormed off to settle it with her mother. Women have the right to change their mind, but Rose's mind seemed to be stuck in first gear. Bud's mind went blank, taken over by panic over Rose's indecision. In desperation, he decided to loose himself in his work. He was distraught, but he was determined to hold up his end of the bargain.

RICHARD C. HARRISON

TERMINAL STRESS

The pressure was on. Bud had to finish winterizing the old farmhouse. He had to provide bedrooms for out of town guests. When Du Wright finished up the job for Mr Jones, Bud asked him to start on the old farmhouse. He had Doug Rhodes tear out the walls in all the upstairs bedrooms. He ran new wiring and a phone line into the master bedroom. When it was hooked up and working, he called the best dry wall man to finish the walls.

Another job came in for an addition. Mr Jones' neighbor had liked the job Du had done. Bud and Du went to inspect the work to be done and presented an estimate. They were able to put him on hold for a week, until Du could put in a new floor furnace and the siding for the crawl space in the old farmhouse.

"There is nothing like being busy," Du said as they left the neighbor's house.

"Nothing succeeds like success," Bud said as he went home to check Mr. Jones' neighbor's credit report.

Rose picked out wallpaper for each room and helped him hang it. They worked on Rose's day off, when she had other things to do. Working together, they got into a fight and nearly broke up, but when it was finished, they admired their handiwork.

The old farmhouse had four bedrooms upstairs and one down-stairs, which Bud figured would have to do. He straightened up the other front room downstairs and set up some old furniture for a sitting room. The drop-leaf table in the kitchen would have to serve as a dining room Bud had planned to leave on a honeymoon from the reception and Bud's family could take care of themselves in the old farmhouse.

By Halloween, the old farmhouse was ready, the reservations were confirmed, RSVP's were flowing back to Lily, and Rose was becoming hostile with the trick or treat attitude of a hobgoblin, holding out defiantly and threatening to have the last word at the wedding. Lily was busy with her plans. Bud lost himself in his work to get his mind off the problem .The constant pressure keeping his nose to the grindstone was more than he could bear.

As the moment of truth drew closer, floating in limbo became more and more frustrating. He had to take the time to sort out his feelings. Sitting quietly in the old farmhouse, Bud went back over his life in his mind.

Each time he moved to a new community, the natives had unique ways of looking at life. As a stranger, he found their ways bizarre, like rats running around in a maze. The fear and greed of Wall Street didn't suit him. He wasn't impressed by the opportunists in the federal city, seduced by power. He could identify with Slower Delaware's lure of nature and the way the "good old boys" played the game.

He had found success by looking inside himself. World Peace worked from the bottom up. He found peace when he took care of his own business and let other people take care of theirs. The more they tried to make Rose conform, the more she resisted . He had to let go and let Rose do her thing.

"That's it!" he said to himself, feeling better already, "If I just mind my business and let Rose mind hers, everything will work out. What I do here is important." He wanted to keep his end of the bargain and let the chips fall where they may.

Bud felt relieved as he went out to check on his latest job. He drove to Rehoboth and turned north on Second Street until he entered Henlopen Acres, just north of Rehoboth. Substantial homes sat back on generous lawns, looking lavish. The utility poles were hidden in the "bridle paths" behind the houses.

When he found the address, it was late in the evening. Bud fixed the problem himself. To get home, he had to go through the town of

Rehoboth Beach. When he got there, the main street was blocked off for the parade. He had forgotten about Halloween.

Bud had missed last year's Halloween parade in Rehoboth, but was glad to be trapped into going to it this year. The community put together a program that solved the vandalism.

There had been a tiny tots' costume parade at the convention center at six, with prizes for each age group. Now, it was time for the big Halloween parade down Rehoboth Avenue and around the U by the ocean and back to the convention center.

He remembered the Fourth of July in Elmira, with speeches and a parade with bands. He loved the hometown festivities. He drove around until he found a place to park. Then he started walking in the direction of the parade. By the time he came to Rehoboth Avenue, the parade had already started.

There was a mother dressed up as Mother Goose pushing her daughter, dressed as a goose, in a baby carriage down the middle of Rehoboth Avenue. People cheered and the little girl loved it and waved back at them.

The parade was forming by the Sea Horse restaurant. Bud saw some of the retired community sitting at a long table in the window, watching the parade with their cocktails. Most everyone else was standing on the side walk, cheering and encouraging their friends, who were marching in the parade.

There was a fireman's convention in town, so there were a lot of fire trucks. The most impressive fire truck was the extra long ladder truck from Bethany Beach for the Sea Colony highrises. A woman's auxiliary hose truck carried stern women, wearing navy blue uniforms, who seemed to have come along to the convention to see that their husbands behave.

The junior high school band was pretty good, because they also march in Halloween parades in Lewes and Milton on different nights. He watched a pick-up truck with the back filled with teenage girls all dressed up. The sign on the side of the truck bed, read, JUNIOR TEEN BEAUTY QUEENS. This was followed by a compact pick-up full of tiny tots in frilly dresses, sporting a sign reading, FUTURE BEAUTY QUEENS.

The Henlopen Senior High School Band was the highlight of the musical features. There was also a man on an old bicycle with an enormous front wheel and a sign advertising WHEELS, the bicycle shop on Rehoboth Avenue.

There were a group of "Z cars" and elaborate vans bringing up the rear, which baffled Bud. By the time the parade was over it was dark and too late for trick or treating.

Bud milled around in the holiday crowd. These were not the revelers , but the solid citizens of the local community. There were a few Washington cottage owners who were civic minded. Bud admired his adopted town and he was glad he came to the parade. The off-season was the in-season for these people.

On the long walk back to his car, he looked over the houses, mostly empty this time of year. The summer crowd only knew the crowded ocean blocks with their hot dogs, pizza, and electronic games on the board walk. They missed the natural beauties of the surrounding countryside.

The next few weeks flew by. Rose was busy renting cottages for next summer and Bud was busy keeping them in condition to rent. Doug Rhodes said he would take the beeper again, while Bud and Rose get married and go on their honeymoon. Gramp and the Tymes were driving down in Gramp's big car on Wednesday before Thanksgiving. Bud had his clothes sorted out and money in order, before they came. He would stay in his downstairs bedroom, until he left for the honeymoon.

On Wednesday afternoon, he hung around, waiting for their arrival. At four o'clock, he got a phone call. They were lost in Rehoboth Beach near the Safeway. "Just stay where you are and I'll be there in ten minutes," Bud said and left to find them.

At the Safeway, he pulled up beside Gramp's car and jumped out to greet them. They all got out and hugged and shook hands. "Just follow me," Bud said as he got back in his car. He kept an eye on the rear-view mirror as he led them to the old farmhouse. He turned in the lane and pulled over to let them park.

"This is it," Bud said proudly, getting out and pointing where they should park.

"Looks a lot like Gramp's farmhouse," Gloria said as they all got out. Bud helped them with their bags into the farmhouse and up the stairs to their rooms. When they all gathered down stairs in the sitting room, Bud said, "How was your trip?"

"It certainly is flat around here," Gramp said "We saw a lot of corn, soy beans, and chickens on the way into town."

"Yes, it is flat," Bud said. "The Rehoboth Ski Club's motto is 'elevation zero.' Excuse me, a moment." Bud heard Rose's car drive in and he rushed out to catch her. "Got a minute to say hello to my folks?"

"Minute is about all I've got. Let's go," she said quickly.

They went in and everyone greeted Rose with enthusiasm. She said, "What a wonderful surprise! I have a million things to do, if I'm going to be married."

Gramp asked, pointedly, "Did you say, if?"

"It isn't over unless the bride says, 'I do,'" Rose said, clouding the issue and leaving everyone in limbo. "I'll be right next door. I'm so glad you came," she said as Bud walked her out the door.

"I'm taking them all to the Lamp Post for dinner," Bud said when they were outside. "They can stop in and say hello to your folks before we go."

"I'll tell them to come say hello when they have a minute. I have to unpack my car," Rose said.

"Need any help?" Bud asked.

"I could use a hand," she said, picking out some paper bags. "Just grab anything you see there."

When Bud took all the rest of the things into Rose's house, he found Mr. Gardner reading in the living room. "My family has arrived," Bud said "Would you and Mrs Gardner have time to pop over and say hello?"

"I'll go see what Lily's doing," he said, getting up. "I can't wait to meet 'em."

Going back to the old farmhouse, Bud found everybody right where he'd left them. "Make yourselves at home. I'll show you around," he said. He took them into the other front room. "This is my office, but I won't be using it till I get back." He led the way to the kitchen. "When I leave for my honeymoon, you'll have the run of the whole house. I'll use this downstairs bed-room till we're married. Master bedroom's upstairs in front."

Bud heard footsteps on the front porch and went to let the Gardners in. "I have the whole gang in the kitchen, showing them around," he said, opening the front door to greet them.

"Well, you can show us around, too," Mr. Gardner said. Bud introduced each one to each of the others. They were thrilled to meet each other. The noise level rose with cheery greetings.

Gloria had never met anyone who had lived in a trailer. She was living in a smaller house than the lavish house, where she had grown up, but it was a house. When she met the Gardners, she said, "I feel like we're putting you out of your lovely house."

Thorny spoke up, "This is Rose's house. Bud fixed it up and kept it going. Can't keep up a place like this and go to Florida all winter. We'd be there now, if it weren't for the wedding."

"Hope Bud hasn't been much trouble to you," Gloria said.

"He's been a big help," Thorny said "I love this old farm-house, but it's too much for me now. Our mobile home is like a new car, all new and no upkeep. It's our lock and leave. What makes a place like this old farmhouse lovely is a lot of tender loving care. It needs young people like Bud and Rose."

"You're right there," Gramp said "I have an old farmhouse very much like this and it takes a lot of work to keep it up. When Rose was in Elmira, she fixed a banquet for us and Bud did all the dishes. It was a pleasure to have her."

"We have a lot of talking to do," Lily said "How long can you all stay with us?"

"We have to drive back Sunday," Justin said.

"I hope you don't mind mixing Thanksgiving dinner with the rehearsal dinner," Lily said.

"It's a good way to get everyone together for Thanksgiving," Gloria said.

"We won't have enough time to talk tomorrow night at the rehearsal dinner," Lily said, "so why don't you drop over when you get settled? We can have a good old time together."

"That sounds wonderful," Gramp said "We've never been in Delaware before. Maybe you can show us around the countryside."

"We'll be looking forward to it," Thornton said.

"Won't that be fun, children," Gloria said Tinny was ready to see the sights, but Nancy wasn't sure yet.

"I'll show Tinny and Nancy the board walk," Bud said as they brightened up. "The shops are closed, but the ocean keeps going all year."

"We have a lot to do," Lily said, "so we'll let you get settled. If you need anything, we're right next door."

"You run along," Gramp boomed out "We feel right at home in this old farmhouse."

"Glad you like it," Thorn said as they went out the door. "See you later."

"Gramp and Mom can check out the kitchen," Bud said. "There's some food for breakfast and lunch, but I'm taking you all out to dinner tonight."

They all went to their rooms to get ready and gathered again in the downstairs sitting room. Tinny and Nancy wanted Bud to show them the farm. "Okay, I'll show you around the place before dinner," he said. "Gramp, Mom, and Justin can visit the Gardners for a drink before dinner. Okay?" Everyone agreed and they all left for their destinations.

Thorny and Lily welcomed the Tymes and Gramp with open arms. Thorny said, "How about a toast to the bride and groom? The doctor has cut me off, but we keep our bar stocked for guests. Lily will be glad to fix you a drink. After forty years of marital bliss, she doesn't trust me near the bar."

"What would you like?" Lily asked They all placed their orders and Lily went off to fix the drinks.

Gramp said, "Forty years! When Lily comes back, I think congradulations are in order."

"You can be first after me," Thorny said.

"Here we are," Lily said, bringing an ornate trayful of drinks and passing them around.

Thorny took his drink and stood up, "Here's to the bride and groom."

They all said, "Hear, hear!"

Rose is a beautiful girl," Gramp said "Her charm is more than skin deep. She has a mind of her own and I'm sure they'll find many years of happiness."

"We are very proud of Bud," Lily said "He performed a miracle on the old farmhouse. He can do anything."

"He can do anything if he puts his mind to it," Gloria said.

"I hope they are together as long as we have been," Thorny said

"We're coming up on our fortieth anniversary."

Gramp stood up and said, "Here's to forty years of marital bliss. May the next forty be just as happy."

"I'll drink to that," Thorny said, raising his glass of iced tea , "but our anniversary isn't until next week."

Gloria had never been inside a trailer. The cozy living room gave her a warm feeling. "Which day next week is your anniversary?" she asked, with feminine precision about detail.

"It's on the real Thanksgiving, before they moved it up a week to allow more time for Christmas shopping," Lily replied.

"Forty years is a long time," Gramp went on "What's the secret to your longevity?"

"Hasn't seemed that long to me," Thorny said, "but you better ask Lily. She knows all the secrets."

"Well, let's see," Lily said, gathering her thoughts. "When Thorny first asked me if I wanted to go out with him, I said I'd try it and see if I wanted to, or not. I still haven't decided whether to stay or not."

She smiled at Thorny as everyone was at a loss for words.Fortunatly, there was a knock at the door. Thorny called out,"Come in."

Tinny and Nancy burst in, both talking at the same time, telling their mother about their big adventure with Bud. Bud followed them in, saying, "Hey! One at a time!" They looked at Bud as he announced, "If you're ready, I think it's time to leave for dinner."

Gloria said, "We'd better be going. Thank you for your warm hospitality."

"Drop over anytime," Thorny said.

When everyone filed outside, Gramp said, "We can all fit in my car. Bud, you can drive and I'll ride in the back with Gloria and Justin."

Bud drove the happy group to the Lamp Post. After dinner, when the live band started playing, Bud said, "Let's dance, Mom. We have to practice for tomorrow night."

Gramp danced with Nancy as Justin and Tinny watched. It was a happy family scene and the other diners watched them with envy. Gramp never liked people who posed on the dance floor, so he and Nancy kicked up their heels.

Dinner was a success and Bud drove them home to their beds.

Thanksgiving morning, everyone gathered in the kitchen, as Bud showed them where he kept things. "We haven't done the kitchen over, yet," Bud said. "When we come back from our honeymoon, we're going to plan a new kitchen with a dishwasher and all the modern amenities. Just leave your dishes and I'll wash them and put them away."

"I think we have everything we need," Gloria said. "If you don't like what I'm fixing, you may pick out what you want to eat and fix it yourself."

They all settled at the kitchen table for a good old family gabfest. When breakfast was over, Bud said, "I'm going to show Nancy and Tinny the ocean. Just leave the dishes. We'll be back in time to get ready for the rehearsal dinner at four o'clock."

Nancy and Tinny jumped up and Bud took them out to the car. He drove into Rehoboth Beach and parked near the ocean in the middle of town. Walking them to the boardwalk, he showed them around. Tinny chased the seagulls and Nancy just stared at the ocean waves. It was the first time they had seen the ocean. A chilly wind blew crashing waves up on the expanse of sand. A hazy sun tried to break through. It was bleak and not like the summertime.

Nancy was cold, so they walked up to the candy store to buy a souvenir box of salt water taffy. Out on the sidewalk, the buildings blocked the chilly breeze. Several shops were open for the holidays, so they walked around and looked in the windows.

Bud took them to lunch in his favorite restaurant and Nancy thought it was a big treat. Tinny tried to act cool, but he had trouble with the menu selections. With a helpful suggestion from Bud, they made their selections and settled back like old timers.

After lunch, as they walked back to Bud's car, Tinny said, "There aren't as many people here as there are in Elmira."

"Not this time of year," Bud said. "This is a resort area and in the summertime there are more people than in Elmira."

"Where do they all live?" Nancy asked.

"They rent cottages. Sometimes two families stay together in the same house. They all crowd down here to have a vacation."

"Maybe we can come here in the summer," Tinny said.

"Maybe so," Bud said as they came to the car. Having seen the sights, he drove them back to the old farmhouse.

As Bud went in, he found the kitchen spotless and everything put away. He dressed for the rehearsal dinner and went out to the sitting room. When the others had all gathered down in the sitting room, Bud took them out to Gramp's big car and drove them all to the Sea Horse restaurant.

The Gardner party had gathered in a private dinning room in the back. It was an intimate Thanksgiving dinner with the two families, Thorny and Lily Gardner, Mary and Thorn, Gramp, Gloria and Justin, Tinny and Nancy, and Bud and Rose. There were also three more bride's maids, Rose's college roommate, a girl from the real estate office, and a childhood friend. Bud and Thorn had become good friends, so Bud had asked him to be his best man.

They stood around chatting with a cocktail Lily ordered Shirley Temples for Tinny and Nancy. Bud caught his mother's arm and steered her to a young couple. Bud said, "Mom, I want you to meet Rose's brother, Thorn, and his wife Mary. Rose picked her sister-in-law, Mary, to be a bride's maid and I've asked Thorn, her husband, to be my best man."

"You have an amazing son," Thorn said "You should be very proud."

"I am," Gloria said, "but a lot of the credit should go to his grandfather. Gramp is here somewhere," she said, looking around the little group.

Regina Lipschidts marched into the room, spotted Gramp, and screwed up her courage to confront him. "Captain Green, I'm looking for a Mrs. Lily Gardner," Regina announced. "Which one is she?"

"Well, Regina," Gramp said, surprised to see her, "how'd you get way down here?"

"Wasn't easy," she snapped "Just point her out."

Gramp caught her elbow as he started across the floor. "Oh,Lily," Gramp called out, as they came up to her. "I want you to meet Regina Lipschidts, Gloria's mother. Regina, this is Lily, the mother of the bride."

"This wedding must not take place," Regina demanded, "and I'll need your help."

"What do you mean!" Lily gasped.

"We have to stop this wedding before it goes any further," Regina ranted.

"But I don't want to stop the wedding," Lily said, aghast,wringing her hands, he dropped her glass. As the glass hit the hard floor, it shattered with a loud crash. As everyone turned toward the noise, Gloria saw her mother. Gramp stooped to pick up the pieces of glass.

"You'll be sorry!" Regina threatened. Turning to go, she added, "I have warned you!"

Gloria rushed to catch her mother as she was leaving. In a shocked tone of voice, she said, "Mother! Wait!" As Regina marched toward the door, Gloria said, "Please stay for dinner?"

"I'm not hungry," she grumped and left in a huff.

"Pay no attention to the old busy body," Gramp said to Lily as he handed the glass pieces to a busboy who had appeared with a mop and bucket. "I'll get you another drink."

Lily was shaken by this outrageous confrontation. "Who was that woman?" she stammered.

"Gloria's mother," Gramp told her, "she's been a thorn in our family, since Bud was born. You shouldn't have invited her."

"Rose said she was hostile," Lily said, "but I didn't expect anything like this."

It was soon time to sit down to a combination Thanksgiving, Rehearsal Dinner, and Double Family Reunion. Gramp sat next to Regina's empty chair. He was glad to pay a handsome price for Regina's dinner, as long as she wasn't there.

When they were all seated, Gramp bowed his head and said:

> "Let us be thankful for this food,
> And this young bride and groom.
> And the happy members of these two families,
> All gathered in this room.
> Amen."

Lily said Amen the loudest. Gloria looked at Justin in a knowing way and watched her children enjoying a happy feast. Bud had missed the significance of Regina's short invasion, busy with his indecisive fiancee. Worrying about what Rose might say at the altar had grown into an obsession with him.

GRASS ROOTS

Everyone else had a good time. These two families either liked each other very much or they had all put on their party manners. Bud wondered if the pilgrims had accepted the Indians as warmly as this.

The next morning, Nancy and Tinny asked Bud to take them to the boardwalk to watch the seagulls again. "We have a rehearsal at the church at ten o'clock," Bud pointed out. "We could go for a short time. Let's check with everyone else."

Gramp offered to drive the others to the church, if the Gardners would lead the way.

Nancy and Tinny cheered as they ran out to the car and Bud drove them back into Rehoboth. They fed the seagulls and looked over the boardwalk. "Get me to the church on time," Bud sang, looking at his watch as they hurried back to Bud's car. He drove to the church, but they found all the doors locked. The Gardners arrived, just as the minister came from his house next door.

Bud greeted the minister and took over the introductions like a member of the congregation. The rehearsal was short and sweet. They walked through the ceremony as the minister gave them their cues. "All right, I'll see you back here at four'clock," the minister said.

Bud thanked the minister as the families began to chatter to each other with excitement. Bud looked at Rose and said, "When you have your things packed for the honeymoon, I'll put them in the trunk of my car."

Lily answered for Rose, "I've been helping her pack and I'll show you where the bags are."

"You aren't supposed to talk to each other until after the ceremony," Thorn said, taking on his best man role. "Rose has to go home and make up her mind whether to say *I do* or *I don't*."

Bud, struck dumb with this remark, muddled through his panic crisis, hoping it was Thorn's weird sense of humor. Bud called out to Rose, "I'll be waiting for you at the altar."

"I just told you, you are not supposed to talk to each other the day of the wedding," Thorn reprimanded him. "You go home and get everything ready. Mary is going to drop me off at your house about three o'clock. I'll help you pack your car and I'll drive you to the church in it."

Bud went home to get ready for the wedding. He packed a bag for the honeymoon, because he and Rose were to leave right from the reception. His mind wandered from the packing, to absent minded doubts and fears. *What if she says, "I don't," and leaves me in the lurch*; *'leaves me waiting at the church,'* he thought to himself. The old rhyme had lost all claim to humor.

He remembered the sinking feeling he had when he missed his airplane connection. His eyes blurred over as he sat in a daze, staring at his half-packed bag. A sudden noise broke through his concentration, jarring him out of his trance.

"Oh, Bud," a man's voice called from the front porch.

He jumped up and tried to pull himself together hastily as he went to the door, wondering who it could be. As he flung open the door, Mr. Gardener was standing there smiling. "Lily asked me to bring out Rose's bags for your trip."

"Hi," Bud said, trying to regain his composure. "Let's take them to the car." He grabbed the larger bag and headed for the car. He opened the trunk and set the bag in. As Mr. Gardner brought the other bag, Bud took it and set it in on top and closed the trunk. "Sorry to be so confused," Bud explained.

"I'd think you would be," he said. "Rose has been driving her mother crazy, saying, 'If I go through with it.' She says that a lot of things could happen until the ceremony and no one can predict the future, but I know it will all work out."

"It's a woman's prerogative to change her mind," Bud mumbled, feeling numb.

"Yes, but it's a matter of timing. I'm sure Rose's timing's better than that. She doesn't like surprises. I think she'll go ahead with this," Mr. Gardner said, trying to reassure Bud.

"God, I hope so," Bud sighed.

"Everything is going to be all right," Mr. Gardner said as he went back in to get ready.

Bud tried to smile in answer as he went back in to finish packing. He had to hold up his end of the schedule, whatever happened. Packing was a distraction and he began to feel better. When he finished, he zipped up the bag and carried it out to the car. *"All I have to do now is to get dressed,"* he reminded himself as he went back into the old farmhouse.

As he finished dressing, the sound of footsteps bounding up the front steps caught his attention. The door burst open and Thorn said, "Are you ready to be led to the slaughter?" "

"Just about," Bud said. "Hope Rose goes through with it."

"She has to or Mom and Dad will kill her," Thorn laughed.

"But I don't want her to "have to," Bud snapped back.

"She's a big girl, now. If you're all set, let's go."

Thorn led Bud out to the car and put him in the passenger seat. "I have to get you there on time." Bud was in a daze. He wasn't sure what Rose's answer would be when the minister popped the big question. The ride to the church was a blur. Thorn backed the car into the driveway, where Bud parked it for Thorn's wedding, handed Bud the keys, and led him into the church office.

The minister had them each sign the official documents. Then the minister took them to the door, where they were to make their entrance. "If you peek through the little white section in the leaded glass window, you can see who has been seated," he said to Bud. Then, he turned to Thorn and said, in an aside,"That keeps the nervous groom occupied. I'll go in this door by the altar. Wait till they play the wedding march before you two go in and stand at the head of the aisle."

When the organ broke into the march, Thorn led Bud into the church, across the front of the congregation, to their places at the head of the aisle. The church was packed with friends of both families. Both Doug Rhodes were dressed up. Rose's real estate friends were all smiles. Even Buck Pheever came.

Nancy was either a flower girl or the first bride's maid to sashay slowly down the aisle. Mary Thoroughgood Gardner was the last bride's maid. As Mr. Gardner whispered a reassuring word to his daughter, all eyes turned to them. He flashed a proud smile as he escorted Rose down the aisle. Bud looked at the vision of loveliness in the elaborate bridal gown, walking erect and sure. He couldn't see her eyes or her facial expression through the veil. As they came slowly up the aisle, toward him, his anxiety grew, obscuring his thoughts and his vision.

When they were side by side, the minister announced, "Dearly beloved, we are gathered here. . ." Bud felt the closeness and terror of the unknown. When the minister asked, "Who giveth this woman to be married?" Thorny said, "I do." Bud thought he was coaching his daughter, how to answer. As Thorny sat down, the minister announced in a loud voice, "If anyone knows any reason why these two people should not be joined in holy matrimony, let him speak now or forever hold his peace." Then he waited for what seemed like an eternity to Bud. He was in a panic, hoping Rose would say I do.

An electrifying shock went through the church, as they heard a loud, clear voice say, "I have an objection to this marriage." The objection ricocheted across the congregation, sucking the joy out of each of their hearts. Everyone turned in shock to see Regina Lipschidts standing defiantly inside the church door.

As a murmur started, the minister said, "Let me have your attention. Please remain seated, while the bride, and groom, parents, and grandparents confer with me in my office. I'll be back as soon as possible."

As Regina, Gramp, Gloria, Thorny, and Lily, came forward and followed the minister, leading Bud and Rose through the side door to his office, the murmur changed to loud talking.

When they had all gathered in the minister's office, he asked, calmly, "Who made the objection?"

Regina said, "I am Mrs. Lipschidts. My daughter is the mother of the groom."

"I see," the minister said, trying to keep the group calm. "Mrs. Lipschidts, what is your objection?"

"I should have stopped my daughter from marrying the groom's father," she stated. "I stayed away from that wedding and I have regretted it ever since."

"But what was your objection?" he repeated, patiently.

"He was lower class," Regina Lipschidts stated.

Gramp started to respond, but Gloria put a hand on his arm.

Regina went on, "She married beneath her class."

"And is that your objection to this marriage?" he asked

"It's the same!" Regina stated.

Bud had not recognized her at first, but suddenly blurted, "You must be my grandmother." Rose took Bud's hand, gave it a reassuring squeeze, and held on, hissing through her teeth,"Well, that did it!"

"Perhaps I can help," Gramp said, rising to his feet "When Regina, or Mrs. Lipschidts, didn't come to my son's wedding, I figured she didn't approve of the marriage. My son was killed overseas, when the groom was born. Since then, the only time the groom ever saw his grandmother was when he was a baby. She has never even sent him a birthday card. I think you will agree, it's too late for her to disrupt my grandson's wedding."

"Perhaps we should ask the others," the minister said "Does anyone else object to this wedding?" After an uneasy silence, he quoted, "Speak now or forever after hold your peace."

There was some uneasy squirming. No one of the little group had ever been in a situation like this. After an uncomfortable, and seemingly endless pause, the minister spoke, "Mrs. Lipschidts, I admire your courage for coming here and speaking up. However , this church does not recognize the class system in the United States. There are many reasons for stopping a marriage, but class is not one of them."

Regina Lipschidts drew herself up, declaring, "I have warned you," and stalked out the back door with her nose in the air.

The minister stood and stated, "Now, let us all return to our places in the church and continue with the ceremony." Rose, following the minister, led Bud back to their place.

When they were settled back in their places, the minister said to the crowd, "Thank you for waiting. The objection was inappropriate, so we will continue with the wedding."

Bud, still in shock from seeing his other grandmother trying to stop his wedding, stood numbly listening to the minister. The minister seemed to be droning nonsense syllables and everything was a blur, until the minister said, "Do you, Archibald, take this woman to be your lawful wedded wife, for better or for worse, in sickness and in health, for richer or poorer, until death do you part?"

As Bud listened for his cue from the minister, he cleared his throat and in his deepest baritone voice said, "I do?"

The minister repeated, "Do you, Rose, take this man to be your lawful wedded husband. . ." Bud watched the minister's lips as he slowly recited the familiar vows. A deafening silence filled the church as the congregation seemed to be straining to hear Rose's answer.

Bud was thrilled, when a confident and electrifying, "I do," came forth. Regina Lipschidts' mischievous disruption had turned the tide and inspired Rose to make up her mind.

"I now pronounce you man and wife!" And in an aside to Bud, he said, "You may kiss the bride."

Bud turned toward Rose as she flipped her veil over her head, revealing a devilish grin. He took her in his arms and kissed her. A sudden burst of applause startled him. With all the excitement of anticipation, he had forgotten that he was kissing her in front of all those witnesses until a thundering round of applause jolted him back to reality.

He offered her his arm and walked her down the aisle, out into the fresh air, and off to eternal bliss.

They did go to the reception. The rip-roaring celebration seemed to be anticlimactic. Bud and Rose jumped through all the usual hoops, but they were anxious to get away together. They danced with each other, danced with their sponsors, threw the bouquet and garter, and cut the cake. Finally, they slipped off and changed into their traveling clothes. Reappearing dressed for their honeymoon just as the coffee and cookies were passed, they thanked everyone for coming and kissed them all goodbye. Bud and Rose each took a cookie and drove off into the sunset.

RICHARD C. HARRISON